I0576648

William Augustus McVickar

The Life of the Reverend John McVickar, S. T. D.

Professor of moral and intellectual philosophy, belles-lettres, political economy,

and the evidences, in Columbia college

William Augustus McVickar

The Life of the Reverend John McVickar, S. T. D.
Professor of moral and intellectual philosophy, belles-lettres, political economy, and the evidences, in Columbia college

ISBN/EAN: 9783337373603

Printed in Europe, USA, Canada, Australia, Japan

Cover: Foto ©Raphael Reischuk / pixelio.de

More available books at **www.hansebooks.com**

THE LIFE

OF THE REVEREND

JOHN McVICKAR, S. T. D.,

PROFESSOR OF MORAL AND INTELLECTUAL PHILOSOPHY, BELLES-
LETTRES, POLITICAL ECONOMY, AND THE EVIDENCES,
IN COLUMBIA COLLEGE.

BY HIS SON,

WILLIAM A. McVICKAR, D. D.

NEW YORK:
PUBLISHED BY HURD AND HOUGHTON.
Cambridge: Riverside Press.
1872.

Entered according to Act of Congress, in the year 1871, by

WILLIAM A. McVICKAR, D. D.,

in the Office of the Librarian of Congress, at Washington

RIVERSIDE, CAMBRIDGE:

STEREOTYPED AND PRINTED BY

H. O. HOUGHTON AND COMPANY.

A SON'S MONUMENT

TO A

LOVED AND HONORED FATHER.

CONTENTS.

CHAPTER I.

EARLY LIFE: 1787–1809.

CHAPTER II.

MARRIAGE AND ORDINATION: 1809–1811.

CHAPTER III.

PERIOD OF PASTORAL WORK: 1811–1817.

CONTENTS.

CHAPTER IV.

CHANGE FROM PASTORAL TO ACADEMIC DUTIES: 1817.

CHAPTER V.

PROFESSORIAL DUTIES: 1817–1824.

CHAPTER VI.

HOME INSTRUCTION, POLITICAL ECONOMY, AND FINANCE: 1824–1827.

CHAPTER VII.

CLERICAL AND COLLEGE DUTIES: 1828.

CHAPTER XVI.

LETTERS: 1832.

CHAPTER XVII.

FOREIGN AND HOME INTERESTS: 1833–1835.

CHAPTER XVIII.

COLERIDGE AND HIS PHILOSOPHY — VARIED INTERESTS: 1835–1844.

CHAPTER XIX.

CHAPLAINCY DUTIES: 1844–1862.

CHAPTER XX.

COLLEGE VIEWS : 1840–1850.

CHAPTER XXI.

CATHEDRAL MISSIONS AND CHURCH BUILDING : 1850–1854.

CHAPTER XXII.

CHURCH INTERESTS : 1854–1864.

CHAPTER XXIII.

RETIREMENT AND DEATH : 1864–1868.

THE LIFE OF

JOHN McVICKAR, S. T. D.

CHAPTER I.

EARLY LIFE: 1787-1809.

JOHN McVICKAR was born in the city of New York, on the 10th of August, 1787. The year, as historic, was one which he was fond of recalling. "The Constitution of the United States and I," he would say, "are of just the same age."

His father, John McVickar, was one of the first merchants of New York. Of Scotch extraction, he came to America in early life, and entered into business with his brother Nathan.

His mother was Anna, daughter of John Moore, of Newtown, Long Island, the descendant of one of the earliest English settlers in the colony, and himself long regarded as a sort of patriarch in that staid old village.

There was the heritage of ancestral Churchmanship on both sides.

As a merchant, his father stood among the highest

in a city then noted for its honorable men of trade.
A nice sense of commercial honor, and a readiness to
grant extensions and give assistance in commercial
difficulty, were his characteristics. " Who has Mc-
Vickar helped to-day ? " is reported to have been a
common question on 'Change.

As a man and a Christian in all the varied duties
of home and society, he was equally exemplary. A
vestryman of Trinity Church from 1801 to 1812, he
still did not allow his duties there either to cramp
his zeal or satisfy his obligations elsewhere. Four
churches within what was then the one Diocese of New
York, owe their origin, in whole or in part, and much
of their prosperity, to the united zeal and liberality
of Mr. and Mrs. McVickar, — Trinity Chapel, on the
north side of Staten Island; St. Michael's, Bloomingdale ; St. James's, New York ; and St. Paul's, Constableville, Lewis County. But though such was the
example of the father, and as one of the sons said in
writing the news of his death, " My father lived for
the happiness of his children," we must rather look
to the mother, as is generally the case, for that personal influence which has its moulding and modifying
effect upon a child's character.

Mrs. Anna McVickar, who died in the seventy-
third year of her age, was one whom every one
loved. " In the estimate of her character," to quote
from the obituary notice at the time of her death,
" it is not easy to say how much was due to natural
temperament, how much to the early operation of
religious principles. Neither is it necessary, for in

her both unquestionably concurred to form a character so peculiarly blameless, that they who knew her
best and longest can now recall to mind no one word
or action, through the varied events of a long life,
and the trying duties of all its social relations, which
did not seem marked by a sense both of Christian
duty and of native kindness. Her religion was truly
that of the heart; it entered into all the daily duties of
life, and under its abiding influences was she formed
to that unpretending truth of character, that single-
mindedness of heart and intention, that unruffled
sweetness of temper, that spirit of quiet yet active
benevolence, and that constant reference of every
question to religious principles by which her life and
conversation were so peculiarly distinguished."

To such a mother, his loved guide in youth, his
honored companion or constant correspondent in
maturer years, my father undoubtedly owed much.
We have it in his own words, when, writing to his
grandfather at Newtown, on occasion of a brother's
death, he says, " My mother writes with calmness,
almost with cheerfulness. She bears it, as she has
ever done her afflictions, with the most perfect resignation to the will of God, referring it to that wisdom and goodness which knows and chooses what
is best. My mother has always been a model to me
of that practical, abiding sense of religion, and I pray
God that I may be able to imitate her in it." Such
are his feelings in 1819, when comparatively a young
man ; and on his mother's death, in 1833, the mature
man of forty-seven years writes, for no other eye but

his own and the All-Seeing One, a series of prayers and meditations, one short extract from which I venture here to produce : —

"O God I thank Thee that from my youth my mother taught me to love and fear Thee, to pray to Thee in secret, to worship in Thy Holy Temple, and to obey Thee in all things — to read diligently Thy Holy Word, and to trust and rely in the merits and mediation alone of Thy Blessed Son."

This reference to parents and parental example is not a mere tribute to a natural curiosity. It has its value. Looking upon each separate life as a worked-out problem, we naturally desire to be put in possession of all the elements, however trivial, which helped to educe that final product of character in which the biographer seeks to interest his readers. It is this which should be the aim of biography, helping to supply, to present workers, data for the formula of life.

My father was the third-born of a large family, nine in number, seven boys and two girls. He was feeble in infancy, and had a delicacy of constitution which, up to middle life, was a trial to himself and a subject of anxiety to his friends. It was only after that period that he attained, through great regularity and activity of life, to that wiry vigor for which, in more advanced age, he was so noted. He was born at his father's city house, 231 Broadway, within sound, as he afterwards loved to recall, of the bell of that college (Columbia) to whose best interests his life was given. Of his early years and boyhood little or nothing can now be told; letters and family traditions are alike wanting. We know, however, that his boyhood was passed in stirring days. A few words written in 1807 show, as was natural, how he was influenced by the spirit of the times and the political complexion of his family. " The son of a Federalist of the old school," he writes, " and having myself worn the Federal cockade, I looked with great reverence to Governor Jay, who, to my mind, stood both as its firmest pillar and its purest representative." How these few lines recall our own experiences of yesterday, and admit us into the boy-life of the close of the last century. The war was ended, but the military spirit was still uppermost, and the youthful members of every household, with true instincts, thought themselves, as they really were, deeply interested in the vast and momentous political questions of the hour. Hence the cockade and the bands of little patriots, and the fireside hero by which each swore, a Jay, a Hamilton, a Washington.

A sole anecdote of these, his early years, survives as having been employed afterwards in home education. " I was just entering my seventh year," my father used to say, " and was quite unable to pronounce the letter S, when one day a friend calling at the house took me by the hand and said, ' How old are you, John?' — ' Going into *he*ven,' said I, at which there was a general laugh and I retired in confusion, mentally resolving that I would not rest till I could sound an *S* as well as any one, a result which perseverance and I soon attained." Those who remember his clear utterance and distinct articulation of after years, and his high appreciation of the virtue of perseverance, can readily see how this anecdote of the boy reveals the hidden man.

Of schools and schooling I know nothing more than what a bare memorandum discloses. It appears from this that he first went to a select school taught by a Mr. Ely, and established by a few gentlemen for the benefit of their sons. Then he went to the school of a Mr. Rudd, of which the remark is made " ordinary but best, eager to go farther." This was soon exchanged for the exclusive services of a private tutor, a learned Scotch clergyman of the name of Barlas. He was a man much devoted to the classics, and probably a good teacher, as he fitted his pupil, at the age of thirteen, to enter Columbia College, head of his class by merit, the youngest of a class numbering forty-five. This was at the beginning of the century. He entered in the year 1800. The examinations for entrance in those days were markedly different from what they are at present. The students were then entered according to merit, and Latin composition was the chief test, written at the time, and handed in with a fictitious signature. Of this examination of the year 1800, which placed the young McVickar of thirteen at the head of a class numbering forty-five, I can give no record. The following, however, from the successful candidate's own pen, describing the similar triumph in 1819, of his young pupil and after friend, Griffin, whose early death was so widely mourned, will doubtless, mingling as it must have done with his own recollections, give us a true picture of the scene.

"In the autumn of this year, when just fifteen years old, Edmund appeared among the candidates for admission into Columbia College. The examination for entrance into this college was at that time long and rigid, continued for several successive days, and terminating in a public arrangement of names in the order of merit. Such a contest between scholars brought together for the first time, and proud of the reputation of their respective schools, was to all a scene of interest; and to sensitive young minds, when thus thrown into the arena, seemed to realize the fables of the classic games of ancient Greece. Most of the teachers, and many anxious fathers, were in constant attendance to encourage their sons or pupils by their presence, or perhaps to become judges of the impartiality of the decision."

It may not be amiss to add here the comment which my father makes upon this practice, after the double experience of his own success in 1800 and the effects of failure long witnessed, as a professor.

" While we call this victory honorable," he writes, " we cannot deny that it was painful, and dearly purchased by the mortified feelings and injured prospects of others ; so much so that it may well awaken the doubt whether such highly excited emulation in the education of youth be not productive of more evil than good. How often do we see the bold heart wearing out the feeble body in the contest ? and when that contest is over, though some generous spirits may rise above the disappointment, yet how often do we see it turning into gall and bitterness, and weighing down the heart with the double load of sorrow and envy.   Nor is the moral injury of such emulation greater than the intellectual.   When made the great engine of education, as in our country it is, it weakens the mind by premature exertion, cultivates the memory at the expense of the judgment, and invariably tends to enfeeble the character by building it upon the sandy foundation of temporary excitement.   Hence the anomalous fact we are so often called to lament and wonder at, that the praised and honored youth turns out the feeble and nerveless man.   Like the boy taught to swim on bladders, in a quiet bath, he goes smoothly on, so long as he is buoyed up by praise; but when called to act unnoticed and alone, to walk unmoved through good report and evil report, he feels as the same artificial swimmer would do, without his aids, in the rough and stormy ocean."

The presidency of the College in the year 1800 was vacant.   Dr. Johnson, in his seventy-fourth year, had just resigned, and though Dr. Wharton of Philadelphia, and Bishop Moore of New York, were successively elected during the next four years, the entire care and instruction of the students fell upon the professors, Doctors Kemp, Wilson, and Bowden, all highly respectable and able men.   Of my father's college course I know but little.   That it was creditable there can be no doubt, as he continued to hold the position which he had gained at his entrance, and in 1804 graduated at the head of his class. A volume of compositions is all that remains to attest the character of his college work and though neatly written and well expressed, their chief merit is perhaps their simplicity and briefness, confirming what was afterwards the successful student's own judgment on himself, that whatever success he attained was due to plodding industry and not to talent. By the closing words of the composition on " History," written in 1800, we are forcibly reminded of what must have been the experiences and exciting subjects of talk to the college boys of these days, " And within *our own memory* we have seen a Washington conducting these States through various hardships, difficulties, and almost innumerable obstacles to a safe and honorable peace." Washington had died not a twelvemonth before. And at the final examination of the class in 1804 an event was announced which must have aroused to the full their youthful feelings, as it did the sorrow and indignation of a mourning people. Young Alexander Hamilton, the eldest son of the General, was a member of this class. On the morning of the 11th of July, 1804, he was not among his class-mates at examination, and on some inquiry being made by the professor, young McVickar said that he had seen him but an hour before galloping up Broadway at a most furious pace, and that he feared something must have been the matter. That day's duties were not over before it was known that General Hamilton, to whose talents and patriotism all

men looked with reverence, had fallen in a duel, by
the hand of Aaron Burr, and that he was at that moment lying fatally wounded, at the house of a friend
at Bloomingdale. The sad but exciting event was
thus brought closely home to these young minds, and
we are not surprised to find that the Latin salutatory
at the approaching Commencement, which belonged
to my father, as head of his class, should have had
for its subject, " Eloquence and Hamilton."

Thus in the Commencement Hall of Columbia
College, draped in mourning for the sad event, did
John McVickar, in his seventeenth year, pronounce
the first public eulogium on General Hamilton.
" The boast of our college and the glory of our
country, just fallen on the field of mistaken honor ;
a doubter in the days of a busy life, but a sincere
and humble believer on his dying bed." Such are
the words used on a later occasion, in recalling this
circumstance, which had so deeply impressed his
youthful mind.

In 1805, Mr. John McVickar went abroad to visit
his aged father, look after his business, and try to
recruit his own failing health. He took with him
his son John, the subject of this memoir, just fresh
from college. Beyond the bare facts of a visit to
Oxford, a day spent at " Peter House " to see a
brother who was a student there, and an interview
with Lord Stowell, then Sir William Scott, and a
short tour in Scotland, I find no records of the
journey or its incidents.

We gather, however, a single touch for our portrait at this time, in a mother's solicitude for her absent son. In a letter addressed to him while abroad she says, " Miss C—— is very well and often speaks of you, and I dare say regrets your absence, as you appeared to be a favorite beau. She is in my opinion so lovely a girl that I should be proud to have her for a daughter. . . . . I hope, my dear John, that although you may mix with the thoughtless and the gay, your mind will never lose those serious impressions which I with pleasure observed before you left home ; and however a certain writer may remark, that travelling unsettles all principles, I hope you will prove an exception, for were you to acquire ever so much knowledge or worldly advantage, yet, if it tended to unsettle your mind with respect to religious and moral principles, I should lament it as the most serious evil which could befall you."

These " serious impressions " must have been deepened rather than disturbed by foreign travel, for shortly after his return to New York he recommenced his studies, which, after a year's time devoted to general subjects, resulted in his offering his name to Bishop Moore as a candidate for Holy Orders. This was in 1807. For the next three years he pursued his theological reading. There being no theological course or seminary of any kind at that early day of our Church's history, the reading of candidates for Holy Orders was usually conducted under some clergyman approved by the Bishop. In this case, Dr. afterwards Bishop Hobart was the one selected, and thus commenced an intimacy, which, with much reverence on the one side, soon ripened into a mutual attachment, which only ended with the Bishop's life. It found its appropriate monument in the extended memoir which afterwards appeared from his former pupil's pen.

During these years of study my father wisely took advantage of a country-seat at Bloomingdale, belonging to the family, to obtain that quiet which the home in Broadway and a large household was not likely to afford. In summer the family were there, but in winter he was sole occupant of the large mansion on what was then the quiet banks of the Hudson, far removed from the great city, whose northern suburbs were just beginning to straggle above Chambers Street. The property had belonged to Mr. Constable, whose son William married one of my father's sisters, and was deservedly considered one of the most beautiful of the once celebrated Bloomingdale Places. The house, shorn of its groves and acres, may still be seen at the foot of Eighty-sixth Street, forming a portion of the present buildings of the " House of Mercy." It was a congenial residence for the young student, who was fond of the country and horticultural pursuits, and to whom the care of the place was now intrusted by his father. Though giving most of his time, as we shall see, to his books, he still paid much attention to beautifying the grounds, planting out many English elms, imported direct from England, which he afterward transplanted to the green of Columbia College when he became its Professor. The planting of trees was ever to him a delight, and he seldom failed to leave his mark in this way on the landscape, wherever he found even a temporary home.

His reading and the division of his time during this period of study was remarkably systematic. I have before me a little book of " memoranda," dated January 7, 1807, which begins with an exact division of time and subjects or books for every day in the week. Then follows a diary, not of thoughts, but of accomplished work. His chief studies during this year appear to have been Hebrew, Italian, and French, with such reading as Paley, Sir William Jones, Robertson's " Charles V.," and Shakespeare. On February 2d, he writes, " Determine henceforward to learn ten lines of poetry before breakfast every morning, to begin with Horace's " Ars Poetica." A few days after, " Formed a scheme of artificial memory by letters and applied it to Bossuet's ' Chronology.' "

The latter part of the year a fuller diary is commenced, with notes upon his reading. The first page is entitled, " The Economy of my Time," and beside the schedule for each day, shows this proportion per week : Latin, six hours ; Greek, six ; Hebrew, twelve ; Divinity, eighteen ; French, three ; Italian, three. It may not be without interest to give two brief specimens of these notes of the young student of twenty, now left so much to his own guidance, as exemplifying that practical straightforward habit of mind which displays itself throughout, and which became a life characteristic.

" *Monday, December 7th.* — Virgil's ' Æneid: '

read four hundred lines, which finishes lib. XII. The battle between the two heroes is not the masterpiece I expected from the pen of Virgil. The one is a braggadocio, the other a coward; the gods arrange the matter among themselves, and the reader is left to wade through the description, without interest as to the combatants or anxiety as to the event."

" *Saturday, 20th December.* — Greek Testament: read sixth and seventh chapters of Matthew. Began to study Greek on a new plan, *i. e.* not to plague myself with the critical acquaintance of every word, but having a sufficient idea of the grammar to judge of the parts of the verbs, &c., to devote myself to the acquisition of words, and thus facilitate the reading of the language. 'Tis wonderful the small stock of words that is gained by a boy in this or the Latin language after three or four years' hard application in the common way; and of course how difficult he finds it to read at first sight a common sentence. Youth is the proper time for the acquisition of words, when the memory is both quick and retentive, and when as yet they are content to heap up arbitrary sounds without adding to their stock of ideas."

During 1808 the same diary is kept up, but now in French, and some little French book is always kept in the pocket for chance moments of reading. For a small portion of the year the diary is kept in Latin, and a volume of " Discerpta " shows a very fair range of theological reading.

Thus was passed a youth marked by the self-dis-cipline of the determined student, added to the gen-

eral self-restraint of a Christian young man. How
far it was a preparation for happiness or the reverse is a question to which the succeeding pages
of this thread of an individual life should supply an
answer.

CHAPTER II.

THE year 1809 brings us to the event which more or less shapes and colors the future of most lives.

Early in this year my father became engaged to Eliza, youngest daughter of Dr. Bard, of Hyde Park. The family with which he thus connected himself was one of distinctive if not remarkable characteristics. Like many of the older families of New York, such as the Jays, Bowdoins, Pintards, and Boudinots, the Bards were descended, and in their case on both sides, from French refugees, who, preferring their faith to their country, became exiles to America at the revocation of the Edict of Nantes. Dr. Samuel Bard, grandson to the refugee, was educated in the medical schools of Scotland, then justly celebrated, and became one of the first physicians in New York city. Not troubling himself much about politics, and finding plenty to occupy him in his profession, he still was a Tory in feelings and had more than once to leave the city during the Revolutionary War. His character and reputation, however, and the preference given to him by General Washington, soon re-established him in full practice, and in 1778 and at the age of fifty-six, having made a competency, and taken Dr. Hosack as his partner, he retired to Hyde Park, a most beautiful spot, about eighty miles up the Hudson River. This property was part of a patent right which his maternal grandfather obtained when private secretary to Lord Cornbury, governor of the province of New York, and favorite cousin of Queen Anne. This was the origin of the name, the tract being called " Hyde Park," as a sort of compliment to his patron.

To this romantic and beautiful spot Dr. Bard had retired about eleven years before the event which was now to add a new member to his family, and join a new and influential current to the life stream whose course we are pursuing. He was a sort of a patriarch in his neighborhood. His only son, William Bard, was married and resided near; his elder daughter, married to Judge Johnston, was also with a large family settled close by; while his own household consisted of his wife, his aunt, Mrs. Barton, his sister Miss Sally Bard, and his only unmarried child, Eliza, now engaged to be married to the subject of this memoir. If this detail seems over minute, it must be pardoned as necessary to enable the reader to enter into the happiest if not the most influential portion of my father's life.

One letter from father to daughter, shortly before the engagement, is here inserted to help to picture the home into which my father was about to enter : —

Hyde Park, *December* 27, 1804.

My dear Child, — Your mother tells me I must

fill this page; but where shall I find matter? Our uniform life affords neither variety nor anecdote. Had I indeed the talent to dress the same sentiments in all the beautiful variety of Madame De Sévigné, I might say again and again how much we love you, and that we are proud of you; and that even at a distance you gild the evening of our lives with the sunshine and joy of youth. But you know all this already, and repetition cannot make it more true; I will, therefore, only charge you to return us that portion of our treasure which is in your keeping — your own health and happiness, bright and unalloyed.

I have received great pleasure in the beautiful specimens you have sent me of your skill and industry in drawing; and from your future improvement, I promise myself a source of delight all the rest of my life. I have placed them up against the wall opposite my seat, that I may have the pleasure of constantly viewing them and anticipating the pleasure we shall enjoy when we come to apply your talent to a thousand useful and ornamental subjects. Your fondness for gardening and painting have ever been strong passions of mine, and we will now cultivate them together; which will add the greatest zest to my enjoyment, and lay up for you a never failing source of the most innocent delight. Everything connected with gardening, drawing, and the study of nature is virtuous, feminine, and elegant; every sentiment and feeling they excite is peculiarly becoming in a female mind: they soften and harmonize the affections, smooth all the asperities of char-

acter, and even allay the bitterness of disappointment
and sorrow. Let nothing, therefore, my good girl,
slacken your industry in this pursuit; and be careful
not to divide your attention between too many objects, as mediocrity in any accomplishment will satisfy neither me nor you.

But I had almost forgot to bestow upon you your
just praise for the readiness with which you have
complied with my desire to avoid large parties ; they
consume a great deal of time, with little pleasure,
and no improvement. It is my boast to have children who know how to submit to what is right without repining.

God bless you, my dear child,

S. B.

Our subject is well carried on by a letter from Miss
Sally Bard, Dr. Bard's sister, to a friend in England.
The minute and interested detail is accounted for by
the fact that the two families had been separated by
the war, one, the Kempes, going to England, the
other, the Bards, remaining in this country, while
the same affection and interest in each other's affairs
was kept up by letter for sixty years. These letters
are now in the writer's possession, and he does not
hesitate to give in full the following one as affording
just such home touches of portraiture as the biographer generally finds it impossible to obtain, or, if he
does, is too apt to think beneath the dignity of his subject. The marriage took place November 12, 1809.

Hyde Park, December 18, 1809.

I ought long since, my beloved friend, to have answered your last most welcome letter: shall I say I waited to tell you my beloved Eliza has changed her name to McVickar, and though the honeymoon was over last Sunday, yet I have scarcely found time to return to my normal habits of thought and occupation. Contrary to Eliza's wishes, we had a large and consequently a gay wedding. He had a large family and many friends to be invited, and, besides, our own home circle, our vicinity to Governor Lewis, Chancellor Livingston, and Mr. Cruger's family, with many in New York who had been too kindly affectioned to her to be left out (unless we had quite a private wedding), swelled our number not only to filling our own house, but Mr. Pendleton's, William Bard's, and Mr. Johnston's. She was married on Sunday evening, the 12th of November, — a most solemn moment to those who have had her so long exclusively to themselves, and who it has been the study of her life to make happy. But then, what cause of gratitude have we in the prospect of her's and our happiness — character, talents, temper, family, and fortune agreed to our fondest, our warmest expectations. My brother says he never knew a young man — not much above two-and-twenty, only two months older than Eliza — so excellent a scholar in the languages, and so well read and perfect a master of every subject of science and polite literature; and I can say few that I have seen equal him in a retentive memory to bring forward agreeable things in conversation; and he has a peculiar gayety, almost sportiveness of temper, that diffuses cheerfulness all around him; and oh, with what pleasure can I add that the turn of his mind is all for domestic joys.

He was in England two years ago with his father. Oh, could we have looked forward to this day, how I should liked you to have seen the lad, and more because he is pleasing to look upon; for though a handsome face and person is of no great consequence, yet, added to better things, I always thought it very agreeable both in man and woman. I am almost ashamed of reaching nearly to the bottom of the second page on the subject of our young people, but this is their day of consequence, and in future I will be more laconic. There were ten days of dancing and festivity, when, by degrees, we sobered down to our usual habits of spending our time. Mr. McVickar's mornings are always occupied in study till twelve or one, when, if the weather is good, they walk, ride to the farm, and sometimes snow-ball each other; if not, they amuse themselves within doors with chess, battledore, or some other recreation. You know how it is in our family; every one lives in their separate apartments till dinner. The afternoons are short, but he gives them to us, reading aloud works of taste and improvement. Tea brings us all together till bed-time. The early part of the evening brother either reads while we work or plays chess with John McVickar. At eight the whist party is formed, and we have our little table at the other side of the fire, where we pass two hours very pleasantly, varied ac-

cording to our humor; reading, chatting, drawing
characters, writing verses, making conundrums, or
anything that comes uppermost, — I making myself
younger, perhaps, than I ought to do, to give the
young people pleasure. He does not expect to take
Orders till next spring twelve-month. . . . .

Most affectionately,
S. BARD.

How truly religion went hand in hand with cheerfulness and even gayety, in this household of the olden
time, is shown by the following prayer used by Dr.
Bard at the ordinary evening devotions on the day
on which the marriage took place. It was his custom
to add something of the kind at family prayer, on all
marked occasions, either of joy or sorrow.

"O, most gracious God, bless with Thy favor and
protection our children, who have in Thy presence
become united in marriage. May they place their
hopes of happiness first in love to Thee, faith in Thy
promises, obedience to Thy commands, and submission to Thy will; and next to these, in a sincere,
tender, and generous friendship for each other. May
these affections brighten all their prospects and joys
in life; and may they always fly to these for comfort
under the misfortunes or afflictions with which Thou
shalt see fit to prove them. May we, their parents,
enjoy, while we live, the unspeakable blessing of wit-
nessing their virtues and happiness: and, when death
approaches, may the blessed hope of meeting again
in Thy presence forever, cheer our last hour, and
soften the pain of parting."

With the exception of occasional visits to his own family in New York, this happy and congenial Hyde Park household was my father's home for the first year of his married life. His expectant profession stimulated and gave shape to Dr. Bard's long cherished idea of a church on his own property, and it was not long before the site was determined on and given, the plan settled, and the work commenced. My father had already purchased, some two miles above Hyde Park, a wooded slope on the river bank, and was there building for himself. He was naturally fond of planning and building, and was not without some skill in architecture, which had already brought him credit through plans for Grace Church, New York, which when quite young he had elaborately prepared and handed in anonymously for competition. We may, therefore, picture him this year as both a busy and a happy man.

The same year, 1811, saw both home and church completed ; the home first, which received the name of "Inwood," and to which my father and family, consisting of wife, infant daughter, and Miss Sally Bard, who thenceforth was to be a cherished member of his household, removed early in June. In after years, writing for a great niece, Miss Bard thus describes the new home : —

" In June, 1811, we removed to Inwood, a place chosen in the romantic days of your father and mother, built in the same taste, more for beauty than convenience ; the road to the house, from choice, difficult of access, among dark and winding paths, over rocks and stones, and much further round than was necessary."

This judgment was probably correct, for two years saw a change to a comfortable cottage about equidistant between the church and the Hyde Park mansion, and not five minutes' walk from either.

The church, erected mainly through the liberality of Dr. Bard and Mr. McVickar's father — a counterpart of which can now be seen in old St. Luke's, New York — was ready for consecration in the month of October. The young candidate was to be ordained deacon at the same time. Bishop Hobart, who had just passed through the stormy times of his own election and consecration to the episcopate, officiated, and we can easily imagine, if imagination were not rendered unnecessary by the following graphic picture from the pen which has already aided us, how full of happiness must have been the occasion : —

" My brother has lived," says Miss Bard, writing to her English friends, " to see completed, and more than answer his expectations, the pious work he so arduously undertook and prosecuted, and after the vigor of life passed in a constant course of usefulness and active benevolence, closes his career with the delightful consciousness of having his last his best work, and already seeing and enjoying the blest effects of it. With little more than the assistance of his own family he has built a church, a lovely one that strikes every eye with its taste and beauty. It is near the mansion-house, half a mile from the village, and near a grove of locust-trees.   On the 12th of October it was consecrated, and on the following day our beloved friend was ordained to the ministry. Never was there a more affecting and solemn scene ; the hubbub of a city consecration can give no idea of it.   But the ordination was still more interesting. The Bishop and two clergymen attended, his father, mother, and others of his family, and every one of ours, formed a group that seemed to touch every heart in the church, and the Bishop, on his return, said he had never witnessed so deeply affecting a scene.   He preached the sermon, and took occasion to speak with high but modest praise of his knowledge from infancy of John McVickar's character, and touched very handsomely on brother's being the founder, father, and patron of the church.   On Sunday, Mr. Mc-Vickar preached his first sermon.   It would be natural for me to be partial in its praise, but indifferent persons spoke highly of it, and Governor Lewis in particular, who, observing the pallid looks of his father, laboring under a lingering and painful disease, said to Mr. Pendleton, ' But who would not take his complaints to be the father of such a son ? ' "

To this picture of Mr. McVickar's early married life, thus drawn for me by other hands, it is not for the writer to add a word.   I may, however, be allowed to close it with a few lines bearing a date some years later, and found among my father's papers : —

TO ELIZA, 12TH NOVEMBER, 1817.

DEAR was the mistress, when with downcast eye,
And glowing cheek, she breathed a kind reply ;

DEARER the bride, when first by right divine
I kissed her virgin lips, and called her mine;

DEAREST the wife, when to her bosom prest
She soothes each anxious care, and lulls my soul to rest.

CHAPTER III.

THE religious destitution of the banks of the Hudson then, even as with the West now, compelled the relaxation of the good ecclesiastical rule that the deacon should always be the assistant of the priest. Thus my father, immediately on his ordination, though still a deacon, was elected rector of St. James' Church, Hyde Park, and became responsible at once for full pastoral duty.

" This country," writes Miss Bard, " had no Episcopal Church nearer to the southward than Poughkeepsie, nor to the northward within twenty miles, so that our common people either attended ignorant Methodist meetings or spent their Sundays in idleness. Since Mr. McVickar's entrance into the ministry, now about six months, he has conscientiously devoted himself to the improvement of his own mind and the good of others, visiting the sick, attending the poor, and instructing the ignorant, in which his wife joins him most sincerely, never having enjoyed admiration and gayety as much as she now does joining him in acts of charity and piety."

This devotion of the young rector to the improvement of his own mind, might have become a snare to him had it not been joined with a strong practical conscientiousness, for he was still a student and a real lover of study. This year he began reading Blackstone, "resolved," as a line in his note-book says, " to obtain a general knowledge of the principles of law." But some months after, in the same note-book, comes the following: " Finished the first two volumes, but resolved to give up this study, at least for the present, from finding the duties of my profession more than enough to engage my whole time."

In 1812 he was ordained priest in Trinity Church, New York, by Bishop Hobart, immediately after the opening services of the Diocesan Convention.

In the episcopal address before the Convention of 1814, we have the following satisfactory evidence of parochial industry, the Bishop having just visited his parish to administer, for the first time, the rite of Confirmation : —

" The congregation of St. James, Hyde Park, which originally consisted of a few select families, has been greatly increased in number by the assiduous labors of its rector, who has been particularly attentive to catechetical instruction, not merely in the church, but in his parochial visits to the families and schools of his parish."

Through his after memoir of Bishop Hobart, we are enabled to give, in the rector's own words, the remembrance of this first Confirmation in his church : —

" The author, indeed, can call to mind few scenes of deeper pathos than the one he saw exhibited on that occasion. The youthful circle, unbonneted and bareheaded, with here and there one in middle and advanced life among their number, deeming it becoming, thus 'to fulfill all righteousness;' the youth, with streaming eyes, trembling and agitated, some to the very verge of sinking beneath their feelings; the interested and eager circle behind of parents, and friends, and congregation, hanging, as it were, upon the words of their spiritual father, — all tended to form a picture lovely to the eye of the philanthropist, and overpowering to that of the Christian."

During the year 1813 a long nervous fever prostrated my father's strength and led finally to his change of residence from " Inwood " to " The Cottage," directly opposite the church. Dr. Roosevelt Johnson, one who knew and loved him well, his successor in the parish, writes: "There, on a site which challenges comparison with any single view on the banks of our beautiful Hudson, he resided five years, distinguished, even so early, for his maturity of mind, his activities, his attentiveness, and his able, eloquent, and touching discourses. Busy among his parishioners, fondly regarded by them then, he was also cherished by them long years after. Though he had the disadvantage of a voice not powerful, and somewhat peculiar, yet it was clear as a bell and musical; and his delivery was impressive, commanding the attention and moving the affections."

I judge that this estimate of him as a preacher must have been correct, from a remark made to me not long since by Mr. Samuel B. Ruggels: " I was

a school-boy at Poughkeepsie, when your father was
rector at Hyde Park, and many a time have I slipped
away and gone up there seven miles to hear him, because I was fond even then of a good sermon and good
preaching."

The " Cottage " here spoken of was commenced by
Dr. Bard, while my father was absent on account of
ill health. He did not believe in his clergyman being so far away from his church, or his children and
grandchildren so far away from him. Hence this
lovely spot was arranged, as a home, midway between his own house and the church. It was the residence of the family for the rest of their stay at Hyde
Park, and soon became a marked centre of quiet
church influence and genial home life.

The following note in Miss Bard's diary reminds
us that this was in days long since gone by, at least
for the State of New York: " Had a letter from Mr.
McV. mentioning the purchase of a black man and
his wife for the term of seven years." This gives
point to the remark which I often heard my father
make, that slavery, beside its inherent evils, had a
most injurious effect upon the character of the master, adding always, " I know it from experience."
The law in New York at that time set the slaves free
after a certain age. This gave rise to circumstances
often annoying doubtless, but sometimes, as in the
following case, ludicrous. A self-constituted committee, one of them a Quaker, determined to call
upon Dr. Bard, then resident in the city, to inquire
the age of his colored boy, imagining that he was un-

lawfully detained in servitude. They were courteously received, until the object of their visit was
declared, when the Doctor drew himself up with dignity and rang the bell. Pompey, the boy in question, answered the call. " Pompey," said he, " go
and get your hat " — the Quaker as was usual with
his sect was wearing his. This having been done,
he added, " Pompey, put your hat on and take my
seat." " Gentlemen," he said, turning to the committee, " I leave you to discuss the questions which
you and Pompey may have in common," and bowed
himself out. One of the committee afterwards re-
marked that he got a lesson then which kept him out
of all such scrapes in the future.

The salary as rector of this little country parish
during these years, from 1815 to 1818, was but
$250. A small amount, I do not know how much,
had been received annually from Trinity Corporation, New York, but even that in 1815 was stopped.
The circular announcing the fact, signed by Richard
Harrison as " Comptroller," and sent, we presume,
to other parishes, reads curiously under the light of
1871. " The enhanced prices of the necessaries and
comforts of life, and the depreciation of money,"
demand increase of salary for their own clergy and
officers. " The requisite endowments for Grace
Church and St. George's Church, lately separated
from them, and the great calamity experienced in
the destruction of St. George's Church by fire,"
" enhance necessary expenses and involve their
affairs in perplexity and embarrassment."

" The permanent annual revenue of the Corporation of Trinity Church, including pew rents, does not exceed twelve thousand dollars, upon the most liberal estimate ; whilst their certain and necessary annual expenses amount to at least double that sum, beside the expenses of repairing and cleaning three churches, and fire-wood, and other contingent charges. . . . . The Corporation are persuaded that this plain exposition of facts must be sufficient to justify them in the eyes of their brethren. They hope, that by the coöperation of the several congregations which compose their body, and by the adoption of some prudent plans for the management of their property, the situation of the Church may, in a short time, be materially improved. They are also persuaded that no assurance can be necessary to convince their brethren in the country that, as they have heretofore done, they will again pay proper attention to them as soon as the situation of their affairs will permit them to do so."

It is about this time that I find the fragmentary beginnings of that volume which was first published long after in 1835, under the title of " Devotions for the Family and the Closet, from the Manual of a Country Clergyman." It was in truth the outgrowth and the fruit of these few years of early pastoral work. Prepared for his own family and private use, enriched, according to his father-in-law's example, on every special occasion of joy and sorrow with the outpourings of both a thankful and a submissive spirit, it is undoubtedly the true record of my father's spiritual

experiences during these years. True in its measure of the whole work, this is especially so of the
latter portion, " Devotions for the Closet," which the
preface says " are from a more private diary, and are
added not without many misgivings." This " diary,"
if ever existing in a formal shape, was probably long
since destroyed, and this book of devotions alone remains to testify to that hidden life, only the outward
evidences of which belong to the biographer.

" These words of Christian prayer," says the
preface, " lay claim to no merit beyond simplicity
and sincerity ; but it may be that to some hearts
they may come more home, on that very account.
In this hope they are made public ; their author casts
them in as his secret mite, into the treasury of the
Church of God ; if they add but one living stone to
the temple, he is more than repaid."

The volume was published anonymously, and has
been used by many, even clergymen, without any
knowledge as to who was the writer. Several editions have been exhausted and yet it is still in demand. Letters might here be inserted from many,
who expressed most warmly their obligations, but it
is unnecessary. Whatever the author may have
looked for in his other literary works, in this he
sought not, or rather he shrank from praise. It was
too truly the child of those joys and sorrows in
which the stranger intermeddleth not, to admit of
any desire to receive for it the meeds of authorship. We therefore close this somewhat anticipated
subject, though in reality one which throws its light

3

back upon these years of pastoral work, with two
letters, one from the author himself accompanying
his gift to Miss Sally Bard of a copy of the printed
volume, and the other from a brother clergyman on
first discovering its authorship.

My dear Aunt, — This little work, which I may
well term our common property, will be, I trust and
doubt not, a new bond of affection between us.   The
beautiful prayers you gave me for it make it yours as
well as mine, but that which above all makes it *common*
to us, is that it has reference to those who were equally
near and dear to us, and from whom, though separated for a season, we shall not be long.   Even now
I feel them nearer to me as I read what I then wrote,
and it is my greatest happiness that, day by day, this
sense of their nearness increases.   It is not space or
time that separates us, but the world and worldly affections, and as these under God's blessing lose their
hold upon my heart, I feel that, even before death,
I may almost embrace them there — through the
atonement of my blessed Saviour I doubt not.

In putting forth this work, I have done it, partly
as a debt to my profession, from which my more
worldly occupations separate me, but mainly in the
hope that it will react upon myself, and make me
what I would teach others to be.

Accept it, then, as a pledge alike of my future resolutions and my present affection, from

Your affectionate nephew,

J. McV.

Monday, 24*th June*, 1835.

The following is from a late prominent clergyman of a neighboring city. It tells its own story, and gives evidence of fruit that the young "country clergyman," as for convenience he committed to writing the prayerful outpourings of his own thankful heart, could then have little imagined.

PHILADELPHIA, *October* 29, 1847.

DEAR DOCTOR, — I purchased some time ago "Devotions, etc.," by a "Country Clergyman," but never knew that I was indebted to you for this valuable little work. I ascertained the fact that you were its author during my recent visit to New York. I intended, while there, to express to you my thanks, and to tell you how excellent and useful I find it. I can truly say that it seems to me to be the very best manual of family prayers I have ever used. Dear Doctor, if your heart dictated those devotions, as I am sure it did, you must know indeed 'how to pray.' And surely you have helped me greatly in learning that important and precious duty. The private prayers are delightful. They suit my poor self exactly. In my family, too, I find them everything I could wish. I shall often think of you now while on my knees before God, and send up a supplication for his blessing to attend you. I frequently think of your kindness to me, many years ago, at a trying period of my life, when I needed friends. You have perhaps forgotten what you did to me so kindly, but I have not, and God Almighty has not, and now you have laid me under a new obligation.

With every sentiment of respect and attachment, I am, most esteemed sir,

> Your friend and brother,
> H. W. DUCACHET.

In 1814, memoranda of monéys received from his parishioners and neighbors for the relief of the Niagara frontiers, reminds us that the War of 1812 was then pressing heavily upon the country, and involving all, if not in its horrors, at least in its calls for charity.

The next year, however, brought peace, and the news found its way to the Hyde Park circle, not in a couple of minutes by telegraph, as it would now, but through the following characteristic letter from my father's eldest brother, and, as it was mid-winter, probably taking at least twenty-four hours to reach its destination of eighty miles.

NEW YORK, *Sunday, February* 12, 1815.

DEAR JOHN, — PEACE: in this small word is comprised all that I have to tell you. It is uttered by every tongue in the tone of exultation and gladness. The only salutation of friends this day has been, joy, peace, and most sincerely and heartily do I congratulate you on the restoration of its blessings to ourselves, our families, and our land at this period, when we had but tasted the bitter calamities of war. Mr. Carrol, the messenger and bearer of the treaty, arrived in town from the Hook between eight and nine last evening. The night was dark and gloomy, and most persons had retired to their firesides for the evening, whence they were roused by distant and repeated huzzas. The word "peace" passed from mouth to mouth and from street to street. Instantly the streets blazed with lights in the windows and boys bearing torches. The hour was forgotten, and friends ran from house to house pouring forth congratulations and joy, and this scene lasted till midnight. I am not yet sobered enough to express my feelings coherently. Again I repeat, joy, peace, and love to you and all friends at Hyde Park.

Your affectionate brother,
ARCH. McVICKAR.

The pastoral work of the remaining years of parochial duty at Hyde Park afford but little of special interest. It would seem to have been earnest, systematic, and conducted on wide and generous principles. We find him doing missionary work many miles back at Pine Plains; corresponding with Edward P. Livingston respecting the erection of a church and the support of public services near Clermont; writing to Chancellor Kent to obtain his official aid to check the unlicensed retailing of liquors; and to Bishop Moore of Virginia, invoking his assistance in a general effort to put down dueling. Memoranda also show him to have been practically engaged in the first efforts to establish a charity for the relief of the deaf and dumb, and to have been deeply interested in Mr. Gallaudet and Mr. Clerc on their first arrival in this country. In his own parish we find, beside the Sunday-school, what was not at that time so common, a sewing-school of young people, and a society of ladies to relieve sick-

ness and distress in the neighborhood.   There was
also " The Christian Association of Dutchess County,"
in which, if not the founder, he was at least deeply
interested.   In an address before it in 1815 we find
him taking that economic view of social questions
which seems to have been natural to his mind, and
which, when his duties afterwards compelled that direction, made him one of the first political economists
of his day.

" In this country," he says, " wretchedness is but
the shadow of vice.   The demand for labor is so great
and the wages of it so high that the means of comfortable subsistence are never wanting to the indus-
trious and the sober.   The money spent for spirits
needlessly drunk in this neighborhood would support
its poor twice over.   It is the heaviest tax we pay,
and costs the country more than all its other taxes
beside.   It cuts off its industry, weakens its strength,
debases its morals, corrupts its principles, and, in the
loss of virtue, paves the way for loss of liberty."

But especially did my father interest himself in
efforts to elevate the social condition of the blacks of
his neighborhood, a large and more or less degraded
class, some free, and some, as we have seen, still in
partial bondage.   In 1816 he formed and put in operation a systematic plan for their improvement, which
seems so happy in its conception, and so well fitted
to the present needs of many Southern parishes, that
we regret that its length forbids its insertion here.
The use of the district school-house and its teacher
was secured for Sundays and certain week-day even-

ings. A Sunday-school and Bible Society was then
formed, to embrace all, if possible, from heads of families to youngest children. To learn to read the Bible
was the professed object of the first, to supply every
member of the society with a Bible the object of the
second. The address closes in these words: " Of
this society your wives and children may all become
members, and I hope to see it excite among you all
a sense of self-respect, a feeling of religion, and a desire of improvement which will make you an example
to the neighborhood. One Sunday afternoon in every
month I will meet you in this church, and do what I
can to encourage and support all your good endeavors, and advise and direct you, as I do now, like a
true and sincere friend."

Among the pleasant excursions of this period was
a drive to the hospitable mansion of Governor Jay
at Bedford, whose son had married my father's
younger sister. On one of these occasions, writing to
Miss Bard, he says, " Through a day that seemed to
partake of the four seasons, we pushed on our way
so cheerily as to drink tea at Governor Jay's. . It required, I believe, all the love of kind friends to be glad
to see our carriage load approach, as the house was
brimful before our arrival. My comfort was that our
family was but a drop in the bucket, so I made myself quite easy on that score. Bating this little difficulty, of packing us by night and seating us by day,
our visit proved a very agreeable one, and the theological discussions to which Mr. and Mrs. G. gave
rise roused Governor Jay to all his early energy.

He was well acquainted, as you know, with old Lady
Huntington in Bath in 1783, and heard from her
many anecdotes of the geniuses of Queen Anne's
reign, with whom she was intimate. Addison, according to her, was a scholar, and a gentleman, and
a Christian ; Pope was a mere poet, testy and not
pleasing in society ; Bolingbroke was the superior of
them all in talent, manners, and conversation.

"We had some talk, also, about the Rev. Dr. Pe-
ters, whom I met in London in 1805. At the commencement of the Revolution he was mobbed in
Connecticut for his Tory principles. He fled to
Boston, and thence to England. He was then employed by Lord North to give information relative
to this country, and was subsequently chosen Bishop
of Vermont, but the Bishop of London declined to
consecrate him, it was said, merely from the want of
proper testimonials. He afterwards became a violent
Oppositionist.

"The Governor certainly fails, but it is an unper-
ceived decay, and few seem either better prepared or
more willing to depart."

In 1816, the Rev. Timothy Clowes, Rector of St.
Peter's, Albany, was presented for trial on charges
affecting Church discipline. In the Convention of
that year, an effort was made to dismiss the present-
ment, but failed on the ground that the Convention
had no jurisdiction in the matter. The present-
ment, therefore, was allowed to take its course, and
my father found himself one of the selected members
of the court, — a serious and responsible position for so

young a man. There is no necessity to enter here into
the merits of this case, long since buried in the past.
The following letter, however, is of interest, as giving a cotemporary view of the proceedings. It is
addressed to Miss Bard, who was then in Burlington,
N. J.

THE COTTAGE, 23d *July,* 1817.

MY DEAR AUNT, — I suppose, ere this, I have
been scolded by you, mentally, a dozen times, for
my long silence, but if so, it has been unjustly bestowed. I left home with the expectation of a week's
absence, but instead of one, I was detained near
four weeks in as steady occupation as I ever had.
I was recorder of the board, and generally wrote
down twenty folio pages of testimony every day.
We always met at nine o'clock and sat till two;
adjourned for an hour and generally continued to do
business until six or seven in the evening. Knowing
Eliza to be anxious, and as the only relief in my
power to my protracted return, I resolved not to
let one post pass without a letter, which I was
obliged to write by being in a little before the board
assembled, and catching every minute I could through
the day from delay of witnesses, or any other circumstance. The early morning, I devoted to exercise, to enable me to bear the application and
confinement of the day. Mr. Jarvis we made president. He proposed our being room-mates. I believe I received the proposition rather coolly. I
was very soon, however, well pleased with the arrangement, finding him an amiable, unassuming, well

instructed companion. As a young man he deserves
to be called learned, and we differ just enough to
keep up the spirit of our argument. He is a little
more attached to forms than I am, but mixes up
with them the spirit, I believe, of unaffected piety.

Of the other members of the board it is not necessary to say much.

We found Mr. Clowes disposed to throw every
impediment in the way of our proceeding. I told
him candidly at first, that the business had been too
long delayed by these trifling objections, and that I
had come up with one settled resolution in the
business, and that was to bring it to a conclusion —
if innocent to acquit, if guilty to condemn him. We
had before us between forty and fifty witnesses, — in
fact all his principal friends and all his great oppo-
nents. It has been as thorough a revolution in the
affairs of the Church as the French one was in the
State. The wealthy and respectable have been put
out and the rabble brought in. The truth of the case
seems to be this. Mr. Clowes on going there found
this democratic spirit existing, and being not much of
a gentleman, either in manners or feeling, he fell
naturally into their society, and led on that spirit to
serve his own interested purposes; but these, when
in power, had their own views in continuing there,
and Mr. Clowes has fallen into the degraded situation of their tool and instrument. Mr. Duer is on
the side of the presenters; Mr. Yates on the part
of Mr. Clowes. It has been a very tedious business,
but it has been impossible to shorten it. Such

warmth of public feeling existed that the board were forced, in order to satisfy both parties, to listen to everything that could be brought forward in relation to it. The senate chamber in the capitol, in which we sat, was in general crowded with auditors. Clowes has the faculty of making warm personal friends; some middle-aged men sat there who wept like children when anything unfavorable to him appeared in evidence. . . . .

Yours affectionately,
JOHN McVICKAR.

The result of this trial was unfavorable to Mr. Clowes, and he was suspended from the ministry.

The two room-mates thus accidentally thrown together during an ecclesiastical trial at Albany, and both destined to do good work in their different spheres, were soon again, as we shall see, to cross each other's path.

In the mean time, an intimacy, if not a friendship, grew up between them, and a correspondence commenced, which, on one side at least, was started in Latin.

CHAPTER IV.

IN the year 1817 the Rev. Dr. Bowden, Professor of Moral and Intellectual Philosophy in Columbia College, died. My father's name was soon mentioned in connection with the vacant professorship. The matter is thus touched upon in Miss Bard's diary: —

"*August 8th.* — I have this day received a great shock, though the circumstances that occasioned it may be designed by a wise Providence ultimately for our good. Dr. Bowden, one of the professors of the college, is dead, and some of Mr. McVickar's friends think, if he would accept the station, it could be procured for him. He has been written to on the subject and I am waiting in the most painful anxiety to know the result. He will do what he considers his duty, and what will be best for the interests and happiness of his family, and my dear brother will urge him to that effect. But O, what a blow to his and my sister's happiness, and, indeed, to all our families, to have him and their beloved daughter separated from them. And what shall I do, or who shall I part from? 'Why art thou so full of heaviness, O my soul, and why art thou so disquieted within me. Put thy trust in God.'"

The following few lines from one with whom my father was then quite intimate, would seem to lead to the conclusion that he did not interest himself much in the result : —

NEW YORK, *September* 5, 1817.

DEAR SIR, — .... We have parties running very high here respecting the vacant professorship in Columbia College. I hope to talk over this and other matters with you ere long under your own vine and fig-tree, which I am happy to learn you have determined not to abandon ; for, you may rely upon it, you are happier and more useful where you are than if you were, professor of moral philosophy, rhetoric, and belles-letters, etc., etc., in Columbia College.

Believe me, my dear sir,

Yours most respectfully,

CLEMENT C. MOORE.

The fact that parties were running very high respecting this professorship was unfortunately true, and still more unfortunate was it that Mr. McVickar's Albany room-mate, Mr. Jarvis, afterwards the learned historian, between whom and my father quite an intimacy, as we have seen, had sprung up, should be his chief rival. But so it was, and, as is often the case, the confident one was disappointed, the careless one successful. The following letter from Mr. Jarvis, though long, is given entire, as being in every way interesting, showing the friendly spirit between two of the rival candidates, and also as markedly characteristic of the future Church historian. It seems to have been in reply to one from my father, in Latin, which is fair evidence that the parochial work of the last six years had not broken up the old habits of systematic study : —

BLOOMINGDALE, *September* 25, 1817.

MY DEAR SIR, — I have too much to say and too little time to say it in to reply to your letter in the same language. My thoughts are so impatient to be with you that they choose the lightest and most rapid vehicle, and will not wait for the more dignified, slow, and solemn pace of the old Roman state coach. You kindly inquire about my health, my family, my studies, and the books I have read — at least you suggest them as topics of correspondence. As to the last you mention, ' de libris imprimendis,' [1] it does not come within the circle of my acts or even of my projects. Since my return my time has been much occupied by business, which had suffered some derangement from my long absence, and by parochial duties which have been more than ordinarily numerous. I have made out, however, to read one book of Quintilian, Longinus, a portion of Lord Kames, and some other critical works, and am at present examining, or rather commencing an examination of the Chronology of Syncellus, the Chronicon Paschale, Eusebius, and Josephus, as compared with the Samaritan, Greek, and Hebrew Bibles, and the modern system of Usher, Blair, and others. For this purpose I have been making chronological notes from Josephus, and have proceeded as far as the Ninth Book,

---

[1] Of publishing.

and I think it very evident that his chronology has
been corrupted, and that it must have been originally
the same as what now appears in our Hebrew copies.
These, with Riley's narrative and the Reviews, make
up the total ' de libris legendis.' With respect to
the Church, I can say but little, as I have seen
scarcely any of the clergy since my return. They
have been so much out of town, that Mr. Milnor
told me he had been called upon to perform the
parochial duties of Trinity, not one of the clergy of
that parish being in the city. What shall I say to
you with regard to the college? On Monday Dr.
Bard favored me with a visit and informed me that
you are a candidate for the vacant professorship.
This information, I must confess, gave me some pain,
because it places me in a situation which I hoped
never to have been in with regard to you. Early this
month one of the trustees asked' my permission to
nominate me, to which I assented, and I find that
my name is publicly mentioned. Mr. Bristed has
been and still is very active in soliciting votes, and
the warmest of his supporters, I understand, is your
friend Clement Moore. I concluded, therefore, that
he also could not have known of your wishes. For
myself, I have not taken any step to secure an election, nor shall I stoop to solicit a single vote. However the matter may terminate, my dear sir, I hope
and trust that it will produce no difference in our
feelings of friendship so happily begun. It pains me,
indeed, to think that my gain should ever be your
loss, and I most heartily wish that some course could

be adopted which would bring us together in the same institution, where I am sure we should be brothers. I do not see that after matters have gone thus far, I can well retreat consistently with a proper degree of self-respect. Notwithstanding all Bristed's exertions, I have reason to believe that I should command a superiority of votes. How it will be now I know not. In a contention with you victory will be almost as bad as defeat. But let me turn from this subject and inquire, in my turn, ' de tuis, de salute tua, de studiis, de libris legendis.' Whatever concerns you, be assured, my good friend, will always be a subject of interest to me, and you can never write without conferring a most sensible pleasure upon

Your affectionate friend and brother,

Samuel F. Jarvis.

Rev. Mr. McVickar.

The following from Bishop Hobart shows that others felt the difficulty of two such candidates even more than the candidates themselves : —

New York, *October* 7, 1817.

My dear Sir, — At the request of Dr. Bard I took much pleasure in nominating you yesterday at the board of trustees, for the vacant professorship, but felt it my duty at the same time to state that I did not intend thereby to express a preference for you over Mr. Jarvis, who was also nominated by Mr. William Johnson. My situation is an embarrassing one, but I must endeavor to do what on the whole seems best. Be assured, however, that whatever may be the issue of this matter you have the sincere esteem

Of your friend,

J. H. HOBART.

REV. MR. McVICKAR.

The result of the election is best told in extracts from a home letter, where the sanguine hopefulness of the mother's disposition is strongly, not to say quaintly, exhibited : —

NEW YORK, *November* 3, 1817, 11 A. M.

MY DEAR SON, — The important question is now agitating at the college, whether you shall obtain the professorship or no. Our hopes stand high, and a few hours will decide whether they were well founded or not, but so sanguine have I been that I have engaged a woman to clean the house.

Dr. Bard, Judge Johnston, and Frank are to dine with us to-day. It will look somewhat like a dinner to celebrate your election, but it was purely accidental and without design ; yet should you gain it I dare say they will have no objection to drinking a bumper to your health, long life, and usefulness in it ; and in which I shall sincerely join them, if not in the bumper, yet in all the good wishes for your health and prosperity. . . . .

Judge Livingston has this minute brought the result of the election to me with congratulations on your success. The vote was taken, when it stood thus : 8 for you, 7 for Bristed, and 4 for Mr. Jarvis ; the second, 13 for you, 6 for Bristed, and 2 for Mr. Jarvis.

4

. . . Dr. Bard has just been in expressing his joy at your election, but was unable to dine with us, as he was sent express for to Mr. King on Long Island, who is ill. . . . . I have been so often broken in upon the last hour, and so many things occupy my mind, that I know not hardly what I write, and lest I should become unintelligible I conclude,

Your ever affectionate mother,

A. McVICKAR.

This event colored the whole future of my father's life. It removed him, almost unwillingly, from country scenes and pastoral duty, and threw him, in the prime of early manhood, into the centre of the intellectual thought of the young but growing American metropolis, as an instructor of its youth and a companion of its maturer minds. We cannot, however, pass into this new and apparently more important period, without first making an effort to show the depth of the impression made upon his character by those subtle forces of a parochial and social circle, like that of Hyde Park, exercising their influence during the first six years of ministerial and married life. Fortunately the " Domestic Narrative of the Life of Dr. Bard," written by him, now out of print, enables me to do this, not directly, but by the stronger testimony of inference. I therefore, without hesitation, avail myself freely of it.

" In the year 1817, the first breach was made in the family circle at Hyde Park, by the removal of the writer of the present memoir, with his family, to

New York, upon being chosen to a professorship in the college at which he was educated.

"How actively Dr. Bard labored in its procurement is gratefully remembered by one who already owed to him more than gratitude could repay. The influence he was able to exert at so advanced an age, and after twenty years of retirement, affords a strong proof of mental vigor.

"An extract from a letter to his wife, while this matter was pending, is an evidence of his exertions and feelings on this occasion, while it makes public a debt of gratitude which the author is proud to acknowledge.

"New York, *September* 1, 1817.

"My dear Mary, — I have been working with all my might for that in which, now that there is some chance of success, I begin to be almost afraid I shall succeed; but I comfort myself, and I hope the consideration will comfort you, that I verily believe it will contribute to the general happiness and interests of our family. Hitherto, my dear wife, we have been as happy in our retirement as we could ever hope to be; and in the health and character of our children, and the promise of our grandchildren, have reaped an ample reward for all our exertions. But our family has now become so numerous that, like the bees, we must be content to swarm; and, like them, I am striving to furnish the young colony with a king and queen, who shall lead them forth, and establish them in their new habitations: nor can I think of any plan upon which we can do this with so little deprivation to ourselves, and so much benefit to our children. We shall not lose them altogether; we shall still enjoy their society in summer, when our pastor will pray with us, and preach for us, and administer to us all the consolations of religion, and foster his little church, and do good to his old friends as heretofore. This I look to for my pay, nor will I abate him one jot of it. In the spring, too, we can visit them; and once a week we shall expect the boat, or the post, with that kind of anxiety which gives a spur to our wishes, and, like a good appetite, seasons our enjoyments.

" In short, my dearest friend, I think it my duty; and if it please God to bless my endeavors, why then we must submit to any privations to which it may subject us : but if it fail, why then I shall firmly believe it ought to fail; and we shall all be equally content and happy without it.

Yours affectionately,   S. B.

" That argument and reflection should be necessary to reconcile those concerned to a change so beneficial, in a worldly point of view, is the strongest proof of the degree of that family union and happiness of which it required the sacrifice; and now that death and removal have so thinned its ranks and dispersed its members, that it appears but as a dream of an earlier and happier state, it may be allowed to one who participated largely in its pleasures, to recall a few touches of a picture of domestic felicity, rarely clouded by sorrow; and still more rarely, by want of sympathy or affection.

" Although the noble mansion at Hyde Park formed
the central point of attraction for children, grandchildren, and kindred, still each member of the circle, claiming on all festive occasions their turn of
entertainment, diffused and multiplied the sources of
an innocent hilarity which none more than Dr. Bard
enjoyed or promoted.

" Among these he seemed especially to enjoy the
simple entertainments of the parsonage, as looking
round on a scene of happiness more peculiarly of his
own creation: and I think I see him yet, with a countenance beaming pleasure, praising the productions of
the children, encouraging the arrangements of their
parents, or joining in the chorus of some little song
prepared for the occasion. This was sometimes
made the vehicle of sentiments which brought tears
into his eyes. A trifle of that kind which has been
preserved, will indicate, at least, the feelings of love
and veneration which he excited.

> " Hail to the sire, that in calmness reposes,
>   Circled by those whom his kindness has blessed;
> Round him, as life with its evening closes,
>   He sinks in the arms of affection to rest.
>   On his dear and reverend head,
>   Heaven long its blessings shed,
>   His presence to bless us, example to mend;
>   While loud the Hudson banks
>   Echo our grateful thanks,
>   Health to our father, companion and friend!
>
> " Hail to the sage, who, when old age advances,
>   Crowns in the shade of retirement his days;
> Ended his full task, his eye upward glances,
>   Waiting the meed of his great Master's praise.

> Heaven long the blessing spare,
> 　Of his kind and watchful care;
> Wisdom to guide us, and skill to defend :
> 　While loud the Hudson banks
> 　Echo our grateful thanks,
> Health to our father, physician, and friend !

> "Hail to the stem, from which we're descended,
> 　Or grafted, like scions, on its evergreen root;
> Round it we cling, by its branches defended,
> 　Rest in its shadow, and feed on its fruit.
> 　　Long may that root be fed,
> 　　Far may its branches spread ;
> 　Flourish in beauty, with fruitfulness bend ;
> 　　While to the Hudson banks
> 　　Echo our grateful thanks,
> 　Health to our father, our guardian and friend!

"Cottage, *December* 31, 1816.[1]

" Among the partakers in these rural festivities, and one whose presence always gave them a peculiar interest, was the venerable Mrs. Barton, a lady whose warm attachment to Dr. and Mrs. Bard, through a long life, demands some passing record, — a tribute now doubly due, since the shock of their united death seemed to break the last feeble thread which detained her in this state of mortality ; and within a few days she followed them at the advanced age of ninety years, neither overcome by disease, nor broken down by infirmity. Mrs. Barton was aunt both to Dr. and Mrs. Bard, being sister to Dr. De Normandie, and widow to the friend and brother-in-law of our eminent countryman, David Rittenhouse.

" At the period to which the preceding poetry re-

[1] J. McVickar.

fers, she had attained the age of eighty-seven years.
Independent in her occupations, actively and benevolently employed, participating in all family festivities, and with a tremulous though sweet voice
(which, in youth, had gained her the title of the
' American Nightingale '), leading at the supper
table a united chorus, in which the voices of four
successive generations emulously contended. As a
trait of superior character, of a mind that could rise
above the besetting weakness of old age, I subjoin
the following letter, conveying to a niece one half
her fortune.

" HYDE PARK, *December* 9, 1803.

" DEAR SALLY, — I beg your acceptance of the inclosed bond, dated on the day which closed the
allotted time of man's life, three-score years and ten ;
and, although I have a proper sense of the great
blessings I enjoy of health and understanding, yet I
am sensible of my own infirmities, and would not
leave to chance, or the caprice of old age, the power
of altering my purpose of seeing you, before I die, in
some measure independent. I beg you will make
me no answer to this letter, as it is far greater happiness to me that I have this little to give, than it can
possibly be for you to receive it ; and I am well convinced, from your temper and disposition, that, were
the case reversed, you would have the same sentiments. To make you perfectly easy, be assured I
am not the poorer by parting with this sum : it is
nothing more than shifting it from one hand to the
other ; and I still retain more than double the in-

come I ever spent upon myself, at any period of my life. God bless you, my dear niece; and that you may long live to enjoy every happiness this frail life can bestow, is the sincere prayer of

" Your affectionate aunt,

" S. BARTON. '

" This rare union of qualities, alike estimable and amiable, produced their corresponding affections, respect and love, in all around her; which, added to the natural emotion excited by so advanced an age, amounted, in the younger members of the family, to a feeling almost of veneration.

" Among other remembrances placed in my hands, of this happy family society, and which are now valued, like other relics, not for what they are, but for what they recall, is the following little address to Mrs. Barton, on the celebration of her eighty-eighth birthday.

'When years to worth, to worth when wisdom's joined,
Instinctive springs the homage of the mind:
But when religion, from her throne above,
Crowns that assemblage in a friend we love,
Gilding life's close with faith's unfading ray,
Like the calm sunset of a summer's day;
'Tis then we think, that Heaven in kindness shows
How age may sink, 'mid blessings, to repose;
How short the passage that to faith is given,
From bliss on earth to higher bliss in heaven.
Long may that bliss be thine, dear aunt, to see
Encircling friends, who love and copy thee:
Learning from thee to blend, in gentle truth,
The voice of wisdom with the charm of youth;

And, when thy spirit bursts from bonds of clay,
To seek the sunshine of a brighter day,
Then may they learn how smooth the bed of death
To a calm conscience, and a Christian faith.

"*December* 8, 1818.[1]

"It may not be uninteresting to add, that the pious wish with which the above closes, was realized in no common degree; gently sinking in the possession of all her faculties, and for two days hourly expecting dissolution, her time and thoughts were occupied with making it a lesson to her young relatives who crowded around her dying bed, giving to most of them some appropriate memorial of the scene before them, — some prayer, or form of devotion (of which her desk contained many, either composed or transcribed by herself), and receiving with them the last consolations of religion, — to them the commencement, to her the termination of the Christian race.

"The last winter of Dr. Bard's life was passed by him in more than usual enjoyment. Preceded by a long and satisfactory visit to his daughter in town, it rolled rapidly by in his usual interchange of study and amusement. Engaged in preparing an enlarged edition of his chief medical work, he found no time to hang heavy on his hands; and it was difficult to say from which of his varied employments, whether of labor or amusement, he derived the greatest pleasure."

Having carried the reader thus far in the closing

[1] J. McVickar.

scenes of this Hyde Park circle, it will not be taken amiss if there is here added, from the same pen, the few concluding lines which chronicle the end.

" In the month of May, 1821, while preparing for the annual spring visit to the city, Mrs. Bard was attacked with a pleuritic affection ; which, after a few days, gave evidence of a fatal termination. Dr. Bard, though laboring under a similar attack, would not be separated from her, but continued to be, as formerly, her companion, nurse, and physician. Such a long and affectionate union as theirs had been, had early excited the wish, the wish the prayer, and the prayer the expectation, that in death they were not to be divided. What was thus both wished for, and expected, had become, it seems, the subject of their sleeping thoughts ; and a remarkable dream of Mrs. Bard's to this effect was now remembered, and repeated by her husband, with feelings not of super- stition, but pleasing anticipation.

" The last effort of his pen was to give comfort to those who were absent. This letter, which con- veyed to his daughter the first intimation of dan- ger, brought her to her paternal home a few hours too late to receive a mother's blessing, but in time to spend a few short ones of affectionate intercourse with her dying father. It was passed with calm- ness by both ; indeed, there was no room for sorrow in such a tranquil, peaceful departure. His calm, but affectionate inquiries about absent friends, his rational directions as to future arrangements, and his freedom from all perturbation of spirit, were so foreign to the conception of departing humanity, that the feelings could not realize it, — there were in it no images of grief from which imagination might draw her pattern.

" Under these circumstances, not of stoical but Christian composure, he sank to rest at five o'clock in the morning of the 24th May, in the eightieth year of his age, twenty-four hours after the death of his wife ! A common grave received their remains.

" Their affectionate relative, Mrs. Barton, sank under the bereavement, and within a few days joined them in the land of rest. . . . .

" Of that which has been the great aim of the author, the display of private character, he has spoken confidently, because he knew intimately ; and in the varied relations of social and domestic life, having proposed him as a model to himself, he is not afraid to hold him up to others as an example worthy of imitation."

Whatever may be thought of this picture, it is certainly very unlike anything of the present day, and as such, like some portrait of the old masters, will be gazed upon with interest. But may I not claim more for it ? Is there not in it a something which the families of this restless generation, without knowing exactly what it is they lack, are constantly sighing after? Repose of mind, united with a pervading faith, intellectual activity, and general cheerfulness, which, if we picture to ourselves at all, seems more what we are hoping for in heaven, than a condition possible on earth. Yet here it was, not only on the earth, but on the familiar banks of the Hudson River, and attained, too, at a very economic expenditure of money. One of the worst quarrels occurring in this family circle, and which lasted nearly a week, arose from sending a party home from the mansion-house, on a stormy night, in the farm wagon instead of in the family coach, which had only lately been freshly painted. This was considered a pitch of meanness not easily forgiven, and a heavy sacrifice to the muses in the shape of poetical letters back and forth was necessary before tranquillity was restored. It may not be easy to analyze a family's happiness, but when we have the character of their faith, their occupations, pleasures, causes of quarrel, and modes of peace-making, the elements of a fair judgment are in our hand. Then by placing these alongside our own and comparing the two, we approach at least, that which must have a distinct existence as truth, *the formula of earthly happiness.*

CHAPTER V.

THE close of the year 1817 found my father and his family, of which Miss Bard was now an acknowledged member, settled in New York city. Their residence at that time was in the old college building at the foot of Park Place, the wings — to one of which they afterwards removed — being then in course of erection. "Comfortable but not fashionable," are the epithets used in writing to absent friends. In fact, it must at that time have been but a dreary looking place, especially to those fresh from the beauties of the country and of Hyde Park. The larger trees of the college green, planted by Dr. Bard, were indeed there, but the space between the buildings and College Place was filled with small wooden houses occupied by a low class of the colored population of the city. The terraces and plantings of after years, and the fine private residences of College Place, had not yet made their appearance. It was then almost what the worst surroundings of Central Park are at present. It is now, having been in the mean time one of the most beautiful and fashionable neighborhoods of this changeable city, given over entirely to the requirements of commerce, and only here and there a forlorn house hides its diminished head amid towering stores. This oldest of the college buildings was erected and first occupied in 1760. It was then in the country, and is thus described by a traveller of the day: "The building forms one side of a quadrangle fronting Hudson's River, and will be the most beautifully situated of any college, I believe, in the world." This was its still earlier phase, and illustrates the wonderful growth of New York city. A hundred years sees one and the same spot the centre of rural beauty, of suburban nuisances, of fashion, and of commerce.

The chair to which my father was appointed in Columbia College was that of " Moral Philosophy, Rhetoric, and Belles-lettres." He entered at once upon his duties, being then in his thirty-first year and youthful in appearance.

" Well I remember," says Dr. Johnson in the discourse already quoted from, " the youthful professor, with his dark hair, his quick glance, his brusque manner, as he was introduced to us, the collegians in the chapel, and how we found fault with him for his youthful look."

This youthfulness of appearance must have been so decided as to be, at that time, almost an annoyance. It brought upon him, at the very first meeting of the college board, the somewhat embarrassing question from the venerable Dr. Wilson, " Pray, Mr. McVickar, how old are you?" But the ready reply, " Between thirty and forty," silenced such questions for the future, and proved that neither years nor wit were wanting.

This must have been a year of hard work to the young professor in the preparation of his different courses of lectures, and yet, with that characteristic boldness, and forgetfulness of self in all matters of duty, which ever characterized him, he did not hesitate the ensuing year to ask permission to enlarge the duties of his chair. He already identified himself with the interests and reputation of the college, and at his urgent request the subjects of Intellectual Philosophy and Political Economy were, in 1818, without any extra emolument, added to his department. This was the first course of political economy lectures established in any American college.

But college duties, however onerous, were not allowed, from the very first, to shut out entirely those of his more sacred profession. In Grace and Trinity churches he often rendered assistance by preaching and otherwise, and if we may judge by the following lines from his mother the year before he came to the city, there must often have been the need: —

"The bishop is still on his eastern tour through Connecticut. I hope this will be the last, and that they will select some one to preside over them, exclusively their own, as we are too much in want of his services ourselves. Unless we have aid from the country next Sunday we shall be obliged to shut two of our churches."

On the 29th of January, 1818, he delivered an address in St. Paul's Chapel, before the New York Bible and Common Prayer Book Society, which was published by request. This was his first publication.

It is not remarkable as a composition, and yet was probably effective from its simple directness.

In another way, also, did my father keep up his professional tone of mind, though I have no reason to suppose that it was done for that purpose. He was in the habit of writing short lectures on some portion of Scripture, suitable to the day or season, for use at family worship. They were short, simple, very much to the point, and loving in tone. This was kept up for many years, and must have had its influence on both himself and others.

The question respecting a regular course of theological study for candidates for Holy Orders was then attracting considerable attention in the Church. The House of Bishops had lately put forth an authoritative course of reading for candidates. Mr. C. C. Moore, the only son of the Bishop of New York, had given in trust, to meet the wants of this demand in the future, a large property on the outskirts of the city. The regents of the University of the State had also made propositions to Columbia College and Trinity Church respecting a new college on Staten Island, without theological restrictions respecting its President, but with a theological school attached. Thus the whole subject, in all its bearings, was being forced upon the thinking minds of the Church. Bishop Hobart, though looking with interest upon the proposition of the regents, doubted their motives, and as far as personal inclination went, favored a diocesan seminary. The plan of a general seminary of the whole Church was, however, the most popular, and, as we know, was finally carried into successful operation ; though many of the difficulties which Bishop Hobart foresaw have since been painfully realized. My father naturally took a deep interest in these questions. When the general seminary was determined on, he threw himself with all cordiality into the carrying out of the plan, and was himself chiefly instrumental in the gathering and endowment of its noble library, still his mind first turned to other plans in connection with the college of which he was a professor.

I find among his papers of the year 1820 one entitled " Plan of Theological Professorship to be attached to Columbia and other colleges." The plan, which is first given in brief, is as follows : —

" The endowment for the support of the professor to be created by donations from individuals attached to the Protestant Episcopal Church until it reaches a revenue of $2,500 per annum.

" The appointment of the professor to rest with the Bishop of the Diocese of New York, subject to the approbation of the Board of Trustees.

" The duties of the professor to be —

" 1. A sub-graduate course of lectures on the evidences of revealed religion, to be delivered weekly to such of the classes as the trustees may see fit to appoint, of which course the president of the college to be visitor.

" 2. A course of theological instruction confined to the students of divinity, in accordance with that prescribed by the canons of the Protestant Episcopal

5

Church. Of this course the Bishop and Standing Committee of the Diocese of New York to be visitors."

A somewhat similar plan for a law professorship, drawn out two years later, shows the working, at that early period, of my father's mind towards that principle of a university which has now become so popular.

" As this law professorship," he writes, " will probably serve as a precedent for connecting with the college other graduate courses of study, it requires consideration to place it under such guards that it may not interfere with the good order and discipline of the institution.

" To prevent the degradation of the existing college course, the course of law should be based upon it, thus making the former necessary, this being regarded as a graduate course, taking up the student where the sub-graduate one has left him. But though ostensibly intended for graduates of the college, it need not in practice be restricted to them. . . . .

" It is not sufficient that this lectureship be *added* to the college; it must be *ingrafted* into it. It must be made part of a great whole so as to unite aptly with it, and have a common interest and common feelings."

This fear of degrading the sub-graduate course through unrestricted contact with professional lectures, and the importance of binding the latter to the college corporation by common interests and common feelings, sounds more like the experiences of 1870 than the warnings of 1822.

In a little bundle of scraps marked " Sweepings of my Portfolio, 1820," I find one entitled " Greek Epigram written in Miss H——'s Album." The Greek is classical and shows the scholar, but I content myself with the English version which accompanies it : —

> " Mary, to try my wit, a verse demands,
>   And gives her album to my trembling hands,
>   But guile befriends me where my wit is weak :
>   To hide the faults her critic taste would seek
>   I shade my dullness with a veil of Greek."

This readiness to gratify others with a few lines of rhyme, which not unfrequently rose to poetic merit, was with my father quite proverbial. And though it must often have been something of a trial added to the exactions of a busy life, good-nature seldom, I might almost say, judging by the following incident, never failed.

A young relative, a school-girl, sought him one day for an acrostic. She met him within the college green, cloak on arm and bag in hand, bound for the country. Seeing her look of disappointment, and drawing from her her errand, he gave into her charge his cloak and bag, and sitting down on the steps of a brother professor's house, wrote on the back of a letter, in a few moments' time, the desired lines, and then hurried on his way with, we cannot doubt, a light heart. A request for verses was nearly always put aside with the plea of want of time, but in spite of that the verses generally came.

The summer vacation after Dr. Bard's death was

passed by my father and his family at the residence
of his brother-in-law, Judge Johnston, near Poughkeepsie.   How it was spent the following portions of
a letter to his mother gives us some idea.

POUGHKEEPSIE, 11*th September*, 1821.

MY DEAR MOTHER, —. . . . On Saturday I
got up a long wagon filled with straw and took a
loadful of children out to a pond a few miles back
from the river to fish, where we spent the day in
high frolic.   This is the only idle morning I have
spent since I have been up.   I am generally near
five hours with my pen in my hand.   About two
o'clock I break off, take a dive in the river, which I
find wonderfully refreshing, shave, dress, and am
ready for our late dinner after three.   The afternoon
I always have my gig up and drive some one of our
invalids eight or ten miles.   Our evenings are en-
livened with the organ and very pleasing singing, and
I sleep sound at night so that for myself my vacation
never passed happier nor more to the benefit of my
health.

Beside my weekly duties, I have preached every
Sunday since I left town, and now have charge of
Mr. Reed's church in his absence.   I leave a space
for my wife, whose warm and sincere expressions I
know you love (as all do) to hear, and who puts as
much in one of them as I can in a whole letter.

Your affectionate son,

JOHN McVICKAR.

He was then engaged on a memoir of his father-in-law, entitled, " A Domestic Narrative of the Life of Samuel Bard, M. D., LL. D.," which was published the next spring, and from which quotations have already been made in these pages. In the short prefatory remarks he says : —

The following narrative was drawn up last summer, during the leisure of a short vacation from academical duties, with a view simply to preserve and arrange the fading recollections of a highly valued friendship. It is now made public, partly from the interest taken in its subject by a large circle of personal friends, but chiefly from the hope that the delineation of Dr. Bard's character, as displayed in the events of his life, may lead others, and especially the young of that profession of which he was an ornament, to tread in his footsteps — to pursue worldly success by exertion, by perseverance, and by the conscientious discharge of professional duty ; and to seek for happiness in the exercise of the benevolent and social affections, under the control and guidance of religion.

Col. College, *March* 30, 1822.

A few notices from those whose opinions in that day carried weight will show how this his first literary work was received.

Governor Jay, then an old man, writes in that staid style which especially belonged to him, and somewhat to his generation : —

Bedford, Westchester Co., N. Y., 28*th July*, 1822.

Dear Sir,—I have received, and we have all read, your Life of the late Dr. Bard. Accept my thanks for this interesting work. It appears to have done justice to the merits of that worthy gentleman, and in a style and manner reputable to the author.

With the best wishes for your and Mrs. McVickar's health and welfare, I am, dear sir,

Your obliged and obedient servant,

John Jay.

Mr. William Moore, a valued friend and relative, says : —

" Those who can read your Life of Dr. Bard without being made thereby the wiser and the better, might as well never have been taught to read. You have erected for him a monument that says in strong terms to every person who sees it, ' Go thou and do likewise.' "

And a well known physician of New York, Dr. A. H. Stephens, writes : —

" To say nothing of its value in other respects, I am determined that it shall be the first book I shall place in the hands of those whose studies in medicine are directed by your obliged and humble servant."

We close this subject with a letter of greater length, from one, who, however necessarily partial in his judgment, still deserves notice in these pages as being, besides a brother-in-law, one of my father's most valued and honored friends. The following lines from Mr. William Bard, on the subject of his father's life, depicts, as in a glass, his own character:

My dear Sir, — I have just risen from finishing the perusal of your memoir. You deserve the thanks of us all, and mine you most sincerely have for this delineation of my dear father's character. It would be scarcely prudent for me to say what the public will think of it, from my own opinion of its merits; but if my feelings do not greatly deceive me it must be well received. I know it gives a just character of my father, and the manner in which that is done, will add, I have no doubt, to your reputation. In addition to the pride justly felt in the world's knowing from what parents we have descended, the making such a character known cannot, I think, but be of service. He was made happy and successful through life by the performance of his duty in every station. His obedience to his parents protected his childhood from error; his industry as a student gave him knowledge and reputation as a physician; his attention to his business procured him independence; his active philanthropy, the esteem of the public; his kind and affectionate manner, the love of his family and friends; his piety, content, with a calm and quiet conscience.

He affords an instance of the reward a wise and virtuous conduct brings with it, even in this life, and an encouraging example of what may be done, by·perseverance, industry, and honor, in securing whatever of good this world has to offer.

While I feel proud of such a parent and of such ancestors, I feel entailed on me greater obligations to endeavor, as far as my abilities and opportunities permit, to maintain the reputation of a name so supported by those who have gone before me. I shall offer your book to my children as a manual and guide, in the hope that, influenced by the same feelings, they will make greater exertions to become the worthy representatives of such ancestors. It will, I trust, be a benefit to us all, and not only to us, but to many less interested, who may read it. Thus will the influence of my father's character extend even beyond his life ; and you be rewarded in the most grateful manner for the labor you have accomplished with so much skill and elegance.

Yours, etc.,

WM. BARD.

June 17, 1822.

This, a reflected picture of Mr. William Bard's own character and life, true in most points, fails, unfortunately, where it speaks of perseverance, industry, and honor as being able to secure whatever of good this world has to offer. Mr. Bard was himself both an example of industry and the acknowledged soul of honor, yet, at an advanced age, he was sacrificed for another's fault, and forced to resign the presidency of a wealthy moneyed institution of this city because of the dishonesty of a trusted clerk.

A tour to Niagara, during the vacation of 1824, gives us the following in a letter to Miss Bard : —

" *August* 31. — In the whole course of our journey we have not passed so interesting a day as yesterday. Meeting General and Mrs. Gaines at Buffalo, the General proposed that we should journey together to the Falls, and visit in our way the battle-ground on the Canada frontier. We accordingly engaged an Extra to meet us at Waterloo, but ourselves took boat across the lake to Fort Erie, the scene of his exploits. We there 'fought all his battles o'er again' amid the ruins which he left behind him. Chippeway, Lundy's Lane, and Queenstown Heights were all visited by us in the course of the day, the latter commanding a noble and delightful view of fifty miles of lake and land. . . . .

" I will not describe the Falls, for I cannot ; neither painting nor description can touch them. It is as much as one can do to bear the awful impressions which rush in upon the mind."

Under date of the 11th of September, Miss Bard writes in her diary, " This evening arrived in perfect health our beloved party, after having enjoyed five weeks to the utmost extent of their wishes and expectations, and are now preparing with a large party to witness the reception given at West Point to the Marquis de Lafayette."

CHAPTER VI.

HOME claims and the education of his children were matters that my father never neglected because of professional and outside duties. Rather did he gather up the experience which these latter gave him to apply them with practical and loving perseverance to those in whose improvement he was most interested. As this is not the universal experience in the case of busy professional men, I here add some extracts from home letters to show how strikingly it was exemplified in his case.

To his eldest daughter, now in her sixteenth year, spending the winter away from home, he writes : —

My dearest Daughter, —. . . . From nine to three is not too long to study, but it is too long to sit; you must, therefore, break in upon its sedentary character as much as you can. It is the division I have always liked, the morning for study, the afternoon for exercise, and the evening for cheerful amusement. Or, in other words, the morning for the mind, the afternoon for the body, and the evening for the social affections.

To the same, at Miss Roberts' school : —

" *October* 30. —. . . . I have long wished for you to have an opportunity of a short residence from home. The fault of character which I wished to see corrected is that of reliance on the care and attention and direction of others, which is destructive to all firmness and independence of character.   Home fosters this weakness ; a residence abroad corrects it, by forcing you to the exercise of your own understanding and to depend on your own exertions.

" Another error to which you are naturally inclined is a reserve which wraps you up in your own feelings, and indisposes you to enter with cheerfulness into the society and concerns of others.   Throw this off, my dear daughter, for if indulged in it will make you less amiable and less useful.   Force yourself to find occupation, if you cannot pleasure, in the company of your equals ; enter into their innocent amusements and conversation, and after a time you will find it agreeable, and your own happiness and your power of bestowing it upon others will be greatly increased. We are generally happy as well as good in proportion as we are forgetful of ourselves and thoughtful of others."

To the same, while staying at Hyde Park : —

"*February* 8. —. . . . We are all well pleased with your proposed jaunt.   Whatever adds to your health and spirits is giving a new value to book learning. It brings it into play, turns learning into conversational powers, history into anecdote, and poetry into taste. . . . . . The ball last night passed without any of us to witness its splendor, or partake of its gayety, so that I am afraid you will receive but a lame account of it. Indeed, I do not know when we shall get to a ball again, having fallen into the error of the golden age of believing that they have little to do with true gayety of heart. You may perhaps correct our notions a little next winter, but I forewarn you they are very stubborn, and will require you to wean us from them by very slow degrees. We have found out by our philosophy that there are very few free in this world, and that there are many other slaves beside those in the West Indies, and many other tyrannical task-masters besides those the Man-umission Society tells us of. Instances have fallen under my own observation of their exacting such tasks from their slaves as have destroyed health and cheerfulness, and sometimes even life itself. But such cruelty is too shocking a subject for your sensi-tive feelings, so I pass to the gayer picture of our family fireside."

To the same : —

"*March* 13. — The older children go to school, the younger are left to the teaching of mother wit, whom I have always regarded as an excellent ' instructress, aided by their aunt with her main supporters, Addi-son and Johnson, your mother with the best of books, and your poor father with more anxiety than zeal, more zeal than diligence, more diligence than leisure, and that little leisure armed with an arithmetic in one hand, and Walter Scott and Shakespeare in the other."

A few years later I find the following hints on study prepared for a younger daughter : —

MEMORANDA FOR MY DAUGHTER.

New York, *January* 1, 1828.

First Great Principle. — Your country winter is intended for the benefit of your health. Everything, therefore, must yield to this. Study is altogether secondary. Exercise, gayety, and talk are better than books. Knowledge may be got afterwards, health and spirits are to be secured now.

Second. — Readiness and correctness with your pen is the main point in which you need improvement. So far as regards the reputation of being well educated, and, I may add, for her own comfort, it is more important for a lady to write a good note or pleasing letter, than to know all languages, and the whole circle of sciences.

Third. — In reading, everything depends upon the zeal and interest you take in what you read; to read as a task is perfect waste of time, it makes stupid without making wise.

Fourth. — Do not attempt to remember above a hundredth part of what you read. Choose what is most striking or illustrative of principles ; fix it by repetition, perhaps by writing, and, above all, by associating it with what you already know on the same subject, and if you wish to fix it forever in the memory, bring it forward in conversation as soon afterwards as you can.

Lastly. — I need hardly impress upon you that the value of all education lies in its application. To make your own mind firm, benevolent, and resolute, — to make others happy.

To make this subject of home education at all complete, I here add portions of two consecutive letters written to his eldest daughter, toward the close of a winter at Hyde Park, bearing on her religious duties : —

Columbia College, *Wednesday Morning, March* 1, 1825. ·

My dear Daughter, — I begin my letter before the receipt of yours, taking time by the forelock. I shall not finish, however, until I see whether your apology is satisfactory for the unprovoked attack you made upon my handwriting in your last. Your visit to the North gave us almost as much pleasure as it did you ; we enjoyed it in the double narration of yours and your Uncle Bard's letters, which, while they tallied in the main, varied in their shades of coloring, which belong not to the things themselves but to the eye which sees them. It reminded us of the varying pictures of the same events as given in "Humphrey Clinker," and with more of interest from the narrators.

Your last letter in reference to your studies was highly satisfactory, except that it said nothing of your serious reading and serious thoughts, in which I feel a deeper interest than in anything else that concerns you. I am writing now on the first day of Lent, that season which the Christian Church has set aside from the earliest age as a suitable preparation for the festival of Easter, and I feel anxious to know whether it will so prepare your mind as to lead you then to become a communicant. Remember that on this point I neither solicit nor urge you, but merely express my hopes and wishes that your understanding may be so enlightened as to see it to be your duty, and your heart so touched as to feel it to be your comfort and support. From the reading you have already gone through I am satisfied that your mind must be settled in belief, and that grounded on rational conviction, after which nothing further is needful but such a sense of your own weakness and reliance on the mercy of God as will lead you to receive with thankfulness a sacrament which has been appointed both as a means of grace and as a pledge of pardon. As to the obligations under which it brings you, it neither adds to nor lessens those under which you now stand, any more than the promise of a child to love and honor his parents creates the obligation to gratitude and obedience. You are now bound to a holy and virtuous life, to obey the truth in proportion as you are instructed in it, and the same continues to be your rule as well after as before becoming a communicant; it only increases your ability to do that to which you are already bound. As to restricting your pleasure, it will restrain you from nothing that is innocent, and in moderation, and to none other will your reason, or, I trust, your wishes, tend. To terminate your winter by such an act of religious duty would be the aim to which both mine and your mother's wishes tend, and it would double the pleasure, my dear daughter, with which both you and we will one day look back to it. It would be crowning a winter of intellectual improvement with an act of religious devotion, that, as it were, would sanctify the whole, and be, on your part, an acknowledgment of the great end to which all intellectual improvement is to be made subservient. But in all this we would have it to be what alone can give it value, an act of free-will and conscientious duty. Having said thus much, my dear daughter, in explanation of our wishes, I shall leave the subject free, and refer you to your excellent cousin, Mr. Johnson,[1] for advice and direction, until your mind is definitely made up. . . . . .

COLLEGE HALL, *Thursday Morning.*

MY DEAR DAUGHTER, — Though I plead guilty to the charge of illegibility, I am not likely, at least this term, to correct it, from the very obvious reason that I write during a college examination, at which, from the president's sickness, I am the presiding officer ; so that while my thoughts are with you and my pen on the paper, my eyes must be directed toward the students. So that, if I am able to think intelligibly, it will be as much as you can fairly require, let alone writing so.

Your letter gave your mother and myself the highest gratification. To find your understanding fully satisfied on the great truths of religion, and your heart touched with them, fulfills, my dear daughter, our warmest wishes for you, since it assures us not only of your present but of your future happiness, and that however short may be our union

---

[1] Rev. S. R. Johnson, then Rector of St. James', Hyde Park.

here we may look forward with confidence to a never ending reunion hereafter. This is the only satisfactory basis on which filial and parental affection can rest, and henceforward our mutual enjoyment of all the innocent pleasures of life will be doubled from the conviction that it is not limited to them, but that however or whenever death may part us, whether you be taken from us or we from you, yet that we may part in peace and hope from the conviction that we shall meet again, never more to be parted.

This great security against the troubles of life, and this doubler of all its joys, you are now, I trust, my dear daughter, through the grace of God aiding your own sincere intentions, beginning to acquire. And in partaking of the blessed sacrament a further blessing will, I do not doubt, become yours. But in all this matter I must guard you against an error into which the young and warm-hearted are apt to run, and to which I think you incline. I mean the desire and expectation of some great and decided change of character and feeling from the conscientious use of the means of grace, of prayer and religious reading and the sacrament, and disappointment and self-accusation and distress of mind if the feelings do not accord. Now all this is wrong, and founded on false views of our nature and our duty, and tends to lessen greatly our temporal happiness without increasing our religious comfort or security. Consider what the object of religion and revelation is. It is to be a guide to our feet amid the snares and temptations of life, and a comfort to our hearts

under its trials and sorrows, and an assurance of
pardon to those who, having failed through the frailty
of nature, do yet through a Saviour's grace repent
and amend.   Here, then, are the objects of religion,
and by our practical conformity to them and not by
our feelings are we to try ourselves.   Do we look to
our religion to guide and strengthen us when we are
tempted to wrong ?   Do we derive our comfort from
it when suffering under the sorrows of life ?   Do we
humble ourselves when we have offended and seek
pardon from God through the mediation of our Saviour ?   If our faith have this strength, we need not be
made unhappy by what we may consider the hardness
of our feelings; they are as God has made them by
the physical and mental constitution of our nature.
I have occupied my paper, my dear daughter, with
this subject, because it seems to be uppermost in your
mind, and I am sure it is in mine.   .   .   .   .

The following from a letter of the same winter,
will give us a slight picture of the home life at " No.
8," as the house was familiarly called, and introduce
us to the literary work which was then occupying
all my father's spare hours.

" As you tell me nothing of your studies, I must
tell you of mine.   Since my return I have resumed
my Notes on Political Economy, perhaps for the
press.   To these I devote all my leisure time after
college duties are over and domestic arrangements
attended to.   Till nine A. M. is fully occupied, after
prayers, with breakfast and a short chat around a

warm fire, and a long walk to a cold market. From nine to half-past twelve college-lectures, which fatigue me sufficiently to send me out of my lecture room for half an hour, which, by way of relaxation, I employ in the correction of some pages of your sister's notes on history. Thus strengthened, with perhaps a biscuit to boot, I return to my room, whence I am called to dinner, and generally again after dinner till summoned to tea. After that hour ' *vive la bagatelle* ' — down with the Political Economy — up with family amusement ; at half after nine Aunt S. and I wind up the pleasures of the evening with one or two hits at backgammon, while your mother takes her lounge on the sofa, and the day closes with prayers, which arise from, I think, not unthankful hearts, and in which our dear absent daughter is not forgotten. By this sketch you may see that I am not eating the bread of idleness, and that if I praise study I also practice it."

The mention of the " Notes on Political Economy " in this last letter brings me to a subject which, though perhaps one of the most important in my father's life, I have no right to consider as one of general interest. I refer to his position and influence as a writer on political economy and finance. And yet, though my readers may not incline to be led into the intricacies of either of these subjects, the results of which alone are generally popular, yet I hope to interest them in a short statement of the relation held by the subject of this memoir to the history of matters which have exercised great influence on the prosperity of the country.

In 1818 the subject of Political Economy was, at Professor McVickar's request, added to his department in Columbia College. This was its first introduction into any American college as a distinct chair, and the new professor devoted himself to the subject with great earnestness and zeal. The want of a proper text-book was at once felt. No foreign work, written, as all such were, to meet the wants of a dense population and a different political status, was at all suitable. My father felt this, and a letter from Edward Everett, dated January 8, 1822, shows that he had tried to impress him into the service ; but though acknowledging the need, and his own interest in the subject, he pleads other engagements. Unable from the same reason to undertake the preparation of an entirely original work himself, my father soon set himself to prepare an American edition of an article on political economy which had just appeared in a supplement to the " Encyclopedia Britannica," from the pen of the afterwards celebrated J. R. McCulloch.

In the preparation of this work, with its copious notes on the American bearing of its various problems, he was greatly encouraged by his warm friend, Mr. James Wadsworth of Geneseo, N. Y., the father of the late General Wadsworth, who, with one or two other young men, was then residing in my father's family, while attending school in the city. Writing on the 16th May, 1825, Mr. Wadsworth says : " I am perfectly aware that it is no common undertaking in which you are engaged, and I have no doubt the work rapidly grows upon your hands as you pursue it. I hardly dare trust myself to speak on what I deem the importance of introducing the study of Political Economy in our literary institutions."

This work appeared from the press during the same year with a short dedication to Mr. Wadsworth, one of the clearest and most philanthropic minds of the period. It was the first work on the science of political economy published in America, and was well received. It is interesting now to look back forty-six years and see the principles upon which this Science of national and individual well-being was first presented to the American mind.

" The principles," says the editor in his concluding remarks, " which this science teaches, entitle it to be regarded as the moral instructor of nations. To them that will give ear it demonstrates the necessary connection that subsists between national virtue, national interest, and national happiness.

" It is to states what religion is to individuals, the ' preacher of righteousness.' What religion reproves as wrong, political economy rejects as inexpedient. What religion condemns as contrary to duty and virtue, political economy proves to be equally opposed to the peace, good order, and permanent prosperity of the community. Thus slave labor is exploded for its expensiveness, non-intercourse is condemned for its extravagance, privateering for its waste of wealth, and war for the injury sustained even by the victor; and thus freedom of person, friendly intercourse between nations, kindness even in hostilities, and, if possible, universal peace, which are the highest blessings as well as the greatest virtues, are supported by the all-powerful considerations of self-interest. . . . .

" This picture, however, presupposes virtue in the people. Political economy is a science which guards against involuntary, not voluntary error. It enters into harmonious alliance with religion, but cannot supply its place. It must find public men true to their trust."

From his retirement at Monticello, Thomas Jefferson writes approvingly of the work, but in a tone which, perhaps unintentionally, carries its lessons of spiritual rather than political economy : —

MONTICELLO, *March* 30, 1826.

I thank you, sir, for the treatise of Mr. McCulloch, and your much approved republication of it. Long withdrawn from the business of the world, and little attentive to its proceedings, I rarely read anything requiring a very strenuous application of the mind, and none requires it more than the subject of political economy. I rejoice, nevertheless, to see that it is beginning to be cultivated in our schools. No country on earth requires a sound intelligence of it more than ours. The rising generation will, I hope, be qualified to act on it understandingly and to correct the errors of their predecessors. With many thanks, be pleased to accept the assurance of my great respect.   TH. JEFFERSON.

The REV. MR. MCVICKAR, *New York.*

The following is a characteristic note from Chancellor Kent in reference to the same : —

PROFESSOR McVICKAR, Columbia College.

Mr. Kent returns his grateful acknowledgments to Professor McVickar for the " Outlines of Political Economy," which he received some time since. He delayed the acknowledgment until he had leisure to read the book. He has now finished the careful perusal and study of the work, and he is in perfect admiration of the good sense, simplicity, and beauty of the publication, and he begs leave to add that he thinks the " notes " of the editor are just and candid, and display a clear analytical sagacity and a profound and accurate knowledge of the science. He professes to have made himself master of the text and of the notes, and to have derived a vast amount of valuable instruction from both.

He desires Professor McVickar to be assured of his highest respect and esteem.

68 GREENWICH STREET, *October* 19, 1825.

The subject thus entered upon in connection with his chair of political economy was one very congenial to my father's mind. But not theoretically alone. It, like every other subject in which he interested himself, must have its practical applications in the wants of the hour, or else, except so far as duty required, his interest flagged. His mind, though analytic to a high degree, was remarkably practical. At that time the whole financial system of the United States was

in a very crude, unsettled state.   In forbidding anything but gold and silver as a 'legal tender, it was
thought by many that the Constitution forbade likewise all legitimate use of paper money, and thus the
whole subject of banking was misrepresented and mis-
understood. Into these practical questions of finance,
so intimately connected with political economy, my
father entered with deep interest.   A close intimacy
with such men as Isaac Bronson, Albert Gallatin, and
Mr. Biddle, served to keep that interest well alive.

During the succeeding year, 1826, he published a
pamphlet entitled " Interest made Equity."   This
would seem to have been, like his former work, the
republication of an English essay with notes and additions.   I have never seen it, but Mr. Wm. Bard,
writing under the date of March 27, 1826, says : " I
have never thanked you as I ought to have done for
your last pamphlet on the subject of Interest.   That
part of it which belongs to yourself is executed with
your usual ability and strengthens the unanswerable
arguments of the essay, on the proprioty of leaving
money, like anything else, to find its own value."

The next year, 1827, he put forth another pamphlet on a kindred subject, entitled, " Hints on Banking, in a Letter to a Gentleman in Albany."   This
was entirely his own, and evinces a clear grasp of
both the errors and the wants of the banking system,
not alone of this country, but of the world.   For the
unsatisfactory condition of banking then was the same
everywhere, and changes since that time prove that
these " Hints " were correct and needed.   The sub-

ject of a general State legislative enactment in the matter of banking was at this time creating some attention at Albany, all banking being then under individual charter, and this letter was intended to bear directly upon the question. The bulk of the pamphlet of forty odd pages is principally taken up in meeting and exposing the many financial fallacies of the day. Then follow these conclusions, many of which were new, and the first one, then at least, considered over bold.

I. Banking to be a free trade to individuals or associations under the provisions of a general statute.

II. The banking capital to be put in pledge outside the power of the bank for the redemption of its promissory notes, one tenth to be invested at the discretion of the bank, nine tenths in government stock, the bank to receive the dividends, but such stock to be untransferable except at the order of the court on the winding up the affairs of the bank.

III. All promissory notes to show on their face the amount of pledged stock and the necessary signatures. To exceed the amount of pledged stock in promissory notes, or to refuse redemption, to be considered acts of bankruptcy. The deposit of stock to be capable of increase, but not of decrease.

IV. No notes of a denomination under five dollars to be issued.

The few concluding words with which these principles are recommended, remembering that we are listening to a voice of forty-four years ago, deserve consideration.

" That these provisions would free banking from all abuses, it would be arrogance to assert; but that they would remedy many and great ones that now exist, seems to be unquestionable. They would operate no change upon our sound banking institutions, which already rest, not upon their charters, but upon the confidence of the public. The unsound banks, if any such there are, of course would shrink before the test to their natural dimensions, and either be renewed upon sounder principles, or leave their places to be supplied by real capitalists. In short, under this system, banking would lose all its attractions, except to the honest, the economical, and the persevering; it would have no surplus profits to tempt the needy and the speculating, nor any cover for bankruptcy to allure the unprincipled. But we should have for our bankers, men of wealth, integrity, and skill, at the head either of private banks or voluntary associations, and drawing from society, not the gains of monopoly, but the equal profits of free trade, the fair reward of integrity and economy in unfettered and open competition. Under such a system of banking, merchants would be more independent and the public more secure, fluctuations less frequent, speculations less wild, commercial prosperity less transient, and, to crown all with a recommendation that I am sure will enlist you, sir, among its advocates, our legislature would be less beset for banking charters by hungry and pertinacious adventurers."

This " Letter " appeared anonymously, though the dating from Columbia College must have suggested the now widely known Professor of Political Economy as its author. Several letters, both from Albany and other cities, especially Philadelphia, then the theoretic centre at least of banking interests, show that it received marked attention. And when, in 1838, the legislature of New York did enact "A General Banking Law," in it were found embodied many of the suggestions and principles of this "Letter," which, whether due to it or not, have given to the State of New York one of the best banking systems in the world.

I am indebted to my friend, Mr. John E. Williams, the accomplished President of the Metropolitan Bank of New York, for a letter in review of this and other of my father's financial tracts, which rightly belongs in this place, but bowing to the dictum of my publisher, which it is impossible to gainsay, that the general readers of clerical biography are not financiers, I have allowed it, I trust without offense, to meet its interested readers in an appendix.

From this time forward till the close of the brief yet influential history of the "New York Review," in 1842, my father was a constant writer on financial and economic questions, beside the other subjects which employed his pen. And generally, as is not always the case on such subjects, while his views were sound and deep, his style was readable, and his grasp of the special wants of his own country remarkable.

In an article written for the "New York Review" in 1841, and afterward circulated in pamphlet form, entitled, " A National Bank, its Necessity and most Advisable Form," we have this remarkable foreshadowing of our present national system.

" Has not the public been at all times a heavy sufferer by the bills of broken banks, discredited notes, and innumerable forgeries upon local issues, arising from their infinite diversity? Now if this be, as it has ever been, a crying evil in our currency, the question is, Can it now, through the medium of a national bank, be, if not wholly removed, yet further and perhaps indefinitely diminished? We think it can. What would be, we ask, the necessary operation of the paper part of our currency being made to consist *entirely* of issues of the national bank? What would be thought of the principle of separating altogether in banking the *making* of notes from the *loaning* of notes, — thus constituting the national bank the *only* issuer, and leaving to local banks the safer and more rightful business of the banker, — discount and deposit, with circulation of other's paper : which in . truth are all the operations that connect banks with the business wants of the country, the other being but an attribute of sovereignty, in which the public as such has no interest. This is a grave question, and demands to be thoroughly looked into. Experience, indeed, has its weight, but so, too, has advancing knowledge; and it may well be absurd to suppose that the American people should at once have reached the acme of perfection in a practical science, and on a definite question in that science, wherein the most enlightened European nations, with their tenfold experience, still hold themselves to be but learners."

And how true has been the following foreshadowed experience both as regards expectation and result in the case of the State banks.

" But now for the interest of the issuers themselves, how are the State banks to be made *willing* or even *unwilling* parties in this substitution ?   Twelve hundred, at least, State banks, broken or unbroken, now enjoy this privilege, and value it as a source of profit, and will not abandon it.   By what scheme of tyranny, it is asked, shall it be *wrested* from them ?   By what instrument of power shall the federal government *put them down?*   Still more, by what argument justify to the nation such *usurpation?*   But softly, gentlemen !   Your *right of issue* we do not propose to take from you, but simply the *motive of interest*, that alone leads you to issue your own notes ; we propose not to break you down but to build you up.   Suppose, for instance, you were to find it to your *interest* to circulate the notes of a national bank rather than your own, would you not at once pocket both the profit and the affront ?   Surely as *wise* bankers you would, or if you still preferred pride to profit, stockholders, having no pride on that point, would soon put others in your place who would."

It had not been my intention to go even as far as I have into this exposition of my father's views on the subject of finance, but there is an undoubted interest, hard to resist, in thus tracing the prophetic flashes of the true science of yesterday as it discloses the riches of to-day. And such was the character of my father's work as a political economist. He was no second hand retailer of book truths, but a genuine tentative thinker, bent on discovery. As he says of himself in another review on this subject : " We are of that class of reasoners who hold it to be of the nature of truth to work its own way. And we are further well satisfied, that in the long run the world is governed by what practical men so greatly despise — IDEAS — abstract, metaphysical, primal truths, such as —

'Wake to perish never.' "

CHAPTER VII.

THIS was a busy period in my father's life, and he gave himself up without reserve to every call that seemed to him one of duty. For two years or more he had been a member of the missionary committee of the diocese, and soon was appointed its secretary, which brought upon him the chief burden and responsibility of its affairs, This was especially the case during Bishop Hobart's absence in Europe, at which time he entered with much zeal into the interests of the Indian mission of the diocese, at the "Oneida Reservation," where Williams, who afterwards obtained that strange notoriety as a possible Bourbon, was quietly and earnestly officiating as deacon. He himself visited the Reservation, and afterwards so warmly pleaded the Indian's cause at Washington as to obtain from the General Government aid for their mission school. The scene of this interesting mission is thus described in his "Life of Bishop Hobart" : —

"Their rich, extended domains were lying in common, the property of the tribe, not of individuals, some little of it cultivated, more in open pasture, but most in its state of native wildness, and reserved for

hunting grounds. Through these forests, paths there
were many, but roads none, and the generally rude,
though sometimes neat and rustic dwellings of these
sons of the forest lay scattered in wild but picturesque confusion."

Among those who flocked around Bishop Hobart
on his visit to them a few years previous, was one
aged Mohawk warrior, who, amid his heathen
brethren, had for half a century held fast by that
holy faith in which he had been instructed and bap-
tized by a missionary from the Society in England
while these States were still colonies. Through the
catechist, as interpreter, he now recounted the event
in the figurative language of these children of nature,
and pointed out with as much feeling as belongs to
that imperturbable race, the very spot where this early
missionary had been accustomed to assemble them and
to preach. It was an open glade in the forest, with
a few scattered oaks, still vigorous and spreading ;
and within view, as if to perpetuate the association,
now arose the tower of a neat rustic church."

Mr. Williams' name having been mentioned, it
seems due to him upon whom some would have
thrust the doubtful honors of a title to the French
crown, to erect here his truer monument of praise
from the mouth of Bishop Hobart : —

" Mr. Eleazar Williams, educated in a different
communion, connected himself with our church from
conviction, and appears warmly attached to her doctrines, her apostolic ministry, and her worship. Soon
after he commenced his labors among the Oneidas,

the pagan party solemnly professed the Christian faith. Mr. Williams repeatedly explained to them, in councils which they held for this purpose, the evidences of the divine origin of Christianity, and its doctrines, institutions, and precepts. He combated their objections, patiently answered their inquiries, and was finally, through the Divine blessing, successful in satisfying their doubts. Soon after their conversion they appropriated, in conjunction with the Christian party, the proceeds of the sale of some of their lands for the erection of a handsome edifice for divine worship." [1]

A vote of thanks from the board of the general missionary society of the Church to Professor McVickar, dated May 16th, 1828, shows him as supplying at this time the pulpit duties of the Rev., afterwards Bishop Upfold, while the latter was preaching for the society. That preaching had not, in spite of other thoughts and duties, become irksome, is evident from the following scraps of family letters belonging to this period : —

"I have been called, through Dr. Wainwright's absence, more than usual of late to clerical duties, to which I return with so much pleasure that were it not for other considerations I should have strong thoughts of returning to them again."

"Dr. Wainwright, after being away three weeks, has returned. His absence revived my love of parochial duty, and I shall come to it perhaps at last. No duties leave so pleasing an impression on my

[1] Journal of New York Convention, 1818.

7

mind; and in this uncertain life it is a great comfort to have such recollections."

This refers to duty done in Grace Church, then on the corner of Rector Street and Broadway, and in which was the family pew. It was his regular place of worship until the removal of the church to its present site, and whenever needed, his assistance was cheerfully rendered.

The following is from a four-page foolscap letter written to his eldest son at Constableville. President Harris was then ill, and though only in his forty-second year, my father was the senior professor, and hence obliged to preside at the college commencement. It thus happened that Washington Irving received at his hands the honorary degree of Doctor of Civil Laws, which had just been conferred upon him by the board of trustees.

COLLEGE, *Friday Morning, 7th August,* 1829.

MY DEAR SON, — You see by my beginning that I intend to give you honest measure ; but whether I shall fill it or no depends upon the leisure I shall find to finish it. . . . . Henry, I trust, is now with you, and my letter is to you both, and my expressions of love and affection and praise in having two such affectionate and good sons. You seem like my props or supporters — like the lion and the unicorn on the royal arms holding and defending the crown. Mr. Ogilby [1] sets off to-day for the North. His

[1] Rev. John D. Ogilby, first Principal of Columbia College Grammar School, and afterwards Professor of Ecclesiastical History in the General Theological Seminary.

Greek speech at Commencement was admirably de-livered. The young ladies especially vowed that they understood it perfectly. He was so graceful and emphatic, and looked so animated, they declared, it was impossible to misunderstand him.

You have seen, I suppose, by the paper that the Commencement passed off well, for which I was very thankful as all the responsibility rested upon me. The day began with being very damp; we had to walk through a drizzle, and when we came out it poured. Notwithstanding the day, the church, St. John's, was crowded. I was afraid I should have trouble, for soon after we got in, Dugan the janitor, on whom I depended for sending orders, said he was so ill he must go home — and went. The con-stables kept no order; ladies crowded into the stu-dents' seats, and they began to clap violently at the end of the very first speech. Upon this I quitted the pulpit, sent for the head constable and told him if there was any repetition of it I would strike off half the pay they were to receive. This made them alert, and the greatest order prevailed to the close. You would have smiled to have seen me in my doc-tor's dress, with square cap and scarlet hood, confer-ring the degrees. I got through the ceremonials and the Latin, fortunately, without a false step or a false quantity, and was congratulated by all friends. I introduced an alteration in the ceremony that was much approved. Before conferring degrees, chairs to the number of the class were arranged on the stage, which was very large, and as each graduate retired

with his diploma, he took his seat of honor. It
cleared off before the hour of five, and we had the
largest and pleasantest Commencement dinner I have
ever known. The mayor and corporation, and several
strangers of distinction, were present; among them
Sir Hilgrave Turner, governor of the Bermudas, with
whose family we have become very intimate and
highly delighted. .   .   .   .   Your affectionate
father,   J. McV.

A few days later and he too was at Constableville, three hundred miles from New York, enjoying
his freedom from college cares, and rejoicing in
the company of the two boys to whom his last letter
was addressed, and the many relations and friends
which formed its attractive circle. A home letter
gives us a few lines on the results of a self-inspec-
tion, which, however habitual, seldom left its record
on paper.

"*August* 10, 1829. I preached this morning to a
circle of relations and old friends, and was greeted
by many old acquaintances of the neighborhood with
strong expressions of pleasure. On coming home to
my brother's, as I sat down in my pretty cottage
room to indulge in a little reflection on old times
and absent friends, the recollection suddenly crossed
me that it was my birthday. I know not why, but
the idea struck me for a moment painfully, but that
soon passed, and I then proceeded to reflect seriously,
and, I hope, profitably, on the many, many blessings
I had to be thankful for — the many providences

which marked a life of forty-one years ; how often preserved, and pardoned, and blessed, amid much of thoughtlessness and forgetfulness, to say no worse. The train of thought ended in comfort — comfort for the past and hope for the future, and a commending prayer for you and our dear children, and absent friends, that we might be directed and supported, and after a life of love and peace might all meet again in heaven."

The advanced age and prolonged illness of Dr. Harris, — he died in October of this year, — naturally awakened at this time the question of his successor in the presidency of Columbia College. My father, who for some time past, at the request of the board, had been performing all the duties of the office, was naturally a prominent candidate. His devotion to the interests of the college, his high standard of excellence in all that pertained to university education, and his acknowledged ability, all pointed him out as one peculiarly fitted for the post. But his decision of character, firm administration of discipline, and, above all, his earnest Churchmanship, created a strong counter influence out of those elements which, both among the undergraduates and the trustees, would be found naturally antagonistic to such characteristics. We find evidence of this coalition of opposing influences, even before President Harris' death, in a paper presented to the board of trustees on the morning of Commencement Day, in the name of certain members of the graduating class, remonstrating against Professor McVickar's appointment to confer degrees on that occasion. It failed of its object, and though its influence was greatly lessened when among its prompters were found at least one offended father, himself a trustee, and his lately disciplined son, still it was not without its effect in giving color and form to an opposition which was the more unreasonable from the fact that it was doctrinal rather than personal. If, however, it disclosed enemies, it likewise unlocked the hearts of friends. Bishop Hobart, an *ex-officio* trustee of the college, thus writes: —

PARIS HILL, *September* 15, 1829.

MY DEAR SIR, — I regret exceedingly that anything should have occurred to give you the least pain. Be assured that the very high opinion of you which it has yielded me the greatest pleasure to cherish, is too strongly fixed to be in the least degree shaken by the very unmerited attack (as I think I may style it) which has been made upon you. That opinion, too, is fortified by the sincerest sentiments of affection excited by your personal virtues, and by the long experience of your kindness on all occasions to me. I am proud, too, in the consideration that you, who I think I can call my friend, are fitted in all respects for the highest literary stations in our country. This opinion I have long entertained and expressed; I shall continue to express it, and, when opportunity offers, to sustain, and as far as may be in my power, to advance it.

Your path has been an honorable and a happy one.

Some clouds must occasionally cross it.   They will soon pass away.

Believe me,
Faithfully and affectionately
Your friend,
J. H. HOBART.

The REV. JOHN McVICKAR, D. D., *Professor, etc., etc., etc.*

The illness of the president continued to throw upon the senior professor all his official duties.   On the 16th of October, we find him the representative of the faculty in the ceremony of opening and dedicating the new grammar-school building just erected in the rear of the college.   " Old Columbia," as it was even then called, was not above having processions in those days, as is evident by the following from the " New York American," under date : —

" The trustees of Columbia, the faculty, and many of the parents having assembled at the college, at 10 o'clock, a procession was formed ; the boys of the grammar school, to the number of about one hundred, and the students of the college, leading ; the trustees, faculty, the parents and guardians of the scholars and such other gentlemen as attended, following.   Passing up Park Place, and thence through Broadway to Murray Street, the procession entered the school-house in reversed order."

Mr. Ogilby, whose Greek speech at the late Commencement we have seen so highly commended, had been appointed head master of the school, and his induction formed the principal circumstance of the occasion, giving us in the address a fair sample of my

father's happy manner on such occasions. We say
" happy," because that word best describes that re-
sultant feeling of a stirred ambition and a warmed
heart, which was ever the effect produced on others
by his premeditated words.   .

. . . . " You are this day called, sir, to an arduous
and responsible charge ; permit me to say that it is as
responsible as it is honorable, and one which, while it
stamps reputation on your past exertions, will call for
all your efforts to deserve and maintain it.   You are
now no longer a private individual ; you are invested
with an official character.   Your good or ill success are
no longer confined to your own fortunes ; they operate beyond that narrow sphere, and reflect credit or
disgrace both on the school we have founded, and the
college to which we belong.   These are high and
imperative motives, and will operate correspondingly
on the ingenuous and noble-minded.

" When we reflect on your youth, thus called to
govern when your equals in age have scarcely ceased
to yield obedience, I do not deny but that a shade of
apprehension glances across our minds ; but when we
again reflect on the proofs you have already given of
those talents which the station requires ; when we turn
our eyes to that band of ambitious and well-trained
students, you have recently presented to us, our ap-
prehensions are changed into confidence, and we hail
your appointment as a presage of future success ;
and with warmer feelings I add, when we recollect
that it is from our training that you have gone forth,
that in our own bosom that son has been nourished

who now bids fair to return tenfold to his parent that strength he once received at her hands, I say it, sir, without a compliment, our feelings are those of honest pride and pious exultation. We are proud to call you our son ; we are thankful that we are given to behold such fruit of our labors.

" To one like you, who know how small are human attainments when compared with the boundless field of knowledge, I need not fear addressing these words of praise ; I need not add that this language of affectionate commendation should excite in your bosom not vanity but humility, not pride but honorable resolutions to win and deserve all we can say. To repose from labor is not the lot of man, least of all is it the fair attribute of the student ; and the worst of all auguries is it, when it appears in youth. To the good student as to the good man, life is but a course of never-ending duties ; and to run that course with an untiring ardor, with an eye which never wanders from that lofty prize, which lies beyond his reach — this is to him that very happiness which others so vainly seek in indolent repose. Press on, then, in the career of usefulness in which you have so honorably labored. Set to yourself no vulgar model of excellence, and let the candidates you present to us be your speaking witnesses.

"But while you seek for yourself honorable fame, while you seek for the school and college the means of extended usefulness, let me say to you in a higher spirit, seek the direction and guidance of that power who alone can enable you to attain them. Seek His approbation, from whose favor you derive all your talents and all your advantages. In addressing to you on this occasion such solemn considerations, I am sure I do not wander from the current of your own feelings. No reflecting mind can undertake new and responsible duties without some thoughts cast upward to implore grace to perform them. I do not envy the man who *could* do it, and I distrust the man who *would.*

"But I cannot conclude these words of affectionate as well as official recognition, without some reference to the venerated head of our college, who, if health had been spared to him, would this day have addressed you. While I think thereupon, I cannot but image to myself his venerable figure and benevolent countenance, and the delight with which he would, on this day and in this place, have hailed this accomplishment of his dearest and long cherished wishes. I may say that his very heart has been in its success. The establishment of a college school was the first subject on which he consulted me twelve years ago when I took my seat as youngest member of that board of which the rapid rotation of life has now made me senior. It was, I say, the first object on which he consulted me, and it is the last subject, save those which look beyond the grave, on which with dying lips he has spoken to me.

" Had Heaven then given him strength to witness this scene, how would he have poured forth the fervor of his single-hearted, thankful spirit! To my ears I confess it would have sounded like a blessing on this institution; and on your heart, my young friend, his words would have sunk like the dying admonition of a pious parent, never, never to be forgotten. But Heaven has willed it otherwise; he is passing to his blessed account, we are left to follow out the footsteps of his wisdom."

This address seemed to possess so much of unity, and to be so characteristic of my father's addresses generally, that I have ventured to give it entire, more especially as the concluding portion was, in truth, a requiem upon the venerable person whose absence is there lamented. And it was a true lament, for the affection which had grown up between the youthful professor and the aged president in those twelve years of academic and neighborly intercourse had been a very sincere one.

Hardly two days after these words were spoken, President Harris passed away. Under the date of the 18th of October, Miss Bard writes in her diary, " This morning, at one o'clock, our venerated and most respected president changed this painful life for the joys of heaven; nor do I believe he has left behind one soul more pure and fitted to enjoy its rewards and blessings."

Professor McVickar was requested to preach at his funeral. This he did, and I believe that the sermon was printed, but I have never seen it except in manuscript. I quote briefly from it as helping us to carry on the story of our Life by disclosing to us the character of its friends, and also because it enables me, in few and fitting words of his own choosing, to present a picture of my father's own religious faith.

. . . . "If place can-add weight to those lessons which death teaches, here is the spot to speak them, for before that very altar where his body now reposes, eight-and-thirty years ago, our deceased friend first stood and there took upon himself the vows of a Christian minister. Before that altar the earthly tabernacle still is, but where is the spirit that assumed those vows? Gone, my brother, to that place where those vows were registered — gone to that higher tribunal where an account must be rendered of their performance. At that bar no human merit is known, no claim pleaded, save that atonement which God, through Christ, has accepted; and it is only as a pardoned sinner, pardoned through faith and sincere obedience, that the spirit which once dwelt in that tenantless clay can now stand before the bar of judgment. But with frail mortals like us, human virtues have their value because they have their influence; and while our holy Church teaches us to thank God for the good example of those who have finished their course in faith, we do not fear to trace, not for eulogy but improvement, the Christian traits which ennobled the character of our venerable president. They are such as the world might possibly pass by without notice, but in the sight of God they are of great price ; and, permit me to say, have often sunk into my heart, an instructive lesson, and spoke a wisdom beyond this world's teaching. They may be summed up in a few brief words : Singleness of heart ; meekness of tongue ; piety of spirit. . . . .

" Such was his calm and tranquil death, full of hope, answering well to the life he had lived. If asked on what that hope rested, I reply, where alone the hopes of dying man can rest, on the belief of the Atonement.

" In the latest conversation I had with him his language to me was, ' In the Atonement is all my comfort,' while he folded me in a dying embrace, which memory shall long live to recall. And where else, my brethren, can solid hope be built? In that trying hour, philosophy indeed may exhibit calmness, and fanaticism may display the raptures of an excited imagination, but hope, such as the unclouded soul can rest upon, rational, yet heartfelt, such hope nothing can give to the dying sinner — nothing, I believe, has ever given, but the reliance on an atonement. It is a want of the human heart, and, in whatever darkness that heart may be, it will, in its hour of need, grope until it find it. The pious Jew on his death-bed, clung to it in the types and figures of the Law; the pious heathen, trembling on the verge of eternity, searched it out even amid the abominations of his idolatry; and the pious Christian, amid all his blessings, blesses God chiefly for that cheering word, ' Jesus Christ came into the world to save sinners,' — on this hope our venerated friend rested, and to him was the promise fulfilled of support in that trying hour. He has gone to his reward: let us honor his fair fame; let us love his memory; let us cherish the remembrance of his virtues; and let us imitate his Christian example. O that we may die the death of the righteous, and that our last end may be like his."

A few days later a resolution of the board of trustees invested Professor McVickar with all the powers of the presidency of the college, " until the vacancy in that office shall be supplied, or until the further order of this board." From that time till the 9th of December there was, doubtless, much repetition of the feelings and the scenes which, twelve years previous, accompanied the filling of the vacant professorship of moral philosophy. But now as then, in spite of strong feelings, my father made no personal efforts to further his own election, and he even went so far in the opposite direction as to write to Bishop Hobart to free him from a pledge which some years previously he had voluntarily made to cast his vote in his favor under circumstances which had now occurred.

CHAPTER VIII.

THE election to fill the vacancy of president in
Columbia College took place on the 9th of December, 1829. To learn the result we will have
recourse, as usual, to our true but very partial witness, Miss Bard, whose comforting philosophy never
allowed an unmitigated ill to befall those she loved.

" *December* 9. — This day our dear Mr. McVickar,
his family and friends, have met with a great disappointment in his losing the election for president of
Columbia College. Mr. Duer carried it by one vote.
But I consider it a dispensation of Providence for
good. Such a character as Mr. McVickar's, so pure,
so religious, so moral, with talents, ability, and energy, yet withal so cool, so dispassionate, and self-
possessed, in every way so suited for the station,
must have carried it, had not God designed him some
higher blessing by withholding it."

And she was right. My father's own judgment
soon told him so, and his future life confirmed it.
Without entering on possible good that might have
resulted to the college from his presidency, the effect
of the official dignity upon himself must have been
unfavorable. He was, even then, suffering alarm-

ingly from overwork, and those who knew him best knew that nothing would have induced him, immediately after entering upon new duties as president, to ask leave of absence for relaxation and health. Yet the European tour, which he soon made, probably saved his life, or at least made of him almost a new man. Twelve years of steady book and routine labor, from the age of thirty, in a few prescribed courses of study, must have made, even in his elastic mind, deep grooves, which a few years more of unbroken work might have turned into unyielding ruts. But now, under the freedom soon to be his, he was to exchange books for men, and the lecture-room for the world, with the happiest possible result upon his whole character and after life. And finally, that ability to give more and more of his time to the distinct claims of his sacred profession, which increasing familiarity with the subjects of his class lectures allowed, would, as president of the college, have been quite inadmissible. Thus would the Church have lost the benefit of his wise and conciliatory counsels, and he himself been deprived in his declining years of his greatest happiness and richest source of comfort. We may, therefore, agree with his then venerable aunt, that " God designed him some higher blessing by withholding this." And often, in later years, have I heard him express deep thankfulness that his future had thus been ordered contrary to his own desires. Still it would be incorrect to say that this was not a great disappointment. Its depths may be measured from the following letter, which, as the

object of this memoir is to reflect a life rather than
its fairer side alone, is here given entire : —

Columbia College, *December* 19, 1829.

To Mr. William Duer, *President elect of Columbia College.*

Dear Sir, — I have to acknowledge the receipt
of yours of the 15th, and in reply to state that the
trustees had anticipated the request it contained of
my continuing in charge of the college until your
actual entrance on the duties of your new station.   I
have also to thank you for the assurances it contains
of unchanged sentiments towards me.   Which, while
I fully reciprocate, permit me to observe that I am
not aware of anything during the late contest that
could make such assurance necessary.   My college
course has ever been an open one, and in appearing
as a candidate for the presidency, I but pressed a claim
which all admitted to be a natural and obvious one,
and which for years had been kept before me by
more than one leading member of the board of
trustees.   Permit me, therefore, to say that we stood
in such different relations to this object as scarcely
to admit that reciprocity of reasoning you apply to it.
With you it was but one prize out of many to which
your talents might aspire, — one external to your profession and brought before you but at the moment of
decision.   To me it was the only prize which was or
could be offered in life, — one for which I thought
myself fitted by natural talent, for which I knew myself qualified by long experience; — one which had
been kept in view during twelve years of unremitted

8

exertion, and in some measure, I might say, earned
by years of voluntary labor far beyond the requirements of my professorship, and by means of which the
college was allowed to go on unembarrassed during
the almost continued indisposition of the late president. These are circumstances which make the
question to me a singular one, such as no other man's
feelings are likely rightly to appreciate, and the decision of it to be felt by me as a hard, I could almost say,
an ungrateful one, since my zeal was turned to my
condemnation.

Such are my feelings on this subject, and I think
that you will agree with me that no man in my situation, conscious of the fair claims which spring from
undivided faithfulness, and a long course of honorable
exertion, could think or feel otherwise. Still it is a
question remote from personal feeling, and as it is now
decided, I feel it to be my duty not merely to submit,
but, both as a man and a Christian to turn from all
fruitless speculation on the past, and in the duties
which lie before me, and in the thankful enjoyment of
the domestic blessings by which I am surrounded, to
forget the only disappointment, I may say, which life
has yet taught me.

With renewed assurances that my best counsel and
advice shall ever be at your service and in the interests of the college,

Believe me, etc., etc.,

J. M^CVICKAR.

It is but fair to the trustees of the college to state

that they were not forgetful of these extra services. On the 2d of February, 1830, the board of trustees passed resolutions handsomely acknowledging the same, and appointing a committee to procure and present a testimonial in the shape of books. These, large and rare illustrated volumes, with the imprint of the college, are still preserved as cherished heir-looms.

My father was true to the resolve expressed in the conclusion of the above letter. He indulged in no vain regrets. He showed no diminution of zeal, and we quickly find him as much interested as ever in all that tended to advance the usefulness or reputation of the college.

A memorandum in his handwriting, dated a month later than the above letter, gives a sketch of a proposed plan, which was only partially carried out, for enlarging the influence of the college under a modified university system. The subject being one of present interest, I subjoin the chief points of the proposed plan, which was in accordance with a statute then recently passed by the board of trustees.

In addition to the regular classes which were entered for the course of arts, admission was to be granted to those who might desire to attend any part of the scientific, literary, or classical courses of instruction, upon the payment of fifteen dollars per annum for each department thus attended. As soon as numbers justified it, they would be formed by the board into classes according to their respective proficiency. Also, beside the regular instruction in the lecture-room, courses of lectures, accommodated to the wants of the public, were to be delivered in the various branches of literature and science. Applications were to be in order at once for each or all of the following courses, dependent for their delivery on the public demand, namely, Political Economy, Greek Literature, Practical Mechanics, Astronomy, Italian and French Literature, to be delivered by Professors McVickar, Moore, Renwick, Anderson, Dupont, and Verren. After which, other and fuller courses were promised, according to the demand.

Columbia College, while slow to be making tentative experiments in education, had always shown herself willing and able to meet all the legitimate demands of New York city and its neighborhood for high education. The closeness, however, and conservative character of her corporation, her high appreciation of classical learning, and her churchly origin, for hardly anything more denominational than that was ever charged against her, created enemies, and at this time they all combined in the attempt to give her a secondary position, by establishing in New York a great university of practical science, which should unite in itself all the literary and scientific bodies in the city.

The effort failed, and Columbia was none the worse for the attempt she had made to meet what had been claimed to be this large unsupplied demand for a wider university course. The demand, however, was a fictitious one; but few of the outside lectures were called for, and but a small number of students availed themselves of the scientific or voluntary courses which were from that time, by statute, allowed.

The course on Political Economy was the first one delivered. The following from the "New York American" of February 23d and 25th, 1830, is interesting, as probably coming from the pen of its editor, Charles King, afterwards himself president of the college, and as adding some little touches of information respecting the subject of our memoir: —

"On Thursday evening Professor McVickar will deliver in the hall of Columbia College, a lecture introductory to the open course of Political Economy, which, in pursuance of the late statute of the trustees of Columbia College, he is about to give. Of his ability in this branch, our community needs no new assurance, for he has, on several occasions of deep interest to the business and pursuits of the great mass of our citizens, made his voice heard, and proclaimed sound doctrine in plain and forcible language. This is a course which will, we presume, test pretty decisively the extent of that desire and thirst for instruction in useful knowledge which is supposed to exist in this city."

In the same journal, two days later : —

"We attended at the college lecture-room last evening to hear Professor McVickar's introductory lecture, and were more than gratified with the enlarged views and elegant illustrations of the science of political economy which we heard from the professor.

Mr. McVickar's voice and manner are particularly

pleasing, and, on that account, he is admirably qualified for a public lecturer. His introductory was, notwithstanding the weather, numerously attended, and
we are quite sure that his sound, practical views upon
banks, upon general education, and upon the importance of free trade, must have given universal satisfaction. We trust that his lectures will be properly
patronized, believing, as we do, that they will prove
highly beneficial to all classes of society."

This lecture was, at the request of some English
friends, afterwards printed by the author, that same
year, during his stay in London. And from the ad-
vertisement we take these few lines, as showing the
result of the whole university scheme.

" The introductory part of the lecture may require,
not only apology, but explanation. It relates to the
scheme of a university then current in New York,
grounded upon the alleged inadequacy of the college,
to which the lecturer belonged, to supply the wants
of the city. The popular cry was for a new institution ; the friends of the college, while they doubted
the necessity, argued for enlargement, as both more
safe and more economical ; and the mention of it is
here retained as adding another proof, by the failure of the whole plan, that these loose schemes of
education are more showy than sound, and can never
become a substitute for the regular study and academic discipline of youth."

As a part of the university plan then proposed,
the trustees made a proposition to the Navy Department, offering facilities in the college for the instruc-

tion of the midshipmen and young officers stationed
at New York harbor, and Professor McVickar was
sent to Washington to explain to the authorities there
its nature and advantages. It fell through, but from
a home letter we obtain some interesting details of the
visit, and some of the causes of failure : —

WASHINGTON, *April* 1, 1830.

. . . . At nine, I meet by appointment General Hayne (Mr. Webster's opponent). He is chairman of the Naval Committee in the Senate, where
our only hope lies, unless I can effect something with
the President, on whom I call at half past two. I
will add another page to-night and tell you how I fare.
. . . . General Hayne I found in his parlor,
rather a small man, youthful in looks, though called
forty-five, very gentlemanly and conversable, but
with a tone of great decision. He was very frank,
explained his views, and put his opposition on the
ground of its economy. He was for a great naval
school. The government had money, and would
spend it, so expense was no consideration. "But,"
said I, "is there not a previous question a legislator
should ask, Why the Government should have a surplus revenue?"—"True," said he, "but there I despair."—"Then," said I, "you are no good citizen."
This brought on varied talk in which we generally
coincided, and I took my leave with his speeches in
my pocket, with the impression made by a clear, warm-
hearted man, but not a rival to Webster.
At seven o'clock, Mr. Hone, Mr. White, and my-

self drove to the palace, as they term it. We were ushered through a great and desolate looking hall into a splendid parlor, ceilings twenty-five feet high. The room was empty, the President engaged with the heads of department, but we were begged to wait his leisure. He soon came down accompanied by two gentlemen. The three ladies of his family were soon after introduced, Mrs. Donaldson his niece, a young lady, and Mrs. Haynes of Charleston. Tea and coffee were then served, and as Mrs. Webster waited our return, we soon after withdrew. On taking leave, the President begged me to come up early in the morning, and he would have some conversation with me about our plan, and named half past nine, when I shall attend him, and if I can make a favorable impression do not yet despair of bringing General H. to another view of it. The chairman of the committee in the House, though at first very hostile, I have brought over, though he is altogether an unfit man for chairman, and has no influence.

But I have not told you how I like the President. I tell you plainly that could I forget his name was Jackson, and all the associations connected with it, I should describe him as one of the most gentlemanly old men I have ever met with ; mild, courteous, and polite, with an air of sedateness, approaching to melancholy, and with a tinge of disease or feeble health. On the whole, I should describe him as a very interesting man ; but I stop to leave room for a second picture.

This second picture is not to be found, but a few extracts from a subsequent letter may be added : —

" Many old persons to whom I am introduced speak to me of my father, and are very attentive to me on that account, among others General Smith of Maryland. Another came up to me at Mr. Webster's, ' Sir,' said he, ' yours was one of the greatest commercial houses of our country.'

" With Chief Justice Marshall, Judge Livingston secured a bond of acquaintance. We had a long talk and walk together this afternoon ; he beat me in the first of course, but I was a little surprised to be distanced by a man of eighty-four. I accompanied him about half-way to Georgetown, and turned back for church, while he went on his solitary walk of eight or ten miles."

Of an evening party at Mr. Webster's he writes : —

" My time was divided between Mrs. Webster, as in duty bound and pleasure too, and Mr. Calhoun, whom I find rather a talented than a great man. Indeed, I have found but one great man and that is Webster. He walks among others with a weight of character and talent that overawes. What he says you remember ; there is a power and truth in it that one cannot forget."

The following letter from Mr. Webster, written shortly after this visit to Washington, carries on our narrative. To some, perhaps, it will seem a good illustration of the above encomium, but though my father's views, as he grew older, became less enthusiastic on the subject of political economy, he never was

willing to bow to Mr. Webster's prophetic dictum of
its practical uselessness, only granting that " it must
find public men true to their trust."

WASHINGTON, *April* 24, 1830.

MY DEAR SIR, — I cannot but be glad to learn
that you contemplate a voyage to Europe, which
promises so much for health and so much for information and reasonable gratification. I almost envy
those who have the means of enjoying so high a
pleasure.

As it happens, I do not feel authorized to give you
letters to Mr. McLane. If you propose to go to
France, I will with pleasure give you, or send to your
address in England, a letter to Mr. Rives.

You will receive in a day or two, half a dozen of
my speeches. I hope you will have with you other
and better samples of our American efforts in debate.
I take the liberty to send a copy or two of a speech
on the tariff in 1824. Probably you never read it.
It purports to treat some subjects which belong to
your department.

Will you allow me, my dear sir, to hazard one little
prophecy. It is that when you shall have read everything ever published on political economy, and seen
and studied the states of Europe, you will come to
the conclusion that political economy is a science of
wise and clear general rules, but so vastly diversified in their practical application as to be worse than
useless in the hands of any who have not the broad-
est knowledge and the nicest discrimination ; and

that so many circumstances belong to each particular case that no wide general principle can be safely trusted to govern it.

Mrs. Webster begs you and your wife and daughter to accept her very best wishes and kindest regards. We all hope for you a pleasant tour and a happy return.

I am, dear sir, with much regard,
Your obedient servant,
DANIEL WEBSTER.

REV. JOHN McVICKAR, *New York.*

This proposed voyage to Europe had become almost a necessity through failing health. Thirteen years of steadily increasing intellectual work had naturally told upon my father's not over hardy constitution, and his physician had lately insisted on the necessity of rest and change of scene. This was not to be wondered at when we think what he was then doing. The whole of the historical, rhetorical, intellectual, moral, and political departments of the college, with the three higher classes rested upon him, without even the aid of a single tutor, which he had often asked for in vain. His report as professor for this year takes up four pages of closely written foolscap, principally detailing the work done. The mode of doing it is thus stated : —

" In reference to the whole course, the professor would observe that his aim is rather to form opinions and to discipline the mind by leading the student to exercise his own judgment, than to load his memory with the language or thoughts of others. Though less favorable for display on the part of either teacher or scholar, he is satisfied that it is most to the real advantage of the student, and constitutes, in fact, the only permanent influence of intellectual and moral education."

Add to this the outside course of lectures on political economy and the many questions of finance which had lately enlisted his pen, and we find how well prepared he must have been to enjoy just that kind of rest which foreign travel, better than anything else, is able to give. At such a time, if not actually broken down, a man feels, as it were, his immortality, and the greater the variety of bodily and intellectual excitement the more complete the rest, and in this case never was there a busier six months, seldom a happier one, and never a more complete restoration to health.

On the 24th of April, 1830, the board of trustees of the college gave to Professor McVickar, in a set of complimentary resolutions, leave of absence for six months, or longer if his health should require it, requesting him to suggest some one to supply his place during his absence. Mr. Beach Lawrence was named, and soon after appointed to deliver the lectures on political economy, and his young friend and pupil, the Rev. Edward Griffin, for the department of rhetoric and belles-lettres. To young Griffin my father was much attached. He had hoped in this way to bring him to the notice of the college authorities, and get for him a permanent position in the promised division of his own chair. He entered upon and performed his temporary duties in a most satisfactory manner, but while steps were being taken to carry out the very plan which had been hoped for, he himself was called away by sudden death.[*] "And the task undertaken by him was so performed," writes my father in a memoir afterwards prepared by him, "as to add another pang to the mind of his friend in the recollection of his loss, namely, the inability of returning thanks. He lived but to give evidence how well-fitted he was for the duties he had undertaken, and was then withdrawn to a higher sphere of usefulness, we may trust, as well as happiness."

On the 2d of May, 1830, my father, accompanied by my mother and two elder sisters, sailed for London. New York was a different city then from what it is now. And nothing illustrates it better than finding a short editorial like the following in the chief evening paper : —

"In the packet ship *Ontario*, which sailed this morning for London, Professor McVickar, of Columbia College, with his family, took passage. The impaired health of the professor is, we are sorry to state, the immediate motive of this voyage. Relaxation from arduous duties, a cheerful season, change of scene, and the affectionate attentions of his family, will, it is earnestly hoped, restore this highly respected individual to his wonted health ; and certainly, if there be any healing balm in the solicitude of numerous friends, and in the anxiety of each, as

well among the youths committed to his instruction
in the college as among many of our oldest and most
respectable citizens, to testify at the moment of his
departure, regret for its cause, and personal regard
for the individual, the thronged deck of the steamboat, that bore the professor and his family to the
ship, must have ministered this healing."

CHAPTER IX.

A EUROPEAN tour, in the year 1830, was, to an American, a great event. And if the presence of an American in foreign circles was not the same, it was, what is by no means the case at present, a rare occurrence, allowing of exceptional privileges. A manuscript of journal letters addressed to Miss Bard, affords material for this tour of six months. In days of fewer books and fewer travellers this might properly have made an independent publication. But as it is, my readers will probably be as well pleased to allow me to read it for them, briefly outline the tour, and weave into it, in the words of the journal, whatever may be deemed of special interest.

The voyage was a short and prosperous one of twenty-four days, differing from the steamer voyages of the present time, not only in its greater length, but in its united social intercourse. An editor was found among the passengers for a semi-weekly gazette, and wit and humor made friends and shortened tedious days.

After arrival, London was, for the time, made the head-quarters of the party, and a suite of rooms taken in Regent Street. Here, calls from Mr. DeRham of New York, and Washington Irving, at once made the strange city seem somewhat homelike.

Sunday Night. — I hardly know whether to call this Sunday, it has been so little like one. I never felt so great a longing for the solemn, quiet services of our Church as I do after being excited by the eloquent vehemence of Dr. Chalmers, and disgusted by the rant and grotesque acting of the once celebrated Edward Irving. To listen to the first was a real treat; to the last, I can only say I felt, on quitting his chapel, as if I required a lustration to purify and cleanse me from such folly and insanity. . . . .

On returning from Richmond to-day, Tuesday, we strolled through the Park, the seat of Lord Sidmouth; the Marquis of Wellesley has also a small seat here; though I gazed at neither with the same interest I did at a small but neat old almshouse, over the stone gate of which was cut these words: "I will pay unto the Lord the vows I made in my trouble."

We drank tea at home, having ordered the carriage at half past nine for Mrs. Bates' musical party, and as this is our first London *soirée*, I must give you some idea of it. Mr. Bates is an American by birth, but now the leading partner in the great house of Baring, Brothers & Co. He is also the entertaining partner, and has an allowance on that score of twelve thousand dollars a year. They occupy a noble house on Portland Place. On entering, our names were announced from the foot of the stairs to the landing, and again to the drawing-room door, both folds of which were thrown open as we entered. The etiquette is an awkward one, the ladies walk in alone, the gentlemen following. The party was small, with some rare musical talent, and a moderation in the refreshments which, in New York, would be termed mean, but which here is universal in good society, and is, I think, in better taste than our overloaded and extravagant profusion. Among the rest, I was introduced to Leslie and West the painters, and to O'Meara, Napoleon's medical biographer. In the case of the latter I fell into an awkward mistake, confounding him with Dr. Stockoe, who also attended Bonaparte, and who had visited us at the College. Fortunately I stopped short when I found myself going wrong in reminding him of his visit, and changed the topic, instead of blundering on with explanations as one often does, making bad worse.

Friday, June 4. — Joined by Mr. Richmond at four, we drove to the palace of St. James to inquire after the health of his Majesty. We alighted in the midst of guards and gentlemen in waiting, were ushered through passages and *salons* up-stairs into the receiving rooms, where Lord Fife, the lord of the bedchamber, in waiting, stepped forward and presented to us for our inspection, the written bulletin of the morning, signed by the attending physicians.

After our royal visit we drove to Mrs. Heber's, to whom we were engaged for this evening. Her residence is in Clarence Terrace, one of the most beautiful ranges of buildings in Regent's Park. Admitted by a servant in livery, we were announced and ushered into a moderate sized but beautiful library, where Mrs. Heber sat at a table covered with books, and writing. From what I had heard of her personal appearance I expected little, — so little that I was agreeably disappointed. Though large, she is graceful, with a very sweet voice, and pleasing, courteous, and even kind manners. She has engaged us to a breakfast on Tuesday next. On inquiring for her daughters

she sent for them. They were both sweet children;
Harriet the very image, judging from his portrait, of
her sainted father. We parted greatly, and, we
would fain hope, mutually pleased.

Carriage at the door again, after dinner, to take
me to visit Coleridge at Highgate. Mr. Ker was my
conductor. We stopped, on our way, for Rev. Edward Irving, much to my annoyance. We found
him in a great house, miserably furnished, at tea,
with his wife and two little children. After tea,
with a solemn air, he laid his hand on the heads of
the two children, prayed for and blessed them. We
then set off for a four mile ride to Highgate. Mr.
Irving grew upon me. I found in him much simplicity, and better sense than I expected. Coleridge
was talked of, — an enthusiast, worshipped and idol-
ized by enthusiasts. On reaching our destination we
were ushered in and introduced to the idol. But let
me first tell you something of his early history. The
son of a clergyman, a Blue-coat boy, an Oxford
scholar, in early life a skeptic, and wild enthusiast,
in concert with Southey and Lovell, he planned a
retirement from the world and all the errors of a
social state. The three then married three sisters,
but Coleridge proved most unfortunate ; he became
an opium eater, separated from his wife, and sank
into almost a lost character. At that time his present kind host, Dr. Gilman, by accident being called
in as his medical adviser, from a feeling of pity and
respect, invited him to his house for a fortnight that
he might better attend to him, and has kept him for

fifteen years in every comfort and luxury. His appearance is of a man over sixty, of powerful make, large head, massive features, and large and expressive eyes, though rather dreamy. There was no company, but his married daughter, Mrs. C——, one of the prettiest and most learned women in England. His conversation is that of a lofty religious enthusiast, but full of deep and original thought, with a flow and power of expression I have never heard equaled. His topics were varied, but with a continued tendency to the deep and personal truths of Christianity. On one point I ventured to oppose him, and found him a powerful, though courteous opponent.

This circumstance is referred to more at large in a communication on the subject of Coleridge sent by my father to the " Churchman," after his return, in which is the following : —

In the course of the evening the Rev. E. Irving, who was one of our small circle, drew from his pocket a letter, and prefacing it by a call on Mr. Coleridge, to counsel him in his spiritual doubts, as " being the man," said he, " from whom I have gained more wisdom than from all other men living," proceeded to read a communication just received from the celebrated Thomas Erskine, of Edinburgh, containing the particulars of the first wonderful effusion of tongues, as it was termed, in the family of the Campbells, near Greenock. The anxious inquiry of Mr. Irving was, " How is this to be regarded ? " Mr. Coleridge, to whom it probably was not new, being thus addressed as an oracle, answered with

corresponding solemnity and certainty, without the
ambiguity complained of in oracular responses of old,
" Sir, I make no question but that it is the work of
the Holy Spirit, and a foretaste of that spiritual
power which is to be poured forth on the reviving
Church of Scotland." Though evidently in a circle
who eagerly hailed the decision, I felt myself impelled to speak, and press upon him its want of accord
with the Scriptural account of the gift of tongues,
and its unworthiness not alone of the wisdom of God
but of the reason of man. To my protestation he
listened respectfully, though evidently unwillingly,
and immediately replied, " Was not the case the same
in the Apostles' days? Is not St. Paul's argument
in the fourteenth chapter of First Corinthians founded
upon the supposition that the saints often spoke in
tongues which no man understood ? " Pressed again
by its incongruity with Scripture facts, more especially
with the record of the first day of Pentecost, he
finally cut short the argument with denying the
genuineness of the chapter that contained it, and
concluded with reiterating his first assertion. Such
is Mr. Coleridge, and such are some of his wild opinions. But with all his errors he both was and is a
wonderful man. " Sir," said Edward Irving to me
after this interview, " his words sink into my mind
like seeds into the ground ; they grow up afterwards,
I know not how, and bear fruit."

Strangely enough, my father was destined to awaken in others, as
well as experience himself, this very feeling, so aptly expressed by
Irving, and so true, respecting one against whom he was, at this

time, so evidently prejudiced. His preface to the American edition of the "Aids to Reflection" having done much to make Coleridge a favorite with thinking minds on this side of the Atlantic.

Monday, June 7. — Our dinner at Lady Affleck's was quite gay, though the party consisted but of four octogenarians, three ladies and one gentleman, beside Lady Affleck and ourselves. The ladies were of a species we know little of in America, wealthy old dowagers who keep up at eighty the spirits and fashion of their youth. These were, besides, clever in their way, and might have sat to Walter Scott as originals. The gentleman — but you may judge of his years when I tell you he was the confidential secretary of Warren Hastings in India, and retained the dress and manners of those most aristocratic days. He and I occupied the head and foot of the table, and entertained each other after the ladies had gone ; he with tales of " auld lang syne," and I with the wonders of our western wilds. He is enthusiastic in his praise of Hastings, and insists that instead of being cruel or rapacious in his government, he was kind and liberal even to a fault.

Such, my dear aunt, is London life, and certainly not without its attractions. To me it is full of interest and improvement, and thus far of health. The last will, I trust, continue, that I may return and be to my dear children what a father should be. God bless you all.

Friday Morning, June 10. — At twelve yesterday Mrs. Heber called and we drove out to Clapham, about four miles, a little beyond which we approached

Battersea Rise, Sir Robert Inglis' very noble country mansion. Among the company were Sir Thomas and Lady Acland, with whom we are to breakfast on Wednesday next; Sir James Mackintosh, who is the ablest man I have yet met with, — his conversation strongly marked and not a little Johnsonian; and Mr. Wilberforce, full of kindness and warm-hearted enthusiasm, who insisted on our giving him a day next week at his seat, Highwood Hill, about ten miles from London. His appearance is that of deformity rather than decrepitude, and would be painful in the extreme were it not redeemed by the cheerful expression of manner and voice; but his mind is full of activity and intelligence, though certainly he cannot be less than seventy-five years of age, having entered Parliament, as he told me, in 1780. It was delightful to listen to his conversation with Sir James Mackintosh, which turned on the changes they had witnessed in public life. . . . .

Sunday Evening. — From Mr. Hume's we reached Lady Newton's last evening at a late hour. I had scarcely entered when Captain Franklin, now Sir John, came up to me, and in the kindest manner welcomed me to England, reproached me with not letting him know at once of our arrival, and introduced me to Lady Franklin. Lady Franklin is a most lovely woman, and we had a long and pleasant talk about her husband's travels, etc. They seem truly kind, and in proof we found on our return to-day from our long church that they had been to see us, and soon after got a pressing invitation for Saturday next.

At half past nine this morning we entered Westminster Abbey while the organ was pealing through its aisles. There is no describing the feelings which this building inspires. I am confirmed by it in my preference of Gothic architecture for religious uses, and am pleased that I have labored to introduce it in America. But of all churches give me that in which we shall all meet again on our return, to unite in grateful thanks for all the mercies of our Heavenly Father. That will be to me as a temple not made with hands.

Monday Evening. — I went out this morning to pay some visits. My first was to Lord Lyndhurst's, to see his mother, Mrs. Copley, Mrs. Startin's sister, at whose house I was intimate twenty-five years ago. She was down at their seat, so I left my card. My next was to Sir H. Parnell, who read me a note from Mr. Tooke, begging him to engage me at their great politico-economical dinner next week. I found him up to his ears in papers, being full of Parliamentary business. . Leaving this, I drove to Lord Stowell's (Sir John Scott), whom I had also known well twenty-five years ago. On sending up my card with the mention of my being from America, he immediately received me with great friendliness, and recalled with wonderful accuracy the circumstances of our earlier acquaintance. His health is much broken, so that he lives altogether retired from company and seldom quits the house, which he regretted, he said, on my account, but proffered every kindness, and promised, if admissible, to get our ladies admitted behind the throne in the House of Lords, a privilege now less easily accorded, in consequence of some indiscretion, I think, of Lady Holland's. He asked me what changes I saw in England. I answered, " An equal increase of wealth and democracy." " Ah," said he, " too true ; you find us in a bad way ! " He speaks warmly of America as a friend, and benevolently and kindly on all subjects. It is a great gratification to have had this friendly conversation with him. He is the great lawyer of the age, and is leaving behind none equal to him on the great questions of belligerent and mutual rights, and in general of international law. I have sent him, at his request, Mr. Webster's great speech.

Tuesday, 15*th*. — We drove, to-day, to Pimlico, to Chantry's. His works have genius and truth in them ; no personifications, no allegories. I noted it to him, " No Fauns," said I, " blowing trumpets, etc.," " Ah," said he, " I leave that to greater geniuses." Three splendid pieces of Canova's are here, belonging to the king. I never was more struck with the progressive steps of art. Canova's at once cast all around into the shade. Chantry's castings in brass are on a great scale. We found the men at work putting together a gigantic brazen figure of the poor dying king.

Friday Morning, 11 *o'clock*. — Bustle, bustle, nothing but hurry and bustle in London. It has kept me from my journal since Tuesday night, and I can now hardly remember the world of scenes that lies in that long interim. On Wednesday morning we had a delightful breakfast at Sir Thomas Acland's with Lady Newton, Mrs. Heber, Mrs. Thornton, etc., etc. He is a baronet of old family, a descendant of the Accalans who came over with the Conqueror, a leading member in the House, very wealthy and hospitable, a religious and an educated man. The Right Hon. Wilmot Horton, whom I was to have met, sent an apology, but with a particular request to see me as soon as convenient after breakfast. I called, and found him in committee of the Colonization Society, of which he was president, into whose views and weaknesses I was soon initiated by being requested to take part in their deliberations. I found them disjointed and at utter variance among themselves, and each party looking to new settlements in the United States for proofs, and to my testimony of the facts as likely to be in their favor. The views I gave agreed, I found, with the chairman, Mr. Horton, who stood alone, clear and intelligent, among visionary or interested men. It was an amusing scene. Mr. Horton and myself planned to meet again, and yesterday I received a long communication from him containing queries, etc., with his works.

Saturday, June 19. — Taking a hasty dinner after a short visit to my medical friend, Dr. Johnson, we bade adieu to London, having entered it as strangers three weeks ago, and now leaving it as if it were a second home.

CHAPTER X.

I TOOK a seat this morning, June 26, on the Bristol coach, starting with the rising sun. At eight we learned the news of the king's death, as we passed Windsor with the flags half-mast, and carried on the news westward, the horses at full speed, for one hundred miles. The rate was fifteen miles an hour saving the short stops in changing our four panting steeds for fresh ones, which seldom took more than one minute and a few seconds, they always standing ready at the door, brilliant with harness and high keeping, and grooms at their heads. I thought that my neck would have been broken; but such was the excellence of the roads, the coach, and the driving, that the motion was scarcely sensible, and at eight P. M. arrived in safety at Clifton, at the friendly home of Mrs. Church, where the ladies had preceded me.

Sunday afternoon we went into Bristol to hear the celebrated Robert Hall, a friend and classmate of Sir James Mackintosh, and not unlike him in talent. I had rather listen to him than Chalmers. There is less of splendor but more repose of manner, like a consciousness of power, and, I think, a more logical mind. I never heard such a calm full stream of thought and language in which there was nothing to alter, either in sentiment or expression. For power over his hearers he is too rapid in delivery, and a little too monotonous.

Thursday Evening, July 1. — LANGOLLEN. — The windows of our inn looked out on the lovely winding Dee, just as it quits the most beautiful vale that eye ever rested on. Our ride to-day has had the drawback of almost constant rain. On leaving our excellent inn at noon, we drove fourteen miles to Shrewsbury on the Severn, which we found dressed out in its holiday garb, the bells ringing a merry peal while the ceremony of proclaiming the new king, William IV., took place.

Friday Morning. — We rose early and joined a family of tourists in a morning walk to Miss Ponsonby's cottage. On the cottage was hung out, strange union, the armorial bearings, on a mourning hatchment, of her lost companion, Lady Eleanor Butler, daughter of the late Duke of Ormond, whose tomb we afterwards visited. The character of both these ladies, as I learned by minute inquiry in the cottages around, though strongly marked by eccentricity, has long been that of active benevolence, and warm attachment to each other. Report gives them credit for a wise though romantic choice. For myself, I doubt, and I felt an anxious wish to learn from the survivor the result of their experiment in seeking in retirement what the world could not give. However, as it was not a question to be asked, we contented ourselves with conjectures, only concluding

that the choice of a spot could never have been more
happy.   Though what is singular in those who had
the power to choose, the cottage itself does not command any of the views which have made the vale so
celebrated, nor does it exhibit. much other external
proof of a refined taste.

Saturday, July 10. — Low Wood Inn. — This
is the most beautiful point of Windermere, a lone
house on the very brink of the lake, and only six
miles from where we slept last night.   Yet we have
not been idle.   After breakfast, at Bowness, took
boat and crossed the lake, sketching a little, and
quarreling with our sketches because they would not
convey the hundredth part of the beauty we saw.
Returning from this delightful excursion, we drove on
to our present inn, and hence to Mr. Wordsworth's
"Rydal Mount," leaving our plans for the night to
be settled on our return.   Our reception was most
hospitable.   Mr. Wordsworth, a tall, grave, simple
mannered man, apparently about sixty ; his wife, kind,
beyond what strangers had a right to expect, and his
sister pleasing though less decided.   We came upon
them at the most awkward time of early dinner, but
this caused but a short delay, after which a walk and
animated conversation made all easy.   The house is
small and old-fashioned, but comfortable and roman-
tically situated ; Rydal Water is beneath you, and
Windermere in the distance. Mr. Wordsworth talked
much of Bishop Hobart's visit, remembered a discussion they had had about a word, and desired me to
tell him that *Capel* was the Welsh corruption of

Chapel. He lives in retirement, with some local salary from government. He may be called a pure ·contemplatist. Speaking of Wellington, he said he regarded his power as a military usurpation, and gave some anecdotes of his uncourteous demeanor towards the council, lying on the sofa, and uttering his dictum, " That won't do," etc. I could not make him understand that no danger existed of military domination in the United States. After giving us a letter to Mrs. Hemans, who is staying in the neighborhood, and engaging us to an early tea to-morrow, we parted.

Returning to our inn, we received a friendly message from Mrs. Hemans and spent the hour till bedtime, partly in the romantic solitude of " Dove's Nest," and partly in an excursion with Mrs. H. and her interesting boys on this most lovely of lakes, and this most lovely of evenings we have yet had in England.

Sunday, 11*th.* — Keswick. — Rode across the mountains, by Wordsworth's advice, to the retired village and model church of Conistone, on the banks of its own placid lake. Heard a sermon full of simple truth from a young clergyman of the name of Sands, with whom after church we formed acquaintance, and gave a seat in our roomy barouche as far as his home, which was a retired inn at the head and on the very shore of the lake, where we also stopped and took an early dinner. By half after four found ourselves again at Rydal Mount with a family toward whom we now feel as friends. It is a family full of simple-hearted, kind feeling, and as for Wordsworth himself, from my knowledge of the author, I think I must retract whatever I have said or thought against his poetry. His conversation is full of interest from deep feeling and talent, and marked by peculiar simplicity and modesty. We felt quite at home before we parted; and bear with us many pleasing memorials of our short but delightful visit, among them the following lines written by the poet in A——'s album : —

> " Hast thou seen with flash incessant,
>   Bubbles gliding under ice,
> Bodied forth and evanescent,
>   No one knows, by what device ?
> Such are thoughts — a wind-swept meadow
>   Mimicking a troubled sea;
> Such is Life, and Death a shadow
>   From the Rock — Eternity.
>
> "WM. WORDSWORTH.

"RYDAL MOUNT, 11*th July*, 1830."

Having sent back to our inn for fresh horses, we delayed parting to a late hour, and blessed the long twilight which enabled us to see our way through the intervening mountains to Keswick, our present home, sixteen miles, where we arrived safely a little after ten o'clock. I forgot to mention Miss Curzon, staying at Wordsworth's, a lineal descendant of the great Alfred. Wordsworth mentioned this to me aside, and then got down a great volume of genealogy, which made it clear to my doubting eyes.

Monday, July 12. — Just returned from a delightful evening at Mr. Southey's, where we found equal talent as at Wordsworth's, more an air of the world, more of fashion and elegance, but less, I would say, of that warm-hearted simplicity which delighted us at Rydal Mount. Our morning was wet and cold ; the ladies employed themselves within doors, while I found my way to Southey's residence prettily situated on a rising ground at the outskirts of the village. I found Southey in his library with his only son, his last hope, a promising and pleasing boy of twelve, and a young man whom he introduced as his nephew. On returning to the inn, we took an early dinner, then ordered horses and took the tour of the lake, Derwent Water, visiting the fall and the rocks of Borrowdale. The hour of six brought us round to Southey's, according to promise, where we were kindly received. Mr. and Mrs. Southey, her sister, three pleasing daughters just grown up, a handsome cousin from Oxford, and two beaux from Cambridge, constituted the party. The house is splendidly furnished with literary treasures, and fashionable in all its arrangements. Wordsworth's noble bust is one of the greatest ornaments of the sitting-room here, as Southey's is at Wordsworth's. Southey has a striking face, very like, I should say from the portrait, to that of his friend Henry Kirke White. He is free in conversation, but without the flow that gives interest and poetic power to Wordsworth's. He seems to me a true Englishman in the best sense of the term, looking with reverence and pride to the old virtues and institutions of his country, and seeing in their preservation the only safety in this age of revolution.   His views are full of anxiety and apprehension for the future.   The property of the Church will not long, he said, rest untouched.   Unless the Whig leaders can be frightened into its defense the next session of Parliament will organize the attack ; which would have been made the present, he said, had the Duke felt himself strong enough.   Wellington has, he thinks, broken the arm of his strength in yielding the Catholic question.   Speaks well of Oxford, ill of Cambridge, and fears that this generation may not pass before the temple falls and another colony be transferred to our shores.

This day, Tuesday, has been spent most agreeably and profitably.   After breakfast, Mr. Hill, the young Cambridge graduate, whom we had met at Southey's, came over by appointment with some papers and A——'s book, in which Mr. Southey had written for her the following lines : —

> — "Both in civil and in barbarous states,
> The course of action takes its bias, less
> From meditation and the calm resolve
> Of wisdom, than from accident and temper.
> Private advantage at all cost pursued,
> Private resentments recklessly indulged,
> The humor, will, and pleasure of the leaders,
> The passions and the madness of the people,
> Under all climes, and in all forms of rule,
> Alike the one, the many, and the few ;
> Among all nations of whatever tint,
> All languages, these govern everywhere ;
> The difference only is of less or more,
> As chance, to use the common speech, may sway ;
> In wiser words, as Providence directs.
>   ROBERT SOUTHEY, Keswick, 13*th July*, 1830."

From an unpublished poem.

The lovely morning had tempted us to plan an excursion to the top of Skiddaw; in this Mr. Hill immediately joined, and after running back for his mineralogical hammer, etc., we set off with a guide, two ponies, a cloak, sketch-books, and provisions. I will not waste words in description; it was a new and inspiriting journey, and we grew stronger the higher we mounted. A bright sun, flying clouds, lakes, mountains, and rich valleys, like gardens, were above, around us, and beneath us. As we returned we found Mr. Southey waiting for us about half-way up the mountain. The more I converse with this celebrated man the more I am delighted. Moral and religious truth, and sound political principles, are all elevated in his mind into a warm-hearted enthusiasm, and expressed in choice language but with the greatest simplicity and unpretendingness of manner. His views of the present state of England are, as I have said, gloomy. " Prepare," said he, as he shook my hand in parting, " prepare to receive in your happy country a new emigration of pilgrims." Finding we had no letter to Sir Walter Scott, while we were dining, he went home and wrote one for us, also to Mr. Morrison of London, and proffered others which I thought we would not need. Bidding farewell with much regret, at five we left Keswick for Ullswater, the last of the lakes we shall visit.

Mr. Hill accompanied us, and next morning, having taken boat on Ullswater, we landed near the head of the lake and walked some distance with our young friend, who was going to find his way across pathless moors and over the mountains, twenty miles, alone.

10

We parted with him with regret and some anxiety for his safety, as the day soon after became dark and stormy. He is a fair specimen of educated young Englishmen, not over refined in sentiment or manners, but simple and polite, having learning without pedantry, and science and accomplishment without conceit. Science being common makes it sit more easily upon the young men here than with us. Mr. Hill, for instance, is a learned and skillful mineralogist and entomologist without thinking his knowledge anything peculiar. Nor, in truth, is it. Thus, on Skiddaw, we meet at least six or eight young men strolling over its varied surface, some botanizing, with their tin cases at their backs, some with their hammers and bags of specimens, and one with his little net for catching insects and bottles for preserving them, all earnest in their own pursuits and happy in them. Thus does education tell more here than with us for the gratification of after life. The same difference, too, I have noticed in female education. Modern languages, when acquired, are more familiarly understood, and such skill with the pencil as with us would make an artist, seems to belong here to every well-educated young woman.

Returning through a storm of rain, which almost flooded us in our open boat, to our inn, we took a hasty lunch and came on to Penrith, six miles; quitting with regret the region of the lakes, where the gratification of months, I may say, has been crowded into the space of a few days. The scenery in leaving Ullswater immediately changed, and, though rich, was no longer picturesque. After leaving Penrith, twelve miles brought us to Carlisle. This began again to be classic ground. We thought of the Roman wall, and we looked with respect at the castle where the unhappy Mary was confined, the spot where McIvor suffered, and the Solway Sands, where Redgauntlet made his abode among the fishermen. From Carlisle, nine miles to the last English village on the border. Three miles further, two turnpike gates, close together, mark the now peaceful boundary line, one on the English the other on the Scotch side. Immediately after crossing we entered into a most romantic region. The banks of the Esk, with precipitous sides and noble woods and dark ravines, reminding us of Scott's finest pictures, and justifying them all. A good Scotch tea with all its accompaniments is now sending us to a welcome bed at Langholm.

CHAPTER XI.

AT Selkirk we struck off from the direct road to Edinburgh, to take Abbotsford and Melrose in our way. On approaching Sir Walter Scott's we were struck with the noble castellated mansion, the splendid liveries, etc., an air of luxury, in short, I had not anticipated. Finding them not at home, I left our letter, together with my card, and drove on about two miles further, to " Chiefswood," where resides his daughter, Mrs. Lockhart, to whom we had also a letter from Mrs. Heber. Leaving our letter here also, from the same cause, we proceeded to visit an old friend whom we were certain of finding, I mean Melrose Abbey. While wandering among these splendid ruins, monuments equally of Gothic taste and modern barbarism, which filled us all with anger as well as admiration, a rather tall gentleman came in, and approaching us, introduced himself as Mr. Lockhart, saying that he and Mrs. L. and her father had reached home very shortly after we had quitted the house, and that he had followed us with all speed, the bearer of an invitation from both to spend that day with him and the next with Sir Walter and Miss Scott. The invitation was so complimentary, and

the manner of it so kind, that the temptation to accept
was great, but, on the whole, we thought it best to
go on, promising, at his request, a visit on our return.
Mr. Lockhart's appearance and manner are rather
American than British; of a thin and rather slight
figure, black hair, face pallid, approaching to sallow,
and with a dash of bilious in his sentiments as well
as his complexion. After some talk he introduced us
to the clerk of the parish, a gossiping old man who
just then entered the abbey, as the original of one of
Scott's characters, and he again to his friend, Captain
C——, another original. With so many topics of interest, though near five o'clock, we could hardly break
away, but, though the dinner might wait our leisure,
we had thirty five miles to drive before we reached it,
and these became very long as the night drew on, if
this may be called night where there is no darkness.
At half past ten we could still read large print by the
twilight. We arrived about midnight at the metropolis of the north, and found our rooms at 19 Princess
Street. . . . .

Saturday, July 17.—Up betimes and favored
with a clear day, which is a rare thing with us.
Walked to Dr. Chalmers', where we were kindly
received by his wife, a very lovely and intelligent
woman, three silent daughters, and the doctor, with
characteristic frankness and simplicity. Some half
dozen students or licentiates completed our breakfast
circle. A chapter in the Bible and family prayers,
all kneeling, was a preparation for breakfast which
made us think of home. Three hours passed away

quickly and pleasantly at and around the table, and by that time we were so much pleased with each other that instead of separating we went out together, and made a new engagement for Monday morning. Before parting Dr. Chalmers wrote me a bundle of notes addressed to professors and leading literary men, in order that I might extend my acquaintance at my leisure.

At two o'clock Mr. Jeffrey called on us with an apology from his wife, who had been prevented from coming in town by the weather; we had already received a note asking us to dine with them to-day. Soon after his visit we ordered the carriage and drove out, about six miles, to Milburn Tower, the very beautiful castellated mansion of Sir Robert Liston, taking it on our way to dinner at Craig Crook, Mr. Jeffrey's country-seat. The ladies remained in the carriage. I was ushered into a splendid Gothic drawing-room, panneled with cedar, and after a short time Sir Robert came in apologizing for the delay, as he was dressing to go out to dinner. At the age of eighty-six he is as hale and hearty as with us are most men at sixty.

Just saved our distance for dinner at Craig Crook. We were received by Mrs. Jeffrey like old friends. She declared she would have known us both, and we certainly should her, by looks, probably, but, without question, by voice and laugh, which, in this land of Ossian, I may say, came o'er me like the days of very youth. Their mansion is a modernized chapelry of the palace of Holyrood, having the picturesqueness of

the old and the luxury of modern days united, while
the style of living is well calculated to set off both.
Mr. Jeffrey's conversational powers seem to me perfectly unique. It is a singular compound of knowledge, talent, satire, and badinage, covering much
natural kindness and good feeling. . . . .

At two P. M. walked through sunshine and rain with
all its intermediate gradations, to hear Dr. Andrew
Thompson, the most powerful reasoner and the most
eloquent speaker I have yet heard. He is a little-
big man, with broad shoulders, a coarse face, and an
enormous head, fitted for a leader either in battle or
argument. Mr. Jeffrey called him the sledge-ham-
mer of divines. He put me in mind of Willie
Garlas in Macniel : —

> "Hap what would Will stood a castle,
> Or for safety, or for war."

His sermon was written and read, but then it was
read as it was written, with freedom and earnestness.
I have heard no extemporary preacher but Robert
Hall; Chalmers writes and commits to memory. Mr.
Jeffrey, who speaks in the highest terms of his talent,
mentioned some anecdotes showing how timid and
distrustful he is of his extemporary powers. When
engaged in preparatory labors, he cannot bear interruption. After church, paid a queer visit to a queer
man, Professor Wilson, and agreed to breakfast with
him to-morrow, when, perhaps, I may think better
of my wild brother.

Monday Night, July 19*th.* — Though quite unwell
to-day I have done and seen much that is interesting.

At nine went to breakfast with Professor Wilson,
the successor of Brown and Stewart. We were alone
and had much talk. He is a strong minded, unpol-
ished man, but not of the kind one expects to see in
the chair of morals. He came in as professor under
the influence of Scott and Lockhart, with much
opposition from Jeffrey. Disputes as to government
in the university arise here as elsewhere, and a royal
commission is now sitting in order to determine the
relative powers of professors, patrons, visitors, etc.
In fact, as it now is, each professor governs his own
class, and the body of professors the whole college
according to usage or opinion, with little interference
from higher powers. The whole number of matric-
ulated students this year is about twenty-five hundred. The largest class is that of chemistry about
five hundred, — that of moral philosophy about one
hundred and fifty. For each course £4 10s. is paid
to the professor by each student, which, with a small
salary from the city funds,• makes their situation
pecuniarily rather better than ours, and, with a vacation of seven months, quite another thing. The
majority of the students have other occupations during vacation. They are teachers, tutors, writers,
etc. Professor Wilson reads his lectures and has no
examination of his students. He receives, however,
from his class voluntary themes, and aids them by
advice in their studies.

. . . . Returning home, found Mrs. Jeffrey with
the ladies, and was soon joined by Dr. Chalmers and
Sir Robert Liston. Going out with Dr. Chalmers,

we directed our course to the house of Mr. Thomas
Erskine, once a literary, now a religious leader in
Scotland. He is the great upholder of the miraculous
effusion of the spirit in the cases at Greenock, a
mania which is working up the minds of many here
into enthusiasm, and, I fear, into insanity. Leaving
Dr. Chalmers to conduct the ladies to the Botanic
Garden, Mr. Erskine accompanied me to the new
Academy, an institution which has been raised within
a few years as a rival, though not so acknowledged, to
the High School. It is distinguished from the latter
by being more aristocratic and more upon the English system. I had a letter to Dr. Williams, the
rector, an Oxford man of Baliol, whom I found intelligent, learned, and full of candor. The curriculum
in this school is seven years. Of their thoroughness
in Latin I had fair proof. For my satisfaction Dr.
Williams called out a student, a lad of fifteen, and
in order to show his general knowledge of the language requested me to give him a passage in Livy,
an author he had never read. The result astonished
me. His examination, after an attentive perusal of
the passage, was that of one familiar, not only with
the language but with the author; others followed
him with the same general result; I have been
delighted. From this I proceeded with Mr. Erskine
to the splendid Botanic Garden, where we lounged
till near five o'clock, delighted with all its arrangements and still more delighted, or to speak with more
exactness, interested by my companion; a noble,
pure, talented, and pious mind, but too likely, I fear,

to become a wreck through religious enthusiasm.
His conversation saddened while it charmed me, and
left an impression I shall not soon lose. . . . . .

The history of Sir Robert Liston, with whom we
breakfasted this morning, is that of a self-made man,
and his success the result of honorable conduct. His
mother was the farmeress, as it is termed here, of
the place he has now adorned with a splendid Gothic
residence, and the cottage she occupied he piously
preserves alongside of his castellated mansion. At
the age of fifteen he still held the plough. An incidental but warm attachment on the part of the son
of Sir G. Eliot, a neighboring youth of his own age,
made him travelling companion, first to his friend
and then to Lord Bute, who afterwards sent him
abroad attached to a foreign embassy. Here he rose
regularly. A long and romantic attachment, delayed
but not lessened by mutual poverty, was at length
rewarded. His long residence at Constantinople
made him wealthy, though, contrary to custom, he
refused all presents. He then married, being about
fifty, and for thirty-six years lived with his wife more
like a lover than a husband. He lost her eighteen
months ago, and such and so long had been his devotion to her that his friends thought that he could not
long survive it; but in active, useful exertion he finds
a resource, and he is now zealously engaged in all
such labor, and especially in restoring a decayed village on his property, which is a very extensive one.

Speaking of Mrs. Grant of Laggan, the author-
ess, he said he had a message for me from her,

namely, that I was her cousin, her maiden name
being McVicar, and that she desired much to see
me.   After breakfast Mr. Fletcher, a young artist
who was one of the guests, offered to ride before us
and inform her of our coming, so we agreed to call.
Mrs. Grant we found living in a large house, in very
comfortable style, in the outskirts of Edinburgh.
We were ushered into an empty but not unfurnished,
literary-looking drawing-room.   She came in supported by crutches, and aided by a servant, looking
old and broken by years, but still with much dignity.
The moment she sat down, however, she was full of
life and interest.   The history of the family name,
the crest, the motto, she entered upon with all her
Scottish feeling.   Her first question was as to the
coat of arms I bore, then proceeded to tell of the
former wide possessions of the clan, and how the
Campbells derived all their property and power from
them by an intermarriage with the heiress of the
McVicar's.   The Earl of Glasgow, she said, was the
present head of our clan, and that I must go and see
him, as she often discussed these matters with his
lordship.   So full, indeed, was she of these thoughts
that she wrote in A———'s album the following lines,
evidently impromptu, expressive of what she deemed
our feelings : —

> " Who the kindly heart would blame,
>   That glows at a congenial name ?
>   These kindred names, well known and dear,
>   Are music to a Highland ear,
>   Oft waking in a Highland eye
>   The sacred fount of sympathy.

These home-bred feelings to restrain,
The wide Atlantic rolls in vain.
Where lovely maids and gallant men
Dwell sheltered in their shady glen,
With Pilgrim steps their exiled race
Shall fondly come to view the place,
And tho' assigned a happier lot,
Shall bless the old ancestral spot.

"Anne Grant — born McVicar."

Wednesday, July 21st. — Dined and spent yesterday night at Craig Crook. The company at dinner consisted of Mr. Murray, one of the leading advocates of Edinburgh, Mr. Morehead, Dean of St. Andrew's, and several others. The conversation was literary and interesting. Of Sir James Mackintosh, Mr. Jeffrey spoke, as the ablest man of his time, a man brimful of learning without being oppressed by it, and gifted with the most prodigious and retentive memory, of which he gave some wonderful instances. He spoke of Professor Wilson as a talented and strong-minded man. Professor Wilson, himself, told me of his own manner of work, that when he did study or write it was generally for fifteen hours at a time, from 6 A. M. to 9 P. M., without moving or eating, which fits of intellectual labor were succeeded by equally immovable fits of indolence. . . . . .

CHAPTER XII.

DEAR Aunt, I now resume my pen here at Rushby Ford, Durham, which at Abbotsford I did not touch, for it seemed a kind of treachery to our kind and noble host. But you must not lose my recollections. At half past nine, Saturday morning, we bade a final farewell to Edinburgh, and to the many kind friends our short stay had given us. Went six miles out of our way to visit Roslyn, with its romantic castle and splendid abbey. This delayed us so long that it was near half past five when we arrived at Melrose, where a note was handed me before we alighted, from Mr. Lockhart, to whom I had written, as I promised, begging us to meet Sir Walter at dinner that evening. Great was the hurry with bags and baggage, and dresses to get ready, and with such success that by six we reached their beautiful cottage.

As we approached we had a glimpse of Sir Walter at the door, but when we drove up he had retired, and Mr. and Mrs. Lockhart alone remained to welcome us. On entering the drawing-room, he was standing with his daughter, Miss Scott, leaning somewhat, as I found was his wont, upon his cane. His appearance — but I will not speak of that, for I had no time to scan it. All that I saw was the face of the " Great Unknown ; " all that I felt was the pressure of that hand which penned " The Antiquary " and " The Lady of the Lake ; " all that I heard were the mellow accents of that Northern tongue, which now with courtesy and kindness, welcomed me to Scotland. The company was not large, but sufficiently so to afford a plea for laying the table on the green, an arrangement which, however agreeable it may have been in Arcadia, is but a perilous experiment in the latitude of Scotland ; besides, the outer air is no place for quiet talk — it is fitted for merriment, but not for intellectual conversation — so that a lowering sky became by common consent an apology for an early return to the drawing-room, where music and the song awaited us.

Sir Walter's great delight is in his daughter's harp, and the ballads of the olden time, which she sings with a most winning grace. Thus passed our evening ; and on parting for the night, we received and accepted an invitation to Abbotsford ; so that, as you may suppose, with gay hearts, we returned to our inn. Now, if you ask me the impression of this day, I must confess, in regard to Sir Walter, it partook somewhat of disappointment. He was kind and courteous, but did not say much ; and when he did speak, I missed somewhat of that precision of · thought and power of language, which had so recently charmed me in Southey and Sir James Mackintosh. But further acquaintance has enabled me to see that I was then in the heresy of ignorance. I was bringing to the measurement an inapplicable standard. It was like measuring *weight* by *length* — it was requiring in a boundless scene of natural beauty the polish and proportions of a Grecian temple. The next day being Sunday, we attended service at the kirk, occupying Sir Walter Scott's pew, which was very near the pulpit. " How did you like the preacher ? " said Sir Walter, when I again met him. " I confess," I replied, " I did not hear a single sentence. " You must not complain," said he ; " you have heard as much as any of his hearers for ten years past." This voiceless preacher, as I afterwards found, was the father of the original Dominie Sampson. Had delicacy permitted it, the father would himself have made no bad " study."

On approaching Abbotsford a second time, we paused not, as before, at the gate ; but driving down through the rich young woods that embower it, and, passing through an arched and turreted gateway, found ourselves in a noble court or quadrangle. On our left rose the mansion in its rich and irregular architecture, bearing in some parts the choice remains of an earlier chisel, which Sir Walter has rescued from the contiguous ruins, but generally the result of native genius, working under his own eye, and passing rapidly, as he told me, " from the models of art to those of nature." In front a rich and lofty Gothic screen separated the court from the gardens, — happily attaining what Sir Walter said he had almost despaired of doing, — " distancing without hiding

them ; " while on the right runs an arcade or clois-
ter, embanking the rising ground behind it, and forming a sheltered walk nearly around two sides of the
court. On this occasion Sir Walter met us at the
door, again welcomed us to Scotland and Abbotsford,
and, taking E—— by the hand, led the way to the
library. But of that way, I must give a little description.

The entrance is through an octagonal turret, raised
but a step from the ground, into a hall occupying
the central front of the building : such a hall as
transports you at once into the regions of romance,
and the days of baronial chivalry. Its walls and
ceiling are of dark oak wainscoting. At either end,
on a raised pedestal, stands forth a mailed knight,
with visor down and spear in rest, like sentinels to
challenge all who enter — these are formed of complete suits of ancient armor ; one of steel, inlaid
with gold, the same which was borrowed by the
champion of England at the coronation of George
IV. ; it cost Sir Walter one thousand guineas. Along
the walls hang " shield and spear and partisan," in-
termixed with horns of the bison and the elk, and
the skins of beasts of prey, as if to mark its lord
equally ready for the foray or the chase. The windows, too, throw " a rich and storied light," being of
stained glass, bearing the armorial escutcheons of the
whole clan of Scots, the Laird of Buccleuch, as I
think, standing at their head. Around the circuit of
the walls, near to the ceiling, run those again of the
Border families, richly carved in oak, and underneath

them the following legend, in the old Gothic letter:
" These be the armour coats of thae who, in times of
auld, stood up for the Marches of Scotland : thae
were men of might and fought stoutly, and God did
defend them." From this hall, you have access to
the other parts of the house, and pass *en suite* through
the following rooms: Miss Scott's boudoir; the
breakfast and dining-room ; the armory; the with-
drawing room ; the library, and lastly Sir Walter
Scott's study; which brings you again to the front
of the house and end of the building.

Of these rooms the most splendid is the library;
the most interesting, I need not add, is the study, into
which last we entered not, but under its master's
guidance. The library, with its noble dimensions
and costly furniture ; its book-cases and cabinets of
odorous cedar; its ceiling of the same, paneled
and carved after the model of Melrose ; its well-
filled shelves; its beautiful oriel window projecting
and spreading out over the Tweed; its curtains of
crimson damask with heavy gold fringe ; its varied
articles of use, curiosity, and luxury; all combine
to make it a most splendid room. Of these articles
many are presents. Here, for instance, stands a massive chair, once a cardinal's, the carving of which
ranks it among the productions of genius : this is
from Rome. There hangs an antique lamp, a relic
of the majesty of Venice. Here, in a corner, stands
Dean Swift's walking cane; and that splendid silver
sarcophagus, on its low pedestal, is the gift of the
unfortunate Byron. How many associations does

even that one awaken ? Within it are the bones of
ancient heroes — for over their tombs were built the
old walls of the Piræus — yet who can name them ?
The lines inscribed " Expende Hannibalem," etc.,
feelingly convey this lesson, — while the name of
Byron, which the donor would not put, but which
Scott has added, brings touchingly to mind the danger and the misery of earthly genius unsanctified by
religion. The letter accompanying this gift has been
purloined from its sacred resting-place. When shall
such a theft dare to be shown ? Sir Walter deeply
regrets its loss, for of Byron he often speaks — sometimes with high admiration — always with tender
feelings. " Poor Byron," is his familiar appellation,
which words, uttered in his deep tones, go to the very
heart.

But with all its splendor, the library yields in interest to the room beyond — his private study : for
there stand his table and his chair, calling up the
visions of his past labors ; and there lie his pen and
papers, the evidence of his present ones ; and there,
too, his uncorrected yet hasty manuscripts, which
show from what a rapid fountain his thoughts must
have poured forth. That which lies upon the table
I dare not read ; but from what he says, conclude it
is upon the superstitions of the Highlands. Around
this room, at the height of about ten feet — for the
ceiling is a high one — runs a light gallery, which
gives access by a private door to his bed-room, so
that he can at all times command privacy. In addition to cases made from wood that once formed the

"Heart of Mid-Lothian," filled with books of more frequent reference, the walls of his study are covered with portraits and scenes of Scottish and Border story. Among them, those of Claverhouse and the unfortunate Mary seem his especial favorites. This first day we had company at dinner and until near bed-time. His style of living is with considerable state. The buildings are very extensive, and lighted throughout by gas, prepared in one of the remotest parts. Two servants in livery, and ·his own gentleman in black, are in regular attendance. Of the embarrassments arising from the failure of his publishers, with whom the law adjudged him to be a partner, I have learned but little. The impression given me by Mr. Jeffrey and others in Edinburgh, was that these engagements, amounting originally to near £100,000, were in a great measure liquidated : partly by a heavy policy on his own life of (I understood) £40,000, and partly by the sale of his subsequent works. But to proceed with my story. Monday, 26th July, shall be marked by us henceforth with a " white stone," as having been spent with Sir Walter Scott alone. Then, indeed, for the first time was I made fully aware of being in the presence of " the mighty master ; " for, as with other magicians, the spell increased as the circle narrowed. The truth is, Sir. Walter Scott is not to be judged of in general society : he never argues, never dogmatizes and never talks learnedly ; his head and heart seemed filled with better thoughts and things ; an overflowing benevolence ; sympathy for all breathing things ; an

imagination that teems with all images of natural
loveliness ; feelings that tremble with every touch of
natural affection ; a memory that so lives in the
records of the romantic past, that a metaphysician
might well doubt to which century its possessor in
truth belonged ; and a sweet simplicity and unas-
sumingness of manner that adds the attractiveness
of childhood to the words and thoughts of genius, —
these are the elements of his strength, and when seen
in private they are overpowering in their influence.
Then a book, a portrait, or a chance word, unlocks,
as it were, by magic, some hidden fountain ; then
comes forth at once the splendid train of thought and
feeling and imagery, the Border story, the touching
ballad, and the heart-rending incident ; in the
mean while his eye lightens up, often suffused with
tears, and his voice deepens to a tone that thrills
through the nerves like the deep notes of the organ.
In this I can liken him to nothing but his own picture of the awakened minstrel — when —

> " The present scene, his future lot,
>   His toils, his wants, were all forgot."

But in all this, his true-hearted modesty never for-
sakes him. In all his poetic recollections, which,
on such occasions, came swelling like a tide into his
mind, I never once heard him repeat a line of his
own ; and whenever the subject of his poems was
alluded to, he avoided it with a simplicity which always left me in doubt whether he understood the
allusion. The old adage of " genus irritabile " ap-
plies not to him : a sneer is as foreign to his nature

as it is to the expression of his countenance ; and, as
far as words and manners go, he certainly knows not
what envy is. Of the race of his contemporaries,
there is scarce one of whom we did not speak ; and
not one of whom he spoke otherwise than with respect and kindness ; and what at any time was wanting in praise, was sure to be made up in kindness of
manner. On his repeating one evening a sea-song
of Allan Cunningham's, beginning, " A wet sheet
and a flowing sea," etc., which he did with great
power, I expressed my surprise at its beauty, and
said, " Does Cunningham often write such ? " He
replied, " My friend Allan is like a boy that shoots
many arrows at a mark — some of them must hit."
Of Coleridge, Wordsworth, and Southey he spoke
often ; and his all powerful memory was ever prompt
to bring forth their choicest passages. On mentioning to him Southey's desponding views of political
affairs, " Ah ! " said he, little aware how much the
past had blinded his own eyes, " Southey is a retired
and bookish man." On expressing my agreeable
disappointment in Jeffrey's character, whom before
personal acquaintance I had regarded as a cold and
cynical critic, he replied with warmth, " You never
did man more injustice ; his heart is all tenderness ; "
and of his own family affections you may judge by
his warm exclamation when the conversation turned
to such themes, " I bless God " said he, " that He
has given me good affectionate children." I may
here mention that these are four in number : Walter,
in the army ; Charles, in the foreign department ; Mrs.

Lockhart, and Miss Scott. As we sat alone after
dinner, I ventured to introduce the subject of his
long " Incognito." He entered into it kindly if not
freely. His near friends, he said, always knew it,
though not by acknowledgment, while to the direct
inquiry of others he felt himself under no obligation
to give an answer. " It was not a crime," said he,
" of which I was accused, and therefore I was not
bound to answer ; the secret began in caprice, and
was continued perhaps from other motives." Upon
my mentioning the name of his brother in Canada as
one to whom in America they had often been attributed, he replied with so much feeling that I feared
again to mention the name, " Ah ! poor Tom " (I
think he called him) ; " he could have written *them*,
and *better;* he had great powers, and I often urged
him, but in vain : he never wrote me a line." On
asking him here the metaphysical question, whether
imagination had ever furnished him with materials
not traceable to experience, he replied, after a moment's pause, that his characters were always drawn
from nature, and many of them individual pictures
but slightly altered. " This likeness on one occasion," said he, " betrayed my secret ; the original of
' Oldbuck ' was an old friend of my father's, whom I
well remembered as a boy. It was too faithful a
copy not to be known. Mr. ——, on its publication,
meeting me, said, as he clapped me on the shoulder,
' Ah, Scott, you wrote that ; no one could paint our
old friend to the life but you or I.' " Upon my mentioning some other wild surmises as to their author-

ship, after answering them, he concluded with a smile, as if in reference to my pertinacity, " In truth, I find that I have kept the secret so long and so well as now to find some difficulty in proving my own."

On Monday morning, Sir Walter rose as usual about six o'clock, wakened, as he regularly is, by his favorite dog, a large staghound of the ancient breed, given him, as he tells me, by Dandie Dinmont himself. This dog, by the by, is his constant companion. At meals, he waits behind his master's chair, and not unfrequently puts his paw upon his shoulder to remind him of his presence; follows him through the day in his drives and walks; dozes at his side while he writes; and completes his tour of duty by guarding him while he sleeps, — his bed being a bearskin couch. At break of day, he again arouses his master with a gentle paw, knowing well that he has work to do in which the whole world is interested, and not the least the canine race, of whose virtues he himself has so often sat as the model. In truth, I look upon this dog with equal respect and kindness, as " part and parcel " of the novelist himself. Until breakfast time, that is, for about two hours, Sir Walter writes, and about an equal time after it, which brings him to eleven o'clock; after which he calls himself a free man, writing no more that day, unless perchance in the long evenings of winter. On leaving his study this day, he immediately proposed to A—— and M—— a drive through his plantations, of which he is justly proud, and as far as Melrose; to which they, as you may suppose, well pleased, acceded. His morning's dress accords with his simple rural habits; a well-worn, green hunting-coat, with ample flaps and pockets, a flat cloth cap, and an oft-used whistle pendant from his button-hole, agree well with the large frame and manly figure, though slight stoop, of one whom you might take to be a Scottish laird of high degree and simple tastes, — of one who was beginning to feel the weight of years, without having lost the taste or enjoyment of the more active sports of youth. In this guise I see him now setting forth in his low-wheeled, open barouche, accompanied by our two girls and followed by his deep-mouthed favorite and two others of minor breed. On visiting the scarcely perceptible ruins of the early Melrose on the heights, he expatiated, they tell me, good humoredly on the taste of the lazy monks, who could prefer the fat lands of the valley to such heart-stirring scenes; and on passing at a little distance a Scotch lassie, knee-deep in the river, fishing, he said (whether in joke or earnest), " There stands my Die Vernon." But I must not defraud them of the pleasure of telling of their drive, which they describe as all delightful from his attentive kindness and his unceasing flow of anecdote and ballad, in reference to every spot they visited, or individual of note of whom they chanced to speak.

On his return I met him in the library; as he approached he handed me from a packet of letters just received, a small, hard roll of parchment, tied with cord, and secured by a lump of raw wax. " Open it," said he ; "it will be something to tell, that a Republican dared to break the seal of a writ of the king ; " " At the orders," I would have added, " of one whom kings delighted to honor," but his modesty awed me, and I dared not. It was a writ for the general election, Parliament being dissolved by the king's death, and was addressed to him as high sheriff of Selkirkshire, — the style and form of it have continued unchanged, he tells me, from the time of the, earliest Edward; and hence its rude accompaniments. A reformed Parliament, however, will no doubt order all that much better.

Remembering the dash of superstition which he invariably gives to his fictions, and which always seemed to me to be *ex animo*, I took occasion to ask, after several surprising narratives given by him of individuals possessing the power of second sight, whether he had, in the course of his life, met with any such which could not be rationally explained? He paused some moments before he answered, " I cannot say that I have." Still, however, whether by natural or early association, a lingering respect for such fears, not to say belief in them, often appears in him. And how, indeed, could it be otherwise, with with a mind of such preponderating imagination, of which credulity (I mean it in a poetic sense) must be one of its highest elements. That mind must believe in the reality of its own creations, or it could not give them life, and cannot therefore judge harshly the illusions of other men. Of Coleridge, he quoted with applause the answer, " That he had seen too

many ghosts to believe in them ; " and then in reference to that wayward writer, said, " He is never
ending, still beginning ; could he be tied to his chair
and to a water diet, he would be the greatest genius
living."

One evening as we sat in the library alone, on
some mention of a present he had received, he opened
a cabinet and brought out a store of them, — rings,
seals, snuff-boxes, miniatures, etc., without number:
each had its own little story.   On showing us a
splendid gold snuff-box presented to him by the king,
George IV., with his likeness on the lid, he said, " A
princely return for a little book which the king had
requested of him."   But on one trifle he seemed to
set a peculiar value : it was an antique stone ring,
found in the Highlands of Scotland, believed to be of
Carthaginian origin, and commonly called the Adder's
Stone, of which he said there were but three known,
whose owners he then enumerated, to each of which,
by popular superstition, rare virtues were attributed,
and, more especially, to drop one from the hand por-
tended some great misfortune to its owner.   To guard
against such an event, to this one was attached a small
silver chain, which was to be slipped over the fingers
as a security.   He took the precaution, I observed,
in his own case, and as A—— received it from him,
he said in an apologetic way, as he put the chain on
her fingers, " Permit me," before untwisting it from
his own hand.

Upon my introducing the subject of the printed
editions of his works in America, he spoke of literary

property as a literary man cannot but speak, namely, as one of its most sacred forms; and I in turn spoke, I was sure, the feelings of my countrymen, in saying, that in proportion to our admiration of his works was our regret at the inadequacy of our laws to secure to him his rightful returns. " On one occasion," said he, " after trying in vain to prevent their bribery of some one having access to the press, in order to remind the publishers in your country that they were trespassing on others' property, I sent to my printer a sheet utterly unsuitable, as the conclusion to one of my novels just publishing — which sheet was immediately canceled as soon as I had reason to believe the surreptitious copy was sent off." " Now this," said he, " I call a fair trick. But seriously," he continued, " I think it is but just and becoming that a common language should make common copyright, as is now the case by treaty between the Prussian and Austrian dominions."

As we had just returned from a tour to Loch Katrine, and the abode of the McGregors, with " Rob Roy " and " The Lady of the Lake in our hands, " as our most faithful guide-books, this was an obvious theme ; he entered upon it freely ; and when his heart was warmed, it only wanted that I should have had (as Boswell says), " a short hand or a long head," to have added another tale to those of " Old Mortality," or with but slight addition of melody, another canto to " The Lady of the Lake." " Rob Roy," is, after all, one of Sir Walter's choicest heroes ; he prides himself in showing in his armory the light, short gun of the

far-famed freebooter.   On our mentioning the inn at
the Trosacks : " Then," said he, " you saw my friend
Stewart (the host), the grandson of that ' Ewan of
Briglands,' who paid with his life for his tender heart
towards poor Rob Roy; he cut the belt and let him
slip; he was my authority for that fact."   But details
I must reserve for our long winter evenings, if Heav-
en is pleased to bring us together again ; in the mean
time, I close my long narrative.   On the second day
I sent for post-horses, fearing to trespass by a longer
stay, but Sir Walter countermanded them, saying in
his own kind manner, " You are not quite well, and
I cannot part with you; besides I owe it, for it was
all Lockhart's doing with his ' fête champêtre.' "
Though the indisposition was but trifling, the kindness was great, and the remembrance of it will be
enduring; it has added love to veneration, so that in
my future recollections of Sir Walter Scott, the virtues of the man will come to my heart, before his
merits as an author.   On the third day of our stay at
Abbotsford we took leave, Sir Walter returning to
A——, as he parted from her, a little book, in which,
on a blank leaf, he had written these words : —

> "To meet and part is mortals' lot,
> You've seen us — pray — forget us not;
> Such the farewell of Walter Scott."

·   ·   ·   ·   ·   ·   ·   ·

LONDON, *August* 3. — Our Paris news darkens the
future.   " To go or stay, that is the question," and a
very doubtful one.   To quit England, with all its high
interests so close to our own, and so many kind friends

making it homelike, for a land of strangers, a foreign tongue, and unkindred people — I sometimes feel like one about to leap a gulf which he will afterwards regret. I shall pause a while for guidance. So having closed that question for a few days at least, I took a cab for city business, and to renew the broken links of our London acquaintance. But here again I find the city a different place in August from what it was in June. Sir Thomas Acland, at his seat in Devonshire, but from him a kind letter of invitation ; Mrs. Bates on the wing, but promising to meet us on the Continent ; Mrs. Heber, already gone, accompanied, I was sorry to learn, by Count Valimachi, the Greek noble, to whom she had introduced me at her own house. This was all I then heard ; but my next visit to Lady Morton cleared up the mystery by the information of a secret marriage, communicated only the morning of her departure to her old and best friend, Sir Robert Harry Inglis, by a hasty note, saying, " That knowing his sentiments it had not been communicated to him before ; " and in short, that her friends must make the best of it.

Among the few acquaintances I found in town, was the Hon. Joseph Hume, M. P., preparing for his Middlesex election to-morrow, to which he has engaged me to accompany him.

. . . . At eight, A. M., Thursday, a long and splendid procession of private coaches appeared in Regent Street decorated with blue ribbons and oak favors. Among them I recognized Mr. Hume's chariot, which, drawing up for me, I entered, joining two

gentlemen, strangers, who informed me that Mr.
Hume was before us with his committee, which
cavalcade we joined at the committee-room in Pall
Mall, thence proceeding on our splendid, but tedious
journey of eight miles to the hustings at Old Brent-
ford. On entering Mr. Hume's carriage I had observed that the gentlemen in it, as well as all others,
wore in their button-holes, and also attached to their
hats, a sprig of oak, the badge of their party, but
never thought myself interested till one of the gentlemen, as I afterwards learned, a nephew of the
new member, seeing me without any, very courteously divided his, and handing it to me requested
me to wear it. It was an awkward moment, but
feeling it inconsistent with my position as an American who had come to see rather than to approve, I
declined, good humoredly, on the ground that as an
American citizen I was precluded from accepting all
title or insignia of honor in a foreign land. At the
committee-room my companions were changed, but
not for the better, the new-comers insisting that
without a badge I would not be safe in an excited
crowd, and still more that I could not be received on
the hustings among the special friends of the new
member. I simply replied that all that was a matter
of indifference to me, and concerned only Mr. Hume,
upon whose invitation I had come. The result justified my confidence. ' Through excited crowds we
passed for miles with much applause, some abuse,
but no disorder; and at the hustings Mr. Hume took
me forward within the privileged rail, introducing me

to Sir John Cam Hobhouse, and the other members
of his committee. On the Hon. Mr. Byng's arrival,
the other radical candidate, amid much cheering, his
horses were taken from the carriage, the mob taking
their place, an honor which Mr. Hume had declined.
But the election was still delayed for hours, waiting
the arrival of the high sheriff, Sir James Richardson,
who had gone down with the king in his first visit to
the " Tower." On his arrival, the usual acts against
bribery, etc., were read, proclamation made, the elec-
tors addressed by the candidates, Mr. Hume and Mr.
Byng being the only names proposed ; and, in fine, no
opposition appearing, and no show of hands called for,
they were declared by the sheriff the elected members
for Middlesex. On leaving the stand Mr. Hume was
" chaired " by his followers, borne aloft on their shoulders through the excited multitude. But I paid dear
for my curiosity, for as I gazed upon the scene with
something of a Republican's contempt, my pockets
were skillfully turned inside out, my purse gone, everything except my watch. Remembering at the moment
my dinner engagement with Sir Robert Inglis, and
time pressing, I was forced at once to exchange my
slow chariot for a swift coach, and, by means of a little stray silver that had escaped, to find my way back
to London and Regent Street. Happily I there met
my own carriage with wife and daughters ; they, tired
of waiting, had just set off, intending to make an
apology for my absence.

It was a fortunate meeting, for I should otherwise
have lost one of the most delightful remembrances

of English society. A few choice friends, added to
a large family circle, Sir Robert and Lady Inglis,
with their young wards, the orphan daughters of
Thornton, the eminent banker, philanthropist, and
Christian, formed a doubly attractive picture to
Americans who had been inclined to associate rank
and wealth and social position, with fashion and
worldly display. We here saw the reverse — genuine
simplicity of heart, manners, and character, adorned
by high accomplishments, with a tone of deep Christian sentiment, pervading and dignifying all. With
little taste for music myself, I was still never weary
listening to the grand cathedral anthems played and
sung by the Misses Thornton; so sweet and soothing,
it gave me new ideas as to the melody of sweet
sounds. From this high enjoyment we returned at
a late hour to our lodgings.

Friday, August 6. — At half past six drove to
Mr. Hume's. A splendid dinner, though small, of
about fifteen covers, to the leaders of his party, Sir
Francis Burdett, Sir John Ellis, Sir John Cam Hobhouse, Sir J. Williamson, high sheriff, etc., etc. I
sat between Mr. Byng — the other elected or rather
reëlected member, Mr. Byng having represented
Middlesex for forty years — and Colonel Jones, natural son of the late Lord Landsdown, and had a most
agreeable and spirited talk generally. Sir Francis Burdett, as the popular leader, was first in importance,
though not in conversational powers. In person, he is
tall and thin, with feeble features, a high, narrow, bulg-
ing forehead, and small, gray, twinkling eyes. You

may judge of the expense of contested elections from his telling me that his three Middlesex elections and two consequent examinations had cost him near £100,000, or half a million of dollars; hence in hard times, he added, contested elections were rare. The expenses of yesterday, uncontested, were about £15,000, though upon Mr. Hume asserting that it had cost nothing to any one, I ventured to assert the reverse, on the score of my emptied pockets.

Saturday, August 7. — Mr. Southey having given me a letter to a Mr. Morrison of London, as one who had revolutionized the retail business, and made an immense fortune by it, I determined to seek him out. Having nothing special before me, I this morning set forth. But London does not admit of having but one point of interest. On my way, passing near the Royal Palace I remembered my promise of calling on the king's son, Colonel Fitz-Clarence, residing with his father, as he, more affectionately than reverentially had expressed it, " to take care of him." I left my card, not finding him in, and thence, passing eastward to the city, paid a similar fruitless visit to Bishop Copleston at his London residence. At length I reached Mr. Morrison's actual scene of business, the source of his wealth, the greatest retail store in the world, where the shop had grown up into an establishment, covering a whole square, — with its independent departments, respective heads responsible, each with its array of clerks, and cash sales to the amount of many millions. So much for the petty shop, while the petty shop-keeper himself has grown into one of the grandees of the land for wealth, and is now recently incorporated among its legislators, being just elected Member of Parliament for the Borough of St. Ives, Devonshire. Mr. Morrison being now among his constituents, his partner became my guide through the establishment, and enlightened me as to the secret of his success. But I will not weary you with the details. The principles are self-evident, requiring only the administrative talent. No credit, cash sales, rapid conversion of capital, minute subdivision of labor, above all, the credit of perfect fidelity in prices and quality of goods, with small profits, and nightly closing of every account. These rules, faithfully observed, have, within a few years, wrought the above miracles and brought the shop-keeper to sit with princes.

In the evening I walked to Mr. Bates'. Found him much changed in views after reading my pamphlet on "Reëxchange" with New York; he now favors it. On my praising the perfect silence that prevailed in his large counting-rooms, his answer was striking. "A single word would indicate that some clerk had neglected his duty." He then proceeded to unfold its beautifully quiet organization. On reaching the counting-house, at half-past nine, the letters of the day are laid before him, numbered from one, say, to fifty, and notes are made upon them for inspection, they thence pass into the hands of the corresponding clerks, of whom there are five in constant employ, — two English, one French, German, etc., each taking his own and noting in their own memorandum book " when, how, etc.," to be answered. Thence they pass to the underwriting clerk, to the sale clerk, etc., each noting his own duty performed, all by writing and without speaking, eventually reaching again by three or four o'clock the hands of the principal, the work done.

Monday, August 9. — Received at breakfast a note from the palace from Colonel Fitz-Clarence, favorite son of the king, saying that he would be happy to see me at his head-quarters. This was an honor not to be declined, so, notwithstanding the hurry of a last day in London, I determined to call, though it had to be dovetailed among many visits and much necessary business. Setting out, I first directed my course to the Dutch minister's to learn the actual state of Brussels, which the papers spoke of as in a great ferment from sympathy with Paris, and unsafe for travellers. He, on the contrary, laughed at my fears, and bade me go with confidence. Driving thence to Mr. Hume's, I found him on the wing for Scotland, to boast his new parliamentary honors as representing the metropolitan county, having heretofore represented an obscure Scotch borough. On reaching the Horse Guards, Colonel Fitz-Clarence's head-quarters, I left my card, finding him officially engaged. But calling again on my return, after some matter of business, his secretary stated that he had left orders for my reception. From a small reception-room I was at once ushered in, and in five minutes, to give you an idea of his cordial reception and open natural manners, I found myself engaged as with an old friend. One bond, at least, was clear, his feelings towards my home and country. " I would have been a rebel myself," said he, " for the cause of representation. Without it taxation is tyranny. My father thinks so, and so do I." Respect and kindness were in all that he said or repeated of his father, the king. " The sailor king," as he himself admitted, adding in a tone of familiar confidence, " I am very anxious to get him down into the country. London is not the place for him now among his old associates." After an hour's pleasant talk and giving me a letter of introduction to one of the Savans of Paris, and urging me to give freely to any friend of mine in America a letter to him, we parted. I secretly wished, for England's sake, that he, instead of his imbecile father, had been in the line of succession.

My last visit was to bid farewell to Mr. Herries, my early acquaintance and recent friend, Chancellor of the Exchequer now ; at my former visit, as the son of a ruined merchant, struggling for support. One further visit both of duty and pleasure remained ; it was to our able and kind minister, Alexander McLane and family, including my old friend Washington Irving, Secretary of Legation. Talking of his diplomatic intercourse with the government, Mr. McLane tells me that it has been specifically with Lord Aberdeen and Mr. Herries, with occasional reference to the Duke of Wellington on knotty points for a final settlement. Of Aberdeen he speaks as a highly honorable man, single-minded but slow. Of Herries, as a perfect man of business and master of all questions that come up, and the facts bearing upon them; but still more highly of the great duke as the most candid, satisfactory diplomat he had ever met: patient in listening, courteous in manner, seeking information, and, when his judgment was settled, clear, liberal, and decided in stating it. " 'Now, Mr. McLane,' he would often say to me in such discussions, ' I do not understand that matter. Explain it to me. Up to such a point we are agreed. There we begin to differ. You hold that course, I think this view best; now then explain,' etc. So that," Mr. McLane added, " I never left him in any doubt as to his opinion on any controverted question, nor as to how far we agreed, and where and how we differed."

Returning to a hasty dinner before embarking, the doubtful question arose as to how we were to travel on the Continent. This speculation soon received a solution in a very kind note from Sir Robert Inglis, urging or rather insisting on our use of his travelling barouche, to be found at Ostend, an order for it being inclosed, for our summer tour on the Continent, and to be redeposited, on our return, at an hotel named, either at Calais or Paris. This liberal offer, twice repeated, was at length accepted with thanks, as giving us more of comfort and freedom of movement in our journey than we could otherwise have commanded. And so, good-night to England! Henceforth Germany, or France, or Switzerland is to be my theme, which, if you feel with me, will be a change for the worse. The ladies of our party are confident, and promise themselves great things; but for myself, I cling to England with filial affection doubly strengthened by our present visit.

CHAPTER XIII.

I WRITE from this old town of Ghent on the twelfth day of August. Our passage across the channel was stormy, but daylight soon brought us into smooth water and alongside the pier of Ostend, surrounded by strange faces and strange sounds. The morning opened dark but soon brightened. The custom-house, our dread, gave us no trouble. The revolution in Paris had converted all into Republicans, and the very name of " American " was sacred in their ears. " Je suis Américain," was an " open sesame " for all that I wanted to see, know, or do. My passport was *viséd* without being looked at, my baggage unquestioned, my trunk keys refused when proffered, and the usual fee declined. All this I received as a tribute to my country, and warmly thanked the chief official for it. His rejoinder was " Ah, vous êtes Américain! C'est une Paradis Terrestre ! " Finding, on inquiry, that Sir Robert's barouche was not here, but at Brussels, I made choice of a comfortable vehicle and good driver to take us there. . . . . .

This morning, Thursday, breakfast was scarcely finished when Mr. Cornelisson of the University of

Ghent, to whom I had sent my card and letter of introduction the evening before, was announced. He immediately planned our day for us, and while our carriage was getting ready set off for the university, there to meet us. This is a noble specimen of royal patronage, doing in six years the work of a century in fostering education and science. Its present number of students is five hundred. Fortunately this was the day of the commencement ceremonial, which, however, was not till three P. M., so we bade Mr. Cornelisson farewell till that hour. Finding our way to the cathedral, we entered during high mass, the splendor of which and its impressiveness on the imagination, I had never before witnessed, nor even conceived.

Three o'clock found us again at the university, where, with great pomp, in the *quasi* presence of majesty, amid the flourish of trumpets, the rewards were declared, and medals of honor hung round the necks of the successful students as they kneeled to receive them at the hands of the president of the university. One touching incident occurred. The father of one of the first medalists, a chief burgher of the city, was seated on the stage when his son advanced, about to kneel to the president, but a wave of hands directed him to his father, on kneeling to whom the chain of gold, with its accompanying medal, was hung upon his neck amid the plaudits of all.

After a drive through the public grounds we visited the convent of ——, the last great nunnery remaining in the Netherlands. Having inspected the interior, we attended the chapel at vespers, where seven hundred kneeling figures without form, except here and there two outstretched arms from under their long veils, black below and white above, formed a spectacle as striking as it was new. But the interior of the convent was neither melancholy nor romantic, being self-supporting through teaching and needlework. I heard as hearty a laugh from the lady abbess, in answer to some simple question of mine, as I ever heard. The sisters take no vows, and may quit at any time they please, though my conductress said that in her own case she was not likely to do so, as she was happier than a queen; " for queens," said she, "sometimes have to flee from their homes, as the Queen of France the other day." We parted with mutual kindly feelings.

The Belgians appear to be both by nature and habit a very thriving, contented people. They work moderately, live comfortably, and look healthy and long-lived. The men you see toward evening gathering into circles in their picturesque caps and large silver shoe-buckles, playing at quoits, or with their favorite pipe and pot of ale, not carousing, but quietly sitting on the " dry, smooth, shaven green," or on benches under the shade of some ancestral tree at the door of a temperate-looking, quiet ale-house. The women, meanwhile, at such hour, appear in their best, — gold earrings, rich lace caps, or fringed cloaks and hoods, — spinning or knitting just outside their door, with children in groups of eight or ten engaged in play, or work so light that they make play of it.

In this country, except its level surface, everything
is picturesque. The houses have all a mediæval
look, grouped with angles and projections awakening
curiosity, while the interiors puzzle you with their
numerous and intricate divisions. Their horses look
as if they had just stepped out of Van Dyke's canvas, — war-horses, full-limbed, hollow-backed, with
crested necks, and sweeping tails touching the ground,
and manes as rich and heavy. And they may well
look proud under their master's care, judging at least
from our own hired team. Every few miles the
driver stopped, went to their heads, gave them something from his pocket, and seemed to have a little talk
with them. At length the lunch time having come,
he opened a box in the carriage and taking out a
handsome brown loaf, with his ever ready pocket-
knife proceeded to help, not himself, but his horses,
giving them alternately slice after slice till they were
satisfied. In short, nothing is fed raw to any of their
animals — all ground and cooked. But falling into
conversation with an intelligent tradesman, I found
the people restless and discontented; taxes heavy,
all forms of business under privilege, and all for the
benefit of Holland; nothing for their own Belgium.

Tuesday, August 17.— HUY ON THE MEUSE. —
. . . . . This is our first appearance in our borrowed
splendor, and I must give you some idea of it. Our
carriage is of Russian form, though probably Paris
built, covered or open at pleasure, capacious and comfortable, with cushions and stuffings, with innumerable
pockets at the sides and nettings above, and a boot

below opening from within for convenience and safety, and a seat in front for the courier. To this vehicle are harnessed four post-horses, and at times six, all governed by a single post-boy with more gold and scarlet about him than belongs to a general. His seat is on the off-wheeler, governing the leaders by reins and by the crack of his far-sounding whip. His " jack-boots," come half-way up his thighs, his great spurs rattling like bells, which last, however, are not wanting to the horses, who jingle along, dressed out also with innumerable scarlet tassels. Amid this display, the postilion stands chief, and is in fact an officer of government. In such style we yesterday rattled out of Brussels, and such must it continue henceforward, " coûte qui coûte." . . . .

Saturday, August 21.— On reaching Andernach on the Rhine, we stopped, and finding my host an intelligent listener, I expressed my surprise at what seemed the evident neglect of early education in the absence of school-houses, giving him a picture of our American public schools. He smiled and said, " Ours is still more exact and complete." On my still doubting, he said, " Go with me now and judge for yourself." I went, and was soon convinced of my error. " Law," said he, " overrules parental neglect. No man has a right to throw fire-brands into the community, and such is every ignorant, vicious youth. Education is therefore a matter of police, and so efficient that I venture to assert that in this city of thirty thousand inhabitants not a child is to be found, however poor or degraded the parents, who cannot, at the age of eight, read, write, cipher, and sing noted music from the blackboard. Botany and drawing is also practically studied with a benevolent end, large colored engravings of the poisonous plants of the country, in their various stages, being hung around the walls for the children to copy and thus become familiar with."

After an excellent breakfast with " côtelettes de mouton au naturel," the hardest thing in cookery to get from a German cuisine, we set off on our road to Coblentz, ten miles, in company with a Prussian Prince and suite in command of a " Corps d'Armée," encamped on our way on the very bank of the Rhine. About midway we approached them, and finding their religious services about opening, we waited and joined in them. It was to us not only a novel but a splendid and solemn service. The white tents and varied flags, spread over a noble plain running down to the flowing Rhine, with all its picturesque surroundings, was a most impressive scene ; but still more the congregation of ten thousand full armed troops in their array, in profound silence, before a single preacher, uncovering their heads with military precision at the same moment at the voice of prayer, or pealing forth one of Luther's grand hymns in the deepest tones of dear " Fader-Land,"— this was a service not soon to be forgotten.

Dined to-day at the *table d'hôte* with a numerous and varied party, some English and Russians, but chiefly Prussian officers of high rank. The dinner was a truly German affair, six courses and almost as many hours, with music to fill up the intervals. A painful contrast it was to the poor fare of the soldiers in the camp, one meal in twenty-four hours, and that a slim one; his pay five groschen, two retained for his rations, and his bread to be bought beside. Prussia, next to Russia, has at present the largest military establishment in Europe; nominally 350,000, actually 140,000, and that from a population of but twelve millions; — too much for the prosperity of their people, especially along the Rhine, who complain that the exactions of the Prussians are treble those of the French. To the latter they look as their friends, having broken up the old baronial tenures, dissolved religious houses, and sold their lands, making the occupants generally proprietors. The King of Prussia has long promised the people a " Constitution," but as yet has not found it convenient to give one. The approaching marriage of the prince with his cousin of the Netherlands bids fair to liberalize their policy. But even Holland has its own troubles in its rebellious Belgium, which looks to union with France, on the score both of safety and trade, and above all, as freeing them from their most hated tax, to pay Dutch debts and maintain Dutch dikes. But notwithstanding this grumbling, Belgium has grown rich under Dutch rule. I have been everywhere struck with the good sense and liberality displayed by the king in the employment of his great wealth. In silent partnership with a great English manufacturer and machinist, he has spread his factories over half the kingdom, and is daily bringing the coal and iron

and stone of Belgium into the same great operative
agency they perform in England. Now of this ubiq-
uitous Messrs. Cockrell & Co., the king supplies the
capital, and is the humble ",Co."

Rose early to enjoy a fine morning in the great
square of Coblentz, with military music and parade.
The Prussian drill is certainly the perfection of me-
chanical movement; whether equally favorable to the
higher elements of the soldier may be questioned, but
not that Prussia lives on the reputation of it, and
seeks to rise again into a first-rate military power.
Its policy is essentially preparation for war. From
the age of twenty to twenty-three every man is
necessarily a soldier, though if engaged in a profession he may get off with one year's actual service,
but for this last there can be neither substitute nor
excuse. Its military system, too, is so effective that
within ten days the whole military population of the
kingdom can be equipped, armed, and brought into
the field. .   .   .   .

Friday, August 27. — HEIDELBERG. — Arriving
here about noon, I proceeded immediately to deliver
my letter of introduction to Professor Schlosser of
the university, and one of its most eminent teachers.
Not finding him at home, I groped my way in German to the university, and in it to the great hall,
where a dignitary from his lofty cathedra was trying
the competency of a " Professeur Supplémentaire,"
in the department of History. When over, I found
the examiner to be Professor Schlosser himself, and
with him, polite and friendly, have passed the greater
part of the day.

The professors hold themselves high in this university, on the score of liberal principles, looking with contempt on Austria and all its schools. On my asking about Frederick Schlegel, — "Ah," said he, "il est mort," — he is gone to Austria. To his brother William, at Bonn, he has furnished me with a letter through Niebuhr the historian. While fresh in my memory, I will add a few notes of what I saw in the university. In no lecture-room were there more than twenty-five students, seated at forms, shabbily arranged and scribbled over with names and pictures, chiefly of college duels, etc. When the professor enters, the students, being all seated, neither rise nor show any mark of respect. He lectures standing, beginning immediately with a good deal of action, each student with pen, ink, and paper before him. The professor opens by laying down very slowly and distinctly, reading from his notes, the general propositions of his lecture, and then proceeds, in order, to unfold and prove them. The outline each student takes down *verbatim*, to the rest he listens and takes notes. In no room did I see idleness or irregularity, but constant attention and perfect silence, and this not the result of discipline, of which there is none, — no roll-call, no examination, and even for a degree but one, and that not academic but by government officials. The degree is a legal requisite in every profession, and for that end valued; but still out of the eight hundred Heidelberg students not one tenth take it, the rest receiving merely a certificate from such individual

professors as the student selects. The number of
professors is about thirty-five, and, including supple-
mental, about sixty. Salaries in value from fifty to
two thousand dollars. I still prefer the English system, and have seen nothing yet to rival Oxford.

Saturday Night, August 28. — Baden-Baden. —
. . . . The roads are all excellent, macadamized,
made or making, with heaps of the ready-made material at the sides. Around these the bright-flowering
toad-flax finds shelter, driven from the fields on to
the roads, having been our constant companion
through England, Wales, Scotland, and thus far on
the Continent. The name of " Macadam " bids fair
to rival that of Napoleon here. The usual answer
to our inquiry as to roads, is, " Bonnes, toutes Macadam." The State of Baden, in which we are, is
both the largest and best governed of the small
principalities, and prospering beyond the largest.
The villages, which in Prussia are cramped and
filthy, are here neat, open, and picturesque. The
peasantry are not only comfortable but rich, the land
divided and worked by the owners. The reigning
family is Protestant, but the peasantry generally of
the Romish faith. This being the king's birthday,
he holds court at Baden and crowns the day with a
grand ball, and we have stayed to see it.

I pass over the enormous public rooms and the
unlimited circles of waltzers and musicians, to speak
of that which was altogether new to me, the desper-
ate scenes of gambling. There was something awful
in the aspect of the players and the dread silence

which prevailed, with every eye fixed on the turn of chance, and the various heaps of gold on the table waiting the decision, and above all the rapidity with which the croupier, with his long-handled rake, every few minutes, swept the whole into some unseen pocket. Peasants and princes were freely mixed, and, to my surprise, among them our new courier, in a full suit of black, who, stepping up to the table alongside of Prince Lichenstein, laid down upon it a piece of gold, turning to me and saying, " Master, that is for you." This startled me into my propriety, and directing him to take it up, I turned upon my heel and quitted the rooms.

. . . . Our dinner was more interesting than usual. After a long conversation with my German neighbor, I found I was conversing with an author and brother professor, Dr. Rotteck, Professor of Natural and Political Law in the University of Freiburg. Beyond him at the table sat Tieck, the Walter Scott of Germany. After dinner, being introduced, I had with him much interesting conversation; we hope to meet him again in Switzerland.

Our ride this evening was under the shadow of the Black Forest and the Hartz Mountains, where we beheld, with proper awe, frowning from one of its summits, the fastness of the last of its robber heroes. In the cultivated fields we here met for the first time an old American friend, the pumpkin, showing his yellow face amid the corn.

Monday, August 30. — After an early breakfast at Kehl we engaged a carriage for Strasbourg, crossing the Rhine into France for the day. To avoid custom-house delays we left our carriage and baggage, and armed ourselves only with passports and courier. The latter seems at home wherever he goes, and to-day quite surprised us by appearing in a new *rôle*. As we approached the frontier, taking from his pocket two Revolutionary cockades, and fixing one in his cap, he handed the other to me, saying, " Master, please attach this to your dress." On my refusal, he said, " You will not be safe without it." To my reply, " You are my courier, wear it; that is sufficient," he answered again, " But I have to ask you to excuse me for the day, and take a *valet de place*, as I find that the commandant at Strasbourg was my colonel at Waterloo, and it is my duty to call on him." We now crossed the Rhine on its famous bridge of boats, entering for the first time the territory of revolutionary France. As forewarned, all was bristling with war. To the numerous challenges of sentinels, our courier proved the sufficient passport, but all were under arms, and the tricolor flag floated everywhere, and the tricolor cockade was in every cap ; from the peasant at his work in the fields, to the dirty gamin in the streets, all wore the national badge, and scarce a window was without its little flag. I still, however, trusted to " Je suis Américain," and, on reaching our inn, left free our courier in exchange for a valet. . . . . The university or college was visited, with its solitary Protestant theology, where Professor Hepp, on whom I called, received me with the greatest kindness, and furnished me with all the information

I desired. Our courier reported himself at last, and
we proceeded on our return. On questioning him as
to a splendid pendant he was wearing, he replied,
that on visiting his colonel he had directed him at
once to resume the Cross of the Legion of Honor,
which Napoleon had himself given him, and which,
up to this time, he had worn secretly. . . . . .

Thursday, September 2. — Zurich.—. . . . .
After dinner, the brothers Pestalozzi, so famous for
their schools, called on us and accompanied us to the
chief points of interest in and about the city. How I
envy such old cities their contiguity to the retirement
and beauty of the country, unknown to our ever-build-
ing, never-finished towns. The Pestalozzi say that,
amid all their in-door labors, they find time for daily
country walks. On inquiry into the present state
of Switzerland, I find here, as elsewhere, Napoleon's
rule was felt as a blessing, and the loss of it lamented.
Their great national evil was, and is, want of power
in their confederation. The pacification of Napoleon
corrected this for a time, and now all sensible Swiss
feel the want, and vainly seek a remedy. To help
them to it, I have pressed in conversation our revolutionary experience — the futility of our old " Confederation " and the blessings of our present " Union."
. . . .

Sunday Night, September 4. — Top of the Righi.
— Wakened this morning at the hospice amid the
howlings of the Alpine storm. We looked out, but
we were in the clouds; earth there was none, and the
loaded *chalet* was like a boat rocking in the storm.

About eleven o'clock it cleared somewhat, and as the view opened it was something beyond the power of words to paint. There seemed a bright world spread out before us, alternately closed and seen, as the cloud in which we were enveloped, like a great curtain raised or slit, gave us glimpses sharp and clear of the scene below us. The view from the edge of the cliff is not only splendid but unique. Righi, as being a spur of the Alps, jutting out into level Switzerland in the circle of its many lakes, unites in one view all its beauties. Mountains, lakes, towns, and cultivated fields, all are under your eye. On the north you look over its richest portion, even to the Hartz Mountains and the Black Forest of Germany. On the south you gaze on the ramparts of eternal snow and the glaciers of the higher Alps, which even at this distance glow so brightly that it seems as if you could touch them with your outstretched hand, while all around you lie lakes and villages innumerable, now brilliant with the setting sun, and its magnificent purple tints. . . . .

BERNE, *Saturday, September* 11. —This has been a day of real travel. We left Interlaken at six in the morning, having engaged a boat the evening before for our especial party. Just as our boat pushed off I noticed our boatman turn away two soldiers whom I had seen hurrying down in hope of a passage ; I called after them and took them in. They proved to be two Swiss of the regiment that had suffered most in the late " three days " at Paris, and were now returning to their homes at Meyringen for the first time after an absence, one of fourteen, the other of eighteen years. Their regiment had been literally cut to pieces, mainly through the fury of the populace excited by the cruel pertinacity of their commander, Count de Salis. A summons of surrender being sent to him, he ordered the messenger to be thrown from the third story window. The massacre of fifteen hundred was the revenge. I was glad to help these poor survivors to their home. The Swiss are a home-loving people. Of this the crew of our barge is a sample. The old father and mother row one oar; the eldest son another; the daughter, aided by her little brother, a third; while the youngest, a sickly girl, reposes on a bench by their side. The gay head-dresses accord strangely with the hard work, the old mother's face being almost covered by the deep lace hanging down from her black velvet cap — and such figures we see repeatedly behind wheelbarrows and wash-tubs. . . . .

To while away the time of a rather long voyage, I entered into talk with our courier, Felix, about his great patron, Metternich, on whose recommendation I had taken him. The origin of the name was a title of honor. The family name was Metter. His grandfather was in the last unfortunate battle with the Turks, when the emperor, being told that all fled, replied, 'Metter nich,' — a Metter never fled, — hence the name. The Prince Metternich, he says, is of small stature, quick of temper, yet mild. He has suffered much from domestic misfortune. Wife and children all gone, he is left alone, and busies himself,

not in solitude, but in the turmoils of a busy official
life. Thus has he placed himself at the head of the
diplomats of Europe, and become almost an arbiter in
the affairs of the Continent. . . . .

Monday, September 13. — Giez. — At last at the
ancient mansion of the DeRham family, where we
have been received with a warmth of kindness beyond all claim. Perfect home in all but our native
tongue, though kind hearts at once made our bad
French good. The house itself is extensive and
irregular, of various dates and styles, but uniting
together the comforts and conveniences of all. The
grounds are beautiful by nature, and improved in
English taste and in the neatest order, while the view
around is a perfect panorama of Alps from the Righi
to Mont Blanc. . . . . Mr. and Mrs. Huber,
their highly interesting neighbors, joined us at dinner.
Talking of Pestalozzi, we found he was of this immediate neighborhood, and more than one of this family
his early pupils. Like most warm-hearted enthusiasts
in education, the novelty of his system once passed,
its influence was gone, and an old age of chagrin and
disappointment awaited one of the most benevolent
of men. His school began in the voluntary and
unpaid charge of the orphans made by the French
invasion of the Canton of Unterwalden. It continued in the same spirit and in such success in its edu-
cational system of teaching " things " rather than
" words," that his fame extended throughout Europe,
drawing scholars from every quarter. In early age
his system was very effective, but failed when lan-

guages were to be taught, and sciences founded upon languages and symbolic signs; so that from his school came forth many good citizens but no superior men. Its reputation is, however, renewed by Fellenburg, whom we visited at Berne, a more practical, but less attractive man, though marked by ready talent and great ingenuity of means. The cost of the unpaid school, a large one, is more than met by the labor of the scholars, while the pay school is sustained by its foreign reputation, chiefly from England and Prussia. Its chief influence is on character, encouraging independence up near to the limit of insubordination. Vocal music is much looked to for its moral and moderating power. But enough of education.

Having noticed in our drives many mountain streams bridgeless and impassable, because of the narrow span to which they are confined in their wooden bridges, limited by the length of a single timber, I suggested the recent patent of " triangulation " of timbers as giving stiffness and almost unlimited length to a bridge made of ordinary plank. Mr. DeRham appeared greatly struck with the importance of its application here, and, at his request, I prepared a card model exhibiting it.

Thursday, September 16. — LAUSANNE. — Before parting with our kind friends we drove together to the Hubers', as we had promised, and found them both busy in preparing some little memorials for us. I had much talk with Mr. Huber touching his favorite insects, the ants, and his father's rival, the bees. The elder Huber lost his sight while still engaged in his observations, and completed them through the eyes of a faithful attendant, and with his wife as an amanuensis. Mr. Huber is a man of great simplicity, both of manners and character, but withal a thorough enthusiast. On asking him rather in badinage, which of the two, bees or ants, he regarded the wisest, his answer I felt as a reproof to my levity. " Equally wise," said he, " in the higher sense of instincts, equally fitted to their respective conditions, but I find the condition of the ants most analogous to that of man. In the instinct of the bee," he said, " there was a certain *finesse* of government and intercourse far beyond that of man, but in that of the ants he found what he would term the perfection of human society. It was the perfection of order and self-government. He could never discern that any order was given, but each one knew his place and duty, and of him-self fulfilled it.   It was, in short, the model of a per-fect republic."   Here we took a final leave of our kind friends and Swiss home, and were again on the wide world.

Stopping at a village to rest our horses, I wandered into a blacksmith's shop where two men were en-gaged in setting a horse's shoe. I ventured to in-struct them in our simpler method of a single operator. They first doubted, then admired, and finally ended with preferring their own fashion. Arrived about three o'clock in the afternoon at Lausanne and its beautiful lake.   Having some letters I sent them off by our courier, with cards.   At dinner, met a con-versible Englishman, *rara avis*, one neither too proud nor too suspicious to converse with strangers. After dinner, took a stroll to the public promenade, overlooking the lake, and on returning to our hotel met a gentleman just retiring from the door with a card in his hand. A glance showed me that it was my own, and the bearer of it, on my addressing him, proved to be M. Kock, son of our banker at Frankfort. He greeted us with great warmth, saying they had been on the lookout for us for the month past. He immediately became our guide and host for the remainder of the day, reminding me of the words of Huber on parting, that, for pleasant and instructive travel, one must pass "not from *auberge* to *auberge*, but from man to man." Among the pleasant incidents of our walk with our conductor, was a visit to the Archery Club, a beautiful terrace overlooking the lake, with appropriate buildings. On asking M. Kock, one of the wealthiest and busiest bankers of the city, whether he ever practiced with the bow, in answer, he drew from his waistcoat pocket a small key, and opening one of the numerous little cabinets, exhibited all his outfit as an archer, saying at the same time, "This is my daily exercise and amusement, and equally so with my friends." How I envied for *my* countrymen and friends in business such wise recreation from the slavery of "Rem facias rem," the unending toil for wealth, ruinous alike to heart and head, to the enjoyment of home and the true happiness of life. As I remember Captain Basil Hall saying to me of New York, "I see many here who know how to make wealth, but few who know how to enjoy it."

Sunday, September 19. — Hospice. — Summit of
the Great St. Bernard, 7,668 feet above the level of
the sea, truly a day of rest and religious thankfulness, after the toils of yesterday. After an early
cup of coffee, mules and guides, a trusty one for each,
having been over night provided for by our faithful
Felix, at six o'clock we set forth cheered by a bright
sun peeping over the mountains and the *vivas*
of the crowd of gazers. The " Hospice " was not
as yet within our thoughts ; we were considered too
late in the season for that ; our only doubt being
between the Col de Balme and the Tête-Noir,
the mountain passes, leading to the Vale of Cha-
mouni, at the foot of Mont Blanc. But as we proceeded our courage rose under the influence of strong
desire and the fair day, and when choice had to be
made, I called a council of our guides and asked their
judgment. On the first point they were unanimous,
" No storm to-day ; " as to the second, " It was not
their part to say." So on we went, with good courage and cheerful hearts, though saddened by the
frequent mementoes of desolation from the great
mountain torrent of twelve years ago, arising from
the breaking away of a mountain lake through its
icy barriers. Of the village of Martigny, three
fourths were swept away. The stone house in which
we slept last night bore the inscription and mark of
fifteen feet submerged, and our present path carried
us over the ruins of three or four villages it had
totally destroyed. The story is even now on every
tongue, and our guides tell of it as a thing of yester-

day. It occurred about four o'clock in the afternoon on the 18th of June, 1818. The danger being foreseen and inevitable, every precaution was taken for its early notice. For a long time watchmen were stationed on the intervening heights and beacon fires prepared to give the alarm, but all proved fruitless. Within forty-five minutes it swept the valley for thirty-seven miles, carrying everything before it. In one village but one person escaped, a young woman, still living, who was carried off by the flood and thrown ashore some distance below. While sympathizing with this distant peril, a nearer one came before us, in the narrative of two young Englishmen, perishing on Monday last, on the mountain before us, caught in one of the terrific snow-storms of the Alps. But our own case now pressed upon us. Our fair morning was gone, changed first to heavy clouds, then to settled rain. The half-way village was passed, a perilous bridge, and the Rock Gallery, with a thousand feet of rock above us, when the rain came down in torrents, and the thunder rebellowed through the mountains with vivid flashes of lightning. Meeting a traveller descending, our guides questioned him with eagerness, whether it was snow above. The answer, " Rain," was cheering, though our path was growing more and more Alpine. On reaching a group of rude huts, our guides counseled prudence, and advised us to stop. It was our last choice, but on examination, their filth conquered fear, and our word was " Go on." This they obeyed unwillingly, though prompted by larger pay. The only other work of

man we encountered in our mountain path was the
" Dead House," a low cavernous erection in the snow
filled with the frozen corpses of lost travellers ; but
by the mercies of God we escaped that fate, and at
length reached the long desired sight of the Hospice,
calling into our eyes tears of joy and thankfulness.
A bright gleam of the setting sun cheered our entrance into the dark but blessed shelter.   Not often
has even this Hospice received more willing guests.
We had been nine hours on our mules without rest-
ing, and never before had any of us travelled in such
severity of weather.   But its ever open doors had
now received us, a fire in the room appropriated to
strangers soon made us comfortable, and the kindness
and agreeable conversation of the two " fathers "
who received us, made us quickly forget our perils
and exertions.   The two fathers were our enter-
tainers, the Prieur, Claushal, head of the house, and
the Sous-prieur, Prevot, a younger man of most pre-
possessing manners and conversation.   From him we
received double attention, from the accidental discovery, through a beautiful sketch of Sir Robert
Inglis' seat at Clapham, that our chief English
friends were his correspondents, and had recently
sent him that picture, done by Sir Robert's niece after
their late visit to the Hospice.   Both these fathers
I find to be educated scholars, and, in the best sense,
men of the world, from their living familiarly with
educated and liberal men of every nation during
their frequent visits here.

Sunday. — After yesterday's fatigue, and a comfortable night's rest, we rose early to behold the tempest of snow we had so narrowly and providentially escaped. The dogs and men have been out on search bringing in travellers, but mainly peasants from the Italian side. Their kind friends, the dogs, were all around us, large, sagacious, for centuries a peculiar breed, — a cross, it is said, between the great Danish dog and the native dog of the Alps, trained to gentleness, but on needful occasion capable of great fierceness, as was instanced some years since in saving the Hospice from a band of robbers, who, admitted as suffering travellers, at dead of night, and demanding admission to the treasure room, were admitted to the dog-kennel instead, and in an instant every robber had a dog at his throat, and his life at the mercy of an unarmed monk. But I turn to the Hospice itself, and the life to which it calls its votaries. In the first place it is the highest spot inhabited by man on the Continent of Europe, perhaps of the Old World, where all vegetation has ceased, winter three fourths of the year, the thermometer often at zero in the summer, and in winter often at twenty-five below it. The number of the professed is unlimited, but in fact seldom exceeds thirty, of whom from ten to twelve occupy this station, the remainder at their lower homes, or engaged in travel, and gathering alms for the Hospice, an ever open inn, without charge beyond the voluntary contribution of visitors. On Sunday last four new " applicants " presented themselves. Their course is one year's " novitiate " free, and then the threefold vow of poverty, obedience, and celibacy, taken irrevocably. Ten years' residence at the Hospice is then expected, — as long as most can stand, though two of the present number have exceeded twenty. The older and better educated have among their benevolent labors the training and instruction of the younger.

At half past four o'clock this morning we were awakened by the matin bell, and hastily dressing and groping our way through the long dark corridors at a freezing temperature, we reached the chapel door, guided by chanting voices and the glimmer of the light within. On opening the door we found ourselves alone in the gallery of a small but beautiful chapel richly adorned and brilliantly lighted. The music of the organ and choir, the splendid dresses of the celebrant, all contributed to form a scene as of magic in those frozen solitudes, and deeply affecting to our better feelings. Not neglecting our own devotions, we again attended high mass at ten o'clock and vespers at five. The intermediate time was spent chiefly in their museum, where I lighted on a specimen from the neighborhood, evidently of anthracite coal. This led to some instruction as to the means of using it as fuel, which delighted them, as their only resource is a scanty supply of little sticks brought up the mountain on the back of mules, a distance of nine leagues. A few minutes sufficed to draft a flue capable, I trust, of igniting and using it. In the course of the day, the storm having ceased, I visited the neighboring " Morgue," a low stone erection, buried in snow, where the frozen dead are deposited. Its only door is opened but for their reception, while its only window, low and grated, affords the ghastly view of frozen humanity, ranged around the walls in all the varying attitudes in which death had seized them, some deeply affecting. Among them was a mother with a child still clasped to her breast. The bodies of all uncorrupt through extreme cold, but gradually passing into the state of mummies. From this sight I gladly turned to the historical mementoes by which I was surrounded. This "pass" over the Alps was known to the Romans in their far-reaching arms, and was probably the one by which Hannibal crossed. The remains of a temple of Jupiter are still traceable, and coins and votive offerings are found among them. Among these was one for a safe return from the perils of the summit, which brought to mind the thank-offering we hope to make on the morrow for our safe descent from the same.

Monday Evening, September 20. — MARTIGNY. — Safely down from the mountain. Awakened this morning at the Hospice before day by the early matin bell, and soon after still more thoroughly by the pealing organ, which in these frozen solitudes sounds like enchantment. We rose and attended for the last time services in which the Roman ritual appears in its most attractive form. A bright sun soon illumined the peaks of ice around, and tempted me again to the little lake lying at the foot of the Hospice where a stone column marks the boundary line of Italy, carrying off from it a fragment of a

Roman brick in memory of my invasion. It is with feelings of regret too strong for expression that I here turn my back upon Italy. But time limited and duty, forbid.

After a mountain breakfast and warm adieu to all, accompanied by one of our kind hosts, M. Barras, who insisted on seeing us safe down, we set out on our descent, which, from its perilous nature had to be made on foot, our mules led by the guides. After descending about two leagues destitute of vegetable life, we entered on the region of Arctic growth,— larch, fir, and other evergreens; thence descending to the fruit-bearing trees, we found first the cherry, then the apple. It is pleasing to notice how naturally the mind seems turned to piety in these perilous regions. Scarce a habitation for man appeared without some words of pious thought carved in stone over the door, an ever present memento, as, " La Volonté de Dieu soit faite;" "Dieu soit benin;" and on an overarching rock among the crags, a place of shelter from sudden tempest, I noticed, " L'Eternel est mon Rocher." As we proceeded, our companion from the Hospice was warmly greeted by every peasant we met, and had in return for each some word of kindness. It was a whole year since he had been down or seen aught but ice and barren rock, and as we approached the green fields he observed that the feelings awakened by the sight are such as none but a monk of the Hospice can conceive. At the hamlet of Lydde, having seen us through our dangers, and partaken of our dinner, we parted; he returning to his mountain home, we to our renewed journey, to meet perhaps with older but not warmer friends. . . . .

Such are some of the perils that hedge round the ascent of the Great St. Bernard, but they are not always from the raging elements. Napoleon, in his celebrated ascent in 1800 with all his troops, twice incurred greater risk of life than in all his subsequent battles. Once, from his obstinacy in persisting to ride his war-horse where none but mules could step with safety, being precipitated from a cliff where the horse was killed and the rider only saved by the strong arm of a guide. The second imminent risk was from the enemy. On approaching the summit of the pass, accompanied by two officers, he preceded the march of his advanced guard so far that on a sudden turn among the cliffs he found himself in the face of a small picket-guard of Austrians. They receiving no satisfactory answer to their challenge, leveled their muskets awaiting the word "Fire." Their officer, however, not dreaming of the probability of a French force ascending a path where a mule could scarce find footing, checked them, and advancing claimed them as his prisoners. Napoleon, unmarked by dress, and unknown, without a direct answer, began in his rapid way some unimportant questions, engaging the officer's attention until by a glance of his eye perceiving the approach of his own troops he turned quickly to the young Austrian and said, " Sir, five minutes ago I was your prisoner, now you are mine ; this is the First Division of the

Grand Army of France, and I am its commander."
This was told me on the spot where it was said to
have taken place. . . . .

Geneva, *Monday, September* 27. — This day has
been one of the highest interest through the letters
of Mr. Gallatin, of New York, to his family here, his
cousin being the present Syndic of this little republic. My early hours were given up to literary guidance, Dr. Candolles introducing me into the literary
circle or club of Geneva, which is at present the
school of philosophic thinkers for Europe. Sismondi,
unfortunately, was absent. Their present subject of
zealous benevolence is the penitentiary system, trying
it themselves and recommending it to others. Du-
mont, the banker, bears the expense. I was called
upon to unfold our system. Their present problem
is its introduction into France, in whose revolutionary
affairs they take great interest. The Syndic has
summoned for this very day their great Council, —
two hundred and sixty deputies, representing sixty
thousand inhabitants, — to deliberate on the present
relations with France, and the expediency of recog-
nizing Louis Philippe as its sovereign. To this
solemn meeting I was invited by Syndic Gallatin.
We ascended to the third story of the great square
tower, from whose windows the whole national
domain is visible, and that by a stairway as peculiar
as the surroundings, being a paved road winding
around an inner tower for the convenience of horse-
back which was the official mode of ascent. I was
admitted into the Council, though against rule, the

committee on the recognition not having yet made their report. On their entering I retired, and in a few minutes all was settled, the House concurred, Louis Philippe was acknowledged, and the word passed out " No war with France."

Among the aristocratic peculiarities of Geneva I mention one. It is the existence in all the old families, running back many hundred years, of a common treasury or fund, bearing the family name, growing with the contributions of many generations, to preserve the name from the disgrace of penury, a family council in annual meeting hearing and answering claims. Among those family treasuries, that of the Gallatins, dating back some three hundred years, is among the largest. In an ancestral republic like that of Geneva and in a home-loving people like the Swiss, it has proved to be a wise, patriotic, and benevolent institution.

Breaking away with difficulty from such scenes and such intercourse I returned to our hotel, finding there several friends, among others the Count de Sellon, with some dispatches to be intrusted to my care for Lafayette in Paris and Mr. Gallatin at home. After dinner, arranging our carriage for three horses to drive abreast, French fashion, we set off. The road along the lake shore was beautiful almost beyond imagination; .around us was an all-placid loveliness; on our right Mont Blanc in the distance, with its surrounding glaciers brilliant with the setting sun, and on our left the dark mountains of Jura.

Upon the ascent of these we shortly after entered, night closing upon us in savage solitude, but with a brilliant moon to light us. About midnight, we reached our welcome inn, standing alone on the very summit of the Jura.

CHAPTER XIV.

FRIDAY night, October 1, finds us in Paris, at the "Hôtel Britannique," in a suite of rooms that would elsewhere be esteemed splendid. Last night we passed in our carriage, posting at a rapid rate all night. We have had four days' and two nights' hard driving from Geneva, the most dull, uninteresting country I ever passed through. One little incident varied its monotony and for a time awakened alarm. As we approached the outer environs of Paris, through a desolate tract covered with a wild growth of underwood, we encountered groups of ill-looking fellows prowling around, looking, as they said, for work: driven out of Paris, was their story, for firing on the people in the late revolution. While congratulating ourselves at having passed safely through these, we found ourselves suddenly surrounded by a body of men, armed to the teeth, to the number of at least a hundred, springing forth from the wild copsewood through which we were passing and where they had lain hidden, surrounding our carriage and seizing our postilions, for with our heavy carriage we were posting with four horses, and demanding our passports. On these being shown to the commander of the party, he explained that they were awaiting in concealment the arrival of the first load of the Algerine treasure that day expected to arrive, and to guard it through this dangerous pass and beyond the Faubourg St. Antoine. The groups we had previously met, he informed us, were dangerous men on their way to their place of exile, the Island of Corsica. . . . .

Attended this morning the levee of the Hon. Mrs. Rives, wife of our minister. Among others we there met our old friend Cooper, the novelist, travelling in search of a revolution, though unfortunate in point of time, complaining to me that Dresden broke out the day after he left it, and Paris finished the day before he reached it. I comforted him with my fears that the volcano, though quiet, was still boiling within. Another visit of more than ordinary interest was to the Duc de Broglie, in his family as well as official hotel. Its arrangements partook of both, sofas and work tables at one fire-place of the grand *salon*, business, papers, etc., at the other, and before leaving I found that the duchess was equally at home at both. On entering she rose and received me with great kindness, for my letter was from an intimate friend in England. The duke soon joined us, his manners wanting the prestige of the old *noblesse*, an air of doubt, like one supported on bladders. After many inquiries about his friends in England, an official message being brought to him to attend council, he rose and, apologizing, was about parting, when in answer to my casual wish expressed to visit the Chamber of Deputies in session, I found by his answer that it was a privilege rarely granted in those unsettled times. On consulting his wife, he answered that I certainly should be admitted, but he could not at once name the day. Subsequently, at the termination of a most agreeable visit, the duchess added that she would send me an order for admission the day after to-morrow. On mentioning this act of courtesy to our minister, Mr. Rives, he observed that it was a privilege hard to obtain. The approaching trial of Polignac and the other ministers of the late king, is looked forward to with apprehension. Speaking of Charles X., he said he was in manner the perfect gentleman, and a good man and honest, seeking only what he believed to be for the good of his people. I asked if he could say as much for Polignac; he replied that, though blinded he was sincere, devotedly attached to his master, whom he termed "the best of men," honestly believing that increase of the royal power was essential to the peace of France and hence of Europe.

Dined at home and then to our evening engagement at the Marquis de Lafayette's, " le premier Homme de France." He looks younger than when in America, and now, at the age of seventy-three, passes through all the labors of an arduous office without seeming to feel it, and with manners alike courteous and kind; towards Americans markedly so. As an instance, in the midst of the revolution, he broke off from absorbing engagements for an hour to attend the marriage of Miss S—— to young

Irving, having given her his promise to be there, and
to us he proffers all that kindness and influence can
bestow.   Among the notabilities present, General
Gourgaud was to me particularly interesting in relation to recent events and the course taken by La Fay-
ette, towards whom there seems one united feeling
of admiration for both his firmness and moderation.
" France a republic and himself at the head " rested
on his word, but he chose prudently as well as
honorably, and, as it was said to me last night, " like
the sun, shows grandest in going down."   Returning
to our hotel, we found cards with a note from the
Duchess de Broglie, inclosing an order for the House
of Deputies.

Thursday, October 7. — The Assembly holds its
meetings in the large but not splendid building opposite the bridge of Louis XVI.   On presenting my
ticket I was admitted into what seemed a box in a
theatre, a resemblance running throughout the whole
house.   After an hour's delay the president took his
seat on his central elevated tribune, the members
gradually assuming their respective seats.   The first
question under debate was one of finance.   That
disposed of, the more interesting resolution of M.
Tracy, abolishing the punishment of death, came up,
doubly exciting under its immediate bearing on the
unfortunate ministers of Charles X.   It was introduced in a very ably written speech by M. Béran-
ger, to which all listened with the silent attention
given to a popular lecturer.   When a member is
speaking there is perfect silence, but after he is fin-.

ished great disorder prevails and it requires often five or ten minutes of the president's bell to restore order. The bell, by the way, is a very poor instrument for enforcing silence, and evidently annoys the president more than the members. Again, the necessity of a member quitting his seat and hurrying to the tribune is exceedingly awkward, and to an English or American speaker would be a great "damper." Not so with the Frenchman; he rushes to it as if bursting with enthusiasm, but on reaching it, his words are calm and collected, and, so far as I have observed, less passionate and more to the point than I have ever heard in a popular assembly, seldom more than from five to fifteen minutes in length. Nor is this because of being written, the good sense was evidently extempore, the truisms and rhetoric penned down. The day has been to me an exciting one, and I have listened for five hours without weariness to the revolutionary orators of the " three days " in Paris.

Monday, October 11. — After a morning spent in business arrangements, three o'clock found me at the palace of the Institute, by invitation, to attend a special meeting of the French Academy, to receive Humboldt on his return from the Himalayas. But unfortunately, it seemed, I was too late for admission, as appeared from a formal printed notice upon the closed doors of the splendid library in which their sessions are held. But while bemoaning my misfortune and despairing of relief, I was attracted to a second framed notice wherein I found my own name excepted from the rule under order of the president as having letters of introduction to him. I was accordingly formally ushered in through a crowd of external listeners to a chair within the inner circle of members, and near the table of the president. The paper under reading was the report upon a scientific question of a previous meeting. On the president's elevated tribune sat also three vice-presidents, among them Baron Cuvier. The next paper was a highly scientific one, " On the Motion of Bodies in Elastic Fluids." This was referred to a member for a special oral report. The next awakened more interest. A member approached the table with a manuscript of ominous bulk, which he began but did not finish without interruption. This arose through the controversy it excited with Baron Cuvier, whose teaching and facts were alike denied and rejected on the same subject, — the crocodile and its anatomy, — in a manner so offensive as to call for immediate rebuke. When finished, Cuvier, speaking from his seat, complained in strong yet gentlemanly terms of both the mode and measure of the attack. Rousing himself from his almost lethargic look with his head sinking between his shoulders, he spoke both courteously and forcibly. This brought from St. Hilaire a passionate rejoinder, when Cuvier terminated the discussion by a solemn pledge to the Academy of full proof at its next meeting.

Humboldt now came forward, presenting to the Academy, in the name of their respective authors, papers and books of foreign associates, and then opened upon the great interest of the evening, a rapid *resumé* of his researches and travels in the Himalaya range, just completed under the patronage of the Emperor of Russia. Humboldt's look is that of a true scientific traveller, somewhat weatherbeaten, middle size, firm knit, hair gray, passing on to white, with a kindly expression, equal to a letter of introduction wherever he goes. He spoke with great modesty, assigning the chief merit of the results of his journey to his philosophic companions, Ehrenborg of Germany, and M. Rodé.

The reading of two more papers closed the *séance*, marked, I thought, both by more exact science than what I had heard in the Royal Society in London, and infinitely greater interest on the part both of members and of the public. After the *séance* the president introduced me generally to members, but especially to Barons Cuvier and Humboldt, with both of whom, more especially the latter, whose English was somewhat better than my French, I had much interesting talk. . . . .

After dinner, about eight o'clock, my wife and myself found ourselves *en route* for the Duchess de Broglie, to whom we had promised a visit *en famille,* and found her truly so, as domestic in her occupation and pleasures as if she were neither a duchess nor a prime minister's lady, surrounded by her children, all young, engaged in their usual studies or amusements. We found her alike lovely and interesting. As a daughter of Madame de Staël, literature and intercourse with literary men has been her natural inheritance, but softened and sanctified, as her mother was not, by a Christian faith and a Christian spirit, giving to her whole character a life, a purity, and gentleness particularly attractive, and such as in French society of the present age is seldom found. Such is the impress of religion on her life that she is often sneered at as a "Méthodiste." Among the subjects that brought forth her feelings was my incidental mention of Erskine of Edinburgh, who I found was her frequent correspondent. Of him she spoke, as I myself feel, with equal admiration for his talents and piety, and pity and apprehension for his deepening trials. Our earnest talk was broken in upon· by a political visit of the Count de Bastard, a relative of the Prince de Polignac, whose case and probable fate awakens deep sympathy. The earnest persuasive influence of a Christian lady in high station was here appealed to, and not, it seemed, in vain.

Tuesday, 12*th.* — Busy until one. Then drove to the " Café de la Régence," where, in New York Maelzel had told me I should meet all the great chess-players of Paris. On entering, I found silence, and chess-tables filled. An old Jew with a clear eye but trembling hand, was pointed out as one of the celebrities. I sat and watched his game rapidly played, won, and repeated. Opening always the same, losing his K.'s B.'s pawn, moving out his K.'s bishop and knight and immediately castling. After the games I entered into conversation with him, and mentioning

Maelzel as my introducer, inquired who played his
automaton in Paris. As to Maelzel himself he said,
" Il n'a point de force, c'étoit moi, qui jouoit ici son
automaté." I replied, " Alors c'étoit das la Boite."
His mumbling answer I could not hear beyond the
word "ridicule." He declined a game with me, but
offered for another day.

On returning home I found an invitation from M.
Julien, for his great monthly dinner to-day, at which
I should meet the chief *literati* of Paris, and some
strangers of note. Immediately accepting, I went
accordingly, and in the great reception rooms met
my host and his rapidly assembling guests. Among
them several of the Academicians, Girard the president, and my pugnacious friend, M. St. Hilaire, who
seemed somewhat ashamed of his attack on Cuvier.
Passing in to the *salle à manger,* as most of the guests
did before dinner, I found it formally arranged with
a card at every plate for perhaps sixty ; our host
at the centre of the long line, where he pointed out
to me my place, shifting my card so as to place me
next to himself. While standing there waiting
the summons, a free-spoken Englishman approached,
changed the cards back again, with a " Hallo ! who
did this ? " I observed it was done by M. Julien
himself in compliment to an American stranger.
" Beg pardon," said he ; " I yield ; but called on as I
am to speak under some perplexity, it would be very
convenient to me to sit next the Chair." I then
found that he was the celebrated " Silk Buckingham,"
just returned from his exile in the East, and looked to,

as one of the great apostles of " Liberté, Égalité, et Fraternité," magical words, at the present time, throughout France and especially in Paris. His speech, or rather narrative of what he saw in the East, half French, half English, was still very effective. As he passed through its once rich and verdant plains, and saw all now waste and worthless, he asked of himself, What had worked that change? Had the skies withheld their influences, the earth its productive power, etc., etc. No! Nor heaven nor earth, but man, — man has sunk.   He has lost " Liberté." At this word every tongue was loosed. " Liberté! Liberté!" resounded through the hall. Buckingham's plan, for he had one, was to organize an expedition, benevolent in name, for rejuvenating the East, but political in its influences, tending to strengthen French influence in India, and give a blow to the English East India Company, who had sent him out of the country.   With Buckingham I had much interesting talk — an innovator in education as well as government. His son, just grown up, was with him, trained in a school of self-government; the scholars the legislators, judge, and jury, with a written code, and willing submission to it; and this, according to his account, working well, turning out both fair scholars and true gentlemen. Such was our dinner, the most spirited and diversified I ever was at.   Politicians spoke, poets recited, inventors unfolded their improvements, and invitations were given and accepted for new scenes of interest. At ten o'clock the dinner ended, and the " chiefs" of the party adjourned to attend the *levée* of the Marquis de Lafayette, the head of the military power of France, and at present more the sovereign than Louis Philippe himself. It was a splendid reception. Not French military men alone were there, but those from other lands looking to France for example or aid. Among the marked figures was a noble looking young Pole in his national garb, now proscribed in Poland : a splendid dress, betokening rank ; a glittering diamond in massive setting worn on his right thumb, with a sad though dignified air, speaking to none, though observed by all, and unknown to all with whom I conversed ; a spectral image of their heroic past, and intended perhaps to awaken French enthusiasm for its restoration.

Thursday, 14*th*. — As I returned into town I remembered my chess engagement and drove to the Café de la Régence. My friend the Jew was not there, but I soon had pointed out to me Professor Boncone. On inquiring of what he was professor, I was told of chess ; that instruction in it was his business and living, and that he was the first player in Paris. I accordingly took my station by him, and subsequently played with him two games, both of which I lost. He stated that there was one abler than himself, though not now in Paris, — M. Labourdonnais ; that the old Jew was named Alexander, a good player, but beginning to break ; and that he himself had played the Automaton for a long time and never been beaten, though he said an equal player would have beaten him from the distraction caused by the

mechanism.   I observed to him, " You were not in
the box then ? He answered, " Others less bound by
honor may tell you ; I cannot.   In France it is not
much of a secret, but in your country I suppose it is
otherwise."

Saturday Evening. — Received a note from General Lafayette as I was going out, proposing to introduce me at the palace to-morrow evening. Drove
to the Duc de Broglie's, who was at the Council, and
the duchess out. The ministers have an anxious time
of it. The people and the government are opposed
in relation to the fate of Polignac and the ex-minis-
ters, — the government anxious to save them, the
mob of Paris prepared to rise *en masse* and murder
them if ministers take a step for their safety. Nor
the mob only ; one hundred and eighty thousand men
of the National Guards have given notice that they
cannot be depended upon if the late ministry be allowed to escape. In this emergency the Chambers,
afraid to pass the bill for the abolition of the death
punishment, have thrown the responsibility upon the
king; the ministry dare not act, and throw it back
again; so that even Lafayette acknowledges there is
no chance of escape for these unfortunate men ; at
least, for Polignac and Peyronnet, whose heads must
answer for the blood of the people.

Sunday Evening. — Just returned from my visit to
the Palais Royal, where I was received in what we
should call a cordial manner. Lafayette commands
everywhere a homage which seems to know no
bounds. The moment he was recognized as we de-

scended from the carriage, his name was echoed by
the crowd.   As we passed up through the great ves-
tibules, officers and soldiers pressed forward to address
him, and at the *levée* he divided attentions with the
king.   As introduced by him, the king received me
with an air of kindness, and still more, it would seem,
as an American.   The queen said to me that he always looked back with peculiar interest to his visit to
America.   The king speaks English passably well, as
do all his family.   It is, one of them said, a family
accomplishment.   He is very like his portraits; full,
large features, and a kind, good-humored expression.
The queen is tall, rather pretty, with a very amiable
look and manner.   Mademoiselle Orleans, the king's
unmarried sister, is also very pleasing, though without
beauty.   I persuaded her to try her English, which she
said she had forgotten, and told her she must cultivate
it as a bond of friendship between the two countries.
The young princess, whom Lafayette described as both
beautiful and agreeable, was unwell and not present.
The eldest son, the Duke of Orleans, a young man
of twenty-one, is as pleasing and intelligent and modest withal, as one could meet with in any station in
life.   On Lafayette's introduction, he addressed me
in French, which I answered in English, knowing
that he spoke it perfectly well.   His education has
been a plain, good one, and his sentiments are manly
and liberal.   France has much to hope in him.   The
appearance and manner of the whole family have a
domestic, simple character, which, from all I have
heard, truly belongs to them.   After almost an

15

hour's conversation, a small private door was opened, through which they retired ; and after some time, finding the king did not return, which he generally does, the company retired also.   On reaching the outer door, an inferior officer of the guard, whom I had before noticed, again addressed Lafayette with some expression of attachment.   Lafayette turning to me said, " This is the officer who refused to arrest Manuel."   He then called and introduced him, with which he seemed greatly pleased, especially when I told him I was an American, and had heard of it there.

I have just found out that my host of the other evening, M. Julien, is no other than the celebrated Julien, private secretary of Robespierre, and the instigator of half his proscriptions. . . . .

LONDON. — *Saturday Morning.* — The unsettled state of Paris and the short time that remains to us before sailing has been the cause of our sudden move. The state of Paris, before we left, was grave and alarming.   On Sunday night, while we were at the king's *levée*, the Palais Royal was quite in tumult; the next night a mob of six or eight thousand attempted to fire the Palace of the Luxembourg, and were only prevented by the doors being thrown open, and being satisfied that the ministers were not there. . . . .

Wednesday. — Having promised Miss Douglas to drop in in the course of the evening, drove there about eleven, and was introduced to Campbell the poet, who, after some pressing, gave us a recitation of part of " Julius Cæsar." Campbell is a man of inferior interest to the other great poets we have met. He wants their simplicity as well as power. His conversation, in short, is that of an ordinary man.

Thursday. — My first visit, yesterday, was to the Royal Asiatic Society, to which Colonel Fitz-Clarence's name was a sufficient introduction. Here they paid me the compliment of getting me to designate four American libraries or institutions to which they would send their proceedings. Finding I was near Lord Stowell's, I stopped to leave my card, on parting, as a mark of respect and sympathy, for I had observed in the morning paper an expression of public feeling respecting the failing health of " the great and good Lord Stowell." On inquiry, I was told he saw none but his physicians, but on handing my card, the footman requested me to walk in till he should speak to his master. I complied, and was surprised to receive a message requesting me to see him. I found him still seated in his library, but unable to rise from his chair ; he expressed very warmly his thanks for the interest I most sincerely felt, and his respect for our rising country. I sat near half an hour with him, for he seemed anxious to detain me. All he said was marked by kindness and a peculiar humility with regard to himself. As he told me, he is now eighty-five years old.

Stopping at " Ridgway's " to return a book he had sent me, I found there Sir H. Parnell, just from Paris, where we left him collecting facts, and making himself master of their system of financial accounts, which is infinitely better, he tells me, than the English. This book-store is the lounging-room of the reading members of Parliament, and the political pamphlets of the day cover the tables.

Being in the city to-day, I stopped at the India House, to pay a visit to Mill, the economist. I here made the acquaintance of Dr. Husefield, the librarian, and visited the immense establishment. Dr. Husefield is an American who went out to Batavia thirty years ago, became eminent in the natural history of Java, and is now surrounded by his own labors in the museum of the India House, of which he is the chief librarian.

I forgot to mention, yesterday, the old Countess of Cork, whom we met first at the rooms of Sir Robert Inglis, and afterward, in the evening, at those of Miss Douglas. She is, I believe, the last remnant of the Johnsonian circle, Lord Stowell excepted. She is the Miss M. recorded in Boswell's life, to whom Johnson applied the phrase of "Pretty fool." Pretty she might have been, but fool she certainly never was. She has talent even now, and at the age of eighty-five exercises considerable influence. Another incident crosses my mind, which I forgot. On Tuesday last, returning through Downing Street, where I had been calling on Mr. Herries, I met the Duke of Wellington with his groom behind him, galloping along in rather a hurried style. Turning into Lord ——'s, he jumped from his horse, but instead of entering the house, brushed hastily past me as I came up, and opening a small iron gate descended by a back way to another street. The next day the " Times " explained it. On leaving the House of Lords he had been hooted and assailed with missiles, and was in full retreat when I saw him. Several arrests were made in consequence.

Just returned from a little party at Mr. Senior's. They certainly understand the rational enjoyment of life better here than with us. Ladies are not excluded; on the contrary no good society exists without them; the young do not rule; and literature forms more the topic of conversation. . . . .

After a busy morning, went to the House; while there received a message that the chancellor, Lord Lyndhurst, requested to see me at the wool-sack. This was rather awkward, as this official seat is in the centre of the House of Lords, and I was not sorry that business soon interrupted us. So I waited till he retired to his room, where I sat some time with him. He gave me unlimited orders for any papers or reports I desired, and begged me to write to him direct for any I might hereafter want. He proffered me admission within the bar on Tuesday next, when the king opens Parliament, which unfortunately I cannot take advantage of. Talking of the approaching session, which they expect to be a stormy one, he said, " These levelers would be for taking the wig off my very head;" to which I replied, " There were times when a man might count himself well off in losing only his wig." This brought on much pleasant conversation. Lord Lyndhurst is something of a humorist, and when on the wool-

sack looks always as if he was laughing in his
sleeve. . . . .

The "Quarterly Review" has greatly risen under Lockhart, who is very independent. In the
last number, the article on "Babbage" was too liberal for the government. It was shown at the Council to the duke, the day before publication. He
found fault with it and sent for Crocker, who threw
the responsibility on Murray. Murray was sent for
and threw it on Lockhart; but Lockhart, when applied to, refused to alter. The "Edinburgh Review,"
under Napier, has fallen very low.

Saturday Night, October 30, 1830. — I close this
day my account with London. Spent the day in arranging and collecting. On returning home, found
that Mr. Winslow had been there from Lord Lyndhurst, with an order of admission to the House of
Lords at the opening of Parliament by the king, on
Tuesday. It is quite a disappointment to give it up,
but so it must be, and so farewell London, England,
Europe ; and now homeward.

AT SEA, GOOD SHIP "ONTARIO." — *November* 8.—
Two days' sail from the channel. We have changed
the scene. I know nothing that makes such a
sudden one, as that from the world of a great city to
the waste of waters ; it is like another state of existence. Our last day, Sunday, in London, was chiefly
given, as was right, to thankful recollections, and I
trust not unfruitful resolutions. We had too many
kind friends, however, to be altogether alone. I had
promised to breakfast with my new friends, the Vil-

liers, and there met Wilmot Horton, Mr. Hume, of the Foreign Office, Mr. M'Culloch, and Mr. Senior. All unite in the critical state of England, and especially London, where they apprehend some sudden outbreak. Wilmot Horton rises upon me in talent. He read to us a " Jeu d'esprit " of his, on the duke, " What is the Captain about ? " a piece of great humor. Such English society is of a higher tone than I have seen in any other country. The knowledge, talent, and conversational powers realize all I ever imagined of the society of clever men.

Many crowded to bid us farewell at the last moment, and at seven we joined the mail coach, of which we had taken the inside. Rode all night very comfortably, and reached the Quebec Hotel, Portsmouth, a little after eight. The captain joined us after breakfast and arranged our going on board, and about one we set foot again on the deck of our gallant ship, while it seemed like a dream, all our wanderings, from the time we left it.

Friday, November 12. — As we have a little calm weather to-day, I take my pen again. On Wednesday evening just at dark, in the midst of a heavy squall, there was a cry that the elephant, which was our fellow-passenger, was out of her house. The captain, with great presence of mind, ordered the ship before the wind; and the mate, with equal courage, went up to the huge beast, who had wreathed her trunk around the chains, and crying " Back ! back ! " succeeded in getting her to retire quietly to her house.' . . . .

The distinction between the University and Academy of France had often puzzled me ; let me secure while I can my recently acquired knowledge.

The University is head of all instruction. The Academy of Paris and all other academies, colleges, etc., are integral parts of it. But the Institute is an independent body, composed of savans in all departments. It consists of four academies.

1. The French Academy, or the Academy of France, originally devoted to the establishing and improving the French tongue. It consists of forty members, a president by rotation, and a perpetual secretary. Admission to this has been the highest reward to men of genius and sought after by princes.

2. The Academy of Inscriptions. The object of this was to guard the purity of the language. All public inscriptions in whatever language fall under its cognizance.

3. The Academy of Sciences. It was at its meetings that I attended.

4. The Academy of the " Beaux Arts." It is under its sanction that the exhibitions of drawings, statues, etc., are held, having in its gift prizes for students of art, affording a support in Italy. . . . . .

" GULF STREAM, *December* 12.—After lying awake through one of our usual tremendous gales, during a long, dark, and anxious night I was often cheered by the notes of a canary whose cage hung opposite to our cabin door. His cheering song was always loudest in the height of the tempest. This had often struck me before, but to-night I felt it particularly, and it suggested the following lines, which in listening I wrote : —

Teach lovely songster! teach to me
   That matin hymn of praise ;
Which on the dark and stormy sea
   I hear thee nightly raise.

It cheers me on my restless couch,
   It lifts my soul on high,
It sounds above the rushing surge,
   Like music from the sky.

Say not from thoughtless breast it springs,
   Unconscious of alarm ;
'Tis nature's voice which upward wings
   Its trust upon His arm

By whom the seas lift up their voice,
   And tempests sweep the shore ;
At whose command they still their noise,
   And oceans cease to roar.

To Him thy little voice is tuned,
   His power and love its themes :
His power which in the tempest speaks,
   His love which through it beams.

Hark ! yet again, those heartfelt trills !
   It shames my coward fears ;
With pious trust my breast it fills,
   And gives me smiles for tears.

For how shall I, the heir of life,
   Whom Jesus died to save,
Forget that 'mid the waters' strife
   He walks upon the wave.

Fear not, " 'Tis I :" that word hath given
   New calm within my breast ;
It closes earth, it opens heaven,
   It shows how faith is blest.

Then thanks, sweet bird: thou'st taught to me
  Thy morning hymn of praise ;
And on this dark and stormy sea,
  I'll emulate thy lays.

And through the stormy sea of life,
  In sorrow's darkest hour,
I'll think I hear thy matin song,
  And feel its gentle power.

CHAPTER XV.

RETURN TO COLLEGE DUTIES: 1831.

THE long and stormy voyage of the ship *Ontario* was at last brought to a close by her safe arrival in the port of New York during the Christmas week, which closed the year 1830. She had been out fifty-eight days, and this protracted winter passage had caused both great suffering to those on board, and anxiety to expectant friends at home. But all was soon forgotten over the happy reunion at 8 College Green. Renewed health gave a zest to everything, and professional duties were at once resumed with the usual cheerful and determined zeal. In the matter of health, the chief object of this journey, we have the professor's own satisfactory report in a letter to one of his friends in England.

" As you were kind enough to take an interest in my health, I am happy to assure you it is now quite restored. A month's ramble in Switzerland made a new man of me; I know not whether by a physical or moral influence, but there was a kind of renewal of youth in that country I never felt before; it seemed as if there was no care on its mountains, and nothing but peace in its valleys."

Of the effect generally of this European tour,

upon one who had left home a dispirited and some-what disappointed man, the tone and matter of his journal have given sufficient evidence. It was just what then was needed for the future development and self-education of my father's mind and character. Men at forty have often built, with original talent and superior industry, their railroad tracks, but for the rest of life they too often become mere drivers, plodding backward and forward over them. Pro-fessional and business life is especially prone to this, and needs at times to be rudely interrupted to pre-vent this sort of fossilization. Travel is, perhaps, the best mode of counteracting it, especially when, as Huber advised, it is made from mind to mind, and not merely from inn to inn. Such was this European tour to an extent, which, at the present day, under increased facilities of travel, seems almost impossible. And the fact that such tours and journals belong to the past must be my excuse, if any be needed, for giving to this autobiographic record of a few months more pages than will hereafter be given to as many years.

There is, however, another and a deeper view in which we must regard this season of widening ex-perience and health-giving enjoyment. It was a toughening of the human fibre to bear the strain of coming trial and fit the tempered instrument for higher work.

Almost the last news received before leaving Eu-rope had contained the announcement of the death of my father's promising young friend Griffin, who, as we have seen, had undertaken in his absence his chief duties in college. And now a sorrowing father at once called upon him to add a memoir of his deceased son to a volume of " Remains " which he had himself prepared. This " Memoir of Griffin " was afterwards published separately, and, at the request of the General Book Society of the Church, was placed upon its catalogue, the copyright being presented to the Society.

Its concluding words open the theme and display the direction of mind which for the next twenty years was to be widened and deepened by continuous blows of domestic bereavement.

" Thus closed the life of this amiable, pious, and talented young man. The aged cumberer of the earth is left, while the youthful Christian warrior is taken away, just as he is buckling on his armor for the battle. Yet thus it is that reason is ever baffled when it seeks to enter into the deep counsels of God, and it is perhaps for this very reason, to teach man humility and the nothingness of himself, and all things human, that death is permitted so often to snatch his victims out of the very instruments which God seems to have prepared for usefulness on earth. The shock given to the mind by one such breach upon the hopes and order of nature, does more to break down the barriers of worldly confidence, to arouse the young to reflection, and the thoughtless of every age to watchfulness, than a thousand re- movals in the ordinary course of mortality. But it teaches yet better things; even the heathen in his blindness could say, 'Whom the gods love, die young.' And cannot the Christian see in their early removal a new proof of that better paradise of God to which they are translated, and where preparations for virtuous usefulness, fruitless as to this world, find at once their exercise and their reward ? "

Death, with the exception of that of an infant of a few days, had not yet entered the circle of Professor McVickar's family. Nearly twenty-two years of married life had passed. Father and mother, five girls and three boys, and the great aunt, whose diary has and will still aid us in this life picture, made up the mystic and still unbroken circle of home. That it was a bright and cheerful one may be gathered from the fond way in which all clung to the old Hyde Park traditions, and that there was no lack of Job-like thankfulness we may assume from what we know of the older members.

Miss Bard thus concludes her diary for 1830 : —

" I close these pages with the safe arrival of our beloved family on Tuesday evening, after a stormy passage of fifty-eight days. When I reflect on all the mercies that have accompanied them during the past eight months, — in safety, health, pleasure, and improvement, returning to their happy children and family all in health, with numerous friends rejoicing to welcome them home — what gratitude, what praise can be adequate to such great goodness. My heart, alas ! is not large enough for all I wish to feel. O my God ! increase my love, duty, and devotion, that I may never, never forget thy loving-kindness and mercies towards us."

Two months after this date, the budding flower
and ornament of the family, Anna, the eldest daughter, just entering her twenty-first year, and fresh
from the exciting pleasures of her foreign tour, was
struck down with illness, and in a few days fell
asleep to this earth and its fleeting interests. If
artist and friends were not extremely partial, she
must have had rare beauty, a loving spirit, and high
accomplishments. A letter from her father to one
of her attached young friends gives us many particulars, but I quote only enough to show the character
of his sorrow, and the practical nature of his hopes,
for both were destined to gather and strengthen as
his life advanced.

"Thus far may I say, this visitation has been
blessed to us, and our hearts have been less filled
with sorrow than with gratitude for the countless
mercies which preceded and accompanied it. . . . .
When I reflect, besides, that a peaceful and Christian
death is the most we can pray for at the end even
of the longest life, I can almost feel thankful that
our dear child has not only escaped all that she might
have endured, but that we have witnessed her attainment of all we could pray for her. For when we
look to her life, it was one of innocent and peaceful
enjoyment, with a deep sense of religion. The last
year of her short life was, as it ought to be, the
happiest and most improving. Travel enlarged her
powers, widened her observations, deepened her reflections, and refined both her heart and mind by intercourse with the wise and good.

"I thank God I feel that confidence in the blessedness of that world to which she has gone that I would not exchange my dead daughter for any living one, but those I have. And instead of feeling as if any pains in her education were now lost, I feel, on the contrary, as if not only every virtue she acquired, but every talent and accomplishment to which she was trained, were now called into higher exercise. I know not what more life can do for us than cultivate our understandings and purify and elevate our affections. The life that has done that, is long enough. To that period our dear Anna had attained ; and I can call her blessed that she was taken away before age, sorrow, and the world had time to darken or blight the fair prospect."

With such feelings, bereavement and sorrow tended to strengthen rather than weaken resolution. The following, from a letter of this year to Miss Bard, shows how fully time and thought were now given to his work : —

" The college goes on much as usual. The president courteous as ever, and Professor —— cross as ever, but neither much affect me. I have full and satisfactory duties of my own, partly in and partly out of college. In college, my most agreeable is my new one, the course of Evidences I have undertaken with the senior class. And so agreeable are all my college duties, that neither a cross word nor a dissatisfied feeling have arisen from them since the term began. My external duties are voluntary. I have undertaken to preach a sermon in our principal churches at the request of the bishop for the greatest cause our Church can urge, the Theological Seminary. I have been invited, also, to deliver a course of lectures on Moral Science, before the Young Men's Association.   The grammar school of the college takes up my time more and more every day, and may become my hobby; the " Churchman " also calls me its debtor from time to time, for a communication." . . .

" Bishop White has been in the city, and as he leaned upon my arm, walking to church the other day, I asked him of his knowledge as to General Washington's religious character, but there was little to tell beyond respect and decorum.   He never was a communicant, though his wife was."

The summer vacation of this year was spent in travelling through eastern Pennsylvania.   Mrs. McVickar's failing health suggested an entire change of air and scene, and it was thought that the proposed trip would be beneficial.   But it was soon found that the comfort of American travel in those days, even as is still the case over unfrequented routes, was little short of misery.   The great Pennsylvania wagon, with canvas top, forced to accommodate the whole party of ten, over roads which from the account must have been dreadful, with the usual accompaniment of summer heat and dust, seems fully to justify the concluding remarks of Miss Bard, in her journal:
" To the young and gay-hearted this journey has excited much interest and admiration, but to my feelings it has been totally adverse, and from the day we left

16

Nazareth it has been a scene of fatigue, alarm, and dismay."

At Wilkesbarre, Mrs. McVickar was taken quite ill, and it was four weeks before they could leave the place and move homeward. This must have sharpened the memory of the late loss, thus touchingly referred to in the same journal: "But oh! how does every beauty in nature, as art, recall the beloved object who used to be our constant companion, and whose pure, delicate taste and observations doubled all our pleasures. When her father now reads some noble or touching lines in her favorite Southey or Wordsworth, I think I hear the sound of her sweet voice, as she used to recite the parts she most admired." And yet, in spite of all this, childish memory of sports that summer in which the father was never absent, and childish records, filling many copybooks, with the proceedings of a mock-heroic society, of which he was the founder and animating spirit, show how wonderful must have been the power of self-control, and how full the realization of a parent's duty in his sad and foreboding heart. When we remember, too, that the subject of this memoir had by nature a nervous and anxious temperament, we see here evidences of character which may not improperly be called heroic, though he would have been the last ever to imagine that he was playing the *rôle* of the hero. It was simply that with him the greater duty was never an excuse for the neglect of the lesser.

Term time brought with it, this year, its usual

college duties, much increased by voluntary additions in the enlargement of the course.   The two following notes from well-known names at Washington, show, however, that there were wider thoughts as well as a widening reputation.

WASHINGTON, *March* 3, 1832.

DEAR SIR, — I beg to make you my thanks for your letter of the 28th ult., received yesterday, inclosing a proposition for a new banking company.   I should entertain great respect for any system proceeding from your deliberate research and examination, and receiving the approbation of yourself and the intelligent men around you.

I will take the first leisure moment to investigate the present proposition, and may correspond with you more at large.

Meantime, I am, dear sir,
With great respect,
Your obedient servant,
LOUIS McLANE.

To REV. JOHN McVICKAR, etc., etc.

WASHINGTON, *May* 4, 1832.

MY DEAR SIR, — I inclose you many questions,[1] submitted to Mr. Biddle, which he will probably answer before the close of this session.   I am permitted by the committee to submit them also to other gentlemen, and I know of no one who understands the subject better than you do.   You will oblige me, at your leisure, by looking them over, and making such

[1] Respecting a National Banking System.

suggestions as you may think proper, or answering such of the questions as you may appropriately do.

I am, with great respect and esteem,

Your obedient servant,

C. C. CAMBRELENG.

Rev. John McVickar.

To some, letters like the above, addressed to one who had upon him the vows of Holy Orders, may seem to suggest over-attention to what are called worldly subjects. But I question whether the experience of my father's life will justify any such inference. Rather did his wide range of thought give to him what appears now almost as if it had been prophetic power in dealing with all practical questions of the Church, as they arose. In the sermon preached at the bishop's request, at this time, in the New York churches, in behalf of the general seminary, we find this exemplified.

His subject, " The Signs of the Times," as demanding a learned clergy, is one easier estimated to-day than it was forty years ago; yet the true bearing of science on religion, could hardly be better stated under the advantages of our present vastly increased light, than in the following lines : —

" The last sign of our times is one that makes the learning of the clergy not only a sacred duty but a glorious privilege. It is an age of the fulfillment of prophecy. Science is, step by step, as I may say, Christianizing itself, turning into arguments for our faith those very physical phenomena which it once laid as stumbling-blocks in our path.   The infidelity which science planted, science with its own hand now roots up. . . . . So marked, indeed, is this sign of our times as to have already called forth the conjecture of reflecting minds, that to centuries, as to individuals, may belong each its appointed task ; and that the peculiar task and duty of that in which we live, will be to Christianize science by identifying its results with the truths of revelation.   Noble and cheering prospect !   True it is, that we can here pick up, but, as it were, among the ruins of the temple, piece by piece, scattered fragments of that divine philosophy which once made all nature a glorious mirror of the power, the presence, and the mercy of God.   But still who knows how near we may arrive, or how much may be effected, by uniting learning with piety, in the education of our clergy.   For, if to human endeavor be destined so glorious a reward, to whom belongs that honor before the Christian ministry ? "

Or see how the banker and economist comes out in the following, to teach our Church a lesson she has been so slow to learn : —

" Look, too, at its funds ; do they correspond with the wealth and liberality which unquestionably exists among us ?   Can Churchmen be aware that this unfed mother of their children is consuming, I may say, literally, her own heart's blood in their support ?   Yet such is the fact.   At the rate of near $1,500 a year is its productive capital annually decreasing, through its necessary though most economical expenditure.

Means of relief, it is true, it has in prospect ; but, though ample in name, in reality they are unavailing. Exposed, besides, to all the uncertainties which attend future contingencies, and therefore not to be relied on by prudent men ; above all in a case of such present emergency. What, too, are they in a question of our duty ? When our starving children ask bread, shall we give them what is colder than a stone ? the fair sight of some distant crop which other hands have sown for their future support. Or even if such funds could be anticipated, would it not be a shame in us, as Churchmen, thus prematurely to exhaust a fountain, which, rightly guarded, will one day send forth a perennial stream ; and tenfold shame, as men and Christians, thus to add meanness to sacrilege, to rob the treasures of the dead in order that we may throw off our own responsibilities on a pious liberality which has now gone to its reward ? "

These words are but a sample of what was constantly heard from his lips, at the meetings of the many Church societies to which he belonged, whenever financial matters came up for discussion. He would never give his sanction to anything like a shiftless policy in what concerned money, and if he had enemies, as all strong-minded men have, more or less, they were generally those who felt themselves aggrieved at the unsparing manner in which he exposed their financial fallacies, and opposed their temporizing measures.

Professor McVickar's value to the Church in the Diocese of New York, was, in this respect, a weighty one. All societies, having funds, seemed glad to have him as a trustee, and the following list, in his own handwriting, made by request, in 1864, of itself suggests a valuable life : —

"In 1820, I was elected by Convention a member of the Missionary Committee of the diocese, and, as secretary, had its affairs mainly on my hands, and during Bishop Hobart's absence in Europe, obtained aid from the general government for carrying on our Indian mission and school.

"In 1826, on the establishment of the General Theological Seminary, I was elected one of its trustees, and a member of its standing committee, a position I still hold.

"In ——, a vice-president of the New York Bible and Common Prayer Book Society, and have so continued.

"In ——, a vice-president of the Tract Society, and chairman of its committee for selection.

"In 1840, a vice-president of the City Mission Society; was also among its founders, and for many years its presiding officer.

"In ——, a trustee and soon superintendent of the Society for Promoting Religion and Learning.

"In 1828, a trustee of Trinity School; for many years official visitor of the school, and chairman of the school committee ever since.

"Of the New York Athenæum, president, for some years, till its consolidation with the 'Society Library,' in 1836."

To this, to make it complete, must be added the

very honorable and important position of a member of the Standing Committee of the Diocese of New York, from 1834 to 1868, being its president for the last five years, and also that of trustee of St. Stephen's College, Annandale, from its foundation.

This represents many years of service in many varied positions, none of which were allowed to be sinecures. They were the side-streams of a noble river, pouring their fresh waters and varied interests into the main current of an academic and literary life, preventing alike either one-sidedness or stagnation. And above and around all rose the controlling influence of clear religious principle. As he writes at about this date, in concluding a review on Chalmers, —

" Christianity, truly preached, is to us as to the inhabitants of Great Britain, the only rock of safety, — to them against the outbreakings of a starving multitude ; to us against the abuse of civil privileges. Centuries may pass over us before scantiness of food shall be the provocation to rapine ; but our own age will not probably pass without our feeling that the virtue of the people is our only political security, and the institutions of Christianity our only sufficient safeguard for the existence of that virtue."

It is not necessary to call this prophecy ; it is sufficient that we recognize it as that fruit of wisdom which the grafted tree of religious learning ever bears.

CHAPTER XVI.

THE death of Sir Walter Scott about this time stirred deeply the heart of New York, as well as of all the English-speaking world. Public meetings were held, resolutions adopted, subscriptions toward a monument here, or in Edinburgh, started, and the delivery of a public tribute to his memory determined upon. Seventy names, such as the old New Yorker loves now to recall, commencing with David Hadden and followed by such as James G. King, James K. Paulding, Washington Irving, Robert Halliday, and Jonathan Goodhue, signed a call for a public meeting at the Merchants' Exchange, Wall Street, on the 19th of November, 1832, " to take into consideration the best means of uniting with the committees in Scotland, in a tribute of respect to the memory of the GREAT MINSTREL OF THE NORTH." One of the results of this meeting was the following note to Professor McVickar: —

NEW YORK, *November* 29, 1832.

REVEREND AND DEAR SIR, — At a meeting of our fellow-citizens we have been authorized to adopt. measures to procure an eulogium to be pronounced

upon the late Sir Walter Scott as a suitable tribute
to the memory of that distinguished man, whose works
have delighted and instructed both hemispheres, and
whose death both hemispheres deplore.

In requesting you to undertake this grateful and
interesting duty, we have the honor to subscribe ourselves, reverend and dear sir,

Your friends and obedient servants,
Jonathan M. Wainwright,
Robert Halliday,
W. A. Duer.

The Rev. John McVickar.

This request was, with some hesitation, acceded to,
and the " Tribute to the Memory of Sir Walter
Scott," afterwards published by request, was delivered
early in December, before, what was then a compara-
tive possibility, the intelligent audience of New York.
It was a high-toned and heartfelt eulogium, and de-
served the general approbation with which it was
received. The romantic school in English writing
was then both new and popular. Scott was its ideal,
and we can well understand how sympathetic, to an
audience perfectly familiar with his works, would be
the suggestive reminders of this eulogium.

From many notes respecting it I select the following : —

Stockbridge, *March* 2, 1833.

My dear Sir, — On my return from Boston I
found the " Tribute to the Memory of Sir Walter
Scott " awaiting me, and I am unwilling to receive,

without acknowledgment, so high a gratification as its perusal has furnished me. Permit me first, however, to thank you for an attention which is the more agreeable, as it recognizes on your part an acquaintance I am happy to perpetuate; to this I must be allowed to add my admiration of the beauty, truth, and eloquence of the production itself. If to few in our country has been afforded the great privilege of seeing and personally knowing Sir Walter Scott, we must at least rejoice that such a distinction has been awarded to one so capable as the writer of appreciating justly his character and genius, and of transmitting his impressions to others.

With best wishes for the health of Mrs. McVickar and your family, believe me,

My dear sir,
Very respectfully, your obliged,
SUSAN A. L. SEDGWICK.

REV. JOHN McVICKAR.

The following from Mrs. Grant, of Laggan, shows that it met with as much favor on the other as on this side of the Atlantic, and that, too, from those who knew Scott best: —

REV. DEAR SIR, — It is not easy for me to say how much you have gratified — I may well say delighted me with the beautiful garland you have hung on the tomb of him whom we all delighted to honor. The mere combination of genius so splendid, with virtue so modest, so consistent, and a temper so sweetly benevolent, seemed to touch the hardest hearts with a kind of hallowed influence. Never surely was a person so much admired, so little, if at all, envied. To me he was not merely a warm friend but a benefactor, ever ready to promote my interests and advantages in every possible way. I felt his loss more deeply than in a person drawing so near the verge of time is perhaps excusable. But Sir Walter's death in one sense made me young again, that is, I felt a renewal of that keen anguish which belongs more to the untamed feelings of youth than to the subdued state of a mind inured to suffering. . . . .

The facility with which this rich intellect poured forth the profusion of its fruits always appeared to me a proof that he felt a lively pleasure in composition such as a bird does in singing. James Ballantyne, his confidential friend, who, within a few months, has followed him to the grave, has told me that, in instances which he mentioned, his sense of the ludicrous was such that, in writing, he was obliged to lay down his pen and indulge in a hearty laugh. He gathered thoughts and images from quarters where no one else would have looked for them. What Pope says of some one by way of reproach, was true of him. He indeed —

> " Filled his head,
> With all such reading as was never read ; "

but the gold that he extracted from this lead showed no common chemic powers. There was and is something too near idolatry in the feelings with which I think of this happy specimen of humanity in its finest from.   Yet I do not expatiate in this way except to those of whose full sympathy I am assured.   I hope, dear sir, you will consider it a compliment when I assure you I think I could not have written so fully and freely to another, and I am not afraid of tiring you.   It is pleasant to think of the effect such un-clouded goodness had on Byron in all his splendid wretchedness.   He could not hear him named with-out emotion, his eyes filled, and his color changing. His distrust in human virtue was to him a sense of misery.   He used to say a few more like Walter Scott would have reconciled him to his fellow-men.

.   .   .   .

Your eulogium of our illustrious friend gave much pleasure, not to say pride, to many of his admirers. It is to be printed at the end of the edition of the works now publishing.

It is time to subscribe myself, dear sir, with much esteem and regard,

Yours truly,
ANNE GRANT.

To appreciate Mrs. Grant's beautiful allusion to the effect of Sir Walter's death in renewing her youth, it must be remembered that she, herself, was long past eighty, though her large pages of fine and beautiful calligraphy would seem to pronounce her as young as she felt.

At the close of the " eulogium," my father sug-gested the proposition from America of an inter-national copyright as the truest monument which

Americans could erect to the memory of Scott. This created considerable attention at the time. It was brought before Congress, and the British Consul at Boston, Mr. George Manners, corresponded with the author, Judge Story, and others respecting it; but it seems to have come to nothing. The mother country had taught her independent and growing child a selfish policy in other matters, and the lesson was now turned against herself. Though the time may come, an international copyright was not then, nor would it be now, of pecuniary advantage to this country; and hence courtesy, honorable feeling, and the individual interests of authors must go for nothing.

The abuse by travellers of the opportunities granted through social intercourse, in pandering to the public curiosity respecting great men, was one with which my father had no sympathy. He not only avoided it, but actually dreaded the slightest imputation. In a letter to Lockhart, Sir Walter's son-in-law, accompanying a copy of the eulogium, he says: —

" Having been recently called upon to express my own feelings and those of my fellow-citizens on the death of Sir Walter Scott, I owe it you on every account to remit a copy of what I have said, more especially as I was naturally led to speak in it of that opportunity of personal intercourse enjoyed by myself and family during our short residence at Abbotsford in the June of 1830. I do this in order that you may be aware of all I have said publicly on that subject. I regarded the invitation to Abbots-

ford at the time as an honor to which I had no
sufficient claim, and felt it consequently as a most
sacred obligation not to abuse the opportunity it
might afford to the gratification of idle curiosity in
myself or others. I therefore abstained while there
from the use of my pen, even in the trifling journal
I kept for the gratification of my children at home,
though I could not deny myself or them the pleasure
of my after recollections ; but to their eyes it has
been almost strictly confined, until the late melancholy event induced me to employ it in the 'manner
you see.''

On the 21st of April of this year, after twenty-
four years of married life, my mother died, leaving
seven children. As a man leaning upon a staff that
had well supported him, when that staff breaks,
either falls, or seeks another, or straightens himself
up into independent strength, so was it with my
father in this great loss and sorrow of his life. And
in a moment it would seem that the resolution was
formed. One had fallen in the great copartnership
of life, and the other without hesitation, in hopes of
reunion, takes up and determines to bear for life, be
it long or short, the double burden. Nor is this
merely matter of conjecture. In the prime of life, —
he was then forty-five, — handsome, as his portrait
by Inman shows, with conversational powers which,
even in that day of a brilliant New York society,
were noted, and which he never lost, he thus writes
to his eldest daughter describing the monument
which he had erected to her mother, and the inscription which embodied his deliberate resolve : —

" The words inscribed are few, and have reference only to myself, which my dear children must pardon. The inscription is as follows, the word ' PARENTS ' being above : —

ELIZA BARD M^CVICKAR,
BORN 12 OCTOBER, 1787,
DIED 27 APRIL, 1833.
IN THE CHRISTIAN'S REST
SHE NOW AWAITS ONE
YET STRUGGLING
WITH A CHRISTIAN'S HOPE.

" It occupies but one half the side, the other being reserved for your dear father when God shall see fit to call him to join her, I trust, in those blessed mansions where there is no parting, and where we shall all, through a Saviour's merits, be reunited."

This monument is a plain, solid block of white marble, on the top of which a marble cross now stands. It occupies the centre of a square plot in the rural church-yard which my father's own hands had laid out, when, as a young deacon, he first took charge of the church which his father-in-law had built for him at Hyde Park, on the banks of the Hudson River.

My mother's character, however beautiful and attractive, does not concern the thread of that life which I am endeavoring now to trace, but the love my father bore her does, for it remained within him to the last, a strong motive power. I shall, therefore, close this subject with two extracts, one from a letter written for all his children four weeks after his loss, the other from one written to Miss Bard some months later.

"If then, my dear children, you loved your mother, follow her example. Let religion give strength to your character, consistency to your conduct, and cheerfulness to all your future prospects. Let benevolence be in all your plans, and energy in all you execute; fear neither difficulties, nor danger, nor self-denial in the path of duty; and without losing sight of Providence, keep ever, as your dear mother did, a generous heart, a willing mind, and an open hand, whenever God places before you the means of doing good. Thus living, your reward shall be as hers was, love and affection without bound or limit, and on the bed of death that peace which passeth all understanding; and above all your reward shall be a reunion with your sainted mother where there is no sin and no sorrow, no tears and no 'parting. Thus prays your affectionate and bereaved father."

To Miss Bard.

" 'Tis true there was a dear one for whom my pen was readier, absent from whom I counted not days but hours, for wherever she was seemed to me my only home and resting-place. Now she is gone, my heart is scattered wherever those are who were near and dear to her. Home, in its dearest sense, I have no longer on earth, nor expect to feel till I join her in that Christian's rest where she awaits me. Neither

17

friend, however dear, nor child, however beloved, can supply the void ; it must remain till made up an hundredfold in a future life. Her dear likeness has been my greatest comfort ; I open it on my table ; I have her gentle face as my companion whether I write or read. It is the last object on which I look at night, and the first thing I see in the morning is the same sweet countenance. O, that it could change or speak, and sometimes I look on it till I almost fancy that it does. But these are dreams, and from them I awake when duty calls, stronger and more resolute. Duty, active duty, therefore, must be my support."

The habit thus formed of companionship with the departed spirit of the loved one through a miniature, which except on the rarest occasions was never allowed to meet other eyes than his own, but always stood open at his bedside during the hours of the night, was kept up, probably without a single intermission, to the last, a period of thirty-seven years.

The conscientious effort to be a mother as well as a father to his children was at once made, and a country-house purchased that very year to be their summer home during the three months of college vacation. He wisely went among friends, purchasing from his brother James his cottage and farm at Constableville, or Turin, as it was generally called, in Lewis County, New York, about three hundred miles northwest of the city. It was a long journey of three days, steamboat, canal-boat, and stage-coach,

but at the end everything was such as to contribute
to his children's happiness. There was a large circle
of uncles, aunts, and cousins, a cool summer climate,
a noble country bordering on the Black River and
the region of the Adirondacks, a dairy farm, beside
all the stimulating interests of a vacation. To these
were added, as if for my father's special need, in this
hour of his loneliness, a struggling Church. As he
writes to Miss Bard shortly after the removal of his
family, —

"All looks well here but the Church, which from
various reasons has sunk almost to nothing. The
endeavor to revive it is the great duty which now
opens upon me."

Fortunately this was a year filled for my father
with varied interests. Early in the summer I find
him elected an honorary member of the Literary and
Historical Society of Quebec, and shortly after the
offer of the provostship of the University of Pennsylvania, just vacated by Dr. DeLancey, was pressed
upon him. This last was urged strongly in letters
from Dr. Adrain, and Bishop H. U. Onderdonk. It
is possible that the disappointment in the matter of
the presidency of Columbia College may have caused
him at first to think favorably of this opportunity
to take the head of a rival institution in another
State; but if so, and I only infer it from some delay
in giving his final answer, other considerations must
have prevailed. Among these a strong attachment
to his native State, city, and diocese would doubtless
have much weight. Both in Church and State he

was a New Yorker, and that to him was synonymous with liberal views, and a high progressive conservatism. This was held not comparatively and boastfully, but positively and practically. As a citizen and a Churchman, it would, at any time, have been a hard trial for him to leave New York.

CHAPTER XVII.

IT will be remembered that in the journal of the days spent at the Hospice of the St. Bernard mention was made of the discovery in the museum cabinet of a specimen of anthracite coal, found in the neighborhood, and of my father's efforts to arrange some means for burning it. In this he was but partially successful. But the subject was not allowed to pass from his mind, and on his return to America he interested a few friends, whose names deserve record here, — Edward Laight, William Moore, Frederick Prime, and Miss Douglas, to aid him in sending a Nott's stove to the Hospice. This, after some delay and much difficulty, was accomplished, and the following letters give an interesting account of the event : —

ST. BERNARD, le 20 Février, 1833.

TRÉS HONORÉ MONSIEUR, — L'Hospice du St. Bernard conservera toujours un très précieux souvenir de l'intérêt que vous prenez à sa prospérité, je puis vous assurer et vous prie de vouloir bien aussi assurer vos amis, qu'il n'est aucun Religieux de notre Congregation qui ne sente vivement les bienfaits que notre Hospice a reçus et va recevoir encore par l'offre généreux que vous lui faites d'un fourneau à brûler l'anthracite. Cet objet sera pour nous une précieuse ressource pour chauffer economiquement la maison, et un soulagement pour l'humanité souffrante, car eloigné de cinq lieues (twenty-five miles) des bois, et vu leur rareté et la difficulté du transport, nous étions obligés d'en faire une stricte économie; au lieu que l'anthracite peut être porté sans fais— mais il nous manquoit le moyen de le faire brûler. Ce fourneau sera donc un monument qui constatera la générosité et le dévouement de nos amis en Amérique, en faveur des pauvres passagers au travers des Hautes Alpes, par le grand St. Bernard. Ces bienfaits la reconnaissance les devra à ce sentiment pieux qui intéresse si vivement les amis de l'humanité envers les malheureux.

Votre très humble serviteur,

BARRAS,

Chan., Reg., Clavendier de l'Hospice.

MONSIEUR LE PROFESSOR MACVICAR.

By what might well be called a fortunate providence, the stove, by no means an easy one to handle, as those who remember the eight-foot high stoves of Dr. Nott in the hall-ways of the old New York houses will acknowledge, fell in with a scientific traveller of the name of Saynisch at the foot of the mountain. He, interesting himself at once in the affair, joined company with the stove, which on such an errand of mercy we may well look upon as a living thing, and did not part company with it till it was set up in the Hospice and the good brothers of the Order had rejoiced over its genial glow.

The following letter, coming as it did from an entire stranger, gave to all concerned in the enterprise a very happy feeling : —

Hospice St. Bernard, *April* 26, 1833.

My dear Sir, — It is with the greatest gratification and pleasure that I can communicate to you the fulfillment of your wishes to erect the stove which you had the kindness to send to the St. Bernard. In this time of the year when the snow reaches Lydde, four miles below St. Pierre, it was with the utmost difficulty for me to bring it up. Till Lydde it was brought on wagon ; from there I took six men, who brought it in pieces to the summit. The construction was very difficult, because several were broken when I opened the case. Notwithstanding all this I succeeded to burn the coal, which is more a plumbago than anthracite. Since yesterday the stove is in full operation, and the joy of the brethren has no boundary. They remember you and your dear family with the greatest gratitude. To-morrow I shall go down with the marronnier and the dogs, because the weather is very stormy and the snow enormous.

Your most obedient servant,
L. Saynisch.

Professor McVickar.

P. S. I hope you will excuse my good English ; my dictionary is 6,000 feet below.

These letters, with a few others from M. Barras, appeared in the " New York American " of July 5, 1833, accompanied by some editorial remarks from the editor, Charles King, but with a studious omission, evidently at my father's request, of his own name. A few days afterwards appeared in the same sheet, the following : —

" The fact of the discovery, by an American traveller, of a species of anthracite on Mount St. Bernard, and of the subsequent present, through his instrumentality, of one of Nott's stoves to the brothers of the monastery, as recorded in this paper on Friday, has attracted much notice and inquiry. Among the evidences of this, we offer, without the permission of the writer, the following extract from a note addressed to us by a distinguished man of letters, a German, now resident among us : —

" ' DEAR SIR, — Are you at liberty to give me the name of the gentleman who erected so excellent a monument of American activity and practical sense on the high summit of the St. Bernard ? I should like to mention his name in some proper place, though I do not yet know where. At all events, I should like to know the name ; it gives me always great delight to watch the pulsations of extending civilization. My heart glowed — not precisely like a Nott stove, but at least like a Roman *marito* — when I read the account of the invaluable present to the good brotherhood of the Hospice. How many a traveller will bless the giver of this stove. Imagine a husband who sees his wife, nearly dead by frost, recovering by this thrice blessed stove. Why, if I knew English, I would make an ode on this new victory of human intelligence : compare it to Napoleon's passing the Alps, and who would appear as the greater benefactor ? '

"It can be no harm, though it *is* a liberty, that we should answer publicly the inquiry of our correspondent, and name Professor McVickar of Columbia College."

The effect produced upon the minds of the occupants of that dreary abode by the happy discovery and practical suggestions of my father, was probably not the least of the benefits bestowed. The mental stagnation of cold and solitude combined, must have been a no unfrequent visitor to this cheerless abode, 8,000 feet above the level of the sea. Anything, therefore, which should create universal interest would be a boon to its inmates, and much more if likely to become a panacea for their greatest ills. J. Fenimore Cooper, writing from Paris at this time to a son of Governor Jay, tells of the enthusiasm among the brothers at the Hospice, but does not sympathize as fully in their feelings as he probably would have done had he himself been under bonds to remain up in that freezing atmosphere for two or three years. He writes : —

"I was at the Great St. Bernard the other day, and the lazy monks inquired after Dr. McVickar, who has quite won their hearts by sending them a contrivance to keep them warm. The egotists did nothing but talk of stoves and coal mines."

It will not lessen the interest of this little episode, though it must suggest days of deep disappointment at the Hospice, to hear that, after being successfully used for a year or two, the vein of coal gave out, and that they have since had to have recourse again to the fagots of wood, brought up on the backs of mules twenty-five miles, from the valley below.

My father was at this time, and long after, deeply interested in the work of city missions, and was now chairman of the City Mission Society. . Aided by members of his family and one or two seminary students, he had started a mission school at Union Square, a neighborhood then not unlike to the present approaches to Central Park. Also another at the dry dock on the East River, which, with the Church of the Epiphany that sprang from it, were, until their adoption by the City Mission Society, supported and carried on by him. Of the capabilities of this City Mission Society, which is still doing a noble though restricted work in the metropolis, he had a high estimation. It was through his influence that it was at this time intrusted by the diocese with the exclusive charge of missionary operations in the city of New York. I find evidence also that he then urged both Trinity Parish and the Society for the Promotion of Religion and Learning, to recognize its official instrumentality, and supply funds for increasing the work, and for the purchase of mission sites over the whole island. This broad and bold scheme of missionary work, which would have placed the Church on such vantage ground as the swelling tides of increasing population rolled in around her, failed, as all such schemes in our Church have failed, from parochial jealousy arising from the want of recognized episcopal headship and a cathedral centre. And though his connection with the society continued for many years, he never felt that it had been allowed to do its full or rightful work.

On the 10th of June, 1834, my father was called upon by the students of the college to address them on the death of an honored and beloved fellow-student, William Moore De Rham. Relationship and close intimacy with the family made it to him an occasion of more than usual interest. The address, under the title, " Be ye also Ready," was published by request, and I feel that in rescuing from the dust and oblivion of the pamphlet collector's shelves the following words of wise and much needed advice, I am but doing that which will receive the thankful acknowledgment of most of my readers : —

" And do you ask how you are to be always ready, I answer, by the steady performance upon Christian principles of each daily duty as it rises before you. Concentrate your thoughts on the present duty whatever it be. The present hour, the present moment is all you have of life. The past is gone, utterly, irretrievably ; the future is not, and to you may never be ; ' the present,' therefore, ' calm and wise dispose.' "

" The position of the youthful student is doubtless one of great danger and high trial, and it is among the mysteries of our probationary state, why, at the age

when resolution is weakest, passion should be found the
strongest; and the fiery trial of temptation appointed
unto those who are but novices in resisting even its
ordinary allurements.   Yet thus it is; God has so
willed it, and our only comfort is, that where a righteous ruler has sent trial He has doubtless sent pro-
portionate help.   Nor is that aid far to seek; much
is to be found in that ardent nature which is itself
your betrayer; in those warm and generous emotions
of virtue, which, even in our corrupt nature, still char-
acterize the heart of youth; in a pure and generous
ambition of excellence, at that age most easily excited;
in a deep love of earthly parents, whose hearts would
be broken by a child's misconduct, and their gray
hairs brought down in sorrow to the grave; and
in a natural piety to a heavenly parent, which in the
youthful breast springs up instinctively into feelings
of love and gratitude.   But among human means,
let me urge upon you as the most practical and most
powerful, the habits of a faithful and diligent student.
These preoccupy the debatable ground of the human heart, and leave no room for the lodgment of
traitorous affections.   It is the *idle* mind alone that
is weak to resist allurement; it is the vacant thought
that allows wandering fancy to be caught with the
unreal shows of vicious pleasure.   Therefore, will the
real student, as a general rule, ever be found to be
the *virtuous* student, and the source of his danger seen
to be not so much in the strength as in the unoccu-
pied state of his emotions.   It is the stagnant pool
that breeds the noxious vapors, and from the listless

hours of idleness, as from their head-waters, creep out the dark and deadly streams of gaming, intemperance, and vicious dissipation ! If, unfortunately, any whom I now address are trembling on the verge of this precipice, let me here arouse them to a sense of the danger in which they stand. I would exhort them in the spirit-stirring language of our great dramatist, —

> ' Rouse up, be firm, and wanton love
>   Shall from your neck unloose his amorous hold,
>   And, like a dew-drop from a lion's mane,
>   Be shook in air.'

"But to him who seeks it there are higher aids than mere occupation of mind. Conscience speaks within — *la buona compagnia*, to borrow the thought of the classic poet of Italy, —

> ' La buona compagnia che l'uom francheggia
>   Sotto l'osbergo del sentirsi pura.'

Or, to give it in the almost equally classic words of his late translator, —

> ' That boon companion, who her strong breast-plate
>   Buckles on him who feels no guilt within,
>   And bids him on and fear not.'

"That inward voice is to the student a voice of safety, for it speaks of time and talents and means of youthful improvement, as things to be accounted for in a day of righteous retribution.

"But higher yet is your strength. Do you ask on what aid that youth shall rest, who, with a spirit willing, finds yet his nature weak. I answer, on that grace which is given in return to earnest prayer, and which is never withheld from the sincere and faithful spirit. That aid, unlike to human aid, lessens not in the using; it may be wasted, but can never be wearied; it may be grieved, and offended, and driven away, but, with a friendship as high above worldly friendships as heaven is above earth, it can never be exhausted or overtasked; it comes into the heart at first, small and unregarded, as the seed of the tree which the birds carry to the fruitful meadow; but received in a thankful soil, it grows up like that tree, till it shelters in its branches those winged thoughts of the soul, which are as the birds that brought it, and till its roots are so entwined with every fibre of the heart as to bid defiance not only to the storm of passion and the assaults of temptation, but even to the searching fires of persecution and martyrdom.

"But there is one question more of deeper interest. How shall he who has once fallen, return? How shall the path of innocence be regained, if, through heedlessness or temptation, our feet have slipped from it? I answer you in the dying words of him to whom this debt of respect is paid: 'I have a humble trust in the mediation of my Redeemer; my hope is in Jesus Christ.' Through Him may sin ever be pardoned; through Him may grace be gained; through Him and the blessed Spirit may the path of repentance lead again to that of innocence, and that narrow path be more safely trodden, when the steps of youth are guided by a light from Heaven, and their feet guarded by the preparation of the gospel of peace."

This year appeared from the press, " The Early Years of Bishop Hobart." The relationship between the Bishop and my father had been a very near one. Ordained by him in the first year of his episcopate, he had ever remained the Bishop's warm admirer, and soon became his intimate and attached friend. His loss was deeply felt, both personally and because of the Church; and the importance of a faithful record of his life seems early to have suggested itself to my father's mind. In commenting, in the columns of " The Churchman," on Dr. Strachan's letter to Dr. Chalmers on " The Life and Character of Bishop Hobart," he says, " Where is the domestic monument which some one of his many sons are bound to raise to his memory;" but I do not think that he had then any idea of raising that monument himself. The first contribution toward a life of the Bishop was made by the Rev. J. F. Schroeder, entitled " A Memorial of Bishop Hobart;" then came a " Memoir," by Dr. Berrian, attached to his works; and it may still be said that the life of Bishop Hobart, the most influential and important life that the Church in America has yet known, remains to be written. The " Early " and " Professional Years," by my father, are but the material for such a life.

His object in the " Early Years " was distinctly of this character, calling himself editor, and presenting, through original letters, the outlines of a character so true to its after development as to silence at once the charge of personal ambition as the motive of its untiring energy, or official position as the secret of its

firm devotion to Church principles, charges which
had more than once been repeated.   In the " Professional Years," which appeared in 1836, he rose somewhat higher in philosophic treatment, but even here
was hampered in a way which proves the need of
some later historian.   " The subject and its events,"
he says, in his preface, " are too well known for the
interest of biography and too recent for the freedom
of history.   It is a story, too, which can hardly, now
at least, be told without compromitting both names
and questions, in a way not easy to avoid reviving old
offense or giving new."   Yet how well he performed
his delicate task friends and enemies alike testified,
and I feel that I shall be forgiven the liberty in inserting here the following unprejudiced testimony : —

White Plains, *August,* 1836.

Reverend and dear Sir, — I cannot tell you how
much I have been delighted in perusing your late
work, " Professional Years of Bishop Hobart."   It
should indeed be, as I am sure it is, matter of joy to
the Church that the character of that great man has
at length been so ably portrayed that the more closely
it is investigated the purer it will appear, and the
longer it shall be contemplated the more it must be
admired.   Not having been one of the Bishop's
warmest admirers during his life, I am happy to rank
myself now among the number, and to add that every
year's experience in the ministry strengthens my conviction of the soundness of his views and the wisdom
of his policy.   Robert Wm. Harris.

Professor John McVickar.

My father was, from the first, interested in the welfare of the General Theological Seminary, and especially of its library, which was a very inadequate one for an institution holding its prominent position as the chief nursery of the Church. He was then chairman of the library and building committees of the board of trustees, and exerted himself in every way to raise the sum of ten thousand dollars for the increase and endowment of the seminary library. Drafts and memorials to Trinity Parish and the Socicty for the Promotion of Religion and Learning, in his handwriting, are before me, as well as the following characteristic note from Bishop Doane congratulating him on his finished work : —

St. Mary's Parsonage, Innocents' Day, 1835.

Reverend and dear Brother, — From my heart I thank God that the noble enterprise of the endowment for the seminary library is accomplished, chiefly, so far as human agency is concerned, by *your* persevering energy. What a noble, generous, most magnanimous mother of us all is Trinity Church! Peace be within her walls and plenteousness within her palaces!

G. W. Doane.

Rev. John McVickar, D. D.

The work, thus satisfactorily accomplished, was aided in an unexpected manner by his memoir of Bishop Hobart. Among the many friends made in England had been Dr. W. F. Hook, the Vicar of

Leeds. To him a copy of the two volumes was sent, and at the same time a letter asking him to interest himself in the proposed library endowment. This was practically answered in the affirmative by the unexpected appearance, shortly after, of an English edition of the " Early and Professional Years of Hobart," with a preface of thirty pages from the pen of Dr. Hook himself, containing a short historic sketch of the American Church. There was also an announcement that Mr. Talboys, the publisher, had agreed to place the *whole of the profits* to the credit of the library of the American Church Seminary. " It had pleased God," he said, " to bless him in the basket and in the store, and he should delight in thus evincing his gratitude by showing his devotion to the holy and Apostolic Church of which he was a member." What these profits amounted to I am not now able to state, but this noble act of an English publisher deserves, what we would here give it, honorable and thankful record.

Shortly before this evidence of his interest appeared, Dr. Hook writes: " I feel much interested about your library and am ready to be employed in the good cause. I consider it useless to attempt a subscription without some definite object in view. What I propose, therefore, to do is this, to raise a subscription among my friends for the purpose of presenting you with a full set of the ' Fathers,' including the ' Benedictine Edition,' which I think can be purchased for £350. I have mentioned my plan to my friends, Professor Pusey, Mr. Newman of Oriel, and Mr.

Palmer, the author of the ' Origines Liturgicæ,' who enter very warmly into the business, and I hope that ere long we shall be able to send a handsome present to the brethren in America."

What were then the feelings of the men who, unknowingly to themselves, were becoming the leaders of the great Church movement of the day, is evidenced in another passage from the same letter: " But I trust that there are many with you as there are very many with us, and the number is greatly increasing, who are determined to adhere, though they die for it, to Catholic doctrine and Catholic practice, resolutely opposing Popery on the one hand, and ultra Protestantism on the other. It was, indeed, your manly avowal of these principles in your first letter that excited in me so strong a wish to aid you in the good cause you have at heart."

Hugh James Rose, who, though a Cambridge man, may not unjustly be called the father of the Oxford school, writing under date of April, 1837, says of his volume of sermons on the ministry, a number of copies of which my father had ordered for presentation to the students of the seminary : " It possessed no novelty, but it was put forth at a time when, at Cambridge, such doctrines had rather been talked of for a long period, and while Whatelyism was reigning at Oxford. So far, I trust, it may have been, by God's blessing, useful. *Now*, a host of able men at Oxford are advocating the same principles, and now and then pressing things to an extreme. Still, their learning, ability, and munificent disinterestedness, as private men, must do good in the highest degree, and will give great weight to their public labors."

I venture here upon a few extracts from letters of other English friends of this period, especially those of Sir Robert Inglis.

FROM SIR ROBERT INGLIS, SEPTEMBER 9, 1833.

. . . . "On Friday, the 6th, I went to see our venerable friend, Mrs. Hannah More, who, for some years, had retired here. [Clifton.] I found that in the preceding night a great change had taken place in her state, and she was gradually sinking. She was dying all day ; and on Saturday, the 7th, was summoned from this world. Though her mind has been eclipsed by her advancing years, — for she was in the eighty-ninth year of her life, — and though there was no longer any continuous flow of wisdom and of piety from her lips, yet the devotional habit of her days of health, gave even to the weakness of decay a sacred character, and her affections remained strong to the last. On Thursday last she became more evidently dying, her eyes closed, she made an effort to stretch forth her hands, and exclaimed to her favorite sister, now for many years departed, " Patty — joy." And when she could no longer articulate, her hands remained clasped as in prayer. Her very intimate friend, Mr. Harford, and I, sat by her bed-side, and in succession kissed her hand, and she in turn raised our hands to her lips. To myself it is a somewhat singular circumstance, that having seen shortly before his death, in London, our admirable friend, Mr. Wilberforce, and having attended his funeral, I should, at so short an interval of time, but at a distance in point of place, been permitted to see the last one of his most intimate friends, herself eminent as a Christian character, and with whom indeed he had taken counsel for nearly half a century. Knowing the value you attach to both, I have no scruple in giving you these details. The mode in which Mr. Wilberforce's funeral was attended, is a bright spot in the national character, in the midst of many unfavorable symptoms. Men of all ranks, parties, and creeds, concurred in doing honor to him, — some from gratitude for his book, and some from admiration and respect for his Christian character; others, perhaps the much larger number, from sympathy with his views in the abolition of the slave-trade; but still, round his grave there they all stood, united for once in one common object — two of our royal dukes who differ in politics, also the Duke of Wellington and Lord Brougham, Sir Robert Peel and Lord Althorp; a High-churchman and a Socinian, a Methodist and a Roman Catholic. I must not, however, run on without thanking you for your just and eloquent tribute to another eminent though different person, Sir Walter Scott. Sir Thomas D. Acland read parts with great effect, at the meeting held in the Mansion House, in the city of London, to promote the subscription for the purpose of securing Abbotsford to the family of Scott.

. . . . " You see that I write not about politics, which yet, you may well believe, occupy me almost day and night. The reform of Parliament is to be followed by reform of the Church ; a measure which even more than the other is connected with property ; and as property is the creature of law, anything which shakes its tenure in the hands of one class, may soon shake it in the hands of another. The law which vested half the property of the Church of Rome here, at the Reformation, in lay hands, while it vested the other half in the reformed Church, is as equally able and equally entitled to resume its grants from the lay sinecurists as it is to seize and subdivide the property which for three hundred years has been held, as it is now held, by those who, at all events, do something for it. England is indeed in a troubled state. It may please God's good providence to guard and guide us through the storm. But all analogy has proved that democracy never stops till it ends in anarchy, and anarchy is despotism. It is fearful to write these things, when we consider how much individual happiness, how much national usefulness is at stake. We have been at once the most favored and the most ungrateful of people. But of one thing we are sure, that all things will work together for good to them who love God. *Sursum Corda.*"

. . . . "We were delighted with Bishop Doane : and in return I think he seemed well pleased with 'Old England.' His visit has left a most happy, and I think enduring impression here. I remember to have told you, at the steps of the door of Battersea Rise, that if your country could and would send such a family as yours over to us, it would do more to form and confirm the union between the two countries than a treaty made at Washington : meaning, that the Christian intercourse of leading families from the United States with our people in England would, if repeated year after year, and still more, if reciprocated by the visits of such families, or such individuals to your shores, do more to rub off the angles where collisions might arise, than any diplomacy. In that point of view, your Bishop Doane, — why may we not call him our Bishop Doane, — was most valuable to us. May God grant that we may never be permitted to go to war. It would be a fearful crisis for Christendom : but we should have gone to war if a hair of Macleod's head had been touched. There are too many on both sides of the water who would urge it; on the slave question, a war would be popular in England; but I repeat it, may God direct us both to peace."

Mr. John Kenyon, writing in 1843, to introduce Mr. Macready, says : —

" In arranging my small library here, I put your

books on the shelves which I am fond of making little altars of friendly memories. You will some day, perhaps, come and see them there.

" I propose that this note shall pass to you by the hands of Mr. Macready. He is a scholar and a gentleman in the best sense of that word, knowing, I have no doubt, many of your English friends, about whom he will tell you. I am habitually shy of giving letters, and never make two persons known to each other where I do not perceive what the philosopher calls the ' fitness of things.' I heard Sidney Smith say the other day, speaking of your minister, who is an old friend of mine, ' One likes fitnesses, and Everett is a fitness.' "

The little volume of " Family Devotions," already spoken of, was brought out from the press about this time, having for many years been used in the family in manuscript. Its Saxon purity of style, a peculiarity noticeable in all my father's writings, elicited, from Dr. Hook and other English friends, warm commendation.

My father's pen was now as constantly in his hand as other duties would allow, and his reputation, not so much as an author as of a writer of wise thought and graceful language, was fairly established. The editor of the " Knickerbocker " writes to ask for occasional articles on his own terms, and the " New York Review " seldom appeared without at least one article from him. Dr. Wainwright, then in Boston, writes to thank him for his " First Lessons in Political Economy," which he is himself using with a youthful class, and to urge on the promised larger works in the same department. Mr. Jared Sparks writes to the same effect. The " American Quarterly " asks for an article on the United States Bank, and the Board of Missions passes a resolution requesting him to take the editorship of the " Spirit of Missions," and in the mean time his home letters show the busy man. January 9, 1836, he writes to his eldest son : —

"In Church affairs I have been prosperous. I have succeeded in the $10,000 for the seminary library, and I think in the endowment of another professorship, and at any rate in getting Whittingham [1] there. I wish you could hear his sermons; they are the only ones that come up to my mark. The stereotype edition of ' Hobart's Early Years ' is out. His ' Professional ' ones, at least one volume, for they grow, will be out in a few weeks. The press is slow work, and annoys me by its delays."

[1] Present Bishop of Maryland.

CHAPTER XVIII.

A LETTER from Philadelphia, dated October
28th, 1835, gives these last memories of
Bishop White : —

" I called on the Bishop before church, time enough
to walk with the younger ladies, the Bishop having
gone before by coach very much against his inclina-
tions. His preaching to-day was contrary to the
urgent solicitations of his family. But as it was,
their fears were unnecessary. He preached a sound,
excellent sermon, heard by those, at least, who were
near him, and without any ill consequences, though
I think that in all probability it is his last. It was
deeply interesting on that account, and his first appearance as he passed from the vestry-room, leaning
on a staff, for he refuses all other aid, was touching
in the extreme. His patriarchal figure, and silver
hair, and benevolent, tranquil features, more especially as he kneeled at the altar, or sat down in his
crimson, mitred chair, formed a picture worthy of
the pen of Scott, or the pencil of Rembrandt."

Another, written, I presume, during the same
visit, though undated, touches on many points of interest : —

U. S. HOTEL, PHILADELPHIA, *Saturday Morning.*

MY DEAR AUNT, ETC., — Spite of all my good resolutions, I am afraid I shall come to the practice of scribbling you a letter every morning and ruining you with postage. But Bardie says he will pay all, so here we go.

Our first move yesterday morning after breakfast was through the snow to call, by appointment, upon Mr. Vaughn, who, an old bachelor of three-score years and ten, like his brother in London, lives, they say, to do good. As secretary of the Literary and Philosophical Society, his chambers are in their building. I found him with a book in his hands, in which he was ruling a line for me to write my name as a visitor of the institution. I begged him to rub it out as I always wrote crooked with such aids. I then scored my name just under, as I observed, that of Miss Martineau. This reminded me of her letter, so off we set to call upon her. On our way we stopped to see West's great picture. It is unquestionably his best, but still, in my opinion, a moderate production. Compared with the pictures of the old masters, it is tame and cold both to the eye and mind. It wants power in the conception, skill in the grouping, spirit in the expression, and brilliancy in coloring; it is like a painstaking poet alongside of Shakespeare. I know you think this nonsense, but wait till you go to Italy and you shall judge for yourself. I take credit for saving this from destruction, for, from a broken window, the snow was driving upon it in a way that would soon have given it at least one of the merits of the old pictures.

On reaching the residence of Mr. Furniss, I sent up my card, was introduced and received by a gentleman, who, when Miss Martineau entered a minute after, disappeared. I was agreeably impressed by her appearance and manner, her pleasing countenance, fine eye, and sweet voice. The intercourse was by the trumpet, which, after all, is not so bad. At first it was rather awkward to look in her face and speak in the trumpet, and sometimes I reversed the order, and spoke to her face and looked in the trumpet. But practice makes perfect, especially the willing scholar, so an hour made me quite an adept. What we said, Bardie heard, so, although I do not write it, you may stretch your faith and believe it was nothing wrong ; like all her country, she disdains to inquire ; she means well, however, and I gave her a little of that commodity, I so often deal in, — plain advice, — the results she is to report at the college next summer.

Dined at home, and the afternoon passed at the Athenæum, which is worth a hundred of ours because people are in earnest in the support of it. At seven dressed for a ball, with two engagements between. The first was the Philosophic Society, where we met some old and made some new friends. Among them was Duponceau, who grows old. " Was I thirty years younger," said he, " I should come on to New York and offer myself to my sweetheart, Miss —— ; tell her so." — "Not I," was my answer, "for I fear she will waive the condition, and then we lose her." Among the "bores" that I fell upon was an English doctor, who cures all with the stomach-pump, the theory of which he plied with such success upon me that it came near producing the natural effect, but I fortunately escaped in time. Our next visit was to the lèvee of a great Quaker nabob, Mr. Dunn, who opens his *salon* and library to company every Friday. We adjourned to it in force, Walsh, Colonel Drayton, Dr. Julius, and myself. And here I found Mr. Biddle, the head of the monster, who, taking me aside, not, as you might suppose, for the purpose of devouring me, established me in a snug corner where we had a long talk. But my own I find is too long or my paper too short, so the *finale* I must leave to my next, and tell you what you value most, something about Bard. He is well in health and well in spirits. I put him on his mettle. To the ladies I introduce him as a young beau, to the politicians as a young diplomat, to Mr. Biddle as a young banker, and to jurists as a young lawyer, so he has to rub himself up. In truth he makes his own way well, and I think will soon be off my hands in the way of guidance. He receives as much attention as will do him good. But I am not afraid of conceit. Your fears, I know, are more awake for me than him, and though I do confess myself a little younger in some points, yet still, for good, I trust I shall never be old.

> Since life is thought, then think I will
> . That youth and I are housemates still.

A happy Christmas again to you and all my dear children.   J. McV.

The vacation life at Constableville, during these busy years, was all that could be desired. It gives a happy and gratifying picture of successful efforts on the part of my father to assume among his children a mother's duties as well as his own. Writing to Miss Bard in 1834, he says: —

"Comforts accumulate the longer we stay. The piano arrived in perfect order, and is a great addition to our pleasures. As it came on Saturday evening, its first use was its best, that of a hymn of thanksgiving on Sunday morning, which is now a regular part of our morning devotions, in which our children all unite with, I believe, heartfelt sincerity."

In 1835, to the same: —

" Our habits are domestic as usual. After reading I go out of my room about seven o'clock, prayers and breakfast by eight, housekeeping and music for girls till about ten. I will not say that we always get down to reading aloud and drawing so soon as that, for H—— has fixed up his target, and, with the Swiss bows and arrows which have just arrived, there is a strong temptation to pass half an hour in archery, but down to reading we get at last, while some draw and others work. We shall soon take up the ' Life of Mackintosh' and the new Reviews. By one o'clock there is some ride in agitation or perhaps already in execution, and by two or half past we are ready to obey the dinner bell. Our afternoons are more diversified, and music, reading, and the hay-field, or a little good hard work carry on the day. After tea we adjourn to the north parlor, where is our sofa and piano, both of which are, I assure you, in good use."

In 1836, also to the same : —

" We have just finished reading the 'Life of Mackintosh.' It has both raised and lowered my opinion of him. Few men have labored more strenuously against constitutional indolence. He had great kindness of heart, but he lived too much on others' good opinions to be esteemed a great man.

" Yesterday I took an exploring turn to the limits of settlement on the hills. Knowing that there was a school-house there I took a bundle of tracts, etc., for premiums, but unfortunately found neither mistress nor scholars there. It did not prevent me, however, giving a silent lesson. In the middle of the room stood a table, with a terrific rod standing erect in it, stuck in a hole for that purpose. I took away the rod, and in its place substituted my pile of little books."

These were days of happy refreshment, and they were needed, for sorrow and bereavement were again knocking at the door. Samuel Bard McVickar, my father's eldest son, was a young man of uncommon promise. From a large class in Columbia he had carried off, each year, the gold medal of superiority in everything, and, in 1835, had graduated with the highest honors of the college. During the tour for health and recreation, which followed shortly on his graduation, preparatory to entering on a position of trust which had already been offered to him, he was taken ill. A few lines from my father show the spirit with which such news was then and ever received by him : —

My very dear Son, — I write this in humble confidence in a gracious Father, that you are well enough to relieve us of our great anxiety, but, sick or well, H—— comes to entertain you and nurse you, and bring you back again, if that is thought best, well and happy. I comfort myself and all around me with that *Word* which is our comfort in sorrow, and, I trust, our guide in health. "I will not be afraid of evil tidings ; my heart standeth fast and believeth in the Lord." . . . . God bless you, my dear son ; all send prayers and good wishes, and if these might avail you, your sickness would soon be past, and I trust they do prevail and that you are well. So prays
Your affectionate father,
J. McV.

Two years of uncertain health were granted, when, on another absence from home in search of healthful occupation, the following message had to be sent by an absent father, who had not been able to reach his bedside of severe illness as early as others of the family.

"Should he yet be spared to your tender cares say to him that my blessing rests upon him, and that I am hastening to him ; that my comfort, like his, is not of this world ; and that I part with him as a child called home from wandering in a weary land."

He was again spared to reach the home circle at Constableville, but nothing more. He lingered awhile amid scenes whose retrospect is filled with spiritual happiness, and then passed away.

The calm but sorrowing circle thus broken again, was soon joined by one who felt that all its sorrows as well as joys belonged of right to her, the venerable Miss Sally Bard, whose acquaintance the reader has already made in the course of these pages. She was now in her eighty-second year, and it had been considered that the journey, a long and toilsome one at that time, was too much for her strength and years. Staying at Hyde Park, her anxiety for one whom she regarded as a son, had been very harrowing; but when the blow came, as always seemed her experience, faith spread its shield, and it fell in blessings. The following is the entry in her diary after hearing the sad news:—

"*August* 12, 1837.— After my above anxious utterances of yesterday, I received from my dear Mr. McVickar, that his beloved son was at rest, more than at rest, in the happiness of paradise. All his sickness, pain, and struggles over, all now joy, and peace, and thanksgiving. O let us dwell upon His mercies who gave us such children, who, in life and death, were equally a blessing to us. I pray that their heaven-supported father may be long sheltered under the wings of his Saviour, for the guidance and comfort of his remaining children, before he is called away to perfect happiness above. And, for myself, with a grateful heart I praise thy holy name, for the peace I feel within me, *thy Peace*, let me not be presumptuous in believing, for it surely is not my own."

My father, feeling her loneliness, separated from those she most loved, went at once to Hyde Park, and finding her not only willing but anxious to attempt the journey, immediately returned with her. On the 22d, in clear and beautiful handwriting, she makes the following entry in her diary:—

"I am once more at Turin, returned from Hyde Park with my dear Mr. McVickar; the fatigue was less than I expected, and I have the comfort of being again with my beloved family and received by my dear children with surprise and joy; but O, how I missed one dear face, ever lit up with smiles to receive and welcome me. Yet, let me contrast his present happiness with all this world could give, in its brightest forms, and, instead of repining, bow with heartfelt gratitude to Him who, in mercy, took him from pain and disease and all the vicissitudes and trials of this life, an early offering to his Saviour, to live with Him in endless felicity, and, I trust, to be in sweet communion with beloved ones gone before."

This entry in her diary—a diary of twenty-six years—was the last she ever made. Though apparently in her usual health when she arrived, she soon began to fail, and within a few weeks passed calmly away, to enter upon the reality of those blessings which had so long been hers through faith, and to rejoin the many loved ones whose peaceful departure she had witnessed.

Thus broke away, within a few weeks of each other, from the home-circle, the first-born son, whose opening promise of twenty-three summers was such a bond upon the future, and the aged, motherly aunt, of eighty-two years, whose sympathies in times gone by so bound my father to the past. That he felt both losses deeply, though so different in their character, is unquestioned, but the chief way he showed it was in an increased devotion to the daily duties of his actively useful life.

At the invitation of the Alumni Association of Columbia College, he delivered before them, in October of this year, an address which " The New York American " characterizes as " one of the happiest efforts of one of our best writers." Though several subjects are introduced, among them a sketch of the life and character of his predecessor in the chair of Moral Philosophy, the Rev. Dr. Bowden, the evident object of the address is to urge the establishment, by an Alumni endowment, of a Professorship of the Evidences of Christianity. The matter, in its proposed form, came to nothing, but in substance it was a success, my father having, with the permission of the trustees, immediately, without compensation, assumed the duties. He continued them until the readjustment of the chairs of the college in 1857, when that of the " Evidences " was not only made distinct, but placed first in the list, and my father appointed its first professor.

Written over thirty years ago, this address suggests principles in the study of the Evidences, the truth and importance of which the scientific advances of to-day have simply settled. Witness the following short extracts : —

" The truth of the Bible is a question of evidence cumulative ; not only does its testimony come from every quarter of human knowledge, but it grows and advances with it. It stands, therefore, among the sciences of progressive discovery; day by day its limits are enlarging ; its materials accumulating, and its arguments strengthening. There is no science but brings tribute to it, no branch of learning but bears fruit for it, no discovery, whether of ancient or modern research, but throws some new light upon it. The astronomer, as he watches in the heavens nebulæ of light centring into suns ; the geologist, as he demonstrates out of organic remains the progressive order of creation ; the naturalist, in detecting the edible grasses growing wild on the mountains of Central Asia ; the historian, as he traces up the origin of nations to their common cradle ; the philologist, in following up affiliated languages till at last they stand side by side, alike and yet different, like dissevered rocks which some great organic convulsion of nature had split asunder, leaving an unbridged chasm ; the ancient scholar, recovering some lost passage of Berosus, verifying the Mosaic record ; the antiquarian, reëstablishing, by means of a coin, the impeached veracity of St. Paul, — all bear upon the Bible, and require in the teacher as varied learning to keep pace with the progress of science, and to collect, arrange, and enforce its scattered evidences."

" All truth is ONE, and, come from what source it

may, can never be at variance with itself. As with the rays of solar light, so with those of truth. However bent or reflected, they are traceable back to one centre; however colored, they are still but elements of one primitive, pure beam. With our limited powers of vision, we see truth but in fragments, and to them give the name of varied sciences; but could we, from some loftier stand, take them all in at one comprehensive glance, we would see them to be but parts of one great science — but radii of one circle, of which nature is the circumference, and God the centre."

During these years, which were, in truth, among the most actively employed and influential of my father's life, I find myself, as his biographer, reduced to very scanty material. Bundles of letters from foreign and home correspondents, especially from Sir Robert Inglis and Archbishop Whately, suggest sources of information which it has been found impossible to obtain. I therefore confine myself to the few salient points of interest which appear above the natural level of a very busy academic and Church-society life. Among these stands out with some prominence the question of the Christian character of the philosophy of Coleridge.

Coleridge and his philosophy were becoming at that time as nearly popular, both in England and this country, as such a writer and such subjects can ever be. Not that all agreed with him or even understood him, but he was read widely and his works were producing considerable influence, especially on youthful

thinkers.   The " Aids to Reflection " had been
brought to the notice of the American public in
1829 by an edition published at Burlington, Vt.,
with a thoughtful Preliminary Essay by Dr. Marsh,
of the University of Vermont.   The "Churchman,"
of New York, then ably edited by Dr. Seabury, had
given in its almost unconditional approval to both
Coleridge and his school of thought.   My father, too,
was an admirer of much that he had written, and of
the high spiritual tone of his philosophy ; but he was
never a wholesale approver of any human system,
and in this of Coleridge he thought he saw much of
danger to the simplicity of Christian faith.   He
therefore unhesitatingly sounded the note of warning,
and wrote for the columns of the " Churchman "
strictures on what he thought was a " communication " too indiscriminate in its praise.   The supposed
communication turned out to be from the editorial
pen, and my father thus found himself involved in
what is always hazardous, an editorial controversy.
The following opening of his next communication
will show how wisely and delicately he conducted it,
while it may give us a lesson which the controver-
sialists of the present day would do well to study : —

Mr. Editor, — Had I recognized your pen in
the recent eulogium in your paper on ' The Coleridge Philosophy,' I had probably been more cautious
of entering on that contested field, as I esteem it
alike discourteous and unsafe to attack an editor in
his own columns.   It is not, therefore, in acceptance

of your chivalric challenge that I renew the subject.
Because you look at the *golden* side of the image
and I at the *brazen* is no reason why, knight-errant-
like, we should draw swords on that grave question ;
at least not until we have looked on both sides, and
settled by mutual examination whether the precious
or the baser metal preponderates in the image that has
been set up, and before which some are but too well
inclined, when they hear the trumpet sounded, to fall
down and worship.   Nor shall we, I think, differ in
our conclusions, for I never yet knew difference in
men's estimate of things to be more than skin-deep,
provided there was equal knowledge and sincerity —
the *latter* qualification for peace I am sure there is ;
to attain the *former*, I herewith give you my views
on the subject, in order that, if incorrect, they may
be amended, or if imperfect, enlarged ; being fully
satisfied of the general conclusion that they who
mean well, end, in the long run, in thinking right.

The concluding lines of this communication suggest the danger which, in spite of his own admiration, was ever present to my father's mind in connection with the works of Coleridge, and the fear of
which led him, perhaps, into some unphilosophic
statements : —

" I fear, Mr. Editor, this error ; that of leading
the unlearned to think that human philosophy is to
come in aid of Scriptural revelation, and that the
education of the Christian is to be esteemed imperfect till he has been taught to fathom the depths of

Coleridge or the bottomless abstractions of the German school."

There is a confusion here which displays the weak point in my father's side of this argument. Because the education of the Christian, as such, may not be deemed imperfect through ignorance of human philosophy, it does not, therefore, follow, as he maintains, that human philosophy may not come to the aid of Scriptural revelation. Philosophy and revelation are as two parallel streams : the former fed by innumerable tributaries does still, left to itself, lose itself in the sands of finite speculation ; while the latter, issuing from a single spring, flows undiminished into the eternal rock. Unite them in their early course, and revelation, as well as philosophy, is the gainer : human philosophy, by being preserved from ultimate failure ; and revelation, by being brought to sweeten and strengthen new and lifeless soils.

It would seem as if Coleridge maintained the first of these, as I believe, erroneous propositions, that " revelation *needs* philosophy ; " while my father, in combating it, fell somewhat into the second, that " philosophy can give *no* aid to revelation."

But he was a real lover of all true philosophy, and hence of all the philosophic truths of Coleridge, and it grieved him to see, as he thought, the streams of his influence perverted. This led to a second American edition of the " Aids to Reflection," with a preliminary essay by himself. In it he gives all due honor to Dr. Marsh, the former editor, but maintains that Coleridge cannot be properly understood, or his philosophy wisely studied, except in the light of the faith of the Church of England, of which he was a conscientious member. This was true, but the pressing of it offended minds that were philosophic rather than religious, and gave rise to considerable controversy, and perhaps laid my father open to the charge of some inconsistency.

Henry Nelson Coleridge, the literary executor and first editor of his uncle's works, writing under date of April, 1840, says, " Your preface is very spirited, eloquent, and likely to popularize the volume to readers generally, especially to such of them as are members of the Church of England." And again in August, 1840, " I confess I greatly regret the party character which seems to have attached itself to the two editions to the ' Aids to Reflection.' S. T. C.'s personal habits and sympathies were those of a member of the Church of England ; but his support of it will be found in principle and by influence, and not so much in direct advocacy or defense."

I turn from this little cloud of literary controversy, which was to my father neither common nor congenial, to give a single home letter of this period to show how fully, when absent, he strove to contribute to that fund of family cheerfulness which was ever with him as well a promoter as an evidence of Christian faithfulness : —

Tremont House, Boston, *Tuesday.*

Before I can sleep in peace I must have a little chat with those I love best, that what we enjoy they may enjoy too.   So now for our journey.   Our boat was a splendid one, the afternoon delightful ; F——— in good humor, I not in bad, so we get on pretty well.   And it was well that we were something to each other, for there was nobody else to be anything to us—not a face I had seen before or ever care to see again.   Mr. Goodhue had told me of a Mr. Jackson, of Lowell, on board, whom I would find intelligent, and described him as a gentleman with green spectacles.   As a matter of curiosity, not because I needed him, F——— and I speculated for him among our fellow-passengers.   There were two competitors for the description,— each near it.   One a bandy-legged, long-bodied man, whose fingers came within twelve inches of the deck, with white spectacles and large, green blinders, like a horse that is apt to be frightened ; the other gaunt and tall with glasses, however blue, rather than green.   What between their physiognomies and their dubious claims, I did not trouble them with a new acquaintance.   On going to pay our passage I found the captain's window barred by a new obstacle.   An old woman, in paying her fare, whether from hardness of hearing or anxiety to see that her change was right, had climbed up, forced head and shoulders through, and when I reached it hung about fairly balanced, half in and half out, while the impatient crowd around waiting for their turn were about in an equal balance which way they should help her.   .   .   .   .

To make up old scores, I lay late this morning, and on reaching the parlor, found Dr. Wainwright and his daughter awaiting our appearance. F——came out at the same time, and we had plenty of talk while a nice breakfast was making ready, which (I would add for the reputation of our health) we greatly enjoyed. Our kind friend, Mr. Ward, had last night planned Lowell for us to-day ; so at eleven he called, in his carriage with his daughter, for us and Mr. Stevens, who, with his two boys, made up the party. We joined the cars at the bridge, set off like the wind, and uncommoded by noise, dust, or ill-humor, and having got but half through a good, long, cheerful argument upon which we had entered, we found ourselves twenty-five miles from Boston, in the midst of this little " Manchester " of six years' growth. Though composed entirely of factories and the dwellings of the operatives, I beg you not to think it either dirty or disagreeable. I assure you it is neither ; but neat, clean, and airy. The young girls were just marshaling back to the mills in troops and bands, looking cheerful and healthy. But factories are things you care nothing about and I not much, that is to say, out of political economy. So after a nice little dinner, we resumed our seats at three o'clock in our flying vehicle, and a few minutes after four were again at home, thus having in less than five hours travelled over fifty miles, visited as many manufacturing rooms, eaten a quiet, comfortable dinner, and had two hours of unrestrained, hearty talk, and all without fatigue. So much for the march of improvement ! Mrs. Webster, I forgot to tell you, I called on this morning. She set off for New York an hour

after, and expressed much regret on F——'s account.
After escorting F —— to Mrs. Wainwright's, where
was a little party of young folks, my engagements
were to sit an hour with Mr. Bowditch, and an hour or
two more with one of their scientific clubs. With Mr.
Bowditch I was delighted ; he reminded me strongly
of Dr. Rush in look and manner ; cheerful, intelligent,
and warm-hearted, I could hardly break away, and
have promised to call again.   The club they call the
" *Old* Club." It is one of the applications of the epithet
with which I will not quarrel — but — good-night —
with every prayer of love for you all — good-night.

Such is a letter both unsigned and undated, though
belonging to about this period, which is characteristic
of the happy way in which, when absent, my father
made those that were left behind to feel that they
were not forgotten, and thus ever to insure for himself a hearty welcome home, — a home which, from
this time forth for eight long years, was to have in it
the room of the helpless, though bright and cheerful
invalid.   Never was a sick-room that had a happier
influence, and my father, like all others who strove
to brighten its inmate, had to confess that more
was received than given. Yet this was but the
true reflection of his own teaching.   Absent from
home when the stroke of threatened illness came,
he writes to the one thus afflicted : " Life passes
quickly, and what does it leave behind worth having,
but a Christian's peace and hope. Bear up, then, my
dear daughter ; all is for the best to those who sub-

mit themselves in faith. The day before us is our life. What to-morrow will bring forth, whether health or sickness, who knows save He who orders all for the final good of those who love and trust Him."

In obituary notices, whether of the tongue or pen, my father was remarkably happy, and ever ready at the call of friendship. The following from an ex-tempore address in moving the resolutions of respect on the death of Rev. Dr. Bayard will help to fill out his portrait in this respect, and recall to many the mingled grace and earnestness of his public speaking : —

. . . . " The impression, Mr. Chairman, our friend ever left was that of a true-hearted man, the rarest and the noblest picture which our formalized, degenerate days can exhibit. There was in him a certain honest simplicity and right-mindedness which gave fearlessness to the whole character — the union, I might almost say, of the child and the lion. But what I may well say is, that it was, in human measure, 'that single eye' which our Lord had blessed, and of which the promise was, in our friend, in due meas-ure, fulfilled, that 'the whole body should be full of light.' His heart it was that doubled the powers of his head, and the sincerity and directness of his speech went home to the conviction, even beyond his argument. Now, Mr. Chairman, far beyond all intellectual power do I honor, nay, reverence such a man ; for, inasmuch as the primal curse of our na-ture was the severance of the conscience from the reason, and of the heart from the head of man, so too do I seem to see in every such instance of true-hearted character, the type of man's better nature appearing, the anticipated restoration rather, through grace, of the once defaced image of God in our souls.

"I have said that sincerity doubled his powers. The assertion reminds me of the reply of Mirabeau in reference to one whom he feared, ' I stand in awe,' said he, ' of that man, for he believes every word that he says.' Now, such was our lamented brother. He spoke not the word that he believed not, therefore were his words living words, and had power, for they came home to our inner and better nature. He ever spoke what he thought, and he thought what his conscience made him feel to be true, and right, and just. No man, therefore, doubted him, no man distrusted him, no honest heart ever feared him, and no kind and good heart, that knew him, but loved him. Such was our lamented friend in my eyes; and in the course of an experience, now not a short one, never have I met with a man who bore more visibly stamped upon him, what with reverence I may term Heaven's broad seal — the stamp of TRUTH."

It was in the year 1843 that my father, as superintendent of the " Society for the Promotion of Religion and Learning," brought forward, with the approbation of the Society, his " plan for ministerial education." Up to this time, the funds of the Society, and of the Church, had been distributed by favor, to what were called "beneficiaries," young men recommended by others as fit recipients of the Church's aid. This was, by the proposed plan, changed in principle, and all aid was henceforth to be given only to "scholars" who had borne off the prize in open competition among those whose otherwise good character had admitted them to the trial. The system was not to stop at the Seminary, where a room, free education, and two hundred dollars a year was the prize; this, by special agreement, was to be competed for in a number of our first class colleges; while free education at these same colleges, and a one hundred dollar stipend, was set before the schools; and in the schools themselves, free education and forty dollars a year was an open prize to the best scholar among those whose parents desired them to look to the Church as their profession. This "plan," with such modifications as the practical experience of its working has rendered necessary, has ever since been the system of the "Society for the Promotion of Religion and Learning," whose wisely administered and largely increased funds has made it so efficient a helper to Church education in the State of New York. There is one feature, however, which seems to have been entirely dropped, and the neglect of which is sufficient to account for the burden of the society's annual complaint against the parishes that they take so little interest in aiding by their contributions the spread and increase of its efficient labors. This feature is provided for in the fourth section of the adopted plan — as follows:

"Of the parochial collections or contributions of the diocese, required by canon, one half thereof, if desired by the parish, to be annually funded by the society and placed to the credit of the contributing church, towards the foundation of a perpetual scholarship, to be known forever, when completed, under the name of said church, and the presentation to be vested in its rector or corporation, subject, as above, to the rules and regulations of the society."

In enlarging upon this feature of the plan in the columns of the "Churchman," he maintains, — "1. That it will identify the interests of ministerial education with the interests and feelings of the diocese at large. And, 2. That it will lead to the establishment of the higher classical schools in connection with parishes and under the control of their respective rectors." And in speaking of its ultimate results, he says : —

"Thus no parish in the diocese will be without its organized parochial school ; no school without its perpetual scholarship, no scholarship without its openly tried and worthy scholar; and no scholar in any part of the diocese, however poor or destitute of friends, but seeing before him through these open prizes, the path of advancement up to the very portals of the Church he loves, provided he can but make good his superior claims, step by step, in open competition.

"But if in derogation of such glowing picture, it be objected that it is a far distant one, the churchman's answer is: Nothing is far distant in the policy

of the Church that is progressive and certain. As
the Church has no limited duration, so neither is
the question of time to determine her course. All
that is needed for the Church's decision is, that her
plans be true in principle, and that they work forward on the great moving springs of our nature.
All the rest she leaves in confidence to God's blessing, who demands from man the use of means, but
not the results of them."

"No. 8 College Green," the old familiar city residence of Professor McVickar, where he lived for forty
years, until the college buildings were pulled down,
and the goodly home and academic neighborhood of
Park and College Place given up to business, was the
scene of much pleasant and intellectual society. "The
Club," as it was called and familiarly known by old
New Yorkers, met there regularly in its appointed
turn. It was a dignified assemblage, as I remember
it in my youthful days, confined to twelve members,
and composed of such men as Peter Jay, Judge
Kent, Dr. John A. Smith, etc., and the rule of the
club that each member may bring to the meeting one
distinguished stranger, insured always sufficient
novelty to keep the conversation fresh, and make
this weekly gathering one of real interest. At one
of these meetings at our house, the present Ex-
Emperor of France was a guest, and I have often
heard my father tell in a tone of amusement, of his
serious use on that occasion of the following argument against the employment of paper money, in his
somewhat broken English: "I go out shooting, I

load my gun, I put my hand in my pocket for a wad,
I ram it down, I fire off my gun, and then I say,
Bah ! I've fired off ten dollars.'' And this at a time
when ten-dollar bills were not plentiful with the
ambitious adventurer, whose subsequent course has
drawn so marked a line over the historic page of
Europe.

Letters of introduction from English friends also
brought to that old house pleasant guests. Charles
Dickens was the bearer of such a letter from Mr.
John Kenyon, a short extract from which will be
of interest, as giving the English estimate of this great
author, in 1841, and more especially as telling us
something about Mrs. Dickens, whose misfortune it
would seem to have been to be a retiring, simple-
minded lady.

. . . . . " My object in this is to introduce to
yourself and family, including my young friend
Henry, your son, who should come and see us again,
Mr. and Mrs. Dickens. I will say nothing of him
of whom all Europe, and further countries, ring from
side to side, — as they ought, of a man who employs
so much genius in the service of all humanities and
all generosities, — but would more particularly introduce Mrs. Dickens to you as one of those unpresuming
spirits who will make no claims for herself. And one
claim which I will make for her is, that she is the
granddaughter of Mr. Thomson of Edinburgh, still
alive, the dear and kindly friend of him who had few
peers among men of genius, (Coleridge used, I remember, to put him as one of the four great poets of

the world) — of Burns.   They are going southward,
where I have no friends.   What I wish to procure
for them on their journey is not the opportunity of gay
society, of which they will have more than enough,
but to give them, and more particularly Mrs. Dickens, the opportunity of knowing a few quiet, friendly
persons, who will offer quiet conversation and any information which may be useful, more particularly to
a lady travelling in a new country."

CHAPTER XIX.

MY father had now reached his fifty-sixth year ; a time of life when most men, if they do not think of rest, do still hesitate about adding to their work. Yet we find him this year accepting the chaplaincy of Fort Columbus in the harbor of New York.

He had always been fond of parochial work, and was not only ever ready to assist his brother clergymen, but constantly went out of his way to do so; generally singling out those, whether young or old, whom he had reason to believe were over-worked. A friend and relative knowing his feelings in this respect, and being also acquainted with the officers of this post, mentioned his name and secured his appointment. This unexpected proffer of missionary work, for it was really such, the performance of which was rendered possible by residence at the post not being required, came during the college vacation, and my father accepted and entered upon it at once. He probably never gave a thought to the possibility of its concerning any one but himself. But to the College authorities it appeared differently, and some pressure was brought to bear upon him to induce him to give it up, as inconsistent with his professorial position and the rules of the college. This he stoutly refused to do, and said he would resign his professorship rather than the chaplaincy with its hard work among the soldiers, and its seven hundred dollars a year salary. The old professor, for he had long been the senior member of the board, and had now held his chair for over a quarter of a century, triumphed ; but by some the offense was never forgiven. It was a case where the official red tape failed to appreciate the presence of a higher law. To have insisted on the professor resigning' this work, thus undertaken with the most disinterested motives, would have been to injure his moral self-respect, and thus cause a disadvantage to the college greater than any distraction of thought or absorption of leisure time caused by the new duty. This at least was true of a professor of his years and standing, whatever it might be in the case of one just entering on his duties.

.Fort Columbus was then the great recruiting depot of the United States army, and its chaplain was thus brought in contact with the soldier when most susceptible to his influence. His quarters, unneeded for residence, were soon made the receptacle of lending and gift libraries, for the replenishing of which nearly every publisher in the city was put under contribution, and most of whom gladly responded. Not a soldier left the post under orders without the offer of a Bible and a Book of Common Prayer ; and not an officer who had shown interest in his services, without being taken to his quarters and made to select some work from the library as a memento of their intercourse.

On first entering upon his duties, the chaplain found no place set apart for public worship, except the large room used on week-days as the business office of the post ; and on several Sundays business requirements forced them to vacate even this and go to an inconvenient upper room for service. This quickly determined him to make an effort for a chapel, but he found the matter surrounded with apparently insurmountable difficulties. Government was not accustomed to build chapels ; nor was it willing either to make an appropriation for the purpose, or to allow others, even if prepared, to build on government ground. But there was determined perseverance on the one side, and probably friends at court on the other ; not least among the latter being the then commander-in-chief of the army, General Scott. The result was a personal lease from the government of about one hundred and fifty feet square, on the south side of the island, subject to the exigencies of war ; and within the year, the completion of a most tasteful and church-like building of wood, after my father's own plans, and from funds given and collected by himself. Writing to his eldest son, then a missionary near Lake George, he says : —

" My church goes on beautifully. It grows upon me every time I see it. It has, beyond any little church I know, the two elements I want in a rural house of God — humility and reverence. These are both strongly awakened, and when summer comes you cannot imagine a more beautiful spot. It is true it is something against architectural rule, but I have chosen to work rather with the ' elements ' than under ' models,' and thus to work out the same problem by original methods. I look to the effect, and work it out as I can. This is *great* talk for a little church, but I think you will like it. As to cost, it will sum up when finished to near $2,500. What I can raise by the help of friends I will; what I cannot I must bear, and hold it a consecrated gift, laid on God's altar, a trespass-offering for years of over-devotion to the acquisition of wealth."

This last sentence seems to demand some word of explanation, for if my father be right in representing his life as one of " over-devotion to the acquisition of wealth," then is his biographer at fault in failing, as he knows he has, in so presenting it. But the truth of the case is this. My father, as a political economist, had a clear and far-seeing head in all matters of business, which sometimes led him to make investments which required more business devotion than he ever considered himself justified, as a clergyman, in giving to them, and which, on this very account, became sources of annoyance and perplexity. A case in point was his purchase of the whole north side of Union Square in this city, at the time of the laying out of that square. He saw clearly its future importance, but he did not, perhaps, sufficiently calculate the heavy drain from taxes and assessments which must precede the attainment of its present value, a yearly rental, within thirty years, of more than what the property then cost. The worry and anxiety connected with this purchase, which he was not able to hold, and some speculative investments made in the West, is translated by him into " over-devotion to the acquisition of wealth," and brings forth the following self-condemnatory reflections written out at the close of his account book in 1845 : —

THOUGHTS ON CLOSING THIS ACCOUNT BOOK OF FIFTEEN YEARS.

COLLEGE, *February* 3, 1845.

I am glad to be able to close my eyes, not, I trust, my penitential thoughts, on this long arrear of worldliness and grasping desire of wealth, by transferring to a new book the few accounts that yet remain unsettled. The most of them, after tantalizing for a while with a restless show of profit, terminated in disappointment, and some in lawsuits. All the sorrows of my life from all other causes have not, I think, equaled those from this single source, namely, the speculative purchases into which I was led by persuasion, or perhaps self-prompted, in the years 1835, 1836, and 1837 ; as I verily believe they have brought upon me deeper guilt than any or all other temptations united. God be thanked. that I have survived the shock, the trial, and the disgrace, and that a remnant of days is yet spared me, with an humbler mind and higher hopes, and that God has at length called me to a spiritual charge wherein I may show the sincerity of my faith and repentance.

Through Christ may that call be blessed to me and those to whom I minister. Amen. So be it.

J. McV.

It is but right, as regards a just judgment of my father in this matter, to state that these " Western speculations " were entered into principally to give occupation to the invalid son whose death was lately noticed, and it was his death which threw the whole burden of their care upon one necessarily absent and fully engaged in other duties.

But to return to the little chapel at Governor's Island and the interests that centred around it. The war with Mexico breaking out at this time increased greatly the difficulties to be overcome. These were fully appreciated, as the following extract from a letter shows, on the army side : —

" To me, and I believe all of us, the interest of the Church is greatly enhanced by its erection in war times on the very scene of active preparation for distant service. It seems a happy omen of those times when war shall be known no more. That it is fairly erected and completed seems to me almost a miracle, and to you, dear sir, it must seem almost a creation. It has taught me a lesson in the power of faith and perseverance that I trust I shall never forget. Those of us who knew the peculiar and tormenting discouragements under which you labored, and which seemed to us insurmountable, cannot too highly appreciate a labor which not only benefits Governor's Island but the whole army."

An officer, writing from the far-off field of battle, says : " I am much pleased to hear of your final and complete success in building a church on the island, and shall place my small donation in your hands at the first good opportunity. May its hallowed walls echo back strains of pure devotion from the hearts and lips of its fortunate attendants, and may its erection prove the means of turning many from the power of Satan unto God. If it shall be my privilege to return again to the United States, it will arouse no ordinary feelings of emotion in my heart to enter into the courts of our little sanctuary, and there to join the voice of prayer and praise to Him who is the God of dangers and of protection. Be so kind, my dear sir, in your next letter, as to describe its position and its form, even in details."

Fort Columbus, as has been said, was the great recruiting depot of the army; the numbers, therefore, that came under the chaplain's notice in war times was greatly increased. As the common soldier is not generally considered very impressible, we may judge somewhat of the spiritual power of the work centring round this little chapel by knowing that it received several bequests from common soldiers dying in the hospitals of Mexico. The circle of its influence was a large one. The regiments were often changed, and when they were, a practical symbolism was enlisted to give permanency to the spiritual impressions already made. The communicants among the commissioned officers were assembled by the chaplain and requested to choose a Bible text which should be the motto of their regiment, this was then inscribed, with proper device and color, on a metal shield, with the name of the regiment, and solemnly hung on the walls of the chapel, a binding link to the absent, a suggestive subject of reflection to the present worshippers.

In July, 1849, writing to an absent son, my father says: "The little Church of St. Cornelius is growing in historic interest as well as beauty. The three successive commands of the island have all their mementos on its walls, — texts selected by them, with appropriate shields; and what is more satisfactory yet, I never had better attendance from the officers. College is now over; president and all but Dr. Anthon gone; we shall probably be quiet, and, with my island, not without work. Trinity Church, too, will be a resource; I have supplied the duty there for the last two days; I shall resume German, too, and look over my college notes. At any rate, *ars longa*. No difficulty in finding something to do."

An interesting episode occurred after the close of the Mexican War in the encampment, for a time, on the Island, of what was called the California Regiment of Colonel Stevenson. This was a semi-military colony, under government patronage, going to take practical possession of the newly acquired territory of California. The proposed expedition aroused all my father's clear-sighted zeal, both for the commonwealth and the Church. He saw how much of the future of California, civil and ecclesiastical, might depend on the character and moral impetus of these men. He knew that they were mostly adventurers, but he never doubted the germ of goodness within. He worked among them untiringly, and before they sailed, — they were going by the six months' voyage round the Horn,— he persuaded them to elect a chaplain, determine on daily prayers on shipboard, and take the nominal position at least of a God-fearing body. The American Bible Society and the New York Bible and Common Prayer Book Society were brought into requisition to enable him to make distribution to every man of a Bible and, to every one that desired it, a Prayer Book. This distribution was made the occasion of a farewell address, which, at the request of the officers, was printed and distributed among the men as a memento of home, for California was then a *terra incognita*, and felt to be, as it really was, very far away. The address was earnest and powerful throughout, and in parts, as in the following, rises to eloquence : —

" Even while I thus speak do I see her, the venerable Genius of our Anglo-Saxon land, the common mother of us all. I see her rise up from her watery throne, where she sits embosomed amid the peaceful fleets of an unbounded commerce, to bid you, her armed sons, farewell. I see her followed in dim procession by a long train of patriots, and heroes, and Christian men, — men who not only here but in older lands have toiled and fought and bled, not for conquest, but for right ; not for license, but for law, and that they might build up for posterity that which we here enjoy, a fair and, I trust, an enduring fabric of constitutional freedom. I see her form, I hear her words, and mine, believe me, are their faithful echo.

" ' Go forth,' she says, ' my well-armed sons — the sword in your hands, but peace in your hearts, and justice in your deeds. Go forth from this, my favored land, to bless those to which you go. Remember that you bear a widely honored name. It has ever been a lineage of faith and virtue, of courage and gentleness, of peace, of order, and of religion. Such has it been in the Old World ; such in the heroic times of the New. Let not its fair fame be tarnished, or its institutions defamed by unfilial hands or unworthy tongues. As you bear your country's ensign, so, remember, do you your country's honor. Let not the name of American citizen ever receive a blot through you. Let it not be said, that with Americans, might was the measure of right, or that gold outweighed justice, or that the soldier's sword made heavy the scale of a vanquished enemy's ransom. Rather let that name be known as one of blessing wherever it is heard, even as that of a teacher appointed of Heaven to instruct the nations of the earth ; to exhibit to the world the living proof how liberty may dwell united with law, how individual freedom may stand linked together with public order, and Christian faith in the nation walk hand and hand with an unfettered private conscience.' "

For the interests of the Church in the new territory, my father was equally clear-sighted. A letter from the quartermaster-general of the army informs him that his request has been granted, and that free passage will be given to two missionaries for California and Oregon. If the Church could have risen to the duty then pressed upon her, and consecrated a Whipple or a Morris as a bishop for the Pacific slope, and sent him, with two or three missionaries, to plant the good seed in the hearts of the children, and buttress the future Church with the waste acres that then surrounded the half-populated towns, the churches of California and Oregon might ere this have vied with the East in the missionary work of the centre of the Continent.

The following from Bishop Chase, two years after, shows how earnestly those efforts were continued, and how fully they were appreciated by one who had the largest experience in western missions: —

ROBIN'S NEST, ILL., *March* 17, 1849.

MY DEAR SIR, — Yesterday the " Banner of the Cross " reached us here in the far West, and few things gave me more pleasure to read, than the report of the General Missionary Society on the subject of California.   Your name as the chairman of that committee never before commended itself more to my warm approbation, than when I read it in connection with the noble stand taken in the body of the report. The hearty sincerity of what I now say, I trust will be impressed on your mind by a recollection of what passed in St. Bartholomew's Church on the subject brought forward by you and supported by my feeble voice, touching the duty of the Church's extending the benefit of our holy religion to the shores of the Pacific.   You then gave me the right hand of Christian fellowship; an event ever to be cherished in my memory as a pledge of better things to come.

Your affectionate friend and brother in Christ,

PHILANDER CHASE.

To the REV. DR. McVICAR.

My father did at the time what he could. Though many a well-tried man might have been willing to go as bishop, not from ambition, but because of the power it would give him to meet and overcome difficulties, one only offered to take the hard and depressing position of chaplain to a band of adventurers, and solitary missionary in a new land. And if future events have left the stigma of moral weakness, in the desertion of his sacred calling for a more gainful pursuit, upon the name of J. M. Leavenworth, it may still be a question, whether the Church, which allowed him to go single-handed into such a perilous contest, must not be willing to assume her share in the guilt of his fall. His first letter after arriving would seem to show that then, at least, he had good intentions and a clear head. I give it entire : —

SAN FRANCISCO, *May* 24, 1847.

REV. AND DEAR SIR, — A good Providence permits me to announce my safe arrival and prosperous beginning — when I can give my whole time to the duties of my holy calling. The Church will be well planted in Sonora, San Francisco, Puebla, and Monterey, with ample lands, and soon missionaries will be called for. Oregon calls aloud. Experiments

have well prepared the way for the Church. Will
the Church at home send $1,000 the current year to
California?   If so, whether for salary or donation
for churches, it will do what $20,000 will be required
for in three years from this.   There is no way of
locating lands in and near villages (future cities), but
by extinguishing titles now Mexican.   Soon it cannot be bought.   Under sound advice I can do great
things for the Church during the year.   In the name
of my Master, I ask of Churches to come to his help.

Respectfully and very truly yours,

J. M. LEAVENWORTH.

Rev. John McVickar, D. D.

P. S. — I have organized a Sunday-school in San
Francisco, and wait on God's good providence to sustain me and send me help.   I am alone, yet confident.
The courier for Monterey waits, leaving unexpectedly early, and I can only say I am sincerely and
truly yours,   J. M. L.

The removal of the " Depot " from Governor's
to Bedloe's Island in 1850, was very embarrassing
to the chaplain.   His duties went with the Depot, and
required him to go several miles further down the
bay in open barges to Bedloe's Island, while his heart
was with the little church he had built, and the permanent interests that had gathered round it on Governor's Island.   As was his custom, however, he
undertook the new duty with zeal, but did not let
go of the old.   A daughter writing from home shortly
after the change, says, —

" Father's return in safety from one or other of his islands each Sunday afternoon always appears to me a new and abundant source of gratitude, for he seems to spare himself no duty, and fear no personal exposure at a time of life when so many think that the call for exertion is over. His zeal in his missionary work, ' grows with what it feeds upon,' and whereas he says, formerly he was content with one jewel, now he has two, and he could not tell if called upon to give up one, which would be the dearest. Never, he says, did the church look more beautiful, nor the men work for it with a more loving zeal, and yet there is a daily prospect that every one of them may be ordered off."

In his public ministrations as a clergyman, in these chaplaincy duties, my father was effective, and always acceptable. His manner was dignified yet simple, his offering of the prayers reverential, and his reading of the Scriptures perfectly natural and effective. There were probably few better readers in the diocese. In the pulpit he had the rare gift of always adapting himself to his hearers and his occasion, and seldom failed to awaken sympathy of feeling. As a general rule, his sermons at this time, were extempore, though not always. Latterly, however, they became entirely so from increased nearness of sight, and the impossibility of reading his own much interlined manuscripts. From a sermon on the Fourth of July, 1846, I take the following as an example of this adaptation of subject to

21

occasion, as well as because it embodies interesting personal recollections of Governor Jay.

"Of the pure and self-denying character of Jay, could I speak more largely than time here admits, for I saw him intimately during many of his closing years. Suffice it to say the patriotism of Jay was the patriotism of a Christian. He knew but one law of right — that was the Gospel. He acknowledged but one teacher, one ruler — that was Christ, his Master in heaven, speaking in His Word and through his conscience. Out of this faith, as from a fountain-head, sprang all the virtues of his character. As he truly feared God, so did he fear nothing else. He never feared the face of man, nor did he the frown of power, nor the proscription of party. He set his course, and that was heavenward, and then bade the world go by. Therefore was it that his patriotism stood like a rock, against which the waves of popular opinion beat as idly, throughout the course of his life, as had done the threats of unjust power at its beginning. Therefore, too, was his old age a peaceful and blessed one, not like that of too many, clinging on to public life till finally driven from it by younger and stronger hands; nor like others, retiring gloomily from scenes of public excitement, — but, like one who had been the Christian first, and the statesman afterwards, he retired the Christian, who, having fulfilled one task to which his God had called him, passes on to another, willingly, cheerfully, as following the same great leader; and that task was to him, as it should be to all, in the peaceful retirement of a Christian home, to prepare himself for the new and higher duties on which we may not doubt he has now entered.

" How deeply our country now needs more such rulers and more such examples, to keep us citizens of a later day up to its earlier heroic tone, it becomes not me to say ; but this at any rate is clear, that to remember we once had such pure and great men, and that they were the men by whom, under God, that national blessing was achieved which we have just celebrated, this cannot be a valueless recollection at any time, nor an unsuitable one now to be urged from a Christian pulpit."

Of his ministrations among the sick, it is sufficient to say that he was faithful, and never allowed personal fear, and seldom personal weariness, to interpose a barrier.   When the cholera was raging on the island in 1849, he writes to an absent member of his family: " Dr. —— I was with last night, who, both for his own sake and that of his family, is very dear to me.   I am afraid we shall lose him.   It has terminated in cholera, which has carried off so many.   I shall return after breakfast to a sorrowing, perhaps desolate house, but God's will be done.   It is painful beyond measure to lose, as I do, the mourners also, by their removal from my care and sympathy."

As I copy these lines, evidently written before breakfast, after an anxious night's visitation, and telling of the simple way in which the chaplain went in and out among his cholera sick, I am forcibly re- . minded of his devoted successor in the chaplaincy,

the Rev. Alexander Davidson, who has but just laid
down his young life, a sacrifice to the same sense of
duty, as he went in and out among the sick soldiers,
during the late prevalence of yellow fever on the
island.   His record as given by his commanding officer is a very noble one, and if imagination might be
allowed to picture choice meetings in the spirit world,
it would find here congenial material.

Many letters show the personal interest which my
father took in the new recruits, especially those who
had seen better days, and who, by misfortune or
wrong-doing, had been induced to enlist in the army.
Several, so situated, were through his influence at
Washington freed from their enlistment and restored
to their friends.   Foreigners also, who could neither
speak nor write English, but who were well educated,
and who from necessity had been forced to enlist,
often found in the Latin tongue a means of communication which must have been to them a great
comfort.   From several such preserved, written
generally on mere scraps of paper, suggestive of the
entire literary privation of the recruit's life, I tran-
scribe the following : —

DOMINE PASTOR, — Quod tibi scribo, excusa me.
Te rogare volui, ut tibi curam haberes pro me.   Ma-
jorem optare, ut me in Partem Permanentem trans-
ferret.   Simul curriculum vitæ meæ tibi refero, ut
de me judicare possis.

Filius pastoris, primarii Magdeburgiensis sum.   In
prima classe Gymnasii Latini Halberstadiensis ver-

satus sum.   Postea quinque annos mercator fui, in-
quibus Collegium Carolinum Brunoswigii visitavi.
Capitanus in bello Danico fui, et infelix fortuna poli-
ticio me in hanc partem mundi transtulit.

Non amicum, qui me novit, habeo.   Rogo ut tu
meum optatum audias.

CAROLUS ARMINIUS THRYHSSON.

The " permanent party " referred to in the above
was the permanent garrison of the island, the members of which were not liable to be sent to distant
posts, and had other privileges.   Only the best men
were put upon it, and it was considered an honor as
well as an advantage to belong to it.

These chaplaincy duties, running over a period of
eighteen years, having commenced with one war,
were destined to terminate with another.   My father's
feelings with regard to the War of the Rebellion are
well expressed in the following few lines of a home
letter: —

" *April* 17, 1861. — Our April has been stormy,
but less so than our national affairs.   It is a crisis I
could never have believed in, and even now can
scarcely realize; but it alters not our rule of life —
duty and Christian hope.   When earth is dark, we
must look to Heaven for light.   Civil war is upon us.
It might, perhaps, have been avoided, but must now
be met, and the Federal government supported at all
hazards and any cost.   We must now *conquer peace.*
The interval, long or short, will be one of trials and
self-denials such as we have not been accustomed to,

but, with a brave heart and God's blessing, we shall
go through them."

The following, on the same subject, and of about
the same date, is from one between whom and my
father there had grown up a warm attachment; and
the only justification offered for thus making public
a private letter, without the writer's leave, is, that by
his deeds and worth, he has allowed his name and
all that concerns it to become public property: —

Cresson Springs, Pa., July 22, 1861.

My dear Doctor, — Having a leisure moment
to-day I thought that I would write to you a few
lines. . . . . The telegram this morning reports a
great battle at and in the vicinity of Manassas Junc-
tion. I am very anxious to hear the result. I fear
that, in consequence of our having so few disciplined
troops, and so many officers who have had no experience, our losses will be very great. I feel that this
matter has been forced upon us — the firing upon my
little band at Fort Sumter opened a war from which
our government could not withdraw. Only one
course is now left for us, to meet all the responsibilities as becomes Christians and soldiers. That this
civil strife will be attended with incidents which will
sadden and sicken the firmest hearts, none who know
the decided and sternly bitter determination of our
Southern enemies, can doubt. I feel, and acknowledge too, that as a people, we have far forgotten our
God, and that we have justly incurred his wrath.
Let us pray that He will be, as He has ever shown

Himself, merciful to us, and that He will soon bring
hope and peace and love to our land again.   Mrs.
Anderson joins me in sincerest and warmest regards.

Ever yours truly,

ROBERT ANDERSON.

REV. JOHN MCVICKAR, D. D., *Chaplain U. S. A.,* New York.

The chaplain early asked and obtained permission
to visit and minister to the Southern prisoners who
were confined on the Island, and in the harbor of
New York ; and I judge by the many letters of
thanks from friends and interested persons that the
duty must have been kindly and faithfully performed.
Bishop Whittingham, writing on the 18th of September, 1861, says : —

"MY DEAR DOCTOR, — I was greatly pleased to
find how thoroughly you had anticipated all that I
wished to ask you in behalf of the erring men who
are now prisoners in the port of New York.   For the
kind way in which you meet my interference, and
the loving words in which you express yourself concerning it, I can only thank you with heartiest returns
of grateful affection."

On the 10th of September, 1862, a communication
was received from the commanding officer of the post,
in obedience to the new regulations of the War Department, requiring of the chaplain residence on the
Island.   It was one of the necessary changes in point

of strictness required by war times, but to my father
it came as a sort of death-blow. His varied duties
in New York city forbade his living out of it, and he
combated the order in every possible way, for his
heart was in his work among the soldiers, and though
in his seventy-fourth year he was not feeling old. I
have before me a paper in his handwriting, and
drawn up in legal form, entitled "Grounds for Relief," etc., giving under heads the various, and many
of them strong reasons, why this order should not be
binding in his case. But the War Department had
no time then to be looking into exceptional cases, consequently, when the order was repeated, my father
resigned, and the last settled ministerial work of his
life was brought to a close.

What was grief to him was secret joy to his family
and friends. They saw no prospect of voluntary
resignation on his part, yet they had felt for some
time that his age, and the value of his experience as a
counselor in the Church, made it important that this
duty of great exposure and hazard should be given
up. It was therefore looked at by them as a kind
providence, and my father soon came to acquiesce in
the view, settling, in its own way, a difficult problem.
Thus ended a phase in my father's life which stood
out with a distinctness that made it almost look like
the work of another man, and suggested that separate treatment which requires us now to take up
again the thread of his ordinary life, eighteen years
previous.

CHAPTER XX.

THE requirements of the invalid daughter, of whom mention has been made, led to the giving up of the Turin farm, as too far away, and the purchase of a small place on Staten Island. It was a comfort so far as it gave pleasure and enjoyment to the sick one, but beyond that it never went. This place never was a home, and after a few years, when the sufferer for whose gratification it had been purchased went to her rest, it was parted with without regret. The interests as well as duties of these years, from 1840 on to 1850, centred in the college and flowed out to the chaplaincy and Church societies. There was no lack of interest, however, in general matters, as evidenced by various articles in the current press, over the familiar signature of " M." To show how very familiar it was, and, consequently, how ready as a writer was my father in all the live interests of his day, I venture to quote the following *jeu d'esprit* from the " Churchman : " —

MR. EDITOR, — Having been complimented more than once since the appearance of the last " Churchman," by some friends who know my signature, on my change to *liberal Low-church* principles, it has forced so strongly on my mind the inconvenience resulting, at least to the writers themselves, from there being two contributors to the same paper under the same signature, that I have determined to trouble you and my namesake, " M.," with this notice of it. Hitherto, I am willing thankfully to acknowledge that the balance of divided merit arising from a common name has been greatly in my favor, inasmuch as it has been the means of gaining me credit with my friends, not only for many zealous and good articles which I did not write, but also for much poetry that I could not have written, the reputation of which, with the usual inconsistency of man, inasmuch as nature has denied me the faculty, I prize, even more, perhaps, than it deserves. But be that as it may, now that it has come to doctrine, that, I confess, is a nicer matter, and, as I can, to use a cant phrase, " pin my faith on no man's sleeve," I now feel myself forced, however unwillingly, thus publicly to renounce all claim to the aforesaid poetry, and to state that I am unwilling to undertake the responsibility of my brother M.'s Church opinions, as he doubtless has long been of my metaphysical lucubrations ; and if a mere personal question like this were worth the trouble I would request you to decide between us the priority of use, in order that one or the other might recede. As the world of *letters* lies free before us where to choose, the loss, on whichever side it fall, may be easily supplied ; and the poet comforts us with the assurance that " the rose by any

other name would smell as sweet." Much, therefore,
as I feel attached to my accustomed letter, inasmuch
as it seems to me like an old friend, and indeed to
an anonymous writer may be said to be his *only* one,
yet, valuing, as I do, the substance above the shadow,
and consistency of opinion beyond consistency of signature, I hereby promise to abide contented by your
decision; and if you say so this is the last time you
will be troubled with communications from the

M., NOT OF LAST WEEK.

The next week appeared the following from the
editor : —

" We say, No. Our present correspondent has a
right to the signature, first, by priority, secondly from
its aptitude, as an initial letter, to express the subjects
on which he is accustomed to write. 'M., not of last
week,' is already known to our readers as the successful opponent of Coleridge, by which we do not mean,
as was rather illogically argued at the time, that he
is the follower of Locke. In that controversy he vin-
dicated his claim to the department of *M*etaphysics.
As a metaphysician, his peculiar province is, of
course, the first principles of *M*ind and *M*atter. It
is also no secret that ' M.' is anything but a novice
in moral philosophy, and we must, therefore, count
*M*orals as one of his rightful subjects. It was the
same ' M.' who introduced to our readers the treatise of Dr. Chalmers on Political Economy in
connection with the *M*oral state and *M*oral prospects of society, of which treatise, as we remember,

*M*arriage and *M*oney are the chief topics ; two more articles of mental property which ' M.' may plead in defense of exclusive right to his signature.   More-over the same ' M.'—we hope we are not betraying secrets — has erected *M*onuments, and may each be *ære . perennius !* to the memory of deceased wor-thies ; and if we were disposed to stand on trifles, we might add, that one of these worthies was an *M.* D., another a *M*inister, and the third a *M*instrel.   Where rival claims are to be adjusted, it were invidious to speak of *M*erit ; but leaving *it* out of the question, and *malgrè* all the counter claims that can be set up by other competitors — for it seems there have been several on the ground of *M*usic, or the *M*uses, or *M*oderation, in Church principles, or *M*ysticism, or any other *M*ay-be *M*atters, we think we have shown ample reason for requesting all other aspirants to recede, and leave our present correspondent in sole possession of the signature ' M.' . To a superficial observer the instances adduced may seem an acci-dental alliteration, and of no weight in argument. But the profound thinker, who is not deluded by outward phantasms, but penetrates into the essences of things, will be of a different opinion.   He well knows, however fashionable it may be in modern times to sneer at cabalistic lore, that *letters* have secret affinities which are necessarily expressive of *real* properties.   Such a mind would be easily able to trace the letter ' M.' from its origin in the primi-tive language through all its ramifications, from the confusion of Babel to the worse confusion of Edward

Irving, and show that it has an inherent and necessary aptitude to express, not only the favorite subjects, but the essential character of our correspondent. And now, having thus shown that the said correspondent has an exclusive right both by prescription and in *rerum naturâ*, to the said signature, we hope that no one in future will venture to dispute his *nominal* property, or call in question our editorial decission. The present ' M.,' we repeat, is the true ' M.,' and his rivals, in common with all their fellow *M*ortals, must search for secret affinities in their appropriate *M*otto, *memento mori*."

In the year 1845, the Annual Convention of the Diocese of New York met under the most trying and exciting circumstances. Without consent or concurrence on the part of the diocese, foreign bishops had come in, presented, tried, convicted, and sentenced to indefinite suspension, the Bishop of New York. This was as much a sentence of suspension laid upon the diocese, as it was upon the Bishop. Hence, placing the result alongside of the manner in which it was attained, it was thought by many that envy of the growing power of the Diocese of New York, together with a dislike of her decided Churchmanship, had had somewhat to do, at least, in shaping the sentence. The consequence was a convention of unusual length and of sharp and stormy debate. My father was a member of it, though entering but little into its embittered discussions. Once only, at any length, was his voice heard, and then his words were so characteristic of the bold and clear consistency, yet humble dependence upon a higher power, of his character, that I shall make no excuse for inserting them here. It was towards the close of the session that he rose to speak to a compromise resolution.

" The Rev. Dr. McVickar said he rose to oppose it. It was not what it purported to be, — a true measure of peace. It sought agreement by a union of inconsistencies. It asserts in the preamble what it denies in the body of the resolution, and would build up with one hand what it pulls down with the other. Such action is unworthy of the wisdom of the Church, and would prove utterly valueless for the end it purports to seek. Whether I look at it in my place as a legislator, or in my relations as a presbyter of the Church, I can find in it no one ground either for confidence or approbation.

" As a legislative act it is wanting in any quality to recommend it. It is inconsistent with itself, contradictory to the past action of the house, and, besides, worthless as being but an expression of opinion in a matter beyond our jurisdiction. It reasserts, as an admitted fact, what the house has just negatived — and would smuggle into a preamble what, by a decisive vote on Saturday last, was rejected as a resolution. This, Mr. President, is neither fair, wise, nor prudent, — and, speaking for one, I will not consent to spread upon our minutes, action thus stamped at once with inconsistency and feebleness. As a legislator of the Church I stand on this ground. I will keep within my constitutional powers. I will not go beyond them. I will not spread 'words' upon its journal. But speaking as a presbyter of the Church I have other objections. It trespasses on matters with which we, as a convention, have nothing to do. And here, Mr. President, as others have defined their position, permit me to say a word touching mine. Withdrawn from parochial charge, and thus separated from the more public duties of the ministry, I yet hold myself severed from no duty or interest of the Church or diocese ; and in my humbler sphere have labored, at least faithfully, to advance them. Unconnected, therefore, with the laity of the Church, I claim to speak forth equally with others, an unbiased clerical opinion. It has, at least, this merit, — no man, no body of men, no public opinion · has influenced it.

"It is this. I desire to look and do look at the sentence on our Bishop, and the consequent desolation of the diocese, in the light of a spiritual judgment on us all ; I would humble myself under it, and not sit in judgment on it — on those who moved in it, or on those who adjudged it; they have their own account to render and their own answer to give. For myself, silence and submission towards that sentence are my only duties, and I would await in penitence and prayer, yea, even in sackcloth and ashes, the removal of God's heavy hand from off us. That these may not be taken for mere words, permit me to add, Mr. President, that the published records of that trial, sent to me, I never have read, and, God help me, never will. For why, I argued, should I stain my mind with sinful words, beyond its own native sinfulness, when by no possibility I can ever be called on to sit in judgment on my Bishop, or to review the judgment of the court that condemned him. Such, Mr. President, has been my view of this question. Had my voice prevailed, it would have been so marked by an early action in the Standing Committee of the diocese. A day of fasting or an appropriate form of prayer would, from the first, have converted this into a spiritual question and brought us all upon our knees for our own sins."

My father's subsequent course was in strict accord with what he then said. The record of the trial lay upon his table for a long time. I remember well seeing it there, sealed with his own coat of arms, and indorsed in his own bold hand, " Never opened. To be returned ; " and he continued from that time to visit Bishop Onderdonk regularly up to the time of his death, seventeen years afterwards, five or six times a year, as one in affliction. And this he could well do, knowing only that he was indefinitely suspended from the performance of his episcopal duties. This begat a strong feeling of affection on the part of the humbled Bishop, and, in Dr. Seabury's account of his last communion, he says, " His family were all present, and the only thing that at all disturbed him was the absence, through a mistake, of the two friends, Dr. McVickar and Dr. S. R. Johnson, whom he had desired should have received it with him." Two days before his death my father saw the Bishop for the last time. In his own words, in a note writen to me at the time, he says, " As I entered I saw that the hand of death was upon him, and fearing that I should not see him again, I knelt at his bedside and placing his hand upon my head, I said, ' Bless me, Bishop.' He evidently understood my meaning and faintly murmured the blessing, but was unable to converse."

Of Bishop Onderdonk's guilt on the charges made against him, I never heard my father once speak. He was much opposed to the publication of the evidence, and, as has been said, returned his copy unopened. He was willing to bow to the authority of the court, but ever considered the sentence an illegal one, which judgment future legislation confirmed. An earnest friend, he was no partisan, and ever counseled that submission which is now considered as having so ennobled the Bishop's character. In the Standing Committee he was appointed to draw up the resolutions upon the Bishop's death. This he did, and they were adopted with but a single alteration. " Under a judicial sentence believed to be of doubtful validity," was changed into " believed *by many* to be of doubtful validity," on the ground taken by Judge Hoffman, that the Standing Committee having acted on the ground of its being valid, nothing should now be said that could question the validity of its own acts. He was invited to preach the funeral sermon, but declined.

A vacancy had twice occurred in the presidency of Columbia College within the last seven years ; in 1842, by the resignation of President Duer, on ac-

count of long illness, and in 1849 through the resignation of President Moore. On both these occasions
my father's name had been proposed, but resolutely
withdrawn by himself. The dream of twenty years
before had passed. Writing to a son abroad, Christmas Day, 1849, he says, " Our college has, as you
know, a new president. At Mr. King's inauguration
I was requested by the trustees to address him on
the part of the Faculty. I was solicited to be a candidate, but declined and would not have accepted an
office full of annoyance, and one that would have cut
me off from my little church." Yet there was no de-
cline of interest. His address was, as usual on such
occasions, a bold and stirring one, prepared with care,
and intended mainly to counteract the dependence on
outside influence which the election of Mr. Charles
King to the presidency of the college had too much
suggested.   In it he presses with a strong hand the
necessity of religious training and the impossibility of
a college, governed from without, ever rising to the
height of a university. As this is a subject of present interest, I quote a passage bearing on each of
these points.

" To ' popularize education,' Mr. President ; to accommodate college studies to what are deemed the
practical wants of a business community, is an experiment, as you well know, that has often been tried
and as often signally failed, here and elsewhere, at
home and abroad. Our own partial trial of it, a few
years since, was perhaps too short to be held a con-
clusive one. That, however, of the London Univer-

sity, as being a thorough trial, may be so regarded.
. . . . A deeper cause of ill-success for such
plans must then be found, than want of skill, or
means ; and do we not find it, I ask, in the very principle which it advocates. Education governed from
without — this is its root error, $\pi\rho\omega\tau\text{o}\nu\ \psi\epsilon\upsilon\delta\text{o}\varsigma$. I care
not from what quarter that dictation comes — from
the will of rulers, or from the voice of the multitude
— it is usurpation whencesoever it comes, in the eye
equally of the scholar, the statesman, and the Christian. Education, sir, is a mission from God to man —
the teacher and not the taught, in the community
— giving, and not taking impress — moulding, and
not to be moulded by the mass on which it is sent to
operate ; so therefore, looking not, as such scheme
proposes, to what is, but what ought to be, in the
community. . . . . Your own education, sir,
was in schools of another mark — in the schools of
our ancestral land — where solid learning, and labo-
rious study and careful training — intellectual, moral,
religious training — is made to lie at the foundation
of all other attainments in education. I say ' training,' sir, in contradistinction to mere imparted knowledge — not learning merely, not science only, not
dogmatic opinions at all — but that quiet, solid, unobtrusive ' training ' which constitutes distinctly, Anglo-Saxon education, wherever that race is found. In
my own survey of foreign schools, some years since,
deeper learning I found in the schools of Germany
— deeper science in the schools of France, and more
precocious and versatile talent in our own ; but

deeper elements of national safety, that best product
of education, the union of the gentleman, the scholar,
and the Christian, I found nowhere more truly worked
out than in the higher schools of England."

After giving a picture of the English universities,
he draws the following well-timed inferences : —

" Now is not this, I ask, a more republican picture
of education than our own colleges present ? And is
it not more in accordance with all our boasted democratic institutions and principles ? But what is still
more to the point, does it not afford an adequate solution to their possession, and our want of national
influence and wide-spread patronage ? Does it not
explain why these universities are part and parcel of
the life of the nation, while our American colleges
are found to stand, as they are charged, falsely
through our negligence, with doing, like dead things,
amid the living interests of society ; bolstered up by
laws and patronage from without, instead of a living
force within ; taking so little hold as they do, on the
sympathies even of their own alumni, and gathering
so little as they do, from their subsequent wealth ? Is
not this the solution ? Think you, sir, such would be
the case, were their diplomas made title-deeds to an
estate, giving them an elective franchise in a common
body, and securing to them the privileges of citizen-
ship in that republic ? Would their zeal, money, or
labor, be wanting in our service ? Would libraries,
apparatus, scholarships, prizes, be asked for, as now,
in vain ? Surely not ! At the banner cry, ' Columbia
to the rescue !' how would its hosts start to life, like

the Scottish chieftain's warriors, where least thought of — 'from copse, and heath, and cairn' — from the plough, and the machine-shop, and the manufactory, as well as from the bar, the pulpit, and the desk, to aid and strengthen their common home : or, let me rather say, speaking as I do, before the first soldier [1] of our land, with his laurels fresh upon him, like as when on some doubtful field, he has marked a periled banner, and bade the drums beat, ' To the color ; ' how quick, through willing hearts and united hands, that failing banner has arisen ! risen higher than before, and been borne aloft in the arms of victory, till planted on the highest citadel of fame. So would it be — fellow alumni, to you I speak — with our college pennon ; none in our land, I well believe, would then float higher, or wider, or fairer."

These were not the mere words of a popular inauguration address ; they were the matured results of long reflection based on wide experience, upon the practical difficulties which seemed to surround and impede the advancing steps of Columbia College.

The permanent chaplaincy, which is now attached to the college, was, I should judge from the following, due very much to Professor McVickar's efforts. " Our college affairs are again settled. Dr. Moore resigned, and Mr. King elected. During the ' interregnum ' I introduced a short responsive service, and although Mr. King does not conform to it, I shall use it whenever called on, and thus not improbably, lay the foundation for the chaplaincy."

[1] General Scott, lately returned from the conquest of Mexico.

Many sheets and scraps of paper are now lying before me (it was his custom to tear off the blank page of notes and letters, and place them in his portfolio as a ready receptacle for stray thoughts), closely written with reflections and suggestions concerning college and other matters. The importance and present interest which surrounds the academic and university question justify a few extracts.

From an outline report on proposed changes in college examinations, without date, but not less, probably, than thirty years ago, I quote the following : —

" The point to be attained is the devising such a plan, as, while it removes the reproach from those naturally dull or inadequately prepared, shall yet preserve the excitement required to arouse the abler students to the highest exertion of their powers.

" To this end there shall be in the course of the year two examinations for honors and one for college standing. The first two to be public, semi-annually, the latter private at the end of the year. The public examinations for honors to be voluntary. An abstract of the roll of standing in relation to every student on a printed form prepared for that purpose, to be made out subsequently to each examination and sent to the parent or guardian of each."

The following are scraps : —

" German universities not examples for us. They do not undertake to educate. They are mere seats of learning, open to all, on payment of special fees. No examinations, no care, no note, no report, no knowledge even of names, no degrees, only certificates.

Degrees conferred by government board of examination. Those who attend are of riper age, young men preparing for professions, namely, theology, law, physics, and teaching, for all of which, attendance on lectures is a legal, essential condition. The professors are appointed by government, and the result of the whole system shows, too often, a student's life of wild dissipation and infidel principles.

" The English university is a double system.

" 1. University with professors and open lectures, and examinations for degrees and honors. Governed and taught originally by the graduates.

" 2. Colleges with tutors, daily instruction by them in all branches, with private examinations.

" The complaint has been that the colleges have swamped the university. The tutorial system has swallowed up the professorial, lowering the degree of knowledge acquired by practically throwing all branches upon one teacher."

Under the head of " Suggestions as to Columbia College," I find the following : —

" Necessity of tutors comes from the disparity of students in the class. The dull and idle must be cared for and yet not retard the majority. Add one or more tutors to college faculty, with whom, as a penalty for idleness or neglect, students might have one or more additional hours, during the week, to make up deficiencies. A tutorial in subordination to the professorial is the condition of a perfect system. A combination of both is essential to a practical university. Our chairs, at present, involve duties both of professors and tutors. In the æsthetic and intellectual at least they should be separated. There are sciences of memory and sciences of mind.

" All true education is self-education.

" Attendance should be voluntary, or if enforced, there should be power to transfer to the tutor. Classes, if the attendance is voluntary, may be indefinitely large ; if compulsory, small, not over twenty or twenty-five.

" Our present form of public examination not suited to the æsthetic and intellectual courses. As conducted, they are tests of memory, not of taste or judgment. The truest test is by written theses, and, in its higher form, maintained against a disputant.

" The end sought in the æsthetic course is to awaken taste and form the critical judgment, not to store the memory with dogmatic opinions.

" The end in the moral and intellectual course is training, to settle in the mind great principles of truth, and to train the mind to their quick perception, and their satisfactory defense. For this, free conversational lectures is the best form of teaching, combined with set discussions; and for public examination, written theses, and, if time serve, openly defended.

" The great difficulty, common to all our colleges, is a growing democracy in our homes. Our best students are of well ordered families ; our worst are often of our first families, over-indulged at home."

These last lines embody what was a growing grief to my father in the latter years of his professorship. Neither his subjects nor his ways of imparting knowledge were suited to wayward, headstrong boys, much less to that ungentlemanly behavior of which he sometimes, more latterly than formerly, had to complain. In the lecture-room he was ever the dignified, though courteous gentleman, and expected to rule his students not by fear but by eliciting from them a like sentiment and behavior.

Dr. Bethune, writing from Philadelphia, in 1836, says : —

" I cannot deny myself the pleasure, my dear Dr. McVickar, of assuring you that I ever retain a most gratified sense of your kindness to me when I was your careless and wayward pupil. Your instructions often recur to my mind, and it is with keen regret that I reflect on my abuse of the advantages I then enjoyed. To *no one* so much as yourself am I indebted for any taste for letters."

Many like words from old pupils are before me. One says : —

" If your intercourse, my dear sir, with the class of '63, produced no other effect, it did this, it made one member of the class a more thorough gentleman than he was before, that is a more *gentle man*."

And Professor Elmendorf of Racine College, Wisconsin, writes, in 1868, as follows : —

" Now that the work at Racine is fully inaugurated, I am constantly reminded how much we are indebted to him who showed us how to think and work. This young college, so full of vigor and fresh young life, is most truly old Columbia's child. And could you be with us for even a short time, it would be very evident to you that the teachings we received of old have found their reality and power by reaching to very many who never received them from your own lips.

" I found Professor D—— so fully aware of the value of his early training that he had taken every occasion to apply it from his own chair. And now that the college has assigned to me the same subjects of which I heard for the first time in your lecture-room, I am made to feel more deeply than ever before, the inestimable value not only of the principles but of the methods of study and teaching which I then acquired."

I add a few suggestive scraps from the " portfolio sweepings " of 1849 : —

" Three philosophic truths form the basis of religion : —

1. *Freedom of Will,* so far as to feel a sense of self-condemnation.

2. *Corruption of Nature,* so far as always to fall short of what we feel to be right.

3. *Help,* that comes from prayer."

" Byron confesses a great truth when in his ' Cain ' he makes Lucifer say : —

> " ' He who bows not to God has bowed to me.' "

" Many things are above people's understanding, but nothing is above their misunderstanding, so we must teach all."

This subject of College Views is well closed by the following thoughtful and appreciative estimate of my father as a teacher, from the pen of one of his former pupils, Professor Dean of Racine College. And the Professor will perhaps not take it amiss if we point to himself, as a proof of the truthfulness of that estimate : —

" Your father was one who thoroughly subordinated rhetoric to the purposes of a teacher. While using language with singular precision and skill, and able, as few apprehended, to evoke its subtlest harmonies, making it suggestive, persuasive, and far-reaching, he was, nevertheless, not mastered by it. The matter of his speech remained ever more weighty than its manner. And this fact may, I think, with some propriety, be viewed as a kind of typical one, or key to his whole mind and character. While it was impossible that anything slovenly should ever proceed from him, he would, nevertheless, have preferred infinitely the appearance of carelessness in style to carelessness about the subject-matter. His constant advice to young men was, ' Never use language insincerely : never speak, or write, even in literary debate, upon the side in which you do not believe.' His whole temperament, taste, and habit led him always to subordinate, sometimes sternly, every doctrine and pretension, every claim, either abstract or personal, the charms of style equally with the rulings of life, to the simple requirements of truth and duty. Well do I remember the force and earnestness with which at our first appearance before him he urged upon our class Pythagoras's definition of virtue, ἡ ἕξις τοῦ δέοντος, 'the habit of duty.' 'Do not rely on heavenly favor, or on compassion to folly, or on prudence, on common sense, the old usage and main chance of men: nothing can keep you — not fate, nor health, nor admirable intellect; — nothing but rectitude only, rectitude forever and ever!'

"Your father's whole teaching might, I think, be suitably described by a paraphrase on Wordsworth's unsurpassable lines 'To Duty' — 'stern Daughter of the Voice of God.' To this without reserve would he trust as the Light to guide and the rod to check, to this for victory amid the shock of empty terrors, the shield from temptation, the true peace amid human strife.

"It may be worth while to illustrate this peculiarity by referring specifically to the different branches of his teaching.

"It was sometimes startling, for instance, to hear the unreserved commendation which, in his lectures on philosophy, he would occasionally bestow on the great heathen teachers. He dismissed almost with contempt the objection of those who conceived that the necessity of the Christian revelation was disparaged by the admission of such excellence. He maintained, on the contrary, that Christianity is the perfection of all the scattered rays of wisdom among the heathen. The study and appreciation of their great writers, therefore, he believed would liberalize the mind. He did not shrink even from comparing Plato's criterion of man's duty, ὁμοίωσις τῷ θεῷ κατὰ τὸ δυνατόν, 'likeness to God according to our ability,' with the Christian injunction, 'Be ye perfect, even as your Father in heaven is perfect.'

" But while listening to such statements, every pupil of Professor McVickar was made to feel that they accompanied what is too frequently wanting in the souls of those who make them, namely, a firm, clear, unquestioning grasp of the mysteries of the Faith, held with such absolute assurance that no disturbance or uneasiness of suspicion could be aroused by the acknowledgment of heathen excellence. All of God's rational children, like all of his works, he held to be, in their idea and creation, good ; and it was an habitual remark with him that all systems and institutions which had exercised an enduring control owed this to some element of truth and right in them. Nothing simply false, he would say, can have permanent power. This conviction led him invariably to seek out what was good in every man and system, to acknowledge it without reserve, and to dwell on it with pleasure. This impressed a certain character upon his teaching, which all who were under him will recognize, — a graceful and effective use of commendation, when it was in his power.

" In his lectures on rhetoric, logic, and æsthetics, the leading and vital principles of which he grasped with singular precision and power, and implanted in the mind by brief and pregnant statements, which clung to the memory, he was always anxious to have the merits of the great classical authorities acknowledged. In rhetoric, for example, the prevailing bent of his mind led him to prefer Aristotle's view of it to Cicero's, inasmuch as the analysis of the mind and language of man for the purpose of persuading to believe truly and to act rightly, is a nobler thing than even the ability to express all knowledge with correctness. So in æsthetics, he referred the spiritual theory, which he regarded as the true key to the subject, to the ancient Platonic conception of the unity of the first good and the first fair. This theory raises beauty as it were from earth to heaven. It directs us for study, not so much to the intellect or senses, as to the spiritual nature of man; and thus makes æsthetics, instead of trivial or trifling, to become one of the most ennobling of all studies for training, and for sinking deeply into the character.

" The unity of Professor McVickar's teaching was felt even where he passed into the very different spheres of history and political economy. His judgments of individual character were a vivid and picturesque illustration of his abstract principles. No one could expose with a calmer disdain the pretense and tinsel of many a popular reputation as he put his finger on the fatal taint of baseness or interest in it. Every one of his pupils will remember the enthusiasm with which he was wont to quote Sir Philip Sidney's definition of the gentleman, ' High thoughts seated in a heart of courtesy.' On such names and pregnant phrases he delighted to dwell when he treated of the last and highest view of history, as ' Philosophy teaching by examples; ' in other words, history with its lessons, moral, prudential, and Christian.

" If he had rendered no other service to political economy, — a science whose early principles he had grasped with hardly equaled precision and clearness, — he deserves perpetual gratitude for the emphasis and effect with which he corrected the error, given currency under several eminent names, and among others that of McCulloch, who had confined political wealth to material productions, thus excluding all consideration of the influence exercised upon national prosperity by science and professional labors. We might say with truth that the Professor's own career was the most solid refutation of this fallacy. It is difficult indeed to estimate by any gauge of this world's valuation, the worth and preciousness of such a career. The principles for which he nobly and effectively battled throughout a protracted life-time, are the very salt which preserves human society and its institutions from corruption and dissolution. They became in many a young and enthusiastic heart, where his skillful hand well knew how to plant them, the guide and stimulus of noble and useful lives, whose regulative principles were a scorn of baseness, contempt for mere expediency, the habit of duty, the enthusiasm which counts it honor to pay life for truth, reverence for the spiritual and unseen, and, as the support and lode-star of all these, Christian faith, received with humility, cherished with devotion, modestly yet firmly and fearlessly confessed before men."

CHAPTER XXI.

IN 1850 the New York Ecclesiological Society
found itself without a president under circumstances which gave good opportunity to its enemies
to raise the cry of " Romanizing." The vacant
office was one neither of honor in the Church nor
emolument, at the same time sufficiently prominent
to make its occupant a good butt for party arrows.
In spite of this, and of the fact that neither years nor
pursuits fitted him for special interest in this society's
labors, my father, at the request of its members,
assumed the vacant office of president. He did not
desire it in any way, but he sympathized most fully
with that foundation principle of the Ecclesiological
Society, reverence and love for the house of God,
according to its motto, " Tabernacula tua quam di-
lecta." He also — and it was the crown and blessing
of his declining years — sympathized with young men,
even in spite of their natural rashness, in all aspira-
tions aiming at high and noble ends.

The possible value or use of such a society, might
seem at the present day questionable. But it must
be remembered that at that day we could boast of

many strange things which this society helped to banish. Even a chapel of Trinity, New York, could proudly point at that time to a chancel arrangement somewhat as follows: About six feet behind the chancel rail was a pyramid filling the greater part of the chancel and built up as follows. First, two square kneeling benches, then the holy table, not unlike in size and appearance to a closed card-table, with velvet cushion on either end; then behind, rising five or six feet, and spreading its wings both ways, a huge reading-desk with folio Bible in the centre and folio Prayer-Book on each side, with its plethoric velvet cushion swelling over in voluptuous folds and garnished with wooden fringes of fantastic shapes, and tassels whose shape and huge proportions reminded one of church bells; above this and still be-hind, in true pyramidal effect, the towering pulpit on whose desk the traditional fat cushion again reclined, and flung to the air of that upper region its solid fringes and tassels of turned wood; and higher still, in unapproachable dignity, the sounding-board with its gilded and symbolic decoration. Now people this structure, as it was often seen when at the close of a sermon all the clergy would stand, two on the ground floor, three in the second story, and one in the pulpit above, and you have before you a specimen of the not unusual chancel arrangements at the time when the Ecclesiological Society was formed. to awaken thought and call attention to better things. Its success is written in such churches as St. George's and St. Thomas's, New York, and in the present

23

improved taste in church architecture throughout the country.

The following from one of the first papers written by my father on these subjects will show the tone he then took and ever afterwards maintained : —

" The ecclesiologist should ever have in view a higher end than his own science gives him, as indeed every true workman must have, whatever his craft. . . . . An humble, churchlike spirit, alike quiet and earnest, affectionate and faithful, is a true and sufficient security. In these we have at once our compass, our chart, and our anchor, and, under God, need fear no quicksands, either of Rome or Geneva.

" In addition to this general guidance as Church-men, the society stands pledged already to certain great conservative principles in the science which it teaches, which stand forth as landmarks against wandering in church architecture. The following may be enumerated as the chief: —

1. The adoption of the old parish church of England as our present type, with its lengthened nave and ample chancel. Aisles if needed; open roof; sacristy and south porch; no gallery; and with orientation whenever it may be secured.

2. Open seats instead of pews, and, so far as may be, FREE ; no proprietorship in the house of God.

3. In church building, rather to erect solidly and well, a *portion*, than the whole slightly.

4. To seek beauty in proportion rather than in material ; for it is not roughness or rudeness that

excludes beauty, but false proportion or feeble outline.

5. To study reality and truth everywhere in the building; no sham, no pretense, no falsehood.

6. To decorate construction, only, and never to construct decoration.

7. To repudiate utterly all heathen symbols and words of vanity in churches and on monuments, and to replace them with Christian forms and words, — above all with the cross, that universal emblem of our faith.

8. To have no meanness in the house of God; not wealth at home and poverty there; but to give to God and his house of our best; remembering who hath said, ' Them that honor me will I honor.' "

But the subject which, above all others in this connection interested my father, was cathedrals and the cathedral system as essential to the efficiency of a missionary church, whether in the metropolis or in outlying missions. He fought hard for it in the first mission established in California long before this society was formed, and now he used his position and pen to further it at home.

" Such then," he says, in concluding a paper on the subject, — " such then are cathedrals in their essential nature, origin, and uses, — the original of dioceses, their spiritual centres; the primeval citadels of the Church's strength; the nursing mothers of a thousand parishes; the primitive council of the bishops, aiding and tempering the severity perhaps of solitary rule; the maintaining in the ever open cathedral of the daily services of the Church in all their propriety, dignity, and beauty, and that, too, in the metropolis of the land; thus consecrating as it were, the state itself under God and Christ; and lastly a diocesan home for its clergy, through its ample means and liberal endowments affording a quiet resting-place and leisure, and libraries for training up for the defense and ornament of the Church a continued succession of learned clergy, far beyond what the daily toil of the parish life admitted. Then again, consecrating the learning and the talents thus acquired to their highest and noblest uses, the glory of God and the salvation of men, under the guidance of their own spiritual head, and in accommodation to the varying demands of a growing or full diocese."

The discussion of this subject at the meetings of the society and in the pages of the " Ecclesiologist," gave occasion to the following remarkable and important letter from the present venerable Presiding-bishop of the Church, Bishop Smith of Kentucky.

Diocese of Kentucky, January 19, 1855.

Rev. and dear Doctor, — As one of the pioneers of our beloved Church, earliest commissioned to commence her great work here in these ends of the earth, I have reason to thank you for the kind interest you have felt, not to say in me, but certainly in my work since the days, long time ago, when we used to meet in some of those delightful Christian homes in New York, which the hand of

death has long since made desolate. .   .   .   .
Hoping that dark days to the Church are over and
that a brighter morrow is dawning upon us, I hailed
with singular satisfaction the report in the " Church
Journal," of the important discussion lately had about
cathedrals. .   .   .   . As far as communicating the
impressions made upon my mind in the course of the
observation and experience of nearly a quarter of a
century to you, and through you, to your society,
may be offering them to the Church for her use and
benefit, they are quite at your service.   It is for this
purpose I am now writing.

The first great want I discerned upon coming to
Kentucky, was the want of indigenous, or at least of
semi-indigenous clergy.   Hence my efforts, in vain,
for a theological school ; and hence for Shelby College, alas! thus far also in vain, as a feeder to it.
Twenty years' experience and more, throws us all
back upon a quasi-cathedral theological school, almost
in connection with the bishop's family (quite so, except boarding the young men), in a great city or
near it.

The next conviction forced upon me was, that the
bishop's residence could not be off the banks of the
Ohio, or out of our chief city.   And it is quite remarkable that the Bishop of Ohio, afterwards, and
the Bishop of Indiana, now, have acted on the same
convictions.

I had not been five years in Louisville before I observed the disjointed, ineffective, and often fruitless efforts of the Presbyterians, a very numerous, wealthy,

liberal, and therefore powerful body, in all their plans for Church extension, education, care of orphans, etc.   And in a much shorter time, I witnessed the singular efficiency and success of the Roman Catholics, they too removing their see from Bardstown to Louisville, by means of their singularly convenient Gothic church, for a cathedral, and their close-ribbed centralization.

We are the only Protestant body in a condition to avoid the mistakes of the one, and to imitate the wisdom of the other: but yet we do not!

Now, as to the features of a plan of a quasi-cathedral, suited, as it seems to me, to our purposes: —

1. A parish church to be built, paid for, and supported, under all the usual advantages and disadvantages of a vestry and of the old and almost universal pew-system.   A church with galleries and sittings for fifteen hundred hearers as well as worshippers, with what corresponds to Lady Chapel, for Sunday-school, Bible class, evening meetings, and winter prayers.

2. An adjoining residence for the bishop on one side, and a rector on the other.   A residence for a bishop's chaplain or one theological professor, and for ten or twelve theological students; a parish school, dormitories for transient clergymen, offices for standing committee, Bible, and prayer-book, and missionary societies, two or three deacons for suburban and in-urban missionary work, etc., etc.

Pray begin in New York or Philadelphia, that we may not die without hope of it in this seat of the diocese of   Your ancient friend,

B. B. Smith.

My father said "amen" to this prayer of his friend, the Bishop of Kentucky, but there was little more that he could do. Nor is it clear, that those in authority even had the power. The large and wealthy parishes of our Eastern cities are, practically, little bishoprics, whose strong congregationism is not pleased with the idea of a mother-church setting an example to all, frowning on willfulness, and caring for all alike ; while every year makes it more difficult to graft upon the full-grown tree that which in the order of nature should have been its stock and root.

As applied to New York city, I find the following rough outline of a comprehensive scheme among my father's " portfolio sweepings " of this period.

" In our Diocese of New York, with our vast, half heathen city, we have parishes and extra-parochial work, which we may name *missionary*. The question is, how is this last to be provided for ? I propose all such to be the bishop's peculiar charge, either direct or by appointment, to be known as bishop's parish, to be seen in a church, and felt in a missionary organization, adopting and organizing all voluntary societies engaged in any and every branch of missionary work, confirming their officers, receiving their reports, and giving unity and efficiency to the whole, — uniting freedom of action, whether in labor or financial means, with church order and episcopal authority. The Bishop, the fountain-head of spiritual authority and discipline ; an organized army of free-workers, for Christ and in Christ. A missionary society thus ordered, would soon make our Church triumphant through all the waste places of our city and its surroundings."

To an absent son my father writes about this time: "The ' Ecclesiologist ' and society give some little occupation. Number 8 College Green, must, they think, attend to all its concerns, applications for books, plans, subscriptions, etc. But honors must be paid for, and the president must not complain, and the truth is, it has been a pleasure." And again: " In spite of our difficulties in the society, prudence and perseverance, here as ever, are making headway. Bear this as your motto; it has been mine. If I have accomplished anything, it has been, not by talent, but by *quiet perseverance* in what I deemed good. The world gets out of one's way, under these circumstances, tired out."

In 1851 occurred the third semi-centennial jubilee of " The Society of the Propagation of the Gospel in Foreign Parts," the " Venerable Society," as it is commonly called in England. A jubilee celebration having been determined upon by the English Church throughout the United Kingdom and the Colonies, the primate, the Archbishop of Canterbury, wrote to the Diocese of New York to request it, and its sister dioceses of the United States, to unite. This, so far as New York was concerned, was gladly and promptly acquiesced in. A grand celebration was determined on, to be held in Trinity Church, New York, and my father was invited to preach the sermon. The discourse was a bold and outspoken one, —·cloquent in parts, but rather distinguished for the straightforward manner in which it dealt with the questions of the day, — Romanism and Protestantism, the Greek Church, Indian missions, bestowing the episcopate upon converted tribes, provincial synods, and the like. And all said in a way to stir thought and yet not give offense. The service was solemn and noble, such as to make one feel the power of the simple dignity of our worship when properly performed, as compared with the ornate formality of the Roman and Greek rituals, or the apparent barren formalism of Protestant prayers. And when the venerable parish of Trinity poured its gold, to the amount of three thousand dollars, into its old alms-dish, the gift of William and Mary, and offered it upon the altar for the home missions of the diocese, and also announced that it had, in thankful consideration of the jubilee, bestowed an endowment of five thousand dollars upon the African missionary bishopric of Cape Palmas, it stirred one's heart to thankfulness to see such noble fruit of former faith. And yet many would have been glad to see a more thoughtful reading of their own history by this venerable and wealthy corporation, and part at least of their gift invested in land, in the outskirts of this flourishing African town, in faith, for some future jubilee.

The summer of 1850 was spent at Croton, on the Hudson River. The following lines, from a home letter, show the active and social habits which increasing years had, as yet, made no impression on :

" This fine weather has kept me rambling, selecting choice spots, building rural cottages, instead of castles, and laying the corner-stones of half a dozen little country churches. I have perambulated all the shore farms between us and Sing Sing, and visited all the chief families."

A new and sad break in the family circle occurred this summer in the unexpected death of Mr. George Kneeland, my father's only son-in-law, occasioned by a southern fever contracted in seeking health for an invalid wife. This gave rise to the purchase of a small place at Morristown for the widowed and failing daughter with her young family. The writer, then just ordained, passed his diaconate in the same place as assistant to the rector of St. Peter's. In this old-fashioned house, of what was then an old-fashioned town, were reunited for a very brief period the broken family links. It was a period of great peacefulness as we watched the two, the widowed daughter above mentioned, and a noble-hearted, sweet-spirited son, broken down by over devotion to missionary work in his sacred calling, and saw them gradually detach themselves from earth, and pass away almost together, to join the now longer family chain in the spirit world.

I cannot thus chronicle your death, my dear brother, without at least a word of passing tribute. Eight years my elder, you were to me more than brother, you were an example and a spiritual guide, one who never failed me when I needed direction, or sought advice. And as I now recall your brief ministry of six years, divided into its three, almost equal periods, — one of health, buoyant as a missionary at the north ; one of feebleness, half-hopeful, as a southern missionary ; and one at home, patiently waiting for the end, — I seem able to appreciate, better than ever before, the spirit which throws its deep and lovely life into these few lines of yours : —

> " 'Tis hard to sit by life's fast babbling springs
> And count our joys and hopes, as flow'ry things,
> Which ever grow and creep and rise and twine
> Among the thorny leaves of discipline ;
> But he who'd rise in Christ's self-mastering school,
> Must teach his very heart to beat by rule.
>
> " H. McV., 1849."

The return of four orphan grandchildren to the family home was an event of considerable importance. The once large family had been reduced to three, and though my father faithfully acted on his favorite maxim, " Do your duty with a cheerful boldness," it was not in accordance with human nature, however wonderfully sustained, that this blow upon blow of bereavement should not tell both outwardly and inwardly. But the presence of youth, even if we cannot entirely sympathize with it, — and it was only at times that my father did, — is a great renewer. It makes its own imperious demand on time and thought, and breaks down, rudely perhaps as we think, but always for our good, those carefully formed habits on which, as years advance, we are wont, unwisely, to set such store.

The first result of the presence of these children, and consequent feeling of responsibility, was the

search for a summer country-place. This was soon
found on the banks of the Hudson, adjoining "Sunny-
side," the seat of Washington Irving, and twenty
odd miles from New York. Here my father found
his summer home for the happy years of his remaining life. This place, called, "Inwood," after his
early and romantic residence at Hyde Park, though
now at his children's not at his own suggestion,
was a choice and lovely spot. And, as one of the
things in which my father took both pleasure and
pride, it deserves here a few words of description.
It consisted of about thirty acres on the wooded
banks of the Hudson, at the widest point of Tappan
Zee. A view of three miles across and twenty to
the north, closed in by the varied outline of the softened Highlands, gave it all the charm of an apparent
lake. But at the same time steamboats, and pro-
duce-tows with their long lines of barges, and fleets
of sail, ever passing, added all that life and variety
belonging to a great river, connecting together the
interest of farmer and merchant, which seen but not
heard, as in the present case, harmonizes so pleasantly with the silent activities of nature. The place,
itself, owing more to nature than to art, was what
might be called a half-note between the romantic
and the beautiful. A low, square, stone house,
with piazza all around, was placed on a tongue of
level ground between two richly wooded ravines.
These, uniting below the house, gave some little
foreground between it and the water. To the east
the ground, well planted, rose in gradual and undu-

lating slope a quarter of a mile, up to the old Albany post-road, which, thanks to Irving and Cooper, still holds to its memories of Dutch and English and Revolutionary days.

This spot, though simple, had a charm that was universally acknowledged. And often have I heard Washington Irving himself express his admiration, especially when he caught sight of a distant sail at the further end of a vista which he had allowed to be opened through his own wood, and which he seemed to take as much interest in as if it had been done for his own gratification. With his kind and accomplished neighbor, up to the time of his death, my father was on friendly and intimate terms. It was but the renewing of an old and early acquaintance, and unquestionably added much to the happiness of these years.

But residence of whatever kind, with my father, meant for happiness, work also, and especially Church work. A note, written before even the family had moved up, says, " We will look what can be done at Dearman. [The adjoining village now called Irving-ton.] I shall purchase, or secure at once, ground for a school, to be used as, and after a time converted into, a church."

This same year, the writer, having concluded his engagement at St. Peter's, Morristown, received an appointment under Bishop Wainwright, the Provis-ional Bishop of New York, as missionary to Dear-man and parts adjacent. To this was soon added the rectorship of the neighboring parish of Zion

Church, Greenburg. This gave to my father the great gratification of having a son, the only one now surviving, settled near him, engaged in work which he also loved, and in which he was now, as he had always been, so glad to coöperate.

On the 10th of August, 1852, — this was a favorite day with us for the commencement of any little work in which the family were interested, being my father's birthday, — the first spadeful of earth was upturned, by the youngest grandchild, for the proposed chapel-school of St. Barnabas. On the 17th of the same month, the corner-stone was laid by the Rev. Dr. Creighton, my father delivering the address. He had neither the means nor the desire to do this work by himself alone, and in this address he says, " It is the manifest duty of the residents of this village at the present, when land is comparatively cheap, to secure the blessings of religion and Christian education, not merely for themselves but for those who should come after them, by an endowment in land like those in England which have yielded such blessed fruits." In this, however, he was but feebly seconded, and his own responsibility, about four thousand dollars, in a building that cost six, prevented his doing more himself. By Will, however, he left to the successful parish, which now takes the place of the modest missionary station of 1852, a stone house and near an acre of ground adjoining the church, subject to a life lease. And it now remains to be seen whether the overflowing wealth which has since poured into that neighborhood will be stimulated to follow or simply contented to enjoy the fruits of the example then set and the words then spoken. There was, certainly, no lack of earnest words to accompany these liberal actions. At the dedication, which took place on St. Barnabas's Day, June 11, 1853, my father preached the sermon, from which I quote the following passage : —

"And that we may look at this question aright, let us first deepen our sense of what the act of dedication has done for it. The special dedication of aught we possess to God, has in it something as beautiful and touching, as it is solemn and instructive. We, and all that we have, are HIS; and as Christians, we know and believe that we ourselves are bought with a price. This is our general faith. But then this solemn, special dedication of a part of the debt, does it not become, I ask, an open acknowledgment of the whole, so that we can never after behold that thing dedicated, without remembering whose we are and whom we serve ? God grant such blessing may attend this humble house thus dedicated, and would to God there were more such and better in our land ! — consecrating that overflowing wealth which God is pouring into the lap of this people beyond any former example, Christianizing our too secular education, giving open doors to God's house of prayer, and keeping ever in the world's eye something of which man may not say, ' This is mine.' Would it not be a blessed thing if this spirit of dedication, springing out of self-sacrifice, should grow up and bring forth abundant fruit through our wide-spread domain ?

Would it not be the truest crown of our rejoicing, amid the ten thousand worldly blessings that already make our land preëminent among the nations of the earth ? For, believe me, brethren, nay, believe not me, but the voice of History, that without that corner-stone of prosperity, our wealth is but vanity, and our boast of it sin. Our very national freedom becomes insecure, and our wisest political institutions, with all their boasted strength, will be found in the end to be but like some mighty arch, — an arch of empire, 'tis true, and spanning the gulf of anarchy, — but then an arch from which the key-stone has been removed ; one that will hang together but for a time by the frail cement of worldly interests, to be crumbling and washed out, day by day, by the trickling rain of selfish policy, till it sink dishonored, stone by stone : or else, it may be hurled into sudden ruin in the mad tempest of some unholy popular tumult."

A vote of thanks from the Board of Trustees of Columbia College, dated March 1st, 1852, " for the foundation of two annual prizes in the Senior Class, by the Reverend Dr. McVickar," show that not at Irvington only, but elsewhere and in other spheres of duty, was my father acting up to his own teaching. These prizes were, one for accurate knowledge of Patristic Greek, the other for an English essay on some subject connected with the evidences of Christianity, and both for the encouragement of those looking to the sacred ministry as their profession. This was soon followed by the foundation of two like prizes in the General Theological Seminary ; one of these also for scholarship in Greek, the other in Ecclesiastical History, especially in its bearing on the independence of the early English Church. In both institutions have they already borne important fruits.

24

CHAPTER XXII.

IN 1854, Professor McVickar was requested to preach the sermon before the Annual Convention of the Diocese of New York. A few days before the appointed day, Bishop Wainwright, after a short illness, was suddenly and unexpectedly taken away. This left the diocese without any acting head at a time when party questions were running high, and threw very considerable responsibility upon the preacher who within a few days was to address its convention. My father did not often shrink from any responsibility that Providence seemed to lay upon him, but on this occasion he hesitated. He had already written his discourse, which was now useless from the entire change of circumstances. The time was very limited for the preparation of another, and questions of considerable delicacy had to be touched upon, especially as to whether a new election should be at once entered into. One party, to suit party ends, preferred an interregnum, while the other shrunk from what might seem indecent haste in filling the office of one whose memory was so justly honored; while at the same time, the anomalous position of the diocese with a suspended bishop at its head, made

it very important that the office of provisional bishop
should be promptly filled. As my father sat reflecting on these things, mourning for the departed, for
Dr. Wainwright had been one of his early friends,
and even inclined to plead his years in excuse for
throwing upon some younger man the performance of
this duty, a text was suggested to him as appropriate
to the occasion. The effect was instantaneous; his
eye lightened, he seemed to see at a glance the treatment of his subject, and shutting himself up, he
wrote within the working hours of two days a sermon which, without offense to any, probably settled
the question of immediate election. The opening of
the sermon will best suggest the argument: —

"Brethren, beloved in the Lord! — we meet this
day, in God's house, a chastened and heart-stricken
people. A thunderbolt hath fallen on our Church's
path, and we her sons look around and find ourselves
orphans — *orphans*, I may say, by a double claim —
with a yet living father paralyzed — and now our
only living hope — dead before us. 'Of whom, then,
may we seek for succor, but of thee, O Lord, who
for our sins art justly displeased?' To God's Word
let us then turn, as Christian men should, amid our
doubts, for counsel; under our sorrows, for consolation; and we shall there find, as the Christian ever
does, in his darkest hour, both comfort and guidance,
so long as he looks but to the actual duties to which
God's providence is calling him. As a passage suited
to our needs, and full of holy suggestion, I bring before you these heart-stirring words, which stricken

Israel heard when *their* great leader was withdrawn
from them, — ' Moses my servant is dead; now, therefore, arise, go over this Jordan, thou and all this people, unto the land which I do give to thee, even to
the children of Israel.'   Joshua i. 2.   .   .   .   .

" Yes! Moses is dead. But what follows? not
despair, not despondency, not folding of the arms in
sorrow ; but Faith, and the high active courage which
springs from Faith. Arise, it says, arise, thou afflicted one, from the earth ; put off from thy head
sackcloth and ashes ; Moses has but passed before
thee into the heavenly Canaan. But, as for thee,
bereavement is to awaken strength, and loss to be
converted into gain, through that holy alchemy which
Christ teaches to his suffering servants, and which
can never be learned but through the religion of
sorrow. So let it be with us, brethren. The staff
on which we leaned is broken, and, in breaking, hath
pierced both heart and hand ; but it was broken only
to plant our feet more firmly on the Rock whereon
alone they safely rest. For it is when Death hath
rent the veil ; when gifts of nature, talent, learning,
human guidance, are all withdrawn, or rather, as now,
dashed to the ground, that we then see plainly the
Heavenly Hand that, unseen, was ever guiding human instrumentality. The shadows pass, the substance remains, and the awakened soul falls back,
like a startled child, into the arms of its Father — the
Fountain of all wisdom, the Giver of all good, without whom nothing is strong, nothing is holy, and
' who knoweth our necessities before we ask, as well

as our ignorance in asking.' On that Rock, then, my afflicted brethren, let us this day stand ; on that arm let us rest, but the more firmly, because our human props are removed. ' When we are weak, then are we strong ; ' and to that holy guidance let us this day look but the more trustfully and the more lovingly, because our eyes are blinded with human tears, and our hearts weighed down with earthly sorrow, for the friend and leader whom God's hand hath taken from us. ' Moses is dead,' '*Therefore*,' saith God's Word, ' be strong.' Note, brethren, that wondrous sequence in God's reasoning — ' *therefore* ' — the very opposite to all of man's conclusions. ' Ye are weak,' *therefore* be very courageous. ' Ye are broken-hearted,' *therefore* arise to new conquests. ' *Sursum Corda* ' is the Church's cry. ' Lift up your hearts,' and let every tongue this day answer, ' We lift them up unto the Lord.' "

In this same spirit was the whole discourse written ; all uncertainty and hesitation were now gone, and the bold yet conciliatory spirit with which many of the Church's wants were touched upon, such as " shorter services," " mission organization," " banded labor," and " union among Christians," led many to urge my father, in spite of his sixty-six years, to allow his name to be pressed as a candidate for the vacant office. But now, as on a former occasion, he declined ; and though a few votes were cast for him, his friends knew that he had always been too fearless in his expression of opinion to allow of anything approaching to general popularity. This was true, not only in convention, but in the many Church societies of which he was a member and generally chairman : hence, though carrying every one's respect, and even the admiration of many, he was never really popular ; he was even, I think, somewhat feared as a closer political economist than trustees liked generally to have to deal with.

With respect to organized banded city mission work, his utterances in this sermon were very decided. Referring to the history of the missionary associations of the English Church in the seventeenth century, to the experience of Wesley, and to the judgment of all successful missionaries, he says : —

" As Churchmen, then, brethren, let us not fear to adopt what is thus sanctioned, but rather let us take shame to ourselves that we have allowed that sword of the Church's strength so long to rust in the scabbard ; and as its first field of labor, let us give to it, so soon as we have an acting, consecrated head to order and arrange it, that living yet dead mass of heathen ignorance, wretchedness, and vice lying here at our very doors in this great city — a sight that saddens and sickens the heart of the Churchman as he sees and feels the total inadequacy of the Church as she now stands, to even meet and measure the evil, much less cope with and conquer it. Let, then, I say, *bands* of devoted men be organized under ministerial guidance and episcopal supervision, with their own rules of voluntary discipline, under whatever name they may be known, and with whatever freedom of action the necessities of the case may need, and with them let the Church pass over 'this Jordan' that so long has kept us back. In this matter let not fears paralyze us; let not suspicion bar; let not gold be wanting. Hear and believe the words of God to Joshua, — 'Have not I commanded thee? Be strong and of a good courage. Be not afraid ; neither be thou dismayed; only be thou strong and very courageous, for the Lord thy God is with thee whithersoever thou goest!' Let our only fear be, lest we be too late to cut off from ourselves and our Church, that entail of curses which follows duties neglected, and a brother's blood crying unto Heaven."

This sermon had its effect. The objections against going into an immediate election were really met and answered by the text alone, and when afterwards made on the floor of the House, they fell dead. With the choice made by the diocese, he was well pleased. Writing in the ensuing January to his absent son, he says : —

"With our new bishop, my hopes for the Church rise. Last evening I spent with him, together with leading members of the Standing Committee, to talk over plans. I started that of a great city mission with an endowment, and found it was his favorite scheme. It was, in truth, the scheme of a primitive episcopate, with its church and home, and its fifteen or twenty deacons, organized, and working, and living with the bishop, and carrying on the true missionary work of our heathen babel. He is to draw out his plan and talk it over with leading members of Trin-ity Parish. It is our ecclesiological picture, and if carried out, will be in some measure our work."

This meeting, held at the residence of the Rev. Dr. Haight, was, at the time, considered an important one. My father, with mind filled, as we have seen, with his idea of an organized Episcopal mission, exaggerates, perhaps, his share in the discussion on this occasion, as the meeting was really called to hear the new bishop's own plans upon this very subject. But however this may be, we find him continuing, in his persevering way, to work and even hammer at it, longing for its accomplishment. Two months later, I find a letter from the Bishop of New Jersey, in reply to one from him on this subject : —

RIVERSIDE, *March* 12, 1855.

MY DEAR DR. McVICKAR, — Your letter needs no apology. Nothing of yours ever can. In addition to our long friendship, your words come always to my mind and heart as words of truth and wisdom for the Church : ἔπεα πτερόεντα ; words winged with love.

The plan suggested for New York is just as it should be. I go with it heart and hand ; whatever I can do to promote it shall be done. In Trinity Church you have the means, and I trust the will to carry it out.

Give my love, then, to your most excellent provisional bishop ; say to him that it shall be in my prayers that the " Church Home " be set about forthwith, and prospered with God's own prosperity. It will be the nucleus of great things hereafter. It will eventually, I trust, revive and realize the cathedral plan and work. Nothing for the souls and bodies of sick and sinful men that may not flow from it. To me it seems the great thought of the age. Commended fervently to God, in prayers such as David prayed for the peace and prosperity of Jerusalem, we cannot doubt of that blessing which is complete success.

Affectionately and faithfully yours,
G. W. DOANE.

This note with accompanying documents must have been forwarded at once, to the newly consecrated provisional bishop, as the following earnest and characteristic letter, dated the 28th of the same month, shows: —

60 FIFTH AVENUE, 12 o'clock Night, March 28, 1855.

MY DEAR DR. McVICKAR, — Returning an hour ago from a confirmation in Brooklyn, I found your interesting package. I was very sorry to have missed your call, as I am always sorry to lose the pleasant instruction of your words, *O si sic omnes!* It is a comfort to commune with one whose thoughts instinctively turn to the highest themes. In loftier and purer realms will it not be one of the joys of just men made perfect, that they can muse together, of all that has been and all that is most transporting in holiness and goodness, of Him who is the wonder and the glory of the universe?

Many thanks for your note, and for Bishop D.'s note and printed circular, which last I return. I had never before seen the printed suggestions. They are characteristic, and well worthy of being pondered. If you write again, I beg my thanks and very kind regards to him.

As for the Home, my mind has never wavered as to the importance and necessity of the scheme, whatever my doubt may have been as to its probable reception with the public. My feeling has been that nearly the only hope of the present must be from Trinity Church. I have not proceeded more rapidly because I was willing that the suggestions thrown out should be allowed to work their way a little, as leaven, in private, before making a decided move. I have felt gratified and cheered to find that you have been inclined to advocate the thing in your warm and eloquent way. God said to David that he *did well* that it *was in his heart* to build an house to the Lord, even though he was not allowed to build it. The thought, the desire was approved and honored. Let this be our consolation, and let us not despair. There is a pressure upon all spirits at thought of the poor and neglected, and God will yet draw hearts together for his own work. With kindest love to your daughters and young people,

I am ever, my dear Dr. McVickar,

Most truly and affectionately yours,

H. POTTER.

The REV. DR. McVICKAR.

The above letter seemed to me so beautiful and so interesting, both with respect to the little history of this effort to obtain something of a missionary cathedral system in New York city, as well as showing the high and spiritual tone of intercourse between such men as my father and Bishop Potter, that I ventured to request permission to publish it. This permission has been kindly granted in the following note, which is here added as throwing light upon the former, and showing how fruit has ripened even where plans have failed : —

38 EAST 22D STREET, *March* 20, 1871.

MY DEAR DR. McVICKAR, — I am very much obliged to you for allowing me to look at the note to your father, which it seems I wrote in March 1855, at the house of my ever dear friend, Mr. Robert B. Minturn, where I was then staying. I have no objection to your printing the note. There is nothing in it that I feel any desire to change. My interest in *city mission work* with which the " Home " referred to was proposed to be connected, is as earnest and ever present as it was then.

The idea of such a *Central Mission Home* in the city, and its uses, I had explained to a small company of friends, including, I think, your father, some time in the previous winter, 1854–55, at the house of the Rev. Dr. Haight. My opinion with regard to the value of such a Central Mission Home, if properly organized and sustained by proper *unity of action*, is at this hour precisely what it was sixteen years ago.

Perhaps there is no one subject which I have pressed so frequently and so earnestly in my sermons, and in my episcopal addresses to the diocese as the great work of " preaching the gospel to the poor." And certainly the progress which has been made in that work during the last sixteen years has been very great. We have yet great deficiencies to supply, but it is impossible to compare the Church work of this city in reference to the poor, with what it was sixteen or eighteen years ago, without feeling that we have reason to be thankful to Almighty God for his goodness and that we have reason to be encouraged.

If I have not come before the Church in the city, to press the immediate establishment of a Central City Mission Home, or if I have not given my support to some other plans for prosecuting city mission work, it has been because I saw other modes of advancing the great cause which we all have at heart, that seemed to me to promise, for the present at least, more certain and more abundant success.

I am, my dear Dr. McVickar,

Very truly and affectionately yours,

HORATIO POTTER.

To the REV. DR. McVICKAR.

This interesting letter needs no comment. Anything like a history of city mission work does not come within the present province of the writer. His object is attained when he has given a fair statement of the origin and growth of this idea of a cathedral mission in Professor McVickar's mind, and the way in which, from time to time in his long life, he sought for it practical demonstration.

During the coming year the plan for a " Church College and Home for the sons of the Clergy," to be engrafted on the chapel school of St. Barnabas, at Irvington, was put forth, with liberal offers to the diocese of partial endowment. The plan, as a training school for the ministry and home for the sons of the clergy, was a good one, but it soon became evident that the originators of it must be prepared to carry the whole burden. This they were not able to do; it was, therefore, wisely dropped, and my father soon after interested himself warmly in the almost similar effort and plan of his nephew, Mr. John Bard, at Annandale. To this Training College of St. Stephen's he left by will three thousand dollars and a portion of his library, and up to the time of his death was a trustee and a warm advocate of its interests. How real and how successful this was is evident from the following note from Mr. Bard: —

ANNANDALE, *June* 13, 1859.

MY DEAR UNCLE, — Very many thanks for the warm interest and masterly generalship you have shown in our affairs. The handsome way in which matters appear before the Church is indeed gratifying.

I congratulate you on having the opportunity in your advancing years of adding to your many other acts of devotion this one which seems so full of hope of future greatness. And before I relax the grasp from this growing child, let me thank you again, and from the bottom of my heart, for your very valuable services in the period of our necessity.

With kindest love to all,

I am, my dear Uncle,

Yours affectionately,

JOHN BARD.

This refers to his report to Convention as superintendent of the " Society for the Promotion of Religion and Learning," and to the action of that society in favor of the new Training College.

The year 1857 brought my father to his seventieth birthday. This midsummer festival — August 10 — was celebrated in old Scotch style, with something of a family reunion at his country-seat at Irvington. A favorite nephew, unable to be present, writes: " May you be spared to us still many years as guide and example. I have always looked upon you as the head of our clan, and as having kept the standard well advanced and shown us the way." But he was beginning to feel, somewhat, his age, and this year he petitioned the Trustees of Columbia College to relieve him of some of his duties. The simple record in the college catalogue is a very eloquent one as to what had been their extent and duration : —

" John McVickar, S. T. D., appointed 1817 Professor of Moral Philosophy, Rhetoric, and Belles-lettres. The subjects of Intellectual Philosophy and Political Economy were, in 1818, added to this department. In 1857 this chair was subdivided into four, namely, the chair of Moral and Intellectual

Philosophy, the chair of Ancient and Modern Literature, the chair of History and Political Science, and the chair of the Evidences of Natural and Revealed Religion." To this last my father was now appointed, resigning to others the varied duties which had been his for forty years, and in which he had shown himself, as the resolutions of the board express it, "able and faithful." We may indeed wonder at the amount of work done when we consider him, for this length of time, responsible for two or three lectures a day over such a distracting range of subjects.

Rest, however, did not mean idleness. He was a constant visitor, in the way of calls, among friends old and new, and the increase of time now at his disposal led to the renewing of many old friendships. His pen, too, was also kept busy. During this year he wrote a short biographical notice to append to the sermon preached by the Rev. Dr. Cooke at the funeral of the two sisters, Mrs. Banyer and Miss Jay, daughters of Governor Jay, whose united lives, filled with good works, and united deaths, bright with faith, had presented, what is so rare but so engaging, a family picture of the beauty of holiness. This, during the next year, was enlarged into a "memorial" of one hundred and thirty pages, at the request of their brother and his brother-in-law, Mr. William Jay, and at the earnest solicitation of the publisher. The reasons for its publication are thus briefly set forth in the preface : —

"In the hope, under God's blessing, of extending

beyond the limits of the circle in which they were personally known and loved, the memory of the late Mrs. Banyer and Miss Jay, the following brief memorial has been prepared, and is now put forth with the prayer that it may advance the glory of that Saviour in whose name all their alms-deeds were done, and through faith in whom they were supported under all their trials. Such examples, we all feel, are greatly needed, more especially in our age and country, where abounding wealth and the habits of corresponding self-indulgence are found so often to break down the Christian graces of moderation and self-denial, and consequently the means of liberal charity. God grant that this simple record of the reverse may lead many to follow these Christian sisters in consecrating worldly wealth to his glory who gives it, and unto whom account is to be rendered for the use of it. With this prayer it is submitted."

With the year 1859 came the one hundred and fiftieth anniversary of " Trinity School." This was a New York foundation of which my father was a trustee, and in which he had been long and practically interested. He determined that, for its one hundred scholars who were on the foundation, this should be a grand and long to be remembered day. And in this, aided by his brother trustees and the liberality of Trinity Parish, he was quite successful. The anniversary was held in Trinity Chapel, the late venerable rector of Trinity, Dr. Berrian, presiding. My father preached the sermon, and, as chairman of the school committee, distributed the memorial prizes. It was a sight of no ordinary interest to see him there, in his ripe but vigorous age, at the foot of the chancel steps, surrounded by these hundred youthful forms with their expectant faces, and to hear the impressive sentences with which to each different class he made the formal presentation. To the first and second with the Greek Testament, he said, — " Receive the Word of God, the revelation of Jesus-Christ, in that original tongue in which, under the guidance of the Spirit, it was indited. Receive it, value it, study it, guard it; the record of this day, and of your Christian duty." To the third, — " To each of you is presented, in remembrance of this day, a copy of the Book of Common Prayer ; next to God's Word, the most valued heritage of Churchmen; the Church's best bulwark against every error of doctrine, and every corruption of its pure, primitive, and Apostolic worship." To the fourth class he said, — " We give, on this day, in remembrance of it, to each of you, this Christian History of Greece ; a history of the land, whose language is that of the gospel, and whose literature is the ornament of the scholar, — the land, too, where St. Paul founded churches and consecrated bishops, before boastful Rome possessed either." And to the fifth class he said, — " Receive each of you at our hands, in re-membrance of this day, the record of a good man's life, the Biography of Bishop Ken ; a name dear to the Church and reverenced wherever heard. His morning and evening songs are consecrated in the

hearts and memory of Churchmen. Study his life
and follow his example.''

From the sermon preached on this occasion I feel
impelled to quote what was probably his last public
appeal for what he had so often pressed, individual
endowments in the matter of religion and education.

'' The endowments of religion and education, not
by the state, but by individuals, whether kings or
otherwise, has been to nations that fully adopted it,
the strong arm, even in this world's arena. In which
result let our Church and country read a lesson written for it by the hand, not of man's wisdom but of
God's providence ; showing how the present generation, in our far-spread and thinly-peopled land, with
but little personal sacrifice, but with much prospective
wisdom, — the wisdom that becomes alike the statesman and the Christian, — may, by landed endowment,
now make blessed provision for their children and
their children's children, to a hundred generations ;
securing to them and to their land, learning and
liberty and pure religion.   In this matter take the
Christian poet's advice and warning : —

'' ' O ! while thou yet hast room, fair, fruitful land,
      Ere war and want have stained thy virgin sod ;
    Mark thee a place on high, a glorious stand,
      Where truth her sign may make o'er forest, lake, and strand. '

'' Of such prospective wisdom, the early endowment
of Trinity Church is one of the few specimens our
country exhibits, and may be fairly taken as a test of
the principles here laid down. Its early rent roll,
£35 New York currency, burdened not the age that

gave it. Its growing rent roll, like a swelling stream, has been distributed into a thousand rills, carrying the gospel into the desert, as well as nourishing it at home ; and from time to time creating with its surplus waters new and independent reservoirs of strength, such as Columbia College in 1754, Trinity School in 1800, and the Society for Promotion of Religion and Learning in 1802, to carry out more abundantly over a thirsty land the waters of life."

I would here remark that the adverse influences which many have complained of as flowing from the endowment of Trinity Church, resulted, in my father's opinion, from her standing alone among many parishes which, in all other respects save that of wealth, were according to her construction of her own position, her equals ; and that these would have been obviated had she either been one of several similarly endowed, or, more in harmony with primitive principles, as the bishop's church been the cathedral of the diocese.

Home life in the mean time ran on much as usual, except that the household gradually thinned out again, not now by bereavement, but by marriage. The removal of Columbia College from its original site to the upper part of the city broke up the old home at 8 College Green. After one tentative move my father settled down again in 32d Street, in a house which had belonged to his brother-in-law, Mr. William Jay. Here his winters were passed, with the exception of the many happy days, especially Sundays, which were given to those, whom he knew enjoyed his presence, at the little rectory house of St. Barnabas, Irvington. And when he could not come in person, a bright, cheerful note, or a few lines of rhyme, were sent as a peace-offering. Of the first, this Christmas note of his seventy-second year will serve as an example : —

Xtmas, 5 p.m., 1860.

My dear Son, — If this were not Christmas it would be cold weather. It requires all its warm greetings to keep one comfortable; and upon that text I write to send our warmest to the rectory before Christmas Day is swallowed up in the all-devouring Past. To one and each and all, we therefore say, as in the olden time, " A merry, merry Christmas." Our morning breakfast brought to light our respective " presents," in which I am ashamed to say I was a receiver, and not a giver. Having outrun the constable and overdrawn my bank account, I appeared *in forma pauperis,* and had my crying wants supplied by a splendid razor-strop to keep company with its namesake and make it available in dull times, and an umbrella of silk, too beautiful to be exposed to the storm and not needful at present for the heat; so that till summer comes I shall be content with my headless cotton one. . . . . I have not yet told you of our young people's safe arrival some hours after time, having met with delay, and been saved from imminent danger, in crossing a bridge while burning. The bold conductor dashed over it without a minute to spare, through smoke and flame, having many precious souls on board, among others President Lincoln and Secretary Seward. I am the only one of the household not quite bright, suffering from what I thought I never had, a severe cold, got with running about on our severest day to get together the Standing Committee, at the call of the Bishop, for urgent business. . . . . With love to F., and a kiss to each of the children,

I remain, as usual,

Your affectionate father,

J. McVickar.

At another time came up the following, founded on the effects of a grandchild's cold in the head : —

A CHILD'S MISTAKE THROUGH SYMPATHY.

> " ' It blows, it snows,' young Willie said
> To Harry, as he lay in bed,
> With handkerchief beneath his head.

> " ' Who blows his nose ? ' poor Hal sneezed out.
> ' Has he a cold ? Why then 's he out ?
> All night, d'ye say ? Well, then, I knows
> As well as you, he blows his nose.' "

Yet this was not the exuberance of health, but rather the long formed habit of cheerfulness for the sake of others. Not long after, he wrote : —

" For myself, I have been up with you but little this winter, not through want of inclination or love, for my thoughts are daily with you, but through *years!* My feet are tender, my eye annoying, and my whole *body* more dependent than ever on fireside comfort and the daily routine of my own room.

Though all this is grumbling, and a little exaggerated, for what I say of *years* has not yet stopped me of my duties, though last Sunday it was a trial to get to the island from ice and storm. I met the Roman Catholic priest at the boat, but he withdrew, saying he would not cross such weather."

In 1862 these crossings to the island, as we have seen, came to an end by his unwilling resignation of the chaplaincy ; but he did not, on that account, rest from Sunday duties. On a leaf of a pocket notebook of 1863 I find a list of twelve city clergymen for whom he had preached during the winter, for several more than once, and generally those were selected whom he had reason to think were overworked. One, whom he thought highly of, and to visit whose church required quite a journey, thus writes : —

MONDAY, *March* 14, 1864.

MY DEAR AND HONORED BROTHER, — I cannot deny myself the pleasure of expressing to you my warmest thanks for your services yesterday, and to assure you that your words reached many hearts. I hope we may all remember, and profit by, your wholesome and touching counsels. Your presence at St. James's is always a genuine pleasure to the congregation, and I need hardly say to —

Yours most truly,
P. T. CHAUNCEY.

REV. DR. McVICKAR, etc., etc.

So writes the one who listened, and it is pleasant

to be able to compare the thoughts of the preacher, who, under the same date, writing to his son, says, — " I was with Dr. Chauncey last Sunday, in an old wooden church my father united in building sixty years ago, and which I had hardly seen since I was a boy ; and as I sat on the half-fallen willows of that age, I preached a more effective sermon to myself than it is likely I did to others within the building."

In 1862 my father was elected President of the Standing Committee of the Diocese of New York. This brought upon him some new duties and closer relations with the Bishop. He was now fully engaged, and practically interested in diocesan affairs, and his voice was often heard in the counsels of the Church. It was in the Convention of the succeeding year that he introduced the subject of the " Provincial System." This has since steadily gained approval as a wise, practical measure, till this year, 1870, has seen the first meeting, in the city of New York, of the bishops and the delegates of the five dioceses now included within the State.

The underlying idea in my father's mind was a plan which would allow of the increase of the episcopate, and the multiplication of dioceses, without weakening the position of the Church as coincident with the civil lines of the State. He acknowledged that it was a difficult problem to work out, especially when a State had already been divided, but none the less important on that account, and he therefore boldly pressed it upon the Church in spite of the disfavor with which it was at first received.

This endeavor to hold the Church lines coincident with the civil lines, according to the practice of the early Church, was the important feature in which his plan of Provinces differed from the earlier one of Bishop DeLancey.

CHAPTER XXIII.

IN the early spring of 1864 the Trustees of Columbia College called upon the Faculty to report to them, in view of a memorial to Congress, upon the subject of a uniform system of weights, measures, and coins. The Faculty submitted the question to a committee of their own body, of which Professor McVickar was chairman. The majority of this committee agreed upon two principles, which they embodied in about twice as many lines, and submitted that as their report. The chairman dissented on the ground that it was not worthy of the college or the subject, or in accordance with their instructions, and could not but be inoperative if sent to Congress in that bald shape, bringing in himself a minority report of considerable length. President King, writing to the chairman with respect to it, says, — " The members of the Board of Trustees were much impressed with your report as meeting fully their resolution, and as stating with precision and ability the merits of the whole question, and if the paper had been officially before them, on the part of the Faculty, they would, I think, at once have accepted and ordered it to be transmitted to Congress."

This was one of the last college duties which my father officially performed. Soon after, he and President King retired together, though the title, and in his case the emolument, of " Emeritus Professor," still attached him to the College, a connection only severed by his death.

His last report as professor of the " Evidences " was submitted two months later, and concludes with what we may consider the ripe deductions of a nearly fifty years' professional experience.

In conclusion, I would venture to observe that from the frequent voluntary acknowledgments made to me by students in after life, I cannot but highly appreciate the value of such a religious course in the completion of academic education : and express the belief that such enduring influence on the mind of the student has arisen mainly from the whole subject being treated in the lecture-room, not as a matter of memory, or book learning, but altogether as a question of conscience and individual conviction, thus planting in the mind and heart, when all that was trusted to the memory is forgotten, living seeds that never die.

Respectfully,
JOHN MCVICKAR,

Professor of Evidences up to June, 1864, but at present date Professor Emeritus.

The following to the writer, who had gone abroad for health, is somewhat in the spirit of his earlier letters, which, with the increase of years and infirmi-

ties, and somewhat in conformity with an age that
was giving up letter writing, had become more and
more infrequent : —

New York, *November* 17, 1865.

My dear Son, — I have delayed long writing to
you, waiting for something beyond family news. Your
letters bring back all my own pleasure in the scenes
you describe, doubled by the delight of your improving strength and health. You showed good judgment in avoiding Liverpool, and striking at once on
the antiquities of our ancestral home in cathedral
Chester, and the splendor of her modern science in
the " Menai bridges." These first impressions are
all important in their associations, and most enduring
in remembrance with those who visit England, as
all of your party but yourself do, for the first time.

But now for our land and its mighty interests.
Our Church is advancing, as she has never done before, with national strides. The South is coming in,
I may almost say, bodily. Broken up by the sects
and their endless disputes and divisions, they look to
the Church as the only earthly rock on which they
can rest. Our late General Convention has been a
national blessing, and a great element in the concilia-
tion of the South. The new bishops from that quarter are powerful persuaders. Bishop Quintard, after
his consecration, came on here, when a new bond
arose between us, on learning from him that he was
one of my own " Trinity School " scholars; and as I
was aiding him in his first service here, he brought
with him his old teacher, Dr. William Morris. Of

his preaching you may take, as my opinion, my first words on his leaving the pulpit, "As I listened to you I said to myself, there is a Church Luther."

To the General Convention I went, overpersuaded by S——, and a warm invitation from J. C—— and his wife, where I passed a very delightful week. I was treated with unexpected courtesy by the bishops, invited the first day to lunch with them in their private room, being greeted on my introduction as " Bishop of Governor's Island." The next day I dined with them at their hotel, myself the only "undignified " member, and, worst of all, being called on, English fashion, for an after-dinner speech. " Tell us something " they said, " of Old Columbia," some of my own scholars among the bishops having preceded me. " My Lord Bishop of Montreal," who presided, was very complimentary on the occasion, and proffered many courtesies. The discussions in the Convention (the House) were able and full of interest. The " provincial system " was referred to a large committee, Dr. Mahan, chairman ; a warm advocate for it in *principle*, as he admitted to me, yet averse to going further. And so it passed the House, permission to New York and Pennsylvania, which was all we hoped for. . . . . .

A great shock came to us three days ago, in the total destruction by fire of St. George's Church, in this city, through a furnace carelessly left on the roof by the plumbers. The towers and outside walls alone remain ; the parsonage untouched, on the roof of which Dr. Tyng stood during the whole conflagration, in .

spite of solicitation of friends. The next morning early I went down to see him. He was much excited. He had a MS. sermon before him. " See," said he, " the first sermon I preached in this church, on its opening; mark the date, seventeen years ago this coming Sunday, 19th of November; and note the text, 1 Corinthians iii. 13, ' It shall be revealed by fire;' and on Sunday next I shall finish the text, ' To try every man's work, of what sort it is.' Now," said he, " if my work has been true, it will stand the fire, and I shall renew my strength; if not, my work is done," etc. It was very touching, and I think, when I can learn where he preaches, I shall go and hear him, for I feel deep sympathy for him. He said to me in parting, " I love you, for you have been always kind to me." . . . .

Speaking of the treatment of offenses, in a note of about this time, my father says, —

" Let us live in the present and for the future, not in the past, which is dead and gone and should be buried, except for our own improvement, if we would live either wisely or happily in this world. The world has too many trials, and life too many sorrows for us to add gratuitously to the number by raking up the offenses of our friends, whether real or imagined. On this rule I have ever sought to order my course and discipline my feelings, and the result has been PEACE. I think I have never had, though offenses have come, separation from a friend; I know I have often prevented it by the course I here recommend."

During the spring of the succeeding year, 1866, the Trustees of Columbia College had requested Professor McVickar to sit for his portrait, which, on the 23d of May, was publicly hung on the walls of the Library. This brought about his last public appearance in the halls of that College to whose best interests he had been so long devoted. Friends and a large gathering of former pupils conspired with the authorities of the College to make it an occasion of more than ordinary interest. At least, it seemed so to those who were present; and the mature, not to say venerable age of those who were the principals, both alumni and professor, gave a solemnity to the remarks then made, differing from such occasions generally.

The address of the alumni was signed by over seventy names, beginning with one of the class of 1812 and two from the class of 1818, the first which graduated after Professor McVickar's election.

To this address, an earnest and touching reply was made; but the following letter to the chairman of the committee embodies, in shorter form, its chief characteristics: —

IRVINGTON, July 4, 1866.

MY DEAR DOCTOR, — I return to you, by your son, the precious package of letters you were kind enough to intrust me with, for my perusal, from my old college students, on the late festive college occasion. I return them together with many thanks, both to yourself and them; or rather, I should say, with deep but contradictory emotions of both pride and

humility ; with pride at finding myself so affectionately remembered in long after years, amid the cares
and business of life, to many of whom I have for
years looked up for guiding examples to myself in
the duties of life ; but then again more deeply humbled than proud, in feeling myself wholly unworthy
of such high eulogium.

My highest merit in my varied fifty years' professorship, has been simply that of heartfelt sincerity
in that which I taught. Whatever it was, I ever
sought to unite *Truth with Duty*, to deepen its foun-
dations by bringing it home to the heart and the conscience, as well as to make it clear to the understanding, and imprint it on the memory of the students;
and in these their present letters of thankful remembrance, I feel that I have my sufficient reward. Some
word of earnest teaching must, I conclude, have
stuck fast in the heart as well as memory, or they
could not thus have written. " I remember well the
last words you said to me," was the recent address
to me of an alumnus of thirty years' standing, whom
I had wholly forgotten, " I remember them well, and
have lived on them ever since."

But to one other point of influence in my course,
though unnamed in the Alumni letters, I feel not
unwilling to plead guilty. It is the lesson of quiet,
steady perseverance in the duties to which in early
life God's providence called me, and the blessing that
ever rested upon it. For this one lesson of my life,
—a lesson so rare yet so needful in our land of restless change, — I am willing that my example should

be both quoted, and praised, and followed; and in any future eulogium of my life or character be esteemed and taken for its chief merit and value.

Affectionately and truly,

Your professor, friend, and brother,

JOHN McVICKAR,

Emeritus Professor Columbia College.

To REV. B. I. HAIGHT, S. T. D.,
Chairman of Committee, etc.

The trial of the Rev. Mr. Tyng in 1867, and the Bishop's departure for England to attend the Anglican Council, brought additional work and some anxiety on my father as President of the Standing Committee of the diocese. But, though faithful to all duty, he was quite willing now to let others take the laboring oar; and in the Secretary, the Rev. Dr. Eigenbrodt, he found one ever ready, with unobtrusive kindness, to relieve him of all unnecessary labor.

On the 16th of July of this year he writes: —

MY DEAR SON,— It is very long since I wrote to you; not from forgetfulness, but want of power. Hand and head are both feeble. Amid patriarchal claims, you head the list as my only son and dearest brother in the ministry. . . . . I have again to go down to the city this week, to organize the business of the diocese, the Bishop having sailed for England and made our committee the "Ecclesiastical authority" to call the convention and arrange matters, but Dr. Eigenbrodt relieves me of all trouble. . . . .

My only visit from home was, last week, to St. Stephen's Annandale, where I was anxious once more to be and encourage them by the statement of a new scholarship and an annual prize of fifty dollars for elocution, to make their "candidates" correct and effective readers, both from the desk and pulpit, which so few of our young clergy are. . . . .

This prize was then founded, and at the same time another, of like amount, in "Trinity School," "for the most deserving scholar," annually, in the first and second classes. The scholarship referred to, of three thousand dollars, was provided for by Will. A note, of about the same date as the above, shows that the idea of the cathedral system was still holding its place in my father's mind as a measure of practical importance to the Church.

"Trinity, I understand, is to pay off its half million debt through the Astor lots ; with the remainder to make Trinity Church building cruciform, and cathedral-like, and, if I have a word to say, to have a Bishop's Home as a visible centre of Church influence in the city."

A few weeks later he writes : —

"For myself, my time is short ; my strength fails, but not my health. I still keep up my small work in the Church and its societies, in most of which I am still the presiding officer, and always (?) at my post. It is a great comfort to me to find them all successful. As to Church questions I do not trouble myself, being content to teach as I practice, — *Be faithful in your own work*, and all will be well."

26

This is my last record in my father's handwriting, and as such it is not without its interest. That conscientious little query-point, slipped in afterwards, as if he thought it possible that he had been over bold in stating that he was never absent from his posts of duty, shows a remarkable absence of the almost natural boastfulness of age, while the few emphatic words of closing, " BE FAITHFUL IN YOUR OWN WORK, and all will be well," form a strikingly true, and, as it seems, involuntary summing up of the teachings of his whole life. A few months before, however, he had written some lines on the baptism of his youngest grandchild, bearing a loved family name, which seem with peculiar fitness to close the literary record of my father's life. This baptismal gift, though strictly intended for the home circle, seems, as a polished pendant, to afford a graceful finish to the chain of a consistent and thoughtful Christian literary life. It appears, as read now, to have been a preparatory gathering-up of links from the long buried past, in preparation for the journey which was so soon to restore that past to the writer in a living and unending present. As such, and not because of the poetic merit it may possess, it is here given, though as an evidence of intellectual vigor at the advanced age of eighty years, it is not without its interest : —

"TO MY GRANDDAUGHTER ANNA,

ON HER BAPTISM IN ST. BARNABAS'S CHURCH, IRVINGTON, SUNDAY, 2D SEPTEMBER, 1866, AFTER THE DEATH OF HER LITTLE SISTER.

" Thou precious babe ! ordained to bless
Thy mother in her loneliness, —

The sad, pale face by death removed
From earth to heaven, yet there as here beloved.
Anna! It was my mother's name who gave me birth,
And ever 'mid the childish joys of earth,
Taught me to know and love my Saviour Lord,
His holy church on earth, and his redeeming word.
Anna! It was my daughter's and my first-born's name,
Who gave me first to know and feel a father's claim,
Doubling the earthly joys of married love
With priceless gifts, descending from above.
Beauty and grace were hers, and gentle art,
To warm, to please, and elevate the heart,
While fitting it for higher joy and peace,
In that blest world where sin and sorrow cease.

"Though fifty years have past, since when
God called thee to Himself again,
Anna, thy name still brings to clearest sight
The picture of a youthful angel bright, —
Too bright alas! to linger long below,
'Mid chilling blasts and winter's snow.
In bearing thus a name so dear to me,
Anna! my prayers are offered up for thee,
That thou like her, a joy may ever prove
To friends below on earth, and holy saints above.
But if to thee a longer race be given,
To train up children for their home in heaven,
Then may my mother's name remembrance give,
Of how a Christian mother ought to live,
Winning, of earth's rewards, that only test, —
Her children do rise up and call her bless'd."

The first intimation to those outside his own family that Professor McVickar's health was seriously failing, was given in the few happy and touching words in which it was alluded to by the Bishop of New York in his convention address of October, 1868 : —

"One venerable and honored presbyter of this

diocese, oppressed with the weight of years, but not chilled in his love for the Church or in his devotion to duty, retires from the official station which he has so long and ably filled as President of the Standing Committee — the Rev. John McVickar, D. D., for half a century a professor in Columbia College — what a historical name in this diocese ! How steadfast in his principles, how far reaching in his views, and how elevated in all his thoughts and sentiments ! May the rays of that sun which never sets to the Christian heart shine brightly and cheerily along his path, and in his chamber, until faith, hope, and love change into the bliss and glory of the perfect day ! "

This was in the beginning of October. Before the month closed the subject of this memoir was at rest. The summer had been spent at Bloomingdale, within a short distance of the old paternal mansion where, sixty years before, as a solitary student, we saw him preparing for that life-work, which, nobly finished, he was now about to lay down. Surrounded by his surviving children, he passed quietly away, in his eighty-second year, with the oft-reiterated words, " Pray," " Prayer," " Praise," upon his lips, and was buried in the grave-yard of his own Church at Hyde Park, beside her whose memory he had so faithfully cherished, and in the grave he had marked for himself thirty-five years before.

Thus in peace ended the " life " which I have endeavored to portray. I have willfully kept back nothing that could interfere with a true estimate of the character which that life helped to form. To give shape and outline to this estimate is a duty which the writer, as a son, is unwilling to assume. He lays it upon his readers as their work, and to assist them adds these few lines of autobiography written in 1860 : —

" In concluding, my dear son, at your request, this brief memoranda, let me add what I hold to be its lesson. My life has been a long, and has now become a protracted one. Every such life must give its lesson, like a sum worked out, a story fully told. Mine I think is this, The power and blessing of quiet perseverance. A feeble constitution thus hardened — a treacherous memory thus made retentive — very moderate talents thus fitted for usefulness — fair scholarship thus gained by quiet industry — college duties an early choice and never changed — and through my whole life an abiding feeling that, in a good cause, rightly pursued, nothing is impossible. The single eye and the unchanging mind governs the world, and in proportion as we partake of them we are successful, and in all good works, both blessing and blessed. I repeat, therefore, as the lesson of my life your early learned nursery motto, —

"' PERSEVERANTIA OMNIA VINCIT.' "

APPENDIX.

APPENDIX.

REV. WM. A. McVICKAR, D. D.

MY DEAR SIR,—Your kind and friendly note has remained too long without an answer.

Various engagements, it is true, have occupied my attention, but my excuse is, not so much want of time as want of ability properly to write anything on a subject which your late respected father, as Professor of Political Economy in Columbia College, treated so profoundly and learnedly.

And even now, I should hardly venture any remarks, were it not that a fresh perusal of his "American Finances," "The Expediency of abolishing Damages on Protested Bills, of Exchange," "Notes on a National Bank," and "Hints on Banking," have revived my feelings of wonder and admiration, excited by the reading of the latter several years since.

To a practical man of business, an every-day banker, it really seems wonderful that a scholar, investigating the subject of Political Economy on purely scientific principles, should be able to see, not only the practical workings of existing laws, and understand the indissoluble relations of money and trade, but should also be able to foresee and foretell what changes are necessary to produce the highest prosperity and secure the greatest safety to the community.

To me it seems perfectly clear, that the writings of your father prove that he possessed this power.

Take, for instance, his essay on "The Evils of Divers State Laws to regulate Damages on Foreign Bills of Exchange." Practically, banks, bankers, and merchants now admit the correctness of views promulgated by Professor McVickar more than forty years ago; which Mr. Verplanck tried to get Congress to remedy by law in 1829. Although he failed to do so, the several State laws have now become a dead letter.

Perhaps the most remarkable instance of the application of pure principle to practical finance is found in Professor Mc-Vickar's letter to a member of the Legislature of this State, entitled " Hints on Banking," dated February 17, 1827.

In that communication of some forty pages is foreshadowed the Free Banking Law of this State, passed in May, 1838. It suggested, —

1. " Banking to be a free trade, in so far as that it may be freely entered into by individuals or associations, under the provisions of a general statute."

2. " The amount of the banking capital of such individual or association to be freely fixed, but to be invested, one tenth at the discretion of the bank, the remaining nine tenths in government stock, whereof the bank is to receive the dividends, but the principal to remain in pledge for the redemption of its promissory notes, *under such security as to place the safety of the public beyond doubt or risk,*" etc.

3. " The promissory notes of such individual or association to bear upon their face the nature and amount of stock thus pledged, together with the usual signatures," etc.

The writer adds : " That these provisions would free banking from all abuses, it would be arrogance to assert; but that they would remedy many and great ones that now exist, seems to be unquestionable. Nor would their adoption be attended with the dangers which generally await untried novelties. They are *already established by the experience of other trades.*"

This last sentence, which I have Italicized, shows the principle on which this question had been solved. It was not a groping in the dark, but a clear perception of vital elements, known to be working in " other trades."

Now it should be remembered that this letter was written to an influential member of the Legislature in 1827; eleven years later, the seed thus sown matured; in 1838 the Free

Banking Law was passed.* It contains not only the ideas, but almost the precise form of expression which the letter contained.

Nor was the principle thus evolved confined to this State or country. In 1843-44, when Sir Robert Peel proposed his amendments to the charter of the Bank of England, this security for the bank's circulating notes was not lost sight of.

The *issue* department was made distinct and separate from the *discount* department of the bank. *This* idea was suggested in 1841, by your father, in his review and criticism on the Bank of the United States. He there showed the practicability and necessity of having the issue of circulating notes independent of the discount department, and proposed that it be under the charge of a board of governors, while the other parts of the bank should still be managed by the directors.

If I mistake not, in the discussions which arose in Parliament on the subject of the Bank of England, in 1844, reference was had to the Free Banking Law of this State, then six years in successful operation, to show the feasibility of limiting and securing the bank's issue beyond a peradventure.

The influence, therefore, of Professor McVickar's letter of 1827 was not temporary nor confined to the State of New York, although attempts to introduce the Free Banking System into other States prevailed only partially.

The old unsecured currency of State banks, was more profitable to the stockholders; and when such institutions were faithfully managed, the public rarely suffered a loss on bank bills. This was true as to the Safety Fund Banks, and also in regard to the earlier chartered banking institutions of the several States.

Still, in exceptional cases, the community did lose, and the advantage of the Free Banking System over either of the old systems was that the people were by the former entirely secured from loss, by bonds lodged in the banking department of the State, beyond the control of the bank, and held in trust to pay the bill-holders if the bank should default.

Again, in 1863 we find this system offered to the whole

country, and adopted by Congress in the following Act, namely:
" An Act to provide a National currency, secured by a pledge
of United States stocks, and to provide for the circulation and
redemption thereof."

This *National* Bank Act, with more defects than improvements, — as compared with the original, — is the New York
Free Banking Law of 1838, over again. Possibly, it may yet be
so essentially modified as to be made to perform, satisfactorily,
the work of a proper United States Bank, and its branches.

Under this law the National banks now furnish a paper currency of larger volume, and of more uniform value, throughout the country, than has been known before.

Your father, in common with many of the best thinkers in
the land, was in favor of a National or United States Bank,
with wise restrictions as to undue political influences; and
possessing the power to regulate exchanges, to furnish secured
circulating notes, redeemable (at the parent bank) in coin,
and required to afford facilities to mercantile and commercial
interests in the shape of discounts.

One great truth is now fixed and determined, and that is,
that hereafter, no bank or banks will be allowed by law to
supply a circulating medium not secured to the public *outside
of the bank itself!* And it must be a source of inexpress-
ible satisfaction to you, my dear sir, that your father was
gifted with such powers of reasoning as enabled him to de-
fine and establish a vital truth in political economy, for the
benefit of mankind.

Please accept my thanks for that valuable pamphlet, " Hints
on Banking," and believe me, yours sincerely,

J. E. WILLIAMS.

Strawberry Hill, *October* 15, 1870.

INDEX.

www.ingramcontent.com/pod-product-compliance
Lightning Source LLC
Chambersburg PA
CBHW021333110726
47900CB00005B/1445

9 783337 373603